Adventure Stories
for Girls

Adventure Stories for Girls

Edited by
John Canning

First published 1978 by
Octopus Books Limited,
59 Grosvenor Street, London W1

This arrangement © 1978 Octopus Books Limited

Reprinted 1979, 1980, 1981, 1982, 1983

ISBN 0 7064 0691 5

Printed in Great Britain at The Pitman Press, Bath

CONTENTS

THE ESCAPE OF KING CHARLES AFTER WORCESTER

John Buchan

On Wednesday, the third day of September 1651, the army which had marched from Scotland to set King Charles upon the throne was utterly defeated by Cromwell at Worcester. The battle began at one o'clock and lasted during the autumn afternoon, the main action being fought east of the city. Many of the chief Royalists, like the Duke of Hamilton, fell on the field.

When the issue was clear, Charles, accompanied by the Duke of Buckingham, Lord Derby, Lord Shrewsbury, Lord Wilmot and others, entered the city by Sidbury Gate. There an ammunition wagon had been overturned, and this gave check for a moment to the pursuit. In Friars Street the King threw off his armour and was given a fresh horse, and the whole party galloped through the streets and out at St Martin's Gate. Charles was wearing the laced coat of the Cavalier, a linen doublet, grey breeches, and buff gloves with blue silk bands and silver lace. The little party, dusty and begrimed with battle, galloped to the Barbon Bridge, a mile north of the city, where they halted for a moment to plan their journey.

The nearest and most obvious refuge was Wales, where the country people were Royalist, and where, in the mountains, Cromwell's troopers might well be defied. But there was no chance of crossing the Severn in that neighbourhood, so it was decided to ride north into Shropshire. Colonel Careless offered to act as rearguard and stave off the pursuit, and Mr Charles Giffard, of the ancient family of the Giffards of Chillington, who knew the forest country of the Staffordshire and Shropshire borders, undertook the business of guide. There was a place called Boscobel, an old hunting lodge among the woods, where Lord Derby had already been concealed a few weeks before, so Giffard and a servant called Francis Yates (who was afterwards captured by the Cromwellians and executed) led the little band through the meadows.

They passed the town of Kidderminster on their left, where, at the moment, Mr Richard Baxter, the Presbyterian divine, was watching from an upper window in the market-place the defeated Royalists galloping through and a small party of Cromwellian soldiers firing wildly at the fugitives. The main road was no place for the King when the bulk of the Scottish Horse was fleeing northward by that way, so he turned through Stourbridge and halted two miles farther on at a wayside inn to drink a glass of ale and eat a crust of bread. After that they passed through the boundaries of the old Brewood Forest, and at about four o'clock on the morning of Thursday, 4 September, arrived at the ancient half-timbered manor of Whiteladies, belonging to the family of Giffard.

A certain George Penderel was in charge as bailiff, and at the sight of the party he stuck his head out of the window and asked for news of the battle. The door was flung open, and the King rode his horse into the hall. Charles was taken into the inner parlour, and George's brothers, William and Richard Penderel, were sent for. Richard was bidden fetch his best clothes, which were breeches of coarse green cloth and a leather doublet. Charles changed into them, his hair was shorn, and he was now no more the Cavalier, but a countryman of the name of Will Jones, armed with a woodbill.

It would have been fatal for the party to have remained together, so his companions galloped off in the direction of Newport, where most of them were taken prisoner. Lord Derby was captured and afterwards beheaded; Giffard was taken, but he managed to escape, as did Talbot and Buckingham. Charles was led by Richard Penderel into a wood at the back of the house called Spring Coppice, where he had to make himself as comfortable as might be under the trees.

All that day, Thursday, 4 September, it rained incessantly. Richard Penderel brought him food and blankets, and Charles, worn out with want of sleep, dozed till the dusk of the evening. Then Penderel aroused him and bade him be going. His proposal was to guide him south-west to Madeley, where there seemed a chance of crossing the Severn into Wales. Madeley lay only nine miles to the south-west, a pleasant walk among woods and meadows; but on that autumn night, with the rain falling in bucketfuls and every field a bog, it was a dismal journey for a young man stiff from lying all day in the woods, and stayed by no better meal than eggs and milk. Charles was a hearty trencherman, and had not trained his body to put up with short commons. However, he was given some bacon and eggs before he started.

The Penderels were Catholics, and men of that faith were accustomed in those days to secret goings and desperate shifts, and, since all were half-outlawed, there was a freemasonry between them. Therefore Richard proposed to take the King to a Catholic friend of his, Mr Francis Wolfe, on the Severn bank, who might conceal him and pass him across the river into Wales. That journey in the rain remained in the King's mind as a time of peculiar hardships, though there seems no particular difficulty in an active young man walking nine miles at leisure in the darkness. In after years Charles was a famous walker, and used to tire out all his courtiers both by his pace and endurance. But on this occasion he appears to have been footsore and unnerved.

When they had gone a mile they had to pass a water-mill and cross a little river by a wooden bridge. The miller came out and asked them their errand; whereupon Penderel took alarm and splashed through the water, followed by his King. After that Charles almost gave up. Lord Clarendon, to whom he told the story, says that 'he many times cast himself upon the ground with a desperate and obstinate resolution to rest there till the morning that he might shift with less torment, what hazard so ever he ran. But his stout guide still prevailed with him to make a new attempt, sometimes promising that the way should be better and sometimes assuring him that he had but little farther to go.' Charles was desperately footsore. Perhaps the country shoes of 'Will Jones' did not fit him.

In the small hours they arrived at Mr Wolfe's house. Charles waited 'under a hedge by a great tree' while Richard Penderel went forward to meet his friend. He was greeted with bad news. Every ford, every bridge, and every ferry on the Severn was guarded by the Cromwellians, who were perfectly aware that the King would make for Wales. Wolfe had 'priests' holes' in his house, but he did not dare to hide the King there, for they had already been discovered by the soldiers; so Charles was concealed among the hay in the barn, where he lay during the day of Friday the 5th. There was nothing for him but to take refuge at Boscobel, the hiding-place originally arranged.

That night, after borrowing a few shillings from Wolfe, the King and Richard set off eastward again, guided for the first part of the road by Wolfe's maid. At Whiteladies they heard that Colonel Careless, who was acting as rearguard, had safely reached the Boscobel neighbourhood, and that Lord Wilmot was at Moseley, in Staffordshire, nine or ten miles to the east. All the country was thick woodland interspersed with heaths, and few safer hiding-places could be found in England.

Charles was now in better form. The Penderels had stripped off his stockings, washed his feet and anointed the blisters. His disguise was also perfected, for his face and hands had been dyed with juice, and he made gallant efforts to imitate the clumsy gait of a yokel. But his disguise can never have been very perfect. The harsh features, the curious curl of the lips, the saturnine dark eyes, and above all the figure and the speech, were not such as are commonly found among mid-England peasantry.

Penderel did not dare take him into the house, so he took refuge in the wood, where he was presently joined by Colonel Careless. On the coast being reported clear, the King spent the night in one of the priest's holes in the old manor, an uncomfortable dormitory, which had, however, a gallery adjoining it, where he took walking exercise and surveyed the road from Tong to Brewood. Saturday the 6th was a fine day, and the King spent some time sitting in an arbour in the garden. He was presently induced by Colonel Careless to seek a safer retreat in an oak tree in the wood. A little platform was made in the upper branches, pillows were brought from the house, and there Careless and the King spent the day. The Royal Oak is famous in Stuart history, and this particular tree has long since been hacked to pieces to make keepsakes for the faithful. But it is by no means certain that Charles was in particular danger during the day that he slept in it, or that any Roundhead trooper rode below the branches and 'hummed a surly hymn'.

Careless had the worst part of the business, for the King rested his head in his lap and the honest soldier's arm went to sleep. 'This,' in the words of the *Miraculum Basilicon*, 'caused such a stupor or numbness in the part, that he had scarcely strength left in it any longer to support His Majesty from falling off the tree, neither durst he by reason of the nearness of the enemy speak so loud as to awake him; nevertheless, to avoid both the danger of the fall and surprise together, he was (though unwillingly) constrained to practise so much incivility as to pinch His Majesty, to the end he might awake him to prevent his present danger.'

When the dusk came the two descended and went into the manor-house. There they were met by the news that the enemy cordon was closing round, and that £1,000 reward had been put upon the King's head. Charles, however, was in no way dismayed, and demanded a loin of mutton. William Penderel accordingly fetched one of his master's sheep, which Careless stabbed and cut up with his dagger. The King made Scotch collops of a hind-quarter, which the Colonel fried in a pan, and the two had a hearty meal.

The King slept that night in the house in a 'priest's hole', and next day resolved to join Lord Wilmot at Moseley. He found, however, that his feet were still so tender that walking was impossible, so an old mill horse that had carried provisions in the campaign was found for him. Mounted on this beast, attended by Careless and the Penderels, the King set out in the dusk of the Sunday evening. At Moseley he found Lord Wilmot, and since Moseley was a safer place than Boscobel the King spent a peaceful night in the house. There, too, was a priest, Father John Huddleston, and not far off was Colonel Lane, both devoted Royalists. There he said farewell to his staunch friends, the Penderels.

The King, we are told, spent the evening by the fire while Father Huddleston attended to his unfortunate feet. Charles had stuffed his stockings with paper, but the precaution had not saved him from further galls and sores. He was given new worsted stockings and clean linen and slippers, and was so much cheered thereby that he declared he was now fit for a new march, and that 'if it should ever please God to bless him with ten or twelve thousand loyal and resolute men he doubted not to drive these traitors out of his kingdom.'

Next day, Monday the 8th, it was given out that Father Huddleston had a Cavalier friend lying privately in the house, and all the servants were sent away on errands except the cook, who was a Catholic. Watch was kept at the different windows in case of any roving party of soldiers. The King spent the day largely in sleeping and discussing the future, while messages were sent to loyal neighbouring squires to find out the lie of the land. He saw a sad sight from the windows—many starving Royalist soldiers limping past the door, munching cabbage stalks and corn plucked from the fields. However, he heard one piece of news of some importance. Colonel Lane, who lived five miles off at Bentley, had a sister, Miss Jane, who had procured a pass from the Governor of Stafford for herself and her sevant to go to Bristol, and it was thought that if the King passed as her servant he might thereby get clear of the country. It was accordingly arranged that on the Tuesday night Lord Wilmot's horses should fetch the King to Bentley as the first stage of his journey to the Bristol Channel.

On the Tuesday afternoon, however, the plan all but miscarried. A party of soldiers arrived to search Moseley, and the King was hurriedly hustled into one of the priest's holes. The place is still pointed out—a stuffy little nook behind the panelling, through which liquid food used to be conveyed to the unfortunate occupant by means of a quill through a chink in the beams. The soldiers made a great row, and questioned the owner, Mr Whitgreave, with a musket cocked at his breast, but in the end departed. When dusk fell Colonel Lane's horses arrived, and Charles set out and arrived safely at Bentley. There Colonel Lane gave him, in place of Will Jones's unspeakable clothes, a good suit and cloak of country grey, like a farmer's son, and put £20 in his pocket for the expenses of the journey.

The King is now no longer an aimless wanderer among the Staffordshire woods. A plan of campaign has been evolved, and the fugitive in a reasonable disguise is making for the sea. He arrived at Bentley about midnight on 9 September. The party that set out on the 10th consisted of Miss Jane Lane, her cousin, Mrs Petre, Mr Petre, that cousin's husband, and a certain Cornet Henry Lassels, also a kinsman. The Petres were bound for their house at Horton, in Buckinghamshire, and proposed to go only as far as Stratford-on-Avon. Charles rode in front as

Miss Jane's servant. The route lay by Bromsgrove and Stratford-on-Avon, then through Cotswold to Cirencester, and thence to Bristol.

It was a bold enterprise, for the natural route of flight after Worcester would be down the Severn Valley to the sea. Cromwell's troopers were in every parish, and a large part of the population, knowing of the King's escape and the reward for his capture, were on the watch for any suspicious stranger. The first stop was at the village of Bromsgrove, where the King's horse cast a shoe. In the smithy Charles, in his character of servant, asked the smith the news. 'Precious little,' was the answer, 'except that Cromwell has routed the Scots. He has slain or captured most of them, but I hear the King has made his escape.' 'Perhaps,' said Charles, 'the King has gone by by-ways back into Scotland.' 'No,' said the smith, 'there is not much luck for him that way. He is lurking secretly somewhere in these parts, and I wish I knew where he were, for then I would be the richer by a thousand pounds.'

Nothing more happened till they came near Stratford, riding as far as they could be secluded by-ways. Their plan was to ford the Avon about a mile below the town; but when they drew near the river they observed soldiers' horses feeding in the meadows and many troopers lying upon the ground. This sight made them turn to their left so as to enter Stafford another way. But at the bridge there they ran full into the same troop of soldiers. The troop opened right and left to let them pass, and returned the civil salute which the little party gave them.

They were now among the foothills of Cotswold, and before evening reached the straggling village of Long Marston, a place famous for its morris-dancing. In the village there was a certain Mr John Tomes, and in his house the travellers found lodging. The King, passing as a servant, found his way to the kitchen, where, like an earlier monarch of England, he was scolded by the cook because he had no notion how to wind up a roasting jack. The said jack is still in existence, and is to be seen in the village. Meantime Lord Wilmot and Colonel Lane were following behind, and the latter turned off towards London, in order to arrange the final details of a pass for 'Will Jackson', which was the name the King had now adopted.

On Thursday morning, 11 September, the travellers began the ascent into the Cotswold moors. In that empty country of sheep-walks there was less risk of detection, and accordingly good speed was made by

Stow-on-the-Wold and along the old Roman Fosse Way to Northleach and so to Cirencester, where they arrived in the evening, after a ride of thirty-six miles. Near the market-place stood the Crown Inn, an inconspicuous hostelry, and the travellers, professing great fatigue, went immediately to bed. In one chamber a good bed was prepared for Mr Lassels and a truckle bed for Will Jackson; but as soon as the door was closed the King went to sleep in the good bed and the Cornet on the pallet.

Next day, Friday 12 September, the party rode twenty-two miles south-west to Chipping Sodbury, probably escorted for part of the way by Captain Matthew Huntley, an old soldier of Prince Rupert's, who lived in those parts. They entered the city of Bristol by Lawford's Gate, rode through the streets, crossed the Avon by a ferry, and kept the left bank of the river to the village of Abbots Leigh, three miles west of Bristol. Abbots Leigh, which stands high up on the Downs, was an old Elizabethan house belonging to the family of Norton.

For four days Charles pretended to be sick and sat in the chimney corner, while Miss Jane complained to heaven of the feebleness of her servant. 'That wretched boy will never be good for anything again,' she told all and sundry. One day the King, while eating his bread and cheese in the buttery, fell into talk with a man who had been at Worcester, and asked him if he had ever seen the King. 'Twenty times,' was the answer. 'What kind of a fellow is he?' The man looked at Charles steadfastly. 'He is,' he said, 'four fingers' breadth taller than you.' At that moment Mrs Norton passed and Charles took off his hat to her. The butler, who had never seen him uncovered, saw something in his face which he remembered. He took occasion a little later, when they were alone, to ask if he were not the King. Charles confessed that he was, and the butler—one John Pope, who had been once a falconer of Sir Thomas Jermyn, and afterwards a Royalist soldier—swore secrecy and fealty.

Another person was now in the plot, and Pope was used as a messenger to Bristol to find out what ships were sailing. But the news was bad. No vessel could be obtained there, and since it was clear that the King could not stay on at Abbots Leigh, it was resolved to seek the hospitality of Colonel Francis Wyndham, who lived at Trent on the Dorsetshire borders. The aim was to reach the south coast, where a smack might be hired to carry him into France.

16

The man looked at Charles steadfastly. 'He is four fingers' breadth taller than you,' he said.

Lord Wilmot, who had arrived at Abbots Leigh soon after the King, was sent off to Trent to inquire whether the Wyndhams would hide His Majesty. He brought back a reply that Wyndham 'thought himself extremely happy that amongst so many noble and loyal subjects he should be reckoned chiefly worthy of that honour, and that he was ready not only to venture his life, family, and estate, but even to sacrifice all to His Majesty's service.' There was some difficulty about the departure of Miss Jane. The lady at Abbots Leigh had just had a child and implored her friend not to leave her. An imaginary letter was accordingly fabricated, purporting to be from Miss Jane's father, demanding her immediate return on the ground of his sudden and dangerous illness.

On the 16th Miss Jane, Lassels, and Charles set out for Dorsetshire, going first towards Bristol as if they were returning to Bentley. Presently they turned the horses' heads south towards Castle Cary, where they were to sleep the night. The manor there was occupied by Lord Hertford's steward, one Edward Kirton, who had been advised by Lord Wilmot to look out for the travellers. Next day a ride of ten miles brought the party to Trent, where Colonel Francis Wyndham and his wife, Lady Anne, were waiting to receive them. The Wyndhams, as if taking an evening walk, met their guests before the house was reached. Miss Jane and Lassels were publicly received as relations, but Charles was brought secretly into the old house.

Next morning the King parted with Miss Jane, who had been the Flora Macdonald of his Odyssey. She lived thirty-eight years after that eventful journey, marrying Sir Clement Fisher of Packington, a Warwickshire squire. She became a famous toast to Royalists, and the many portraits extant reveal a lady of pleasing aspect, with a certain resolution and vigour in her air. The King gave her many gifts, the House of Lords presented her with jewels, and she and all her relations had royal pensions. Her brother, Colonel Lane, was offered but declined a peerage. The family were granted an augmentation to their coat of arms, and the motto, 'Garde le Roi' to commemorate their achievement.

Trent was a good hiding-place and within reasonable distance of the coast, so that negotiations could be entered upon for a vessel to carry His Majesty to France. There Charles stayed several days, living in a set of four rooms, which are still unaltered. One day the bells of the neighbouring church rang out a peal, and the King sent to inquire the reason for the rejoicing. He was told that one of Cromwell's troopers was in the village, who announced that he had killed Charles, and was even then wearing his buff-coat, and that the villagers, being mostly Puritans, were celebrating the joyful news.

Meanwhile Colonel Wyndham was hunting high and low for a ship. He consulted his neighbour, Colonel Strangways of Melbury, the ancestor of the Ilchester family; and a certain William Ellesdon, a merchant of Lyme Regis, was named as a likely person to procure a vessel, since he had already assisted Lord Berkeley to escape. Ellesdon suggested a tenant of his, one Stephen Limbry of Charmouth, the master of a coasting vessel, and for £60 the latter agreed to carry Lord Wilmot and her servant to France. Limbry was to have his longboat ready at Charmouth on the night of the 22nd.

The next thing was to get rooms at Charmouth for that night, and Wyndham's servant was sent to an inn there—the Queen's Arms— with a tale of how he served a worthy nobleman who was deep in love with an orphan maid and was resolved to steal her by night. The romantic hostess believed the story, and agreed to give them rooms and keep her tongue quiet. Accordingly Charles set out on the morning of 22 September from Trent, riding pillion with a certain Miss Juliana Coningsby, Colonel Wyndham's pretty cousin, who was to play the part of the runaway heroine. Colonel Wyndham went as a guide, and Lord Wilmot and his servant followed behind. On the way to Charmouth they met Ellesdon, who learned for the first time that the King was the fugitive. Charles made the merchant a present of a gold coin in which he had bored a hole to while away the dreary hours of his hiding at Trent. In the afternoon the little party rode down the steep hill into Charmouth, arriving at the inn of the romantic landlady, while Ellesdon went to hunt up Limbry, the seaman.

It was an anxious moment, for, as luck would have it, it was market day at Lyme and the inn was crowded. Lord Wilmot and Miss Coningsby had to live up to the part of runaway lovers—a part in which Charles would probably have shown more zeal than discretion.

Midnight came, but there was no sign of Limbry. Wyndham and his servant were out all night on the quest, but at dawn they returned to report failure. The first idea was that the man must have got drunk at the market; but later the true story came out. Limbry had gone home

19

to get clean clothes for the voyage. But that day a proclamation had been made in the town declaring it death for any person to aid or conceal the King, and promising £1,000 reward for his apprehension. His wife, knowing her husband's practices in the past, accordingly locked him in his room, and when he would have broken out raised racket enough to alarm the neighbourhood. The prudent man made a virtue of necessity and submitted.

Here was a pretty kettle of fish. Charles could not stay at Charmouth, and it was arranged that he and Miss Coningsby and Wyndham should ride on to Bridport, while Lord Wilmot and his servant should remain behind for an explanation with Ellesdon. A rendezvous was to be made at the George Inn at Bridport. Off went the King, while Lord Wilmot's horse went to the smithy to be shod. The smith, who was a stout Cromwellian, began to ask questions. Whence came these nails if the gentlemen had ridden from Exeter, for these nails were assuredly put in in the North? The ostler in charge of the horse added that the saddles had not been taken off in the night time, and that the gentlemen, though travellers, sat up all night. Clearly they were people of quality fleeing from the Worcester fight, and probably the King was among them. The ostler saw a chance of making his fortune, and marched off to the parsonage to consult the parson, one Wesley, the great-grandfather of the famous John.

But Mr Wesley was busy at his morning devotions and would not move till they were ended. On hearing the tale he accompanied the ostler to the inn, where, being apparently a humorist, he thus accosted the landlady: 'Charles Stuart lay last night at your house and kissed you at his departure, so that now you can't but be a maid of honour.' 'If I thought it was the King, as you say it was,' was the answer, 'I would think the better of my lips all the days of my life. Out of my house, Mr Parson.' So Mr Parson went to the nearest commanding officer and got a troop of horse together, who followed what they believed to be the track of the fugitives along the London road.

Meantime Charles had arrived at Bridport. The town was packed with soldiers who had mustered there for an expedition against the Isle of Jersey. It was no easy matter to get lodgings at the George; but there he must go, for it was the rendezvous appointed with Lord Wilmot. A private room was found with some difficulty, while the King attended to the horses in the yard. There he met a drunken ostler who claimed to have known him in Exeter; the King played up to this part and the two made merry together. A hurried dinner was eaten, for there was no time to linger, and as soon as Lord Wilmot had joined them they pushed on along the London road. A quarter of an hour after they left the inn the local authorities arrived to search it (the news of the Royalists' presence having come from Charmouth), and more soldiers started in pursuit. Luckily the King's party resolved to go back to Trent, and had just turned off the high road when they saw the pursuit dash past in the direction of Dorchester.

After that the travellers seem to have lost their way, but in the evening they found themselves in the village of Broad Windsor, close to Trent. In the inn there Colonel Wyndham recognized in the landlord a former servant and a staunch Royalist, and there they slept the night. It was a narrow lodging and much congested with forty soldiers, who were marching to the south coast on the Jersey expedition. No untoward event, however, happened, and next morning the King got back to his old quarters in Trent. There he lay secure while his pursuers were laying hands upon every handsome young lady for forty miles round, under the belief that it was their monarch in disguise. The honest folk of Charmouth and Bridport seem to have seen the King in Miss Juliana Coningsby, and, indeed, this belief in Charles's female disguise was almost universal. There was another rumour in London that, wearing a red periwig, he had actually got a post as servant to an officer of Cromwell's army; and still another, published on 29 September, that he was safe in Scotland with Lord Balcarres.

The problem of escape had now become exceedingly difficult. It was impossible to stay on the coast, which was strictly watched, and was, moreover, all in a bustle with the Jersey expedition. But the coast was the only hope, and therefore it must be again visited. The only chance was to make a cast inland and try for the shore at another point. While at Trent Colonel Wyndham's brother-in-law, Mr Edward Hyde, came to dine, and mentioned that on the previous day at Salisbury he had seen Colonel Robert Phelips of Montacute, who could probably get them a vessel in one of the southern ports. Lord Wilmot was accordingly sent off next morning to Salisbury to find Colonel Phelips and devise a plan.

Phelips willingly undertook the service and went off to Southampton to look for a ship. He thought he had found one; but it turned out that the barque was pressed to carry provisions to Admiral Blake's fleet then lying before Jersey. He returned to Salisbury, and decided to get the assistance of a certain Colonel Gounter who lived near Chichester. It was agreed that Charles should be brought to Heale House, near Salisbury, the residence of a widow, a Mrs Hyde, and there, on Monday 6 October, accompanied by Miss Juliana Coningsby, the King duly arrived from Trent. At Heale Miss Juliana left him, having faithfully played her romantic part. To dinner came Dr Hinchman, afterwards Bishop of Salisbury, and next day the King behaved like an ordinary tourist, riding out to see the sights, especially Stonehenge.

Meanwhile Lord Wilmot was scouring the country for a man who would hire him a boat, and he and Colonel Gounter thought their likeliest chance was with a certain Captain Nicholas Tattersal, the master of a small coal brig, the *Surprise*, at Brighton. Tattersal, however, had just started for Chichester; but a message reached him at Shoreham, and on Saturday, 11 October, there was a meeting, when, for £60, the captain agreed to carry over to France Colonel Gounter's two friends, who were anxious to leave the country because of their part in a fatal duel.

It was now necessary to get the King from Heale to the Sussex coast. At two o'clock on the Monday morning Charles rode out of Heale by the back way with Colonel Phelips, and took the road for Hampshire. After they had covered about fifteen miles they were joined by Colonel Gounter and Lord Wilmot, who, by previous arrangement, had been coursing hares on the Downs. They spent the night in a house at Hambledon among the pleasant hills of the Forest of Bere, where they parted with Phelips. Colonel Gounter was now in charge, and on Tuesday, the 14th, their way lay through the county of Sussex. Charles's disguise must have been fairly complete, for he seems usually to have been taken for a Parliamentarian, since William Penderel's scissors had left him with very little hair. He took pains to keep up the character, for when an inn-keeper used an oath, he flung up his hands and drawled, 'Oh, dear brother, that is a "scape". Swear not, I beseech thee.' He was clad in a short coat and breeches of sad-coloured cloth, with a black hat, and according to one narrative cut a figure like 'the minor sort of country gentleman'.

22

This last day's ride was in many ways the most hazardous of all. As they neared Arundel Castle they suddenly encountered the Governor setting out to hunt with some of his men. Crossing the Arun at Houghton Bridge, they had beer at a poor alehouse and lunched off two cows' tongues, which Colonel Gounter had brought with him. Then they passed through the pretty village of Bramber, which, as it happened, was full of Cromwellian soldiers who had stopped for refreshment. When they had left the village behind them they heard a clattering at their back and saw the whole troop riding as if in pursuit. The soldiers, however, galloped past them without stopping, and at the next village, Beeding, where Colonel Gounter had arranged a meal for the King, they did not dare halt for fear of the same soldiers. Nine miles more over the Downs and they reached the obscure little fishing village of Brighthelmstone, which was all that then existed of Brighton, and halted at the George Inn, where they ordered supper.

The place was happily empty, and there Lord Wilmot joined them. That last meal was a merry one, and Charles was especially cheerful, for he saw his long suspense approaching its end. He had borne the strain with admirable fortitude and good humour, and whatever may be said of his qualities as a king on the throne, he was certainly an excellent king of adventure. The landlord, one Smith, who had formerly been in the Royal Guards, waited on the table at supper and apparently recognized His Majesty, for he kissed his hand and said, 'It shall not be said that I have not kissed the best man's hand in England. God bless you! I do not doubt but, before I die, to be a lord and my wife a lady.' Tattersal, the shipmaster, also joined them, and they sat drinking and smoking until 10 p.m., when it was time to start.

Horses were brought by the back way to the beach, and the party rode along the coast to Shoreham Creek. There lay the coal brig, the *Surprise*, and Charles and Lord Wilmot got into her by way of her ladder and lay down in the little cabin till the tide turned, after bidding adieu to Colonel Gounter. The honest Colonel waited upon the shore with the horses for some hours, lest some accident should drive the party ashore again.

It was between seven and eight o'clock in the morning of Wednesday, 15 October, before the boat sailed, making apparently for the Isle of Wight, the captain having given out that he was bound for Poole with a cargo of sea coal. At five o'clock that evening they changed direction, and with a favourable north wind set out for the French coast. The King amused himself on deck by directing the course, for he knew something of navigation. Next morning the coast of France was sighted, but a change in the wind and the falling tide compelled them to anchor two miles off Fécamp. Charles and Wilmot rowed ashore in the cock-boat. Thereafter the wind turned again, and enabled Tattersal to proceed to Poole without any one being aware that he had paid a visit to France.

After the Restoration the little coal boat was ornamented and enlarged and moored in the Thames at Whitehall as a show for Londoners. She now bore the name of the *Royal Escape*, and was entered as a fifth-rater in the Royal Navy.

Wilmot, the loyal and resourceful companion, did not live to see the Restoration, for he died in the autumn of 1657, after he had been created Earl of Rochester. Nine years after the events recorded in this tale, on 25 May, in bright weather, Charles landed at Dover at the summons of his countrymen, as the restored King of England. He was met by the Mayor and presented with a Bible, which, he observed, was the thing he most valued in the world. So began a reign which was scarcely worthy of its spirited prelude. In one matter, indeed, the King was beyond criticism. No one of the people, gentle or simple, who had assisted him in that wild flight from Worcester died unrewarded. Until the end of his days Charles cherished tenderly the memory of the weeks when he had been an outlaw with a price on his head, and king, like Robin Hood, only of the greenwood.

THE HAND

Guy de Maupassant

The whole party had gathered in a circle round Monsieur Bermutier, the magistrate, who was giving his opinion on the mysterious St Cloud affair, an inexplicable crime, which had been distracting Paris for a month. No one could make anything of it. Standing with his back to the fireplace, Monsieur Bermutier was discussing it, marshalling his proofs, analysing theories, but arriving at no conclusion. Some of the ladies had risen from their chairs and had come nearer him. Clustering round him, they kept their eyes on the clean-shaven lips which uttered such weighty words. They shuddered and trembled, thrilled by that strange awe, that eager and insatiable craving for horrors, which haunts the mind of women and tortures them like the pangs of hunger. One of them, paler than the others, ventured to break a sudden silence:

'How ghastly! It has a touch of the supernatural. No one will ever find out the truth about it.'

Monsieur Bermutier turned to her:

'That is likely enough. But as for your word, supernatural, it has no place in this affair. We are confronted with a crime, which was ably conceived and very ably executed. It is wrapped in such profound mystery that we cannot disengage it from the impenetrable circumstances surrounding it. Still, within my own experience, I had once to follow up a case that really appeared to have an element of the supernatural in it. We had eventually to give it up, for lack of means to elucidate it.'

Several ladies exclaimed as with one voice:

'Oh, do tell us about it.'

With the grave smile appropriate to an investigating magistrate, Monsieur Bermutier resumed:

'At all events pray do not imagine that I myself have for one instant attributed anything of the supernatural to this incident. I believe in normal causes only. It would be much better if we used the word "inexplicable" instead of "supernatural" to express things that we did not understand. In any case, what was striking in the affair I am going to tell you about was not so much the event itself as the circumstances that attended and led up to it. Now to the facts.

'At that time I was investigating magistrate at Ajaccio, a little town of white houses, situated on the edge of a wonderful bay surrounded on all sides by lofty mountains. My principal task there was the investigation of vendettas. Some of these vendettas are sublime, savage, heroic, inconceivably dramatic. In them, one comes across the finest themes of revenge imaginable; hatreds that have endured for centuries, lying for a time in abeyance, but never extinguished; detestable stratagems, assassinations that are mere butchery, others that are almost heroic deeds. For two years I had heard nothing discussed there but the price of blood; nothing but this terrible Corsican tradition, which obliges a man who has been wronged to wreak his revenge upon the man who has wronged him, or upon his descendants or his next-of-kin. Old men, children, distant cousins—I had seen them all slaughtered, and my head was full of tales of vengeance.

'One day I was informed that an Englishman had just taken a lease for several years of a little villa at the far end of the bay. He had brought with him a French manservant, whom he had picked up while passing through Marseilles. It was not long before universal curiosity was excited by this eccentric person, who lived alone and never left his house except to go shooting or fishing. He spoke to no one, never came to the town, and practised for an hour or two every morning with his pistol and carbine. All sorts of legends sprang up about him. He was said to be an exalted personage who had fled his country for political reasons; to this succeeded a theory that he was in hiding because he had committed a horrible crime of which the most shocking details were given.

'In my official capacity, I was anxious to learn something about this man, but my inquiries were fruitless. The name he went by was Sir John Rowell. I had to be satisfied with keeping a close watch upon him, but I never really discovered anything suspicious about him. Nonetheless, the rumours never ceased, and they became so widespread that I determined to make an effort to see this stranger with my own eyes. I therefore took to shooting regularly in the neighbourhood of his property.

'My opportunity was long in arriving, but at length it presented itself in the form of a partridge, which I shot under the Englishman's very nose. My dog brought me the bird, but I took it immediately to Sir John Rowell, and begged him to accept it, at the same time making my apologies for my breach of good manners. He was a red-headed, red-bearded man, very tall and massive, a sort of easy-going, well-mannered Hercules. He had none of the so-called British stiffness, and although his accent came from beyond the Channel, he thanked me warmly for my considerate behaviour. Before a month had elapsed we had conversed five or six times. One evening as I was passing his gate, I caught sight of him smoking his pipe. I greeted him and he invited me to come in and have a glass of beer. I accepted his invitation with alacrity. He received me with all the meticulous English courtesy; and although he made shocking mistakes in grammar he was full of the praises of France and Corsica and professed his affection for these countries. Very cautiously, and under the pretext of a lively interest, I began to question him about his life and his plans for the future. His replies were perfectly frank and he told me that he had travelled much in Africa, India and America.

' "Oh, yes, I have had plenty of adventures," he added, laughing.

'Then I turned the conversation on sport and he gave me the most curious details about shooting hippopotamus, tiger, elephant, and even gorilla.

' "These are all formidable brutes," I said.

' "Why no," he said smiling. "Man is the worst of all."

'He laughed heartily, like a big, genial Englishman.

' " I have done lots of man-hunting, too."

'Then he talked about guns and invited me into his house to look at various makes. His drawing-room was hung with black silk, embroidered with golden flowers that shone like fire on the sombre background. It was Japanese work, he said.

'In the middle of the largest panel, a strange object attracted my attention; it stood out clearly against a square of red velvet. I went up to examine it. It was a hand, the hand of a man. Not a clean, white skeleton hand, but a black, dried-up hand, with yellow nails, bared muscles, and showing old traces of blood, black blood, crusted round the bones, which had been cut clean through as with an axe, about the middle of the forearm. Round the wrist of this unclean object was riveted a powerful chain, which was attached to the wall by a ring strong enough to hold an elephant.

' "What is that?" I asked.

' "That is my worst enemy," replied the Englishman calmly. "He was an American. His hand was chopped off with a sabre. Then it was skinned with sharp flints, and after that it was dried in the sun for a week. It was a good job for me."

'I touched this human relic. The man must have been a Colossus. The fingers were abnormally long and were attached by enormous tendons to which fragments of skin still adhered. It was a terrible sight, this hand, all flayed; it could not but suggest some savage act of vengeance.

' "He must have been a stout fellow," I remarked.

' "Oh yes," replied the Englishman in his gentle tones. "He was strong, but I was stronger. I fixed that chain on his hand to keep it from escaping."

'Thinking that he was joking, I replied:

' "The chain is hardly needed now; the hand can't run away."

'Sir John answered gravely:

' "That hand is always trying to get away. The chain is necessary."

'I cast a rapid, questioning glance at him, wondering whether he was mad or making an unpleasant joke. But this face retained its calm, impenetrable, benevolent expression. I changed the subject and began to admire his guns. I noticed, however that, there were three loaded

Round the wrist of the dried-up hand was riveted a powerful chain.

revolvers lying about on the chairs and tables. Apparently this man lived in constant dread of an attack.

'I went to see him several times, and then my visits ceased. People had become accustomed to his presence and took no further interest in him.

'A whole year passed. One morning towards the end of November, my servant woke me with the news that Sir John Rowell had been murdered during the night. Half an hour later I was in the Englishman's house. With me were the Superintendent of Police and the Captain of gendarmes. Sir John's manservant was weeping at the door of the house; he was distraught and desperate. At first I suspected him. He was, however, innocent. Nor was the murderer ever discovered.

'When I entered the drawing-room, the first thing to strike me was the sight of Sir John's corpse lying flat on its back in the middle of the floor. His waistcoat was torn; one sleeve of his coat was ripped off. There was every indication that a terrible struggle had taken place.

'Death had been caused by strangulation. Sir John's face was black, swollen, and terrifying. It bore an expression of hideous dread. His teeth were clenched on some object. In his neck, which was covered with blood, there were five holes, which might have been made by iron fingers. A doctor arrived. After a prolonged examination of the finger-marks in the flesh, he uttered these strange words:

' "It almost looks as if he has been strangled by a skeleton." '

'A shudder passed down my spine, and I cast a glance at the wall, at the spot where I had been wont to see that horrible, flayed hand. The hand was no longer there. The chain had been broken and was hanging loose. I bent down close to the corpse and between his clenched teeth I found one of the fingers of that vanished hand. At the second joint it had been cut, or rather bitten, off by the dead man's teeth. An investigation was held, but without result. No door or window had been forced that night, no cupboard or drawer had been broken into. The watchdogs had not been disturbed. The substance of the servant's evidence can be given briefly. For a month past his master had seemed to have something on his mind. He had received many letters, which he had promptly burnt. Often he would snatch up a horse-whip and in a passion of rage, which suggested insanity, lash furiously at that withered hand, which had been riveted to the wall, and had mysteriously vanished at the very hour at which the crime was committed.

'Sir John, said the servant, went late to bed and locked himself carefully in his room. He always had firearms within reach. Often during the night he could be heard speaking in loud tones, as if he were wrangling with someone. On the night in question, however, he had made no sound, and it was only on coming to open the windows the next morning that the servant had discovered the murder. The witness suspected no one.

'I told the magistrates and police officers everything I knew about the deceased, and inquiries were made with scupulous care throughout the whole island, but nothing was ever discovered.

'Well, one night, three months after the murder, I had a frightful nightmare. I thought I saw that hand, that ghastly hand, running like a scorpion or a spider over my curtains and walls. Thrice I awoke, and thrice fell asleep again, and thrice did I see that hideous relic gallop around my room, with its fingers running along like the legs of an insect. The next day the hand itself was brought to me. It had been found in the cemetery on Sir John's tomb. He had been buried there, as no trace of his family was discoverable. The index finger of the hand was missing. Ladies, that is my story. That is all I know about it.'

The ladies were horrified, pale and trembling. One of them protested:

'But the mystery is not solved. There is no explanation. We shall never be able to sleep if you don't tell us what you make of it yourself.'

The magistrate smiled a little grimly:

'Well, ladies, I'm afraid I shall deprive you of your nightmares. My theory is the perfectly simple one that the rightful owner of that hand was not dead at all, and that he came looking for his severed member with the one that was left him. But as for explaining how he managed it, that is beyond me. It was a kind of vendetta.'

Another lady protested:

'No, that can't be the real explanation.'

Still smiling, the narrator rejoined:

'I told you it wouldn't satisfy you.'

RIKKI-TIKKI-TAVI

Rudyard Kipling

At the hole where he went in
Red-Eye called to Wrinkle-Skin.
Hear what little Red-Eye saith:
'Nag, come up and dance with death!'

Eye to eye and head to head,
   (*Keep the measure, Nag.*)
This shall end when one is dead;
   (*At thy pleasure, Nag.*)
Turn for turn and twist for twist—
   (*Run and hide thee, Nag.*)
Hah! The hooded Death has missed!
   (*Woe betide thee, Nag!*)

This is the story of the great war that Rikki-tikki-tavi fought single-handed, through the bathrooms of the big bungalow in Segowlee cantonment. Darzee, the tailor-bird, helped him, and Chuchundra, the musk-rat, who never comes out into the middle of the floor, but always creeps round by the wall, gave him advice; but Rikki-tikki did the real fighting.

He was a mongoose, rather like a little cat in his fur and his tail, but quite like a weasel in his head and his habits. His eyes and the end of his restless nose were pink; he could scratch himself anywhere he pleased, with any leg, front or back, that he chose to use; he could fluff up his tail till it looked like a bottle-brush, and his war-cry, as he scuttled through the long grass, was: '*Rikk-tikk-tikki-tikki-tchk!*'

One day, a high summer flood washed him out of the burrow where he lived with his father and mother, and carried him, kicking and clucking, down a roadside ditch. He found a little wisp of grass floating there, and clung to it till he lost his senses. When he revived, he was lying in the hot sun on the middle of a garden path, very draggled indeed, and a small boy was saying: 'Here's a dead mongoose. Let's have a funeral.'

'No,' said his mother; 'let's take him in and dry him. Perhaps he isn't really dead.'

They took him into the house, and a big man picked him up between his finger and thumb, and said he was not dead but half choked; so they wrapped him in cotton-wool, and warmed him, and he opened his eyes and sneezed.

'Now,' said the big man (he was an Englishman who had just moved into the bungalow); 'don't frighten him, and we'll see what he'll do.'

It is the hardest thing in the world to frighten a mongoose, because he is eaten up from nose to tail with curiosity. The motto of all the mongoose family is, 'Run and find out'; and Rikki-tikki was a true mongoose. He looked at the cotton-wool, decided that it was not good to eat, ran all round the table, sat up and put his fur in order, scratched himself, and jumped on the small boy's shoulder.

'Don't be frightened, Teddy,' said his father. 'That's his way of making friends.'

'Ouch! He's tickling under my chin,' said Teddy.

Rikki-tikki looked down between the boy's collar and neck, snuffed at his ear, and climbed down to the floor, where he sat rubbing his nose.

'Good gracious,' said Teddy's mother, 'and that's a wild creature! I suppose he's so tame because we've been kind to him.'

'All mongooses are like that,' said her husband. 'If Teddy doesn't pick him up by the tail, or try to put him in a cage, he'll run in and out of the house all day long. Let's give him something to eat.'

They gave him a little piece of raw meat. Rikki-tikki liked it immensely, and when it was finished he went out into the verandah and sat in the sunshine and fluffed up his fur to make it dry to the roots. Then he felt better.

'There are more things to find out about in this house,' he said to himself, 'than all my family could find out in all their lives. I shall certainly stay and find out.'

He spent all that day roaming over the house. He nearly drowned himself in the bath-tubs, put his nose into the ink on a writing-table, and burnt it on the end of the big man's cigar, for he climbed up in the big man's lap to see how writing was done. At nightfall he ran into Teddy's nursery to watch how kerosene-lamps were lit, and when Teddy went to bed Rikki-tikki climbed up too; but he was a restless companion, because he had to get up and attend to every noise all through the night, and find out what made it. Teddy's mother and father came in, the last thing, to look at their boy, and Rikki-tikki was awake on the pillow. 'I don't like that,' said Teddy's mother; 'he may bite the child.' 'He'll do no such thing,' said the father. 'Teddy's safer with that little beast than if he had a bloodhound to watch him. If a snake came into the nursery now——'

But Teddy's mother wouldn't think of anything so awful.

Early in the morning Rikki-tikki came to early breakfast in the verandah riding on Teddy's shoulder, and they gave him banana and some boiled egg; and he sat on all their laps one after the other, because every well-brought-up mongoose always hopes to be a house-mongoose some day and have rooms to run about in, and Rikki-tikki's mother (she used to live in the General's house at Segowlee) had carefully told Rikki what to do if ever he came across white men.

Then Rikki-tikki went out into the garden to see what was to be seen. It was a large garden, only half cultivated, with bushes as big as summer-houses of Marshal Niel roses, lime and orange trees, clumps of bamboos, and thickets of high grass. Rikki-tikki licked his lips. 'This is a splendid hunting-ground,' he said, and his tail grew bottle-brushy at the thought of it, and he scuttled up and down the garden, snuffing here and there till he heard very sorrowful voices in a thorn-bush.

It was Darzee, the tailor-bird, and his wife. They had made a beautiful nest by pulling two big leaves together and stitching them up the edges with fibres, and had filled the hollow with cotton and downy fluff. The nest swayed to and fro, as they sat on the rim and cried.

'What is the matter?' asked Rikki-tikki.

'We are very miserable,' said Darzee. 'One of our babies fell out of the nest yesterday, and Nag ate him.'

'H'm!' said Rikki-tikki, 'that is very sad—but I am a stranger here. Who is Nag?'

Darzee and his wife only cowered down in the nest without answering, for from the thick grass at the foot of the bush there came a low hiss—a horrid cold sound that made Rikki-tikki jump back two clear feet. Then inch by inch out of the grass rose up the head and spread hood of Nag, the big black cobra, and he was five feet long from tongue to tail. When he had lifted one-third of himself clear of the ground, he stayed balancing to and fro exactly as a dandelion-tuft balances in the wind, and he looked at Rikki-tikki with the wicked snake's eyes that never change their expression, whatever the snake may be thinking of.

'Who is Nag?' said he. '*I* am Nag. The great god Brahm put his mark upon all our people when the first cobra spread his hood to keep the sun off Brahm as he slept. Look, and be afraid!'

He spread out his hood more than ever, and Rikki-tikki saw the spectacle-mark on the back of it that looks exactly like the eye part of a hook-and-eye fastening. He was afraid for the minute; but it is impossible for a mongoose to stay frightened for any length of time, and though Rikki-tikki had never met a live cobra before, his mother had fed him on dead ones, and he knew that all a grown mongoose's business in life was to fight and eat snakes. Nag knew that too, and at the bottom of his cold heart he was afraid.

'Well,' said Rikki-tikki, and his tail began to fluff up again, 'marks or no marks, do you think it is right for you to eat fledglings out of a nest?'

Nag was thinking to himself, and watching the least little movement in the grass behind Rikki-tikki. He knew that mongooses in the garden meant death sooner or later for him and his family, but he wanted to get Rikki-tikki off his guard. So he dropped his head a little, and put it on one side.

'Let us talk,' he said. 'You eat eggs. Why should not I eat birds?'

'Behind you! Look behind you!' sang Darzee.

Rikki-tikki knew better than to waste time in staring. He jumped up in the air as high as he could go, and just under him whizzed by the head of Nagaina, Nag's wicked wife. She had crept up behind him as he was talking, to make an end of him; and he heard her savage hiss as the stroke missed. He came down almost across her back, and if he had been an old mongoose he would have known that then was the time to break her back with one bite; but he was afraid of the terrible lashing return-stroke of the cobra. He bit, indeed, but did not bite long enough, and he jumped clear of the whisking tail, leaving Nagaina torn and angry.

'Wicked, wicked Darzee!' said Nag, lashing up as high as he could

35

'I am Nag,' said the cobra. *'Look, and be afraid.'*

reach toward the nest in the thorn-bush; but Darzee had built it out of reach of snakes, and it only swayed to and fro.

Rikki-tikki felt his eyes growing red and hot (when a mongoose's eyes grow red, he is angry), and he sat back on his tail and hind legs like a little kangaroo, and looked all round him, and chattered with rage. But Nag and Nagaina had disappeared into the grass. When a snake misses its stroke, it never says anything or gives any sign of what it means to do next. Rikki-tikki did not care to follow them, for he did not feel sure that he could manage two snakes at once. So he trotted off to the gravel path near the house, and sat down to think. It was a serious matter for him.

If you read the old books of natural history, you will find they say that when the mongoose fights the snake and happens to get bitten, he runs off and eats some herb that cures him. That is not true. The victory is only a matter of quickness of eye and quickness of foot—snake's blow against mongoose's jump—and as no eye can follow the motion of a snake's head when it strikes, that makes things much more wonderful than any magic herb. Rikki-tikki knew he was a young mongoose, and it made him all the more pleased to think that he had managed to escape a blow from behind. It gave him confidence in himself, and when Teddy came running down the path, Rikki-tikki was ready to be petted.

But just as Teddy was stooping, something flinched a little in the dust, and a tiny voice said: 'Be careful. I am death!' It was Karait, the dusty brown snakeling that lies for choice on the dusty earth; and his bite is as dangerous as the cobra's. But he is so small that nobody thinks of him, and so he does the more harm to people.

Rikki-tikki's eyes grew red again, and he danced up to Karait with the peculiar rocking, swaying motion that he had inherited from his family. It looks very funny, but it is so perfectly balanced a gait that you can fly off from it at any angle you please; and in dealing with snakes this is an advantage. If Rikki-tikki had only known, he was doing a much more dangerous thing than fighting Nag, for Karait is so small, and can turn so quickly, that unless Rikki bit him close to the back of the head, he would get the return-stroke in his eye or lip. But Rikki did not know: his eyes were all red, and he rocked back and forth, looking for a good place to hold. Karait struck out. Rikki jumped sideways and tried to run in, but the wicked little dusty grey head lashed within a fraction of his shoulder, and he had to jump over the body, and the head followed his heels close.

Teddy shouted to the house: 'Oh, look here! Our mongoose is killing a snake'; and Rikki-tikki heard a scream from Teddy's mother. His father ran out with a stick, but by the time he came up, Karait had lunged out once too far, and Rikki-tikki had sprung, jumped on the snake's back, dropped his head far between his forelegs, bitten as high up the back as he could get hold, and rolled away. That bite paralysed Karait, and Rikki-tikki was just going to eat him up from the tail, after the custom of his family at dinner, when he remembered that a full meal makes a slow mongoose, and if he wanted all his strength and quickness ready, he must keep himself thin.

He went away for a dust-bath under the castor-oil bushes, while Teddy's father beat the dead Karait. 'What is the use of that?' thought Rikki-tikki. 'I have settled it all'; and then Teddy's mother picked him up from the dust and hugged him, crying that he had saved Teddy from death, and Teddy's father said that he was a providence, and Teddy looked on with big scared eyes. Rikki-tikki was rather amused at all the fuss, which, of course, he did not understand. Teddy's mother might just as well have petted Teddy for playing in the dust. Rikki was thoroughly enjoying himself.

That night, at dinner, walking to and fro among the wine-glasses on the table, he could have stuffed himself three times over with nice things; but he remembered Nag and Nagaina, and though it was very pleasant to be patted and petted by Teddy's mother, and to sit on Teddy's shoulder, his eyes would get red from time to time, and he would go off into his long war-cry of '*Rikk-tikk-tikki-tikki-tchkâ*'

Teddy carried him off to bed, and insisted on Rikki-tikki sleeping under his chin. Rikki-tikki was too well bred to bite or scratch, but as soon as Teddy was asleep he went off for his nightly walk round the house, and in the dark he ran up against Chuchundra, the musk-rat, creeping round by the wall. Chuchundra is a broken-hearted little beast. He whimpers and cheeps all the night, trying to make up his mind to run into the middle of the room, but he never gets there.

'Don't kill me,' said Chuchundra, almost weeping. 'Rikki-tikki, don't kill me.'

'Do you think a snake-killer kills musk-rats?' said Rikki-tikki.

'Those who kill snakes get killed by snakes,' said Chuchundra, more sorrowfully than ever. 'And how am I to be sure that Nag won't mistake me for you some dark night?'

'There's not the least danger,' said Rikki-tikki; 'but Nag is in the garden, and I know you don't go there.'

'My cousin Chua, the rat, told me——' said Chuchundra, and then he stopped.

'Told you what?'

'H'sh! Nag is everywhere, Rikki-tikki. You should have talked to Chua in the garden.'

'I didn't—so you must tell me. Quick, Chuchundra, or I'll bite you!'

Chuchundra sat down and cried till the tears rolled off his whiskers. 'I am a very poor man,' he sobbed. 'I never had spirit enough to run out into the middle of the room. H'sh! I mustn't tell you anything. Can't you *hear*, Rikki-tikki?'

Rikki-tikki listened. The house was as still as still, but he thought he could just catch the faintest *scratch-scratch* in the world—a noise as faint as that of a wasp walking on a window pane—the dry scratch of a snake's scales on brickwork.

'That's Nag or Nagaina,' he said to himself; 'and he is crawling into the bathroom sluice. You're right, Chuchundra; I should have talked to Chua.'

He stole off to Teddy's bathroom, but there was nothing there, and then to Tddy's mother's bathroom. At the bottom of the smooth plaster wall there was a brick pulled out to make a sluice for the bath-water, and as Rikki-tikki stole in by the masonry curb where the bath is put, he heard Nag and Nagaina whispering together outside in the moonlight.

'When the house is emptied of people,' said Nagaina to her husband, '*he* will have to go away, and then the garden will be our own again. Go in quietly, and remember that the big man who killed Karait is the first one to bite. Then come out and tell me, and we will hunt for Rikki-tikki together.'

'But are you sure that there is anything to be gained by killing the people?' said Nag.

'Everything. When there were no people in the bungalow, did we have any mongoose in the garden? So long as the bungalow is empty, we

39

are king and queen of the garden; and remember that as soon as our eggs in the melon-bed hatch, as they may tomorrow, our children will will need room and quiet.'

'I had not thought of that,' said Nag. 'I will go, but there is no need that we should hunt for Rikki-tikki afterward. I will kill the big man and his wife, and the child if I can, and come away quietly. Then the bungalow will be empty, and Rikki-tikki will go.'

Rikki-tikki tingled all over with rage and hatred at this, and then Nag's head came through the sluice, and his five feet of cold body followed it. Angry as he was, Rikki-tikki was very frightened as he saw the size of the big cobra. Nag coiled himself up, raised his head, and looked into the bathroom in the dark, and Rikki could see his eyes glitter.

'Now, if I kill him here, Nagaina will know; and if I fight him on the open floor, the odds are in his favour. What am I to do?' said Rikki-tikki-tavi to himself.

Nag waved to and fro, and then Rikki-tikki heard him drinking from the biggest water-jar that was used to fill the bath. 'That is good,' said the snake. 'Now, when Karait was killed, the big man had a stick. He may have that stick still, but when he comes in to bathe in the morning he will not have a stick. I shall wait here till he comes. Nagaina—do you hear me?—I shall wait here in the cool till daytime.'

There was no answer from outside, so Rikki-tikki knew Nagaina had gone away. Nag coiled himself down, coil by coil, round the bulge at the bottom of the water-jar, and Rikki-tikki stayed still as death. After an hour he began to move, muscle by muscle, toward the jar. Nag was asleep, and Rikki-tikki looked at his big back, wondering which would be the best place for a good hold. 'If I don't break his back at the first jump,' said Rikki, 'he can still fight; and if he fights—O Rikki!' He looked at the thickness of the neck below the hood, but that was too much for him; and a bite near the tail would only make Nag savage.

'It must be the head,' he said at last; 'the head above the hood; and when I am once there, I must not let go.'

Then he jumped. The head was lying a little clear of the water-jar, under the curve of it; and, as his teeth met, Rikki braced his back against the bulge of the red earthenware to hold down the head. This gave him just one second's purchase, and he made the most of it. Then he was battered to and fro as a rat is shaken by a dog—to and fro on the floor, up and down, and round in great circles; but his eyes were red, and he held on as the body cart-whipped over the floor, upsetting the tin dipper and the soap-dish and the flesh-brush, and banged against the side of the tin bath. As he held he closed his jaws tighter and tighter, for he made sure he would be banged to death, and, for the honour of his family, he preferred to be found with his teeth locked. He was dizzy, aching, and felt shaken to pieces when something went off like a thunderclap just behind him; a hot wind knocked him senseless, and red fire singed his fur. The big man had been wakened by the noise, and had fired both barrels of a shotgun into Nag just behind the hood.

Rikki-tikki held on with his eyes shut, for now he was quite sure he was dead; but the head did not move, and the big man picked him up and said: 'It's the mongoose again, Alice; the little chap has saved *our* lives now.' Then Teddy's mother came in with a very white face, and saw what was left of Nag, and Rikki-tikki dragged himself to Teddy's bedroom and spent half the rest of the night shaking himself tenderly to find out whether he really was broken into forty pieces, as he fancied.

When morning came he was very stiff, but well pleased with his doings. 'Now I have Nagaina to settle with, and she will be worse than five Nags, and there's no knowing when the eggs she spoke of will hatch. Goodness! I must go and see Darzee,' he said.

Without waiting for breakfast, Rikki-tikki ran to the thorn-bush where Darzee was singing a song of triumph at the top of his voice. The news of Nag's death was all over the garden, for the sweeper had thrown the body on the rubbish-heap.

'Oh, you stupid tuft of feathers!' said Rikki-tikki angrily. 'Is this the time to sing?'

'Nag is dead—is dead—is dead!' sang Darzee. 'The valiant Rikki-tikki caught him by the head and held fast. The big man brought the bang-stick, and Nag fell in two pieces! He will never eat my babies again.'

'All that's true enough; but where's Nagaina?' said Rikki-tikki, looking carefully round him.

'Nagaina came to the bathroom sluice and called for Nag,' Darzee went on; 'and Nag came out on the end of a stick—the sweeper picked him up on the end of a stick and threw him upon the rubbish-heap. Let us sing about the great, the red-eyed Rikki-tikki!' and Darzee filled his throat and sang.

'If I could get up to your nest, I'd roll all your babies out!' said Rikki-tikki. 'You don't know when to do the right thing at the right time. You're safe enough in your nest there, but it's war for me down here. Stop singing a minute, Darzee.'

'For the great, the beautiful Rikki-tikki's sake I will stop,' said Darzee. 'What is it, O killer of the terrible Nag?'

'Where is Nagaina, for the third time?'

'On the rubbish-heap by the stables, mourning for Nag. Great is Rikki-tikki with the white teeth.'

'Bother my white teeth! Have you ever heard where she keeps her eggs?'

'In the melon-bed, on the end nearest the wall, where the sun strikes nearly all day. She hid them there weeks ago.'

'And you never thought it worth while to tell me? The end nearest the wall, you said?'

'Rikki-tikki, you are not going to eat her eggs?'

'Not eat exactly; no. Darzee, if you have a grain of sense you will fly off to the stables and pretend that your wing is broken, and let Nagaina chase you away to this bush. I must get to the melon-bed, and if I went there now she'd see me.'

Darzee was a feather-brained little fellow who could never hold more than one idea at a time in his head; and just because he knew that Nagaina's children were born in eggs like his own, he didn't think at first that it was fair to kill them. But his wife was a sensible bird, and she knew that cobra's eggs meant young cobras later on; so she flew off from the nest, and left Darzee to keep the babies warm, and continue his song about the death of Nag. Darzee was very like a man in some ways.

She fluttered in front of Nagaina by the rubbish-heap, and cried out, 'Oh, my wing is broken! The boy in the house threw a stone at me and broke it.' Then she fluttered more desperately than ever.

Nagaina lifted up her head and hissed, 'You warned Rikki-tikki when I would have killed him. Indeed and truly, you've chosen a bad place to be lame in.' And she moved toward Darzee's wife, slipping along over the dust.

'The boy broke it with a stone!' shrieked Darzee's wife.

'Well! It may be some consolation to you when you're dead to know that I shall settle accounts with the boy. My husband lies on the rubbish-heap this morning, but before night the boy in the house will lie very still. What is the use of running away? I am sure to catch you. Little fool, look at me!'

Darzee's wife knew better than to do *that*, for a bird who looks at a snake's eyes gets so frightened that she cannot move. Darzee's wife fluttered on, piping sorrowfully, and never leaving the ground, and Nagaina quickened her pace.

Rikki-tikki heard them going up the path from the stables, and he raced for the end of the melon-patch near the wall. There, in the warm litter about the melons, very cunningly hidden, he found twenty-five eggs, about the size of a bantam's eggs, but with whitish skin instead of shell.

'I was not a day too soon,' he said; for he could see the baby cobras curled up inside the skin, and he knew that the minute they were hatched they could each kill a man or a mongoose. He bit off the tops of the eggs as fast as he could, taking care to crush the young cobras, and turned over the litter from time to time to see whether he had missed any. At last there were only three eggs left, and Rikki-tikki began to chuckle to himself, when he heard Darzee's wife screaming:

'Rikki-tikki, I led Nagaina toward the house, and she has gone into the verandah, and—oh, come quickly—she means killing!'

Rikki-tikki smashed two eggs, and tumbled backward down the melon-bed with the third egg in his mouth, and scuttled to the verandah as hard as he could put foot to the ground. Teddy and his mother and father were there at early breakfast; but Rikki-tikki saw that they were not eating anything. They sat stone-still, and their faces were white. Nagaina was coiled up on the matting by Teddy's chair, within easy striking distance of Teddy's bare leg, and she was swaying to and fro singing a song of triumph.

'Son of the big man that killed Nag,' she hissed, 'stay still. I am not ready yet. Wait a little. Keep very still, all you three. If you move I strike, and if you do not move I strike. Oh, foolish people, who killed my Nag!'

Teddy's eyes were fixed on his father, and all his father could do was

43

to whisper, 'Sit still, Teddy. You mustn't move. Teddy, keep still.'

Then Rikki-tikki came up and cried: 'Turn round, Nagaina; turn and fight!'

'All in good time,' said she, without moving her eyes. 'I will settle my account with *you* presently. Look at your friends, Rikki-tikki. They are still and white; they are afraid. They dare not move, and if you come a step nearer I strike.'

'Look at your eggs,' said Rikki-tikki, 'in the melon-bed near the wall. Go and look, Nagaina.'

The big snake turned half round, and saw the egg on the verandah. 'Ah-h! Give it to me,' she said.

Rikki-tikki put his paws one on each side of the egg, and his eyes were blood-red. 'What price for a snake's egg? For a young cobra? For a young king-cobra? For the last—the very last of the brood? The ants are eating all the others down by the melon-bed.'

Nagaina spun clear round, forgetting everything for the sake of the one egg; and Rikki-tikki saw Teddy's father shoot out a big hand, catch Teddy by the shoulder, and drag him across the little table with the tea-cups, safe and out of reach of Nagaina.

'Tricked! Tricked! Tricked! *Rikk-tck-tck!*' chuckled Rikki-tikki. 'The boy is safe, and it was I—I—I that caught Nag by the hood last night in the bathroom.' Then he began to jump up and down, all four feet together, his head close to the floor. 'He threw me to and fro, but he could not shake me off. He was dead before the big man blew him in two. I did it. *Rikki-tikki-tck-tck!* Come then, Nagaina. Come and fight with me. You shall not be a widow long.'

Nagaina saw that she had lost her chance of killing Teddy, and the egg lay between Rikki-tikki's paws. 'Give me the egg, Rikki-tikki. Give me the last of my eggs, and I will go away and never come back,' she said, lowering her hood.

'Yes, you will go away, and you will never come back; for you will go to the rubbish-heap with Nag. Fight, widow! The big man has gone for his gun! Fight!'

Rikki-tikki was bounding all round Nagaina, keeping just out of reach of her stroke, his little eyes like hot coals. Nagaina gathered herself together, and flung out at him. Rikki-tikki jumped up and backward. Again and again and again she struck, and each time her head came with a whack on the matting of the verandah, and she gathered herself together like a watch-spring. Then Rikki-tikki danced in a circle to get behind her, and Nagaina spun round to keep her head to his head, so that the rustle of her tail on the matting sounded like dry leaves blown along by the wind.

He had forgotten the egg. It still lay on the verandah, and Nagaina came nearer and nearer to it, till at last, while Rikki-tikki was drawing breath, she caught it in her mouth, turned to the verandah steps, and flew like an arrow down the path, with Rikki-tikki behind her. When the cobra runs for her life, she goes like a whiplash flicked across a horse's neck.

Rikki-tikki knew that he must catch her, or all the trouble would begin again. She headed straight for the long grass by the thorn-bush, and as he was running Rikki-tikki heard Darzee still singing his foolish little song of triumph. But Darzee's wife was wiser. She flew off her nest as Nagaina came along, and flapped her wings about Nagaina's head. If Darzee had helped they might have turned her; but Nagaina only lowered her hood and went on. Still, the instant's delay brought Rikki-tikki up to her, and as she plunged into the rat-hole where she and Nag used to live, his little white teeth were clenched on her tail, and he went down with her—and very few mongooses, however wise and old they may be, care to follow a cobra into its hole. It was dark in the hole; and Rikki-tikki never knew when it might open out and give Nagaina room to turn and strike at him. He held on savagely, and struck out his feet to act as brakes on the dark slope of the hot, moist earth.

Then the grass by the mouth of the hole stopped waving, and Darzee said: 'It is all over with Rikki-tikki! We must sing his death-song. Valiant Rikki-tikki is dead! For Nagaina will surely kill him underground.'

So he sang a very mournful song that he made up on the spur of the minute, and just as he got to the most touching part the grass quivered again, and Rikki-tikki, covered with dirt, dragged himself out of the hole leg by leg, licking his whiskers. Darzee stopped with a little shout. Rikki-tikki shook some of the dust out of his fur and sneezed. 'It is all over,' he said. 'The widow will never come out again.' And the red ants that live between the grass stems heard him, and began to troop down one after another to see if he had spoken the truth.

Rikki-tikki curled himself up in the grass and slept where he was—slept and slept till it was late in the afternoon, for he had done a hard day's work.

'Now,' he said, when he awoke, 'I will go back to the house. Tell the coppersmith, Darzee, and he will tell the garden that Nagaina is dead.'

The coppersmith is a bird who makes a noise exactly like the beating of a little hammer on a copper pot; and the reason he is always making it is because he is the town-crier to every Indian garden, and tells all the news to everybody who cares to listen. As Rikki-tikki went up the path, he heard his 'attention' notes like a tiny dinner-gong; and then the steady '*Ding-dong-tock!* Nag is dead—*dong!* Nagaina is dead! *Ding-dong-tock!*' That set all the birds in the garden singing, and the frogs croaking; for Nag and Nagaina used to eat frogs as well as little birds.

When Rikki got to the house, Teddy and Teddy's mother (she looked very white still, for she had been fainting) and Teddy's father came out and almost cried over him; and that night he ate all that was given him till he could eat no more, and went to bed on Teddy's shoulder, where Teddy's mother saw him when she came to look late at night.

'He saved our lives and Teddy's life,' she said to her husband. 'Just think, he saved all our lives.'

Rikki-tikki woke up with a jump, for all the mongooses are light sleepers.

'Oh, it's you,' said he. 'What are you bothering for? All the cobras are dead; and if they weren't, I'm here.'

Rikki-tikki had a right to be proud of himself; but he did not grow too proud, and he kept that garden as a mongoose should keep it, with tooth and jump and spring and bite, till never a cobra dared show its head inside the walls.

MIRACLE NEEDED

Dodie Smith

In Dodie Smith's story of The Hundred and One Dalmatians *the pups of the Dalmatian Pongo and his Missis are abducted from their London home with the Dearly family by the wicked Cruella de Vil, who aims to make furs for herself out of their skins. They are taken to a remote country house called Hell Hall where they meet other Dalmatians destined for the same fate. But Pongo and Missis, after many adventures, manage to track them down and, soon afterwards, all make their escape. On their way back to London, hotly pursued by Cruella, they have camouflaged themselves by rolling in some soot at the back of the sweep's house. But now serious dangers threaten.*

'Last lap before supper,' said Pongo, as they started off again across the moonlit fields.

It was the most cheering thing he could have said, for the ninety-seven puppies were now extremely hungry. He had guessed this because he was hungry himself. And so was Missis. But she was feeling too peaceful to mind.

They went on for nearly two miles, then Pongo saw a long row of cottage roofs ahead across the fields.

'This should be it,' he said.

'What is that glow in the sky beyond the roof-tops?' asked Missis.

Pongo was puzzled. He had seen such a glow in the sky over towns which had many lights, but never over a village. And this was a very bright glow. 'Perhaps it's a larger place than we expected it to be,' he said, and did not feel it would be safe to go any nearer until some dog came to meet them. He called a halt and barked news of their arrival.

He was answered at once, by a bark that said: 'Wait where you are. I am coming.' And though he did not tell Missis, Pongo felt there was something odd about this bark that answered his. For one thing, there were no cheerful words of welcome.

Soon a graceful red setter came dashing towards them. They guessed, even before she spoke, that something was very wrong.

'The bakery's on fire!' she gasped.

The blaze, due to a faulty chimney, had begun only a few minutes before—the fire-engine had not yet arrived. No one had been hurt, but the bakehouse was full of flames and smoke—all the food spread out for the Dalmatians was burned.

'There's nothing for you to eat and nowhere for you to sleep,' moaned the poor setter—she was hysterical. 'And the village street's full of people.' She looked pitifully at Missis. 'All your poor hungry puppies!'

The strange thing was that Missis felt quite calm. She tried to comfort the setter, saying they would go to some barn.

'But no arrangements are made,' wailed the setter. 'And there's no spare food anywhere. All the village dogs brought what they could to the bakery.'

Just then came a shrill whistle.

'My pet is calling me,' said the setter. 'He's the doctor here. There's no dog at the bakery, so I was chosen to arrange everything—because I took first prize in a dog show. And now I've failed you.'

'You have *not* failed,' said Missis. 'No one could say the fire was act of dog. Go back to your pet and don't worry. We shall simply go on to the next village.'

'*Really?*' said the setter, gasping again—but with relief.

Missis kissed her on the nose. 'Off with you, my dear, and don't give the matter another thought. And thank you for all you did.'

The whistle came again and the setter ran off, wildly waving her feathered tail.

'Feather-brained as well as feather-tailed,' said Pongo.

'Just very young,' said Missis, gently. 'I doubt if she's had a family yet. Well, on to the next village.'

'Thank you for being so brave, dear Missis,' said Pongo. 'But where *is* the next village?'

'In the country, there are villages in *every* direction,' said Missis, brightly.

Desperately worried though he was, Pongo smiled lovingly at her. Then he said: 'We will go to the road now.'

'But what about traffic, Pongo?'

'We shall not be very long on the road,' said Pongo.

Then he told her what he had decided. Even if the next village should only be a few miles away, many of the pups were too tired and too hungry to get there—some of them were already asleep on the frozen ground. And every minute it got colder.

'And even if we could get to the next village, where should we sleep, Missis, what should we eat, with no plans made ahead? We must give in, my dear. Come, wake the pups! Quick march, everyone!'

The waking pups whimpered and shivered, and Missis saw that even the strongest pups were now wretchedly cold. So she helped Pongo to make them all march briskly. Then she whispered:

'But *how* do we give in, Pongo?'

Pongo said: 'We must go into the village and find the police station.'

Missis stared at him in horror. 'No, Pongo, no! The police will take the puppies from us!'

'But they will feed them, Missis. And perhaps we shall be kept together until Mr Dearly has been told about us. They will have read the papers. They will know we are the missing Dalmatians.'

'But we are not Dalmatians any more, Pongo,' cried Missis. 'We are black. They will think we are ordinary stray dogs. And we are illegal— ninety-nine dogs without collars. We shall be put in prison.'

'No, Missis!' But Pongo was shaken. He had forgotten they were now black dogs. Suppose the police did *not* recognize them? Suppose the Dearlys were never told about them. What happened to stray dogs that no one claimed?

'Please, Pongo, I beg you!' cried Missis. 'Let us go on with our journey! I *know* it will be all right.'

They had now reached the road and were on the edge of the village. Pongo was faced with a terrible choice. But it still seemed to him wiser to trust the police than to lead the hungry, exhausted puppies into the bitter winter night.

'Missis, dear Missis, we *must* go to the police station,' he said, and turned towards the village. They could now see the burning bakery and at that moment a huge flame leapt up through the roof. By its light Pongo saw the whole village street, with the villagers making a human chain to hand along buckets of water. And he also saw something else

—something which made him stop dead, shouting 'Halt!' at the top of his bark.

In front of the burning bakery was a great striped black-and-white car. And with it was Cruella de Vil—standing right up on the roof of the car, where she had climbed so as to get a good view of the fire. Her white face and absolutely simple white mink cloak no longer looked white. From head to foot she was bathed in the red-gold flicker of the flames. And as they leapt higher and higher she clapped her hands in delight.

The next instant there was a wild clamour of bells as the fire-engine arrived at last. The noise, the flames and, above all, the sight of Cruella were too much for many of the puppies. Squealing in terror, they turned and fled, with Pongo, Missis and Lucky desperately trying to call them to order.

Fortunately, the clamour from the fire-engine prevented anyone in the village hearing the barking and yapping. And after a little while, the terrified pups obeyed Pongo's orders and stopped their headlong flight. They were very shame-faced as Pongo told them that, though he quite understood how they had felt, they must never, never behave in such a panic-stricken way and must always, always obey orders instantly. Then he praised the pups who had stuck to the Cadpig's cart, praised Patch for staying close to the Cadpig, rescued Roly Poly from a ditch and counted the pups carefully. He did all this as hurriedly as possible for he knew now that they must press on with their journey. There was no way they could get to the police station without passing Cruella de Vil.

Their plight was now worse than ever. They not only had to face the dangers of hunger and cold; there was the added danger of Cruella. They knew from the direction her car was facing that their enemy must have already been to Hell Hall, learned that they had escaped, and now be on her way back to London. At any moment, she might leave the fire and overtake them.

If only they could have left the road and travelled by the fields again! But there were now woods on either side of the road, woods so thick that the army could not have kept together.

'But we can hide in there, if we see the car's headlights,' said Pongo, and explained to the puppies. Then the army was on the march again.

'At least the pups are warm now,' said Missis. 'And they have forgotten how tired and hungry they are. It will be all right, Pongo.'

The pace was certainly good for a couple of miles, then it got slower and slower.

'The puppies will have to rest,' said Missis. 'And this is a good place for it.'

There was now a wide, grassy verge to the road. The moment Pongo called a halt the pups sank down on the frosty grass. Many of them at once fell asleep.

'They ought not to sleep,' said Pongo, anxiously.

'Let them, for a little while,' said Missis.

The Cadpig was not asleep. She sat up in her cart and said: 'Will there be a barn soon, with kind cows and warm milk?'

'I'm sure there will be *something* nice,' said Missis. 'Snuggle down in your hay, my darling. Pongo, how strangely quiet it is.'

They could no longer hear any sounds from the village. No breath of wind rustled the grass or stirred the trees. The world seemed frozen into a silvery, silent stillness.

Something soft and fluffy touched Pongo's head, something that puzzled him. Then, as he realized what it was, Missis whispered:

'Look, Pongo! Look at the puppies!'

Tiny white dots were appearing on the sooty black coats. Snow had begun to fall.

Missis said, smiling: 'Instead of being white pups with black spots they are turning into black pups with white spots—only soon, they will be all white. How soft and gentle the snow is!'

Pongo was not smiling. He cried: 'If they sleep on until it has covered them, they will never wake—they will freeze to death beneath that soft, gentle snow! Wake up, pups! Wake up!'

By now, every pup but Lucky and the Cadpig had fallen into a deep, exhausted sleep. Lucky helped his parents to rouse them, and the Cadpig helped, too, sitting up in her cart and yapping piercingly. The poor pups begged to be left to sleep, and those who tottered on to their feet soon tottered off them again.

'We shall never get them going,' said Pongo despairingly.

For a moment, the Cadpig stopped yapping and there was a sudden silence. Then, from the village behind them, came the strident blare of

'Quickly, pups! Jump into the nice miracle,' said Missis.

the loudest motor-horn in England.

The pups sprang up, their exhaustion driven away by terror.

'To the woods!' cried Pongo. Then he saw that the woods were now protected by wire netting, through which not even the smallest pup could squeeze. And there was no ditch to hide in. But he could see that the woods ended, not very far ahead. 'We must go on,' he cried. 'There may be fields, there may be a ditch.'

The horn sounded again, repeatedly. Pongo guessed that the fire-engine had put out the fire and now Cruella was scattering the villagers as she drove on her way. Already she would be less than two miles behind them—and the great striped car could travel two miles in less than two minutes. But the woods were ending, there were fields ahead!

'To the fields!' cried Pongo. 'Faster, faster!'

The pups made a great spurt forward, then fell back in dismay. For though the woods ended, the wire netting still continued, on both sides of them. There was still no way off the road. And the horn sounded again—louder and nearer.

'Nothing but a miracle can save us now,' said Pongo.

'Then we must find a miracle,' said Missis, firmly. 'Pongo, what *is* a miracle?'

It was at that moment that they suddenly saw, through the swirling snow, a very large van drawn up on the road ahead of them. The tail-board was down and the inside of the van was lit by electric light. And sitting there, on a newspaper, was a Staffordshire terrier with a short clay pipe in his mouth. That is, it looked like a clay pipe. It was really made of sugar and had once had a fine long stem. Now the Staffordshire drew the bowl of the pipe into his mouth and ate it. Then he looked up from the newspaper—which he was reading as well as sitting on— and stared in astonishment at the army of pups rushing helter-skelter towards him.

'Help, help, help!' barked Pongo. 'We are being pursued. How soon can we get off this road?'

'I don't know, mate,' barked back the Staffordshire. 'You'd better hide in my van.'

'The miracle, the miracle!' gasped Pongo to Missis.

'Quickly, pups! Jump into the nice miracle,' said Missis, who now thought 'miracle' was another name for a removal van.

A swarm of pups surged up the tailboard. Up went the Cadpig's cart, pulled from the front and pushed from behind. Then more and more pups jumped or scrambled up until the entire army was in.

'Golly, there are a lot of you,' said the Staffordshire, who had flattened himself against the side of the van. 'Lucky the van was empty. Who's after you, mates? Old Nick?'

'Some relation of his, I think,' said Pongo. The strident horn sounded again and now two strong headlights could be seen in the distance. 'And she's in that car.'

'Then I'd better put the light off,' said the Staffordshire, neatly working the switch with his teeth. 'That's better.'

Pongo's heart seem to miss a beat. Suddenly he knew that letting the pups get into the van had been a terrible mistake.

'But the car's headlights will shine in,' he gasped. 'Our enemy will see the pups.'

'Not black pups in a black van,' said the Staffordshire. 'Not if they close their eyes.'

Oh, excellent suggestion! Quickly Pongo gave the command:

'Pups, close your eyes—or they will reflect the car's headlights and shine like jewels in the darkness. Close them and do not open them, however frightened you are, until I give the word. Remember, your lives may depend on your obedience now. Close your eyes and keep them closed!'

Instantly all the puppies closed their eyes tight. And now the car's headlights were less than a quarter of a mile away.

'Close your eyes, Missis,' said Pongo.

'And don't forget to close your own, mate,' said the Staffordshire.

Now the car's powerful engine could be heard. The strident horn blared again and again, as if telling the van to get out of the way. Louder and louder grew the noise from the engine. The glare from the headlights was now so intense that Pongo was conscious of it through his tightly shut eyelids. Would the pups obey orders? Or would terror make them look towards the oncoming car? Pongo, himself, had a wild desire to do so and a wild fear that the car was going to crash into the van. The noise of horn and engine grew deafening, the glare seemed blinding, even to closed eyes. Then, with a roar, the great striped car was on them—and past them, roaring on and on into the night!

'You may open your eyes now, my brave, obedient pups,' cried Pongo. And indeed they deserved praise, for not one eye had been opened.

'That was quite a car, mate,' said the Staffordshire to Pongo. 'You must have quite an enemy. Who are you, anyway? The local pack of soot-hounds?' Then he suddenly stared very hard at Pongo's nose. 'Well, swelp me if it *isn't* soot! And it doesn't fool me. You're the missing Dalmatians. Want a lift back to London?'

A lift? A lift all the way in this wonderful van! Pongo and Missis could hardly believe it. Swiftly the pups settled to sleep on the rugs and blankets used for wrapping around furniture.

'But why are there so many pups?' said the Staffordshire. 'The newspapers don't know the half of it, not the quarter, neither. They think there are only fifteen missing.'

Pongo started to explain but the Staffordshire said they would talk during the drive to London. 'My pets will be out of that house there any minute. Fancy us doing a removal on a Sunday—*and* Christmas Eve. But the van broke down yesterday and we had to finish the job.'

'How many days will the journey to London take?' asked Missis.

'Days?' said the Staffordshire. 'It won't take much more than a couple of hours, if *I* know my pets. They want to get home to finish decorating their kids' Christmas trees. Sssh, now! Pipe down, both of you.'

A large man in a rough apron was coming out of a nearby house. Missis thought: 'As soon as one danger is past, another threatens.' Would they all be turned out of the miracle?

The Staffordshire, wagging his tail enthusiastically, hurled himself at the man's chest, nearly knocking him down.

'Look out, Bill!' said the man, over his shoulder. 'The canine cannonball's feeling frisky.'

Bill was an even larger man, but even he was shaken by the Staffordshire's loving welcome.

'Get down, you self-launched bomb,' he shouted, with great affection.

The two men and the Staffordshire came back to the van and the Staffordshire jumped inside. The sooty Dalmatians, huddled together, were invisible in the darkness.

'Want to ride inside, do you?' said Bill. 'Well, it *is* cold.' He put the tailboard up and shouted: 'Next stop, St John's Wood.' A moment

55

later, the huge van took the road.

St John's Wood! Surely, that was where the splendid vet lived—quite close to Regent's Park! What wonderful, wonderful luck, thought Pongo. Just then he heard a clock strike. It was still only eight o'clock.

'Missis!' he cried. 'We shall get home tonight! We shall be home for Christmas!'

'Yes, Pongo,' said Missis, gaily. But she did not feel as gay as she sounded. For Missis, who had been so brave, so confident up to the moment they had found the miracle, had suddenly been smitten by a great fear. Suppose the Dearlys did not recognize them now they were black dogs? Suppose the dear, dear Dearlys turned them away?

She kept her fears to herself. Why should she frighten Pongo with them? How fast the miracle was travelling! She thought of the days it had taken her and Pongo to reach Suffolk on foot. Why, it seemed like weeks since they had left London! Yet it was only—how long? Could it be only *four* days? They'd slept one day in the stable at the inn, one day at the dear spaniel's, one day in the Folly, part of a night in the barn after the escape from Hell Hall, then a day at the bakery. So much had happened in so short a time. And now, would it be all right when they got home? Would it? Would it?

Meanwhile, Pongo had his own worries. He had been telling the Staffordshire all about Cruella and had remembered what she had said, that night at Hell Hall—how she intended to wait until people had forgotten about the stolen puppies, and then start her Dalmatian fur farm again. Surely he and Missis would get this lot of puppies safely home (it had never occurred to *him* that the Dearlys might not let them in) but what of the future? How could he make sure that other puppies did not end up as fur-coats later on? He asked the Staffordshire's advice.

'Why not kill this Cruella?' said the Staffordshire. 'And I'll help you. Let's make a date for it now.'

Pongo shook his head. He had come to believe that Cruella was not an ordinary human but some kind of devil. If so, could one kill her? In any case, he didn't want his pups to have a killer-dog for a father. He would have sprung at Cruella if she had attacked any pup, but he didn't fancy cold-blooded murder. He told the Staffordshire so.

'Your blood would soon warm up once you started the job,' said the Staffordshire. 'Well, let me know if you change your mind. And now you take a nap, mate. You've still got quite a job ahead of you.'

The Staffordshire, like Missis, wondered if the Dearlys would recognize these black Dalmatians—and if even the kindest pets would take in so many pups. But he said nothing of this to Pongo.

Missis, lulled by the movement of the van, had fallen asleep. Soon Pongo slept, too. But their dreams were haunted by their separate anxieties.

On and on through the dark went the mile-eating miracle.

TEMPEST

Charles Dickens

Of all Dickens's books David Copperfield *was the author's own favourite. As a child David had become friendly with the family of his faithful nurse Peggotty, and one of his happiest recollections was of the time he had spent with them in the upturned boat at Yarmouth that was their home. Mr Peggotty, Peggotty's brother, was an honest and good fisherman who had brought up his niece Emily and nephew Ham. Emily and Ham were engaged to be married when David introduced Steerforth, a dashing friend whom he had known at school.*

The result is disaster: Emily abandons the unfortunate Ham and goes abroad with Steerforth, only to be deserted by him in due course; and Mr Peggotty devotes his life to finding his niece. Emily eventually returns, and Mr Peggotty decides that they should both emigrate. Ham has meantime given a message to David for Emily, and this is on David's mind as this chapter, which is the book's climax, opens. It describes the deaths of both Ham and Steerforth.

I now approach an event in my life so indelible, so awful, so bound by an infinite variety of ties to all that has preceded it, in these pages, that, from the beginning of my narrative, I have seen it growing larger and larger as I advanced, like a great tower in a plain, and throwing its forecast shadow even on the incidents of my childish days.

For years after it occurred, I dreamed of it often. I have started up so vividly impressed by it, that its fury has yet seemed raging in my quiet room, in the still night. I dream of it sometimes, though at lengthened and uncertain intervals, to this hour. I have an association between it and a stormy wind, or the lightest mention of a sea-shore, as strong as any of which my mind is conscious. As plainly as I behold what happened, I will try to write it down. I do not recall it, but see it done; for it happens again before me.

The time drawing on rapidly for the sailing of the emigrant ship, my good old nurse (almost broken-hearted for me, when we first met) came up to London. I was constantly with her, and her brother, and the Micawbers (they being very much together); but Emily I never saw.

One evening, when the time was close at hand, I was alone with Peggotty and her brother. Our conversation turned on Ham. She described to us how tenderly he had taken leave of her and how manfully and quietly he had borne himself. Most of all, of late, when she believed he was most tried. It was a subject of which the affectionate creature never tired; and our interest in hearing the many examples which she, who was so much with him, had to relate, was equal to hers in relating them.

My aunt and I were at that time vacating the two cottages at Highgate; I intending to go abroad, and she to return to her house at Dover. We had a temporary lodging in Covent Garden. As I walked home to it, after this evening's conversation, reflecting on what had passed between Ham and myself when I was last at Yarmouth, I wavered in the original purpose I had formed, of leaving a letter for Emily when I should take leave of her uncle on board the ship, and thought it would be better to write to her now. She might desire, I thought, after receiving my communication, to send some parting word by me to her unhappy lover. I ought to give her the opportunity.

I therefore sat down in my room, before going to bed, and wrote to her. I told her that I had seen him, and that he had requested me to tell her what I have already written in its place in these sheets. I faithfully repeated it. I had no need to enlarge upon it, if I had had the right. Its deep fidelity and goodness were not to be adorned by me or any man. I left it out, to be sent round in the morning; with a line to Mr Peggotty, requesting him to give it to her; and went to bed at daybreak.

I was weaker than I knew then; and, not falling asleep until the sun was up, lay late, and unrefreshed, next day. I was roused by the silent presence of my aunt at my bedside. I felt it in my sleep, as I suppose we all do feel such things.

'Trot, my dear,' she said, when I opened my eyes, 'I couldn't make up my mind to disturb you. Mr Peggotty is here; shall he come up?'

I replied yes, and he soon appeared.

'Mas'r Davy,' he said, when we had shaken hands, 'I giv Em'ly your letter, sir, and she writ this heer; and begged of me fur to ask you to read it, and if you see no hurt in't, to be so kind as take charge on't.'

'Have you read it?' said I.

He nodded sorrowfully. I opened it, and read as follows:

'I have got your message. Oh, what can I write, to thank you for your good and blessed kindness to me!

I have put the words close to my heart. I shall keep them till I die. They are sharp thorns, but they are such comfort. I have prayed over them, oh, I have prayed so much. When I find what you are, and what uncle is, I think what God must be, and can cry to Him.

Good-bye for ever. Now, my dear friend, good-bye for ever in this world. In another world, if I am forgiven, I may wake a child and come to you. All thanks and blessings. Farewell, evermore!'

This, blotted with tears, was the letter.

'May I tell her as you doen't see no hurt in't, and as you'll be so kind as take charge on't, Mas'r Davy?' said Mr Peggotty when I had read it.

'Unquestionably,' said I—'but I am thinking——'

'Yes, Mas'r Davy?'

'I am thinking,' said I, 'that I'll go down again to Yarmouth. There's time, and to spare, for me to go and come back before the ship sails. My mind is constantly running on him, in his solitude; to put this letter of her writing in his hand at this time, and to enable you to tell her, in the moment of parting, that he has got it, will be a kindness to both of them. I solemnly accepted his commission, dear good fellow, and cannot discharge it too completely. The journey is nothing to me. I am restless, and shall be better in motion. I'll go down tonight.'

Though he anxiously endeavoured to dissuade me, I saw that he was of my mind; and this, if I had required to be confirmed in my intention, would have had the effect. He went round to the coach-office at my request, and took the box-seat for me on the mail. In the evening I started, by that conveyance, down the road I had travelled under so many changes of fortune.

'Don't you think that,' I asked the coachman, in the first stage out of London, 'a very remarkable sky? I don't remember to have seen one like it.'

'Nor I—not equal to it,' he replied. 'That's wind, sir. There'll be mischief done at sea, I expect, before long.'

It was a murky confusion—here and there blotted with a colour like the colour of the smoke from damp fuel—of flying clouds tossed up into most remarkable heaps, suggesting greater heights in the clouds than there were depths below them to the bottom of the deepest hollows in the earth, through which the wild moon seemed to plunge headlong, as if, in a dread disturbance of the laws of nature, she had lost her way and were frightened. There had been a wind all day; and it was rising then, with an extraordinary great sound. In another hour it had much increased, and the sky was more overcast, and it blew hard.

But as the night advanced, the clouds closing in and densely over-spreading the whole sky, then very dark, it came on to blow, harder and harder. It still increased, until our horses could scarcely face the wind. Many times, in the dark part of the night (it was then late in September, when the nights were not short), the leaders turned about, or came to a dead stop; and we were often in serious apprehension that the coach would be blown over. Sweeping gusts of rain came up before this storm, like showers of steel; and, at those times, when there was any shelter of trees or lee walls to be got, we were fain to stop, in a sheer impossibility of continuing the struggle.

When the day broke, it blew harder and harder. I had been in Yarmouth when the seamen said it blew great guns, but I have never known the like of this, or anything approaching it. We came to Ipswich—very late, having had to fight every inch of ground since we were ten miles out of London—and found a cluster of people in the market-place, who had risen from their beds in the night, fearful of falling chimneys. Some of these, congregating about the inn-yard while we changed horses, told us of great sheets of lead having been ripped off a high church-tower, and flung into a by-street, which they then blocked up. Others had to tell of country people, coming in from neighbouring villages, who had seen great trees lying torn out of the earth, and whole ricks scattered about the roads and fields. Still, there was no abatement in the storm, but it blew harder.

As we struggled on, nearer and nearer to the sea, from which this mighty wind was blowing dead on shore, its force became more and more terrific. Long before we saw the sea, its spray was on our lips, and showered salt rain upon us. The water was out, over miles and miles of the flat country adjacent to Yarmouth; and every sheet and puddle lashed its banks, and had its stress of little breakers setting heavily towards us. When we came within sight of the sea, the waves on the horizon, caught at intervals above the rolling abyss, were like glimpses of another shore with towers and buildings. When at last we got into the town, the people came out to their doors, all aslant, and with streaming hair, making a wonder of the mail that had come through such a night.

I put up at the old inn, and went down to look at the sea; staggering along the street, which was strewn with sand and seaweed, and with flying blotches of foam; afraid of falling slates and tiles; and holding by people I met, at angry corners. Coming near the beach, I saw not only the boatmen but half the people of the town, lurking behind buildings; some, now and then braving the fury of the storm to look away to sea, and blown sheer out of their course in trying to get zigzag back.

Joining these groups, I found bewailing women whose husbands were away in herring or oyster boats, which there was too much reason to think might have foundered before they could run in anywhere for safety. Grizzled old sailors were among the people, shaking their heads as they looked from water to sky, and muttering to one another; shipowners, excited and uneasy; children, huddling together, and peering into old faces; even stout mariners, disturbed and anxious, levelling their glasses at the sea from behind places of shelter, as if they were surveying an enemy.

The tremendous sea itself, when I could find sufficient pause to look at it, in the agitation of the blinding wind, the flying stones and sand, and the awful noise, confounded me. As the high watery walls came rolling in, and, at their highest, tumbled into surf, they looked as if the least would engulf the town. As the receding wave swept back with a hoarse roar, it seemed to scoop out deep caves in the beach, as if its purpose was to undermine the earth. When some white-headed billows thundered on, and dashed themselves to pieces before they reached the land, every fragment of the late whole seemed possessed by the full might of its wrath, rushing to be gathered to the composition of another monster. Undulating hills were changed to valleys, undulating valleys (with a solitary storm-bird sometimes skimming through them) were lifted up to hills; masses of water shivered and shook the beach with a booming sound; every shape tumultuously rolled on, as soon as made, to change its shape and place, and beat another shape and place away; the ideal shore on the horizon, with its towers and buildings, rose and fell; the clouds flew fast and thick; I seemed to see a rending and up-heaving of all nature.

Not finding Ham among the people whom this memorable wind—for it is still remembered down there as the greatest ever known to blow upon that coast—had brought together, I made my way to his house. It was shut; and as no one answered to my knocking, I went, by back ways and by-lanes, to the yard where he worked. I learned, there, that he had gone to Lowestoft, to meet some sudden exigency of ship-repairing in which his skill was required; but that he would be back tomorrow morning, in good time.

I went back to the inn; and when I had washed and dressed, and tried to sleep, but in vain, it was five o'clock in the afternoon. I had not sat five minutes by the coffee-room fire, when the waiter coming to stir it, as an excuse for talking, told me that two colliers had gone down, with all hands, a few miles away; and that some other ships had been seen labouring hard in The Roads, and trying, in great distress, to keep off shore. Mercy on them, and on all poor sailors, said he, if we had another night like the last!

I was very much depressed in spirits; very solitary; and felt an un-easiness in Ham's not being there, disproportionate to the occasion. I was seriously affected, without knowing how much, by late events; and my long exposure to the fierce wind had confused me. There was that jumble in my thoughts and recollections, that I had lost the clear arrangement of time and distance. Thus, if I had gone out into the town, I should not have been surprised, I think, to encounter someone who I knew must be then in London. So to speak, there was in these respects a curious inattention in my mind. Yet it was busy, too, with all the re-membrances the place naturally awakened; and they were particularly distinct and vivid.

In this state, the waiter's dismal intelligence about the ships immedi-ately connected itself, without any effort of my volition, with my un-easiness about Ham. I was persuaded that I had an apprehension of his returning from Lowestoft by sea, and being lost. This grew so strong with me that I resolved to go back to the yard before I took my dinner, and ask the boat-builder if he thought his attempting to return by sea at all likely? If he gave me the least reason to think so, I would go over to Lowestoft and prevent it by bringing him with me.

I hastily ordered my dinner, and went back to the yard. I was none too soon; for the boat-builder, with a lantern in his hand, was locking the yard-gate. He quite laughed when I asked him the question, and said there was no fear; no man in his senses, or out of them, would put off in such a gale of wind, least of all Ham Peggotty, who had been born to sea-faring.

So sensible of this, beforehand, that I had really felt ashamed of doing what I was nevertheless impelled to do, I went back to the inn. If such a wind could rise, I think it was rising. The howl and roar, the rattling of the doors and windows, the rumbling in the chimneys, the apparent rocking of the very house that sheltered me, and the prodigious tumult of the sea, were more fearful than in the morning. But there was now a great darkness besides; and that invested the storm with new terrors, real and fanciful.

I could not eat, I could not sit still, I could not continue steadfast to anything. Something within me, faintly answering to the storm with-out, tossed up the depth of my memory, and made a tumult in them. Yet, in all the hurry of my thoughts, wild running with the thundering sea—the storm, and my uneasiness regarding Ham, were always in the foreground.

My dinner went away almost untasted, and I tried to refresh myself with a glass or two of wine. In vain. I fell into a dull slumber before the fire, without losing my consciousness, either of the uproar out of doors, or of the place in which I was. Both became overshadowed by a new and indefinable horror; and when I awoke—or rather when I shook off the lethargy that bound me in my chair—my whole frame thrilled with objectless and unintelligible fear.

I walked to and fro, tried to read an old gazetteer, listened to the awful noises: looked at faces, scenes, and figures in the fire. At length, the steady ticking of the undisturbed clock on the wall tormented me to that degree that I resolved to go to bed.

It was reassuring, on such a night, to be told that some of the inn-servants had agreed together to sit up until morning. I went to bed, exceedingly weary and heavy; but, on my lying down, all such sensa-tions vanished, as if by magic, and I was broad awake.

For hours I lay there, listening to the wind and water: imagining, now, that I heard shrieks out at sea; now, that I distinctly heard the firing of signal guns; and now, the fall of houses in the town. I got up, several times, and looked out; but could see nothing, except the reflection in the window-panes of the faint candle I had left burning, and of my own haggard face looking in at me from the black void.

At length, my restlessness attained to such a pitch that I hurried on my clothes, and went downstairs. In the large kitchen, where I dimly saw bacon and ropes of onions hanging from the beams, the watchers were clustered together, in various attitudes, about a table, purposely moved away from the great chimney, and brought near the door. A pretty girl, who had her ears stopped with her apron, and her eyes upon the door, screamed when I appeared, supposing me to be a spirit; but the others had more presence of mind, and were glad of an addition to their company. One man, referring to the topic they had been discussing, asked me whether I thought the souls of the collier-crews who had gone down, were out in the storm?

I remained there, I dare say, two hours. Once, I opened the yard-gate, and looked into the empty street. The sand, the seaweed, and the flakes of foam were driving by; and I was obliged to call for assistance before I could shut the gate again, and make it fast against the wind.

There was a dark gloom in my solitary chamber, when I at length returned to it; but I was tired now, and, getting into bed again, fell—off a tower and down a precipice—into the depths of sleep. I have an impression that for a long time, though I dreamed of being elsewhere and in a variety of scenes, it was always blowing in my dream. At length, I lost that feeble hold upon reality, and was engaged with two dear friends, but who they were I don't know, at the siege of some town in a roar of cannonading.

The thunder of the cannon was so loud and incessant, that I could not hear something I much desired to hear, until I made a great exertion and awoke. It was broad day—eight or nine o'clock; the storm raging, in lieu of the batteries; and someone knocking and calling at my door.

'What is the matter?' I cried.

'A wreck! Close by!'

I sprang out of bed, and asked, 'What wreck?'

'A schooner, from Spain or Portugal, laden with fruit and wine.

Make haste, sir, if you want to see her! It's thought, down on the beach, she'll go to pieces every moment.'

The excited voice went clamouring along the staircase; and I wrapped myself in my clothes as quickly as I could, and ran into the street.

Numbers of people were there before me, all running in one direction, to the beach. I ran the same way, outstripping a good many, and soon came facing the wild sea.

The wind might by this time have lulled a little, though not more sensibly than if the cannonading I had dreamed of, had been diminished by the silencing of half-a-dozen guns out of hundreds. But the sea, having upon it the additional agitation of the whole night, was infinitely more terrific than when I had seen it last. Every appearance it had then presented, bore the expression of being *swelled*; and the height to which the breakers rose, and, looking over one another, bore one another down, and rolled in, in interminable hosts, was most appalling.

In the difficulty of hearing anything but wind and waves, and in the crowd, and the unspeakable confusion, and my first breathless efforts to stand against the weather, I was so confused that I looked out to sea for the wreck, and saw nothing but the foaming heads of the great waves. A half-dressed boatman, standing next to me, pointed with his bare arm (a tattooed arrow on it, pointing in the same direction) to the left. Then, O great heaven, I saw it, close in upon us!

One mast was broken short off, six or eight feet from the deck, and lay over the side, entangled in a maze of sail and rigging; and all that ruin, as the ship rolled and beat—which she did without a moment's pause, and with a violence quite inconceivable—beat the side as if it would stave it in. Some efforts were even then being made to cut this portion of the wreck away; for, as the ship, which was broadside on, turned towards us in her rolling, I plainly descried her people at work with axes, especially one active figure with long curling hair, conspicuous among the rest. But, a great cry, which was audible even above the wind and water, rose from the shore at this moment; the sea, sweeping over the rolling wreck, made a clean breach, and carried men, spars, casks, planks, bulwarks, heaps of such toys, into the boiling surge.

The second mast was yet standing, with the rags of a rent sail, and a wild confusion of broken cordage flapping to and fro. The ship had

66

struck once, the same boatman hoarsely said in my ear, and then lifted in and struck again. I understood him to add that she was parting amidships, and I could readily suppose so, for the rolling and beating were too tremendous for any human work to suffer long. As he spoke, there was another great cry of pity from the beach; four men arose with the wreck out of the deep, clinging to the rigging of the remaining mast; uppermost the active figure with the curling hair.

There was a bell on board; and as the ship rolled and dashed, like a desperate creature driven mad, now showing us the whole sweep of her deck, as she turned on her beam-ends towards the shore, now nothing but her keel, as she sprang wildly over and turned towards the sea, the bell rang; and its sound, the knell of those unhappy men, was borne towards us on the wind. Again we lost her, and again she rose. Two men were gone. The agony on shore increased. Men groaned, and clasped their hands; women shrieked, and turned away their faces. Some ran wildly up and down along the beach, crying for help where no help could be. I found myself one of these, frantically imploring a knot of sailors whom I knew, not to let those two lost creatures perish before our eyes.

They were making out to me, in an agitated way—I don't know how, for the little I could hear I was scarcely composed enough to understand—that the lifeboat had been bravely manned an hour ago, and could do nothing; and that as no man would be so desperate as to attempt to wade off with a rope, and establish a communication with the shore, there was nothing left to try; when I noticed that some new sensation moved the people on the beach, and saw them part, and Ham come breaking through them to the front.

I ran to him—as well as I know, to repeat my appeal for help. But, distracted though I was, by a sight so new to me and terrible, the determination in his face, and his look, out to sea—exactly the same look as I remembered in connection with the morning after Emily's flight—awoke me to a knowledge of his danger. I held him back with both arms; and implored the men with whom I had been speaking, not to listen to him, not to do murder, not to let him stir from off that sand!

Another cry arose on shore; and looking to the wreck, we saw the cruel sail, with blow on blow, beat off the lower of the two men, and fly up in triumph round the active figure left alone upon the mast.

Against such a sight, and against such determination as that of the calmly desperate man who was already accustomed to lead half the people present, I might as hopefully have entreated the wind. 'Mas'r Davy,' he said, cheerily grasping me by both hands, 'if my time is come, 'tis come. If 'tan't I'll bide it. Lord above bless you, and bless all! Mates, make me ready! I'm a-going off!'

I was swept away, but not unkindly, to some distance, where the people around me made me stay; urging, as I confusedly perceived, that he was bent on going, with help or without, and that I should endanger the precautions for his safety by troubling those with whom they rested. I don't know what I answered, or what they rejoined; but, I saw hurry on the beach, and men running with ropes from a capstan that was there, and penetrating into a circle of figures that hid him from me. Then, I saw him standing alone, in a seaman's frock and trousers: a rope in his hand, or slung to his wrist: another round his body: and several of the best men holding, at a little distance, to the latter, which he laid out himself, slack upon the shore, at his feet.

The wreck, even to my unpractised eye, was breaking up. I saw that

'Mates, make me ready!' said Ham. 'I'm a-going off!'

she was parting in the middle, and that the life of the solitary man upon the mast hung by a thread. Still, he clung to it. He had a singular red cap on—not like a sailor's cap, but of a finer colour; and as the few yielding planks between him and destruction rolled and bulged, and his anticipative death-knell rang, he was seen by all of us to wave it. I saw him do it now, and thought I was going distracted, when his action brought an old remembrance to my mind of a once dear friend.

Ham watched the sea, standing alone, with the silence of suspended breath behind him, and the storm before, until there was a great retiring wave, when, with a backward glance at those who held the rope which was made fast round his body, he dashed in after it, and in a moment was buffeting with the water; rising with the hills, falling with the valleys, lost beneath the foam; then drawn again to land. They hauled in hastily.

He was hurt. I saw blood on his face, from where I stood; but he took no thought of that. He seemed hurriedly to give them some directions for leaving him more free—or so I judged from the motion of his arm— and was gone as before.

And now he made for the wreck, rising with the hills, falling with the valleys, lost beneath the rugged foam, borne in towards the shore, borne on towards the ship, striving hard and valiantly. The distance was nothing, but the power of the sea and wind made the strife deadly. At length he neared the wreck. He was so near, that with one more of his vigorous strokes he would be clinging to it—when a high, green, vast hillside of water, moving on shoreward, from beyond the ship, he seemed to leap up into it with a mighty bound, and the ship was gone!

Some eddying fragments I saw in the sea, as if a mere cask had been broken, in running to the spot where they were hauling in. Consternation was in every face. They drew him to my very feet—insensible—dead. He was carried to the nearest house; and, no one preventing me now, I remained near him, busy, while every means of restoration were tried; but he had been beaten to death by the great wave, and his generous heart was stilled for ever.

As I sat beside the bed, when hope was abandoned and all was done, a fisherman, who had known me when Emily and I were children, and ever since, whispered my name at the door.

'Sir,' said he, with tears starting to his weather-beaten face, which, with his trembling lips, was ashy pale, 'will you come over yonder?'

The old remembrance that had been recalled to me, was in his look. I asked him, terror-stricken, leaning on the arm he held out to support me:

'Has a body come ashore?'

He said, 'Yes.'

'Do I know it?' I asked then.

He answered nothing.

But, he led me to the shore. And on that part of it where she and I had looked for shells, two children—on that part of it where some lighter fragments of the old boat, blown down last night, had been scattered by the wind—among the ruins of the home he had wronged—I saw him lying with his head upon his arm, as I had often seen him lie at school.

HIS FIRST FLIGHT

Liam O'Flaherty

The young seagull was alone on his ledge. His two brothers and sister had already flown away the day before. He had been afraid to fly with them. Somehow when he had taken a little run forward to the brink of the ledge and attempted to flap his wings he became afraid. The great expanse of sea stretched down beneath, and it was such a long way down —miles down. He felt certain that his wings would never support him, so he bent his head and ran away back to the little hole under the ledge where he slept at night.

Even when each of his brothers and his little sister, whose wings were far shorter than his own, ran to the brink, flapped their wings, and flew away he failed to muster up courage to take that plunge which appeared to him so desperate. His father and mother had come around calling to him shrilly, upbraiding him, threatening to let him starve on his ledge unless he flew away. But for the life of him he could not move.

That was twenty-four hours ago. Since then nobody had come near him. The day before, all day long he had watched his parents flying about with his brothers and sister, perfecting them in the art of flight, teaching them how to skim the waves and how to dive for fish. He had, in fact, seen his older brother catch his first herring and devour it, standing on a rock, while his parents circled around raising a proud cackle. And all the morning the whole family had walked about on the big plateau midway down the opposite cliff, taunting him with his cowardice.

The sun was now ascending the sky, blazing warmly on his ledge that faced south. He felt the heat because he had not eaten since the previous nightfall. Then he had found a dried piece of mackerel's tail at the far end of his ledge. Now there was not a single scrap of food left. He had searched every inch, rooting among the rough, dirt-caked straw nest where he and his brothers and sister had been hatched. He even gnawed at the dried pieces of spotted eggshell. It was like eating part of himself.

He had then trotted back and forth from one end of the ledge to the other, his grey body the colour of the cliff, his long grey legs stepping daintily, trying to find some means of reaching his parents without having to fly. But on each side of him the ledge ended in a sheer fall of precipice, with the sea beneath. And between him and his parents there was a deep, wide chasm.

Surely he could reach them without flying if he would only move northwards along the cliff face? But then on what could he walk? There was no ledge, and he was not a fly. And above him he could see nothing. The precipice was sheer, and the top of it was perhaps farther away than the sea beneath him.

He stepped slowly out to the brink of the ledge, and, standing on one leg with the other leg hidden under his wing, he closed one eye, then the other, and pretended to be falling asleep. Still they took no notice of him. He saw his two brothers and his sister lying on the plateau dozing, with their heads sunk into their necks. His father was preening the feathers on his white back. Only his mother was looking at him.

She was standing on a little high hump on the plateau, her white breast thrust forward. Now and again she tore at a piece of fish that lay at her feet, and then scraped each side of her beak on the rock. The sight of the food maddened him. How he loved to tear food that way, scraping his beak now and again to whet it! He uttered a low cackle. His mother cackled too, and looked over at him.

Ga, ga, ga, he cried, begging her to bring him over some food.

With a loud scream the young gull fell outwards into space . . .

Gawl-ool-ah, she screamed back derisively. But he kept calling plaintively, and after a minute or so he uttered a joyful scream. His mother had picked up a piece of the fish and was flying across to him with it. He leaned out eagerly, tapping the rock with his feet, trying to get nearer to her as she flew across. But when she was just opposite to him, abreast of the ledge, she halted, her legs hanging limp, her wings motionless, the piece of fish in her beak almost within reach of his beak.

He waited a moment in surprise, wondering why she did not come nearer, and then maddened by hunger, he dived at the fish. With a loud scream he fell outwards and downwards into space. His mother had swooped upwards. As he passed beneath her he heard the swish of her wings.

Then a monstrous terror seized him and his heart stood still. He could hear nothing. But it only lasted a moment. The next moment he felt his wings spread outwards. The wind rushed against his breast feathers, then under his stomach and against his wings. He could feel the tips of his wings cutting through the air. He was not falling headlong now. He was soaring gradually downwards and outwards. He was no longer afraid. He just felt a bit dizzy. Then he flapped his wings once and he soared upwards.

He uttered a joyous scream and flapped them again. He soared higher. He raised his breast and banked against the wind. *Ga, ga, ga. Ga, ga, ga. Gawl-ool-ah*. His mother swooped past him, her wings making a loud noise. He answered her with another scream. Then his father flew over him screaming. Then he saw his two brothers and sister flying around him, curvetting and banking and soaring and diving.

Then he completely forgot that he had not always been able to fly, and commenced himself to dive and soar and curvet, shrieking shrilly.

He was near the sea now, flying straight over it, facing out over the ocean. He saw a vast green sea beneath him, with little ridges moving over it, and he turned his beak sideways and crowed amusedly. His parents and his brothers and sister had landed on this green floor in front of him. They were beckoning to him, calling shrilly. He dropped his legs to stand on the green sea. His legs sank into it. He screamed with fright and attempted to rise again, flapping his wings. But he was tired and weak with hunger and he could not rise, exhausted by the strange exercise. His feet sank into the green sea, and then his belly touched it and he sank no farther.

He was floating on it. And around him his family was screaming, praising him, and their beaks were offering him scraps of dogfish.

He had made his first flight.

MOUFFLOU
Ouida

Moufflou's masters were some boys and girls. They were very poor, but they were very merry. They lived in an old, dark, tumbledown place, and their father had been dead five years; their mother's care was all they knew; and Tasso was the eldest of them all, a lad of nearly twenty, and he was so kind, so good, so laborious, so cheerful and so gentle that the children all younger than he adored him. Tasso was a gardener. Tasso, however, though the eldest and mainly the breadwinner, was not so much Moufflou's master as was little Romolo, who was only ten, and a cripple. Romolo, called generally Lolo, had taught Moufflou all he knew; and that all was a very great deal, for nothing cleverer than Moufflou had ever walked upon four legs.

Why Moufflou?

Well, when the poodle had been given to them by a soldier who was going back to his home in Piedmont, he had been a white woolly creature of a year old, and the children's mother, who was a Corsican by birth, had said that he was just like a *moufflon*, as they call sheep in Corsica. White and woolly this dog remained, and he became the handsomest and biggest poodle in all the city, and the corruption of Moufflou

75

from *moufflon* remained the name by which he was known; it was silly, perhaps, but it suited him and the children, and Moufflou he was.

They lived in an old quarter of Florence, in that picturesque zigzag which goes round the grand church of Or San Michele, and which is almost more Venetian than Tuscan in its mingling of colour, charm, stateliness, popular confusion, and architectural majesty. The tall old houses are weather-beaten into the most delicious hues.

Well, Moufflou lived here in that high house with the sign of the lamb in wrought iron, which shows it was once a warehouse of the old guild of the Arte della Lana. They are all old houses here, drawn round about that grand church which I called once, and will call again, like a mighty casket of oxidized silver. A mighty casket indeed, holding the Holy Spirit within it; and with the vermilion and the blue and the orange glowing in its niches and its lunettes like enamels, and its statues of the apostles strong and noble, like the times in which they were created—St Peter with his keys, and St Mark with his open book, and St George leaning on his sword, and others also, solemn and austere as they, austere though benign, for do they not guard the White Tabernacle of Orcagna within?

The little masters of Moufflou lived right in its shadow, where the bridge of stone spans the space between the houses and the church high in mid-air: and little Lolo loved the church with a great love. He loved it in the morning-time, when the sunbeams turned it into dusky gold and jasper; he loved it in the evening-time, when the lights of its altars glimmered in the dark, and the scent of its incense came out into the street; he loved it in the great feasts, when the huge clusters of lilies were borne inside it; he loved it in the solemn nights of winter; the flickering gleam of the dull lamps shone on the robes of an apostle, or the sculpture of a shield, or the glow of a casement-moulding in majolica. He loved it always, and, without knowing why, he called it *la mia chiesa*.

Lolo, being lame and of delicate health, was not enabled to go to school or to work, though he wove the straw covering of wine-flasks and plaited the cane matting with busy fingers. But for the most part he did as he liked, and spent most of his time sitting on the parapet of Or San Michele, watching the venders of earthenware at their trucks, or trotting with his crutch (and he could trot a good many miles when he chose) out with Moufflou down a bit of the Stocking-makers' Street, along under the arcades of the Uffizi, and so over the Jewelers' Bridge, and out by byways that he knew into the fields on the hillside upon the other bank of Arno. Moufflou and he would spend half the day—all the day—out there in daffodil time; and Lolo would come home with great bundles and sheaves of golden flowers, and he and Moufflou were very happy.

His mother never liked to say a harsh word to Lolo, for he was lame through her fault: she had let him fall in his babyhood, and the mischief had been done to his hip never again to be undone. So she never raised her voice to him, though she did often to the others—to curly-headed Cecco, and pretty black-eyed Dina, and saucy Bice, and sturdy Beppo, and even to the good, manly, hard-working Tasso. Tasso was the main-stay of the whole, though he was but a gardener's lad, working in the green Cascine for small wages. But all he earned he brought home to his mother; and he alone kept in order the lazy, high-tempered Sandro, and he alone kept in check Bice's love of finery, and he alone could with shrewdness and care make both ends meet and put *minestra* always in the pot and bread always in the cupboard.

When his mother thought, as she thought indeed almost ceaselessly, that with a few months he would be of the age to draw his number, and might draw a high one and be taken from her for three years, the poor soul believed her very heart would burst and break; and many a day at twilight she would start out unperceived and creep into the great church and pour her soul forth in supplication before the White Tabernacle.

Yet, pray as she would, no miracle could happen to make Tasso free of military service: if he drew a fatal number, go he must, even though he take all the lives of them to their ruin with him.

One morning Lolo sat as usual on the parapet of the church, Moufflou beside him. It was a brilliant morning in September. The men at the handbarrows and at the stalls were selling the crockery, the silk handker-chiefs, and the straw hats which form the staple of the commerce that goes on round about Or San Michele—very blithe, good-natured, gay commerce, for the most part, not got through, of course, without bawl-ing and screaming, and shouting and gesticulating, as if the sale of a penny pipkin or a twopenny pie pan were the occasion for the exchange of many thousands of pounds sterling and cause for the whole world's commotion. It was about eleven o'clock. Lolo looked on at it all, and

'Moufflou is beautiful,' said Lolo with pride.

so did Moufflou, and a stranger looked at them as he left the church.

'You have a handsome poodle there, my little man,' he said to Lolo, in a foreigner's too distinct and careful Italian.

'Moufflou is beautiful,' said Lolo with pride. 'You should see him when he is just washed; but we can only wash him on Sundays, because then Tasso is at home.'

'How old is your dog?'

'Three years old.'

'Does he do any tricks?'

'Does he!' said Lolo with a very derisive laugh. 'Why, Moufflou can do anything! He can walk on two legs ever so long; make ready, present, and fire; die; waltz; beg, of course; shut a door; make a wheelbarrow of himself: there is nothing he will not do. Would you like to see him do something.'

'Very much,' said the foreigner.

To Moufflou and to Lolo the street was the same thing as home; this cheery *piazzetta* by the church, so utterly empty sometimes, and sometimes so noisy and crowded, was but the wider threshold of their home to both the poodle and the child.

So there, under the lofty and stately walls of the old church, Lolo put Moufflou through his exercises. They were second nature to Moufflou, as to most poodles. He had inherited his address at them from clever parents, and, as he had never been frightened or coerced, all his lessons and acquirements were but play to him. He acquitted himself admirably, and the crockery vendors came and looked on, and a sacristan came out of the church and smiled, and the barber left his customer's chin all in a lather while he laughed, for the good folk of the quarter were all proud of Moufflou and never tired of him, and the pleasant, easy-going, good-humoured disposition of the Tuscan populace is so far removed from the stupid buckram and whalebone in which the new-fangled democracy wants to imprison it.

The stranger also was much diverted by Moufflou's talents, and said, half aloud, 'How this clever dog would amuse poor Victor! Would you bring your poodle to please a sick child I have at home?' he said, quite aloud, to Lolo, who smiled and answered that he would. Where was the sick child?

'At the Gran Bretagna, not far off,' said the gentleman. 'Come this

79

afternoon, and ask for me by this name.'

He dropped his card and a couple of francs into Lolo's hand, and went his way. Lolo, with Moufflou scampering after him, dashed into his own house, and stumped up the stairs, his crutch making a terrible noise on the stone.

'Mother, mother! See what I have got because Moufflou did his tricks,' he shouted. 'And now you can buy those shoes you want so much, and the coffee that you miss so of a morning, and the new linen for Tasso, and the shirts for Sandro.'

For to the mind of Lolo two francs was as two millions—source unfathomable of riches inexhaustible!

With the afternoon he and Moufflou trotted down the arcades of the Uffizi and down the Lung' Arno to the hotel of the stranger, and, showing the stranger's card, which Lolo could not read, they were shown at once into a great chamber, all gilding and fresco and velvet furniture.

But Lolo, being a little Florentine, was never troubled by externals, or daunted by mere sofas and chairs. He stood and looked around him with perfect composure; and Moufflou, whose attitude, when he was not romping, was always one of magisterial gravity, sat on his haunches and did the same.

Soon the foreigner he had seen in the afternoon entered and spoke to him, and led him into another chamber, where stretched on a couch was a little wan-faced boy about seven years old; a pretty boy, but so pallid, so wasted, so helpless. This poor little boy was heir to a great name and a great fortune, but all the science in the world could not make him strong enough to run about among the daisies, or able to draw a single breath without pain. A feeble smile lit up his face as he saw Moufflou and Lolo. Then a shadow chased it away.

'Little boy is lame like me,' he said, in a tongue Lolo did not understand.

'Yes, but he is a strong little boy, and can move about, as perhaps the suns of his country will make you do,' said the gentleman, who was the poor little boy's father. 'He has brought you his poodle to amuse you. What a handsome dog, is it not?'

'Oh, *bufflins!*' said the poor little fellow, stretching out his wasted hands to Moufflou, who submitted his leonine crest to the caress.

Then Lolo went through the performance, and Moufflou acquitted himself as ably as ever; and the little invalid laughed and shouted with his tiny thin voice, and enjoyed it all immensely, and rained cakes and biscuits on both the poodle and its master. Lolo crumped the pastries with willing white teeth, and Moufflou did no less. Then they got up to go, and the sick child on the couch burst into fretful lamentations and outcries.

'I want the dog! I will have the dog!' was all he kept repeating.

But Lolo did not know what he said, and was only sorry to see him so unhappy.

'You shall have the dog tomorrow,' said the gentleman to pacify his little son; and he hurried Lolo and Moufflou out of the room, and consigned them to a servant, having given Lolo five francs this time.

'Why, Moufflou,' said Lolo, with a chuckle of delight, 'if we could find a foreigner every day, we could eat meat at supper, Moufflou, and go to the theatre every evening!'

And he and his crutch clattered home with great eagerness and excitement, and Moufflou trotted on his four frilled feet, the blue bow with which Bice had tied up his curls on the top of his head, fluttering in the wind. But, alas! even his five francs could bring no comfort at home. He found his whole family wailing and mourning in utterly inconsolable distress.

Tasso had drawn his number that morning, and the number was seven, and he must go and be a conscript for three years.

The poor young man stood in the midst of his weeping brothers and sisters, with his mother leaning against his shoulder, and down his own brown cheeks the tears were falling. He must go, and lose his place in the public gardens, and leave his people to starve as they might, and be put in a tomfool's jacket, and drafted off among cursing and swearing and strange faces, friendless, homeless, miserable! And the mother— what would become of the mother?

No one had any heed for Lolo and his five francs, and Moufflou, understanding that some great sorrow had fallen on his friends, sat down and lifted up his voice and howled.

Tasso must go away!—that was all they understood. For three long years they must go without the sight of his face, the aid of his strength, the pleasure of his smile. Tasso must go! When Lolo understood the calamity that had befallen them, he gathered Moufflou up against his breast, and sat down too on the floor beside him and cried as if he would never stop crying.

The next morning Lolo got up before sunrise, and he and Moufflou accompanied Tasso to his work in the Cascine.

Lolo loved his brother, and clung to every moment while they could still be together.

'Can nothing keep you, Tasso?' he said, despairingly, as they went down the leafy aisles, whilst the Arno water was growing golden as the sun rose.

Tasso sighed.

'Nothing, dear. Unless Gesù would send me a thousand francs to buy a substitute.'

And he knew he might as well have said, 'If one could coin gold ducats out of the sunbeams of Arno water.'

Lolo was very sorrowful as he lay on the grass in the meadow where Tasso was at work, and the poodle lay stretched beside him.

When Lolo went home to dinner (Tasso took his wrapped in a hand-kerchief) he found his mother very agitated and excited. She was laughing one moment, crying the next. She was passionate and peevish, tender and jocose by turns; there was something forced and feverish about her which the children felt but did not comprehend. She was a woman of not very much intelligence, and she had a secret, and she carried it ill, and knew not what to do with it; but they could not tell that. They only felt a vague sense of disturbance and timidity at her unwonted manner.

The meal over (it was only bean soup, and that is soon eaten), the mother said sharply to Lolo, 'Your aunt Anita wants you this afternoon. She has to go out, and you are needed to stay with the children: be off with you.'

Lolo was an obedient child; he took his hat and jumped up as quickly as his halting hip would let him. He called Moufflou, who was asleep.

'Leave the dog,' said his mother sharply. ''Nita will not have him messing and carrying mud about her nice clean rooms. She told me so. Leave him, I say.'

'Leave Moufflou!' echoed Lolo, for never in all Moufflou's life had Lolo parted from him. Leave Moufflou! He stared open-eyed and open-mouthed at his mother. What could have come to her?

'Leave him, I say,' she repeated, more sharply than ever. 'Must I

82

'Leave the dog,' said Lolo's mother sharply.

speak twice to my own children? Be off with you, and leave the dog, I say.'

And she clutched Moufflou by his long silky mane and dragged him backwards, while with the other hand she thrust out of the door Lolo and Bice.

Lolo began to hammer with his crutch at the door thus closed on him; but Bice coaxed and entreated him.

'Poor mother has been so worried about Tasso,' she pleaded. 'And what harm can come to Moufflou? And I do think he was tired, Lolo; the Cascine is a long way; and it is quite true that Aunt 'Nita never liked him.'

So by one means and another she coaxed her brother away; and they went almost in silence to where their aunt Anita dwelt, which was across the river, near the dark-red bell-shaped dome of Santa Spirito.

It was true that her aunt had wanted them to mind her room and her babies while she was away carrying home some lace to a villa outside the Roman gate, for she was a lace-washer and clear-starcher by trade. There they had to stay in the little dark room with the two babies, with nothing to amuse the time except the clang of the bells of the church of the Holy Spirit, and the voices of the lemonade sellers shouting in the street below. Aunt Anita did not get back till it was more than dusk, and the two children trotted homeward hand in hand, Lolo's leg dragging itself painfully along, for without Moufflou's white figure dancing on before him he felt very tired indeed. It was pitch dark when they got to Or San Michele, and the lamps burned dully.

Lolo stumped up the stairs wearily, with a vague, dull fear at his small heart.

'Moufflou, Moufflou!' he called. Where was Moufflou? Always at the first sound of his crutch the poodle came flying towards him. 'Moufflou, Moufflou!' he called all the way up the long, dark twisting stone stair. He pushed open the door, and he called again, 'Moufflou, Moufflou!'

But no dog answered to his call.

'Mother, where is Moufflou?' he asked, staring with blinking, dazzled eyes into the oil-lit room where his mother sat knitting. Tasso was not then home from work. His mother went on with her knitting; there was an uneasy look on her face.

'Mother, what have you done with Moufflou, *my* Moufflou?' said Lolo, with a look that was almost stern on his ten-year-old face.

Then his mother, without looking up and moving her knitting needles very rapidly, said, 'Moufflou is sold!'

And little Dina, who was a quick, pert child, cried with a shrill voice, 'Mother has sold him for a thousand francs to the foreign gentleman.'

'Sold him!'

Lolo grew white and grew cold as ice; he stammered, threw up his hands over his head, gasped a little for breath, then fell down in a dead swoon, his poor useless limb doubled under him.

When Tasso came home that sad night and found his little brother shivering, moaning, and half delirious, and when he heard what had been done, he was sorely grieved.

'Oh, mother, how could you do it?' he cried. 'Poor Moufflou! And Lolo loves him so!'

'I have got the money,' said his mother feverishly, 'and you will not need to go for a soldier: we can buy your substitute. What is a poodle, that you mourn about it? We can get another poodle for Lolo.'

'Another will not be Moufflou,' said Tasso, and yet was seized with such a frantic happiness himself at the knowledge that he would not need to go into the army, that he too felt as if he were drunk on new wine, and had not the heart to rebuke his mother.

'A thousand francs!' he muttered, 'a thousand francs! *Dio mio!* Who could ever have fancied anybody would have given such a price for a common white poodle? One would think the gentleman had bought the church and the tabernacle!'

'Fools and their money are soon parted,' said his mother, with cross contempt.

It was true: she had sold Moufflou.

The English gentleman had called on her while Lolo and the dog had been in the Cascine, and had said that he was desirous of buying the poodle, which had so diverted his sick child that the little invalid would not be comforted unless he possessed it. Now, at any other time the good woman would have sturdily refused any idea of selling Moufflou; but that morning the thousand francs which would buy Tasso's substitute were forever in her mind and before her eyes. When she heard the foreigner her heart gave a great leap, and her head swam giddily, and she thought, in a spasm of longing—if she could get those thousand francs! But though she was so dizzy and so upset she retained her grip on her native Florentine shrewdness. She said nothing of her need of the money; not a syllable of her sore distress. On the contrary, she was coy and wary, affected great reluctance to part with her pet, invented a great offer made for him by a director of a circus, and finally let fall a hint that less than a thousand francs she could never take for poor Moufflou.

The gentleman assented with so much willingness to the price that she instantly regretted not having asked double. He told her that if she would take the poodle that afternoon to his hotel the money should be paid to her; so she despatched her children after their noonday meal in various directions, and herself took Moufflou to his doom. She could not believe her senses when ten hundred-franc notes were put into her hand. She scrawled her signature, Rosina Calabucci, to a formal receipt, and went away, leaving Moufflou in his new owner's rooms, and hearing his howls and moans pursue her all the way down the staircase and out into the air.

She was not easy at what she had done. 'It seemed,' she said to herself, 'like selling a Christian.'

But then to keep her eldest son at home—what a joy that was! On the whole, she cried so and laughed so as she went down the Lung' Arno that once or twice people looked at her, thinking her out of her senses, and a guard spoke to her angrily.

Meanwhile, Lolo was sick and delirious with grief. Twenty times he got out of his bed and screamed to be allowed to go with Moufflou, and twenty times his mother and his brothers put him back again and held him down and tried in vain to quiet him.

The child was beside himself with misery. 'Moufflou! Moufflou!' he sobbed at every moment; and by night he was in a raging fever, and when his mother, frightened, ran and called in a doctor of the quarter, that worthy man shook his head and said something as to a shock of the nervous system, and muttered a long word—'meningitis'.

Lolo took a hatred to the sight of Tasso, and thrust him away, and his mother too.

'It is for you Moufflou is sold,' he said, with his little teeth and hands tight clinched.

After a day or two Tasso felt as if he could not bear his life, and went down to the hotel to see if the foreign gentleman would allow him to have Moufflou back for half an hour to quiet his little brother by a sight of him. But at the hotel he was told that the *Milord Inglese* who had bought the dog of Rosina Calabucci had gone that same night of the purchase to Rome, to Naples, to Palermo, *chi sa*?

'And Moufflou with him?' asked Tasso.

'The *barbone* he had bought went with him,' said the porter of the hotel. 'Such a beast! Howling, shrieking, raging all the day, and all the paint scratched off the salon door.'

Poor Moufflou! Tasso's heart was heavy as he heard of that sad, helpless misery of their bartered favourite and friend.

'What matter?' said his mother fiercely, when he told her. 'A dog is a dog. They will feed him better than we could. In a week he will have forgotten—*chè*!'

But Tasso feared that Moufflou would not forget. Lolo certainly would not. The doctor came to the bedside twice a day, and ice and water were kept on the aching, hot little head that had got the malady with the long name, and for the chief part of the time Lolo lay quiet, dull, and stupid, breathing heavily, and then at intervals cried and sobbed and shrieked hysterically for Moufflou.

'Can you not get what he calls for to quiet him with a sight of it?' said the doctor. But that was not possible, and poor Rosina covered her head with her apron and felt a guilty creature.

'Still, you will not go to the army,' she said to Tasso, clinging to that immense joy for her consolation. 'Only think! We can pay Guido Squarcione to go for you. He always said he would go if anybody would pay him. Oh my Tasso, surely to keep you is worth a dog's life!'

'And Lolo's?' said Tasso gloomily. 'Nay, mother, it works ill to meddle too much with fate. I drew my number; I was bound to go. Heaven would have made it up to you somehow.'

'Heaven sent me the foreigner; the Madonna's own self sent him to ease a mother's pain,' said Rosina rapidly and angrily. 'There are the thousand francs safe to hand in the *cassone*, and what, pray, is it we miss? Only a dog like a sheep, that brought gallons of mud in with him every time it rained, and ate as much as any one of you.'

'But Lolo?' said Tasso, under his breath.

His mother was so irritated and so tormented by her own conscience that she upset all the cabbage broth into the burning charcoal.

'Lolo was always a little fool, thinking of nothing but the church and the dog and nasty field flowers,' she said angrily. 'I humoured him too much because of the hurt to his hip, and so—and so——'

Then the poor soul made matters worse by dropping her tears into the saucepan, and fanning the charcoal so furiously that the flame caught her fan of cane leaves, and would have burned her arm had not Tasso been there.

'You are my prop and safety always. Who would not have done what I did? Not Santa Felicita herself,' she said with a great sob.

But all this did not cure poor Lolo.

The days and the weeks of the golden autumn weather passed away, and he was always in danger, and the small, close room where he slept with Sandro and Beppo and Tasso was not one to cure such an illness as had now beset him. Tasso went to his work with a sick heart in the Cascine, where the colchicum was all lilac among the meadow grass, and the ashes and elms were taking their first flush of the coming autumnal change. He did not think Lolo would ever get well, and the good lad felt as if he had been the murderer of his little brother.

True, he had had no hand or voice in the sale of Moufflou, but Moufflou had been sold for his sake. It made him feel half guilty, very unhappy, quite unworthy of all the sacrifice that had been made for him. 'Nobody should meddle with fate,' thought Tasso, who knew his grandfather had died in San Bonifazio because he had driven himself mad over the dream book trying to get lucky numbers for the lottery and become a rich man at a stroke.

It was rapture, indeed, to know that he was free of the army for a time at least, that he might go on undisturbed at his healthful labour, and get a raise in wages as time went on, and dwell in peace with his family, and perhaps—perhaps in time earn enough to marry pretty flaxen-haired Biondina, the daughter of the barber in the piazzetta. It was rapture indeed; but then poor Moufflou!—and poor, poor Lolo! Tasso felt as if he had bought his own exemption by seeing his little brother and the good dog torn in pieces and buried alive for his service.

And where was poor Moufflou?

Gone far away somewhere south in the hurrying, screeching, vomiting, braying train that it made Tasso giddy only to look at as it rushed by the green meadows beyond the Cascine on its way to the sea.

'If he could see the dog he cries so for, it might save him,' said the doctor, who stood with grave face watching Lolo.

But that was beyond anyone's power. No one could tell where Moufflou was. He might be carried to England, to France, to Russia, to America—who could say? They did not know where his purchaser had gone. Moufflou might even be dead.

The poor mother, when the doctor said that, went and looked at the ten hundred-franc notes that were once like angels' faces to her, and said to them, 'Oh, you children of Satan, why did you tempt me? I sold the poor, innocent, trustful beast to get you, and now my child is dying!'

Her eldest son would stay at home, indeed; but if this little lame one died! Rosina Calabucci would have given up the notes and consented never to own five francs in her life if only she could have gone back over the time and kept Moufflou and seen his little master running out with him into the sunshine.

More than a month went by, and Lolo lay in the same state, his yellow hair shorn, his eyes dilated and yet stupid, life kept in him by a spoonful of milk, a lump of ice, a drink of lemon water; always muttering, when he spoke at all, 'Moufflou, Moufflou, *dov' è* Moufflou?' and lying for days together in somnolence and unconsciousness, with the fire eating at his brain and the weight lying on it like a stone.

The neighbours were kind, and brought fruit and the like, and sat up with him, and chattered so all at once in one continuous brawl that they were enough in themselves to kill him, for such is ever the Italian fashion of sympathy in all illness.

But Lolo did not get well, did not even seem to see the light at all, or to distinguish any sounds around him; and the doctor in plain words told Rosina Calabucci that her little boy must die. Die, and the church so near! She could not believe it. Could St Mark and St George and the rest he had loved so do nothing for him? No, said the doctor, they could do nothing; the dog might do something, since the brain had so fastened on that one idea; but then they had sold the dog.

'Yes, I sold him!' said the poor mother, breaking into floods of remorseful tears.

So at last the end drew so nigh that one twilight time the priest came out of the great arched door that is next St Mark, with the Host uplifted, and a little acolyte ringing the bell before it, and passed across the piazzetta, and went up the dark staircase of Rosina's dwelling, and passed through the weeping, terrified children, and went to the bedside of Lolo.

Lolo was unconscious, but the holy man touched his little body and limbs with the sacred oil, and prayed over him, and then stood sorrowful with bowed head.

Lolo had had his first communion in the summer, and in his preparation for it had shown an intelligence and devoutness that had won the priest's gentle heart.

Standing there, the holy man commended the innocent soul to God. It was the last service to be rendered to him save that very last of all when the funeral office should be read above his little grave among the millions of nameless dead at the sepulchres of the poor at Trebbiano.

All was still as the priest's voice ceased. Only the sobs of the mother and of the children broke the stillness as they knelt. The hand of Biondina had stolen into Tasso's.

Suddenly, there was a loud scuffling noise; hurrying feet came patter,

89

patter, patter up the stairs, a ball of mud and dust flew over the heads of the kneeling figures. Fleet as the wind, Moufflou dashed through the room and leaped upon the bed.

Lolo opened his heavy eyes, and a sudden light of consciousness gleamed in them like a sunbeam. 'Moufflou!' he murmured, in his little thin, faint voice. The big dog pressed close to his breast and kissed his wasted face.

Moufflou had come home!

And Lolo came home, too, for death let go its hold upon him. Little by little, very faintly and flickeringly and very uncertainly at the first, life returned to the poor little body, and reason to the tormented, heated little brain. Moufflou was his physician; Moufflou, himself a skeleton under his matted curls, would not stir from his side and looked at him all day long with two beaming brown eyes full of unutterable love.

Lolo was happy; he asked no questions—was too weak, indeed, even to wonder. He had Moufflou; that was enough.

Alas! Though they dared not say so in his hearing, it was not enough for his elders. His mother and Tasso knew that the poodle had been sold and paid for; that they could lay no claim to keep him; and that almost certainly his purchaser would seek him out and assert his indisputable right to him. And then how would Lolo ever bear that second parting? —Lolo, so weak that he weighed no more than if he had been a little bird.

Moufflou had, no doubt, travelled a long distance and suffered much. He was but skin and bone; he bore the marks of blows and kicks; his once silken hair was all discoloured and matted; he had, no doubt, travelled far. But then his purchaser would be sure to ask for him, soon or late, at his old home; and then? Well, then if they did not give him up themselves, the law would make them.

Rosina Calabucci and Tasso, though they dared say nothing before any of the children, felt their hearts in their mouth at every step on the stair, and the first interrogation of Tasso every evening when he came from his work was, 'Has anyone come for Moufflou?' For ten days no one came, and their first terrors lulled a little.

On the eleventh morning, a feast day, on which Tasso was not going to his labours in the Cascine, there came a person, with a foreign look, who said the words they so much dreaded to hear: 'Has the poodle that you sold to an English gentleman come back to you?'

Yes, his English master claimed him!

The servant said that they had missed the dog in Rome a few days after buying him and taking him there; that he had been searched for in vain, and that his master had thought it possible the animal might have found his way back to his old home: there had been stories of such wonderful sagacity in dogs. Anyhow, he had sent for him on the chance; he was himself back on the Lung' Arno. The servant pulled from his pocket a chain, and said his orders were to take the poodle away at once: the little sick gentleman had fretted very much about his loss.

Tasso heard in a very agony of despair. To take Moufflou away now would be to kill Lolo—Lolo so feeble still, so unable to understand, so passionately alive to every sight and sound of Moufflou, lying for hours together motionless with his hand buried in the poodle's curls, saying nothing, only smiling now and then, and murmuring a word or two in Moufflou's ear.

'The dog did come home,' said Tasso, at length, in a low voice. 'Angels must have shown him the road, poor beast! From Rome! Only to think of it, from Rome! And he a dumb thing! I tell you he is here, honestly: so will you not trust me just so far as this? Will you let me go with you and speak to the English lord before you take the dog away? I have a little brother sorely ill——'

He could not speak more, for tears that choked his voice.

At last the messenger agreed so far as this: Tasso might go first and see the master, but he would stay here and have a care they did not spirit the dog away—'for a thousand francs were paid for him,' added the man, 'and a dog that can come all the way from Rome by itself must be an uncanny creature.'

Tasso thanked him, went upstairs, was thankful that his mother was at mass and could not dispute with him, took the ten hundred-franc notes from the old oak *cassone*, and with them in his breast pocket walked out into the air. He was but a poor working lad, but he had made up his mind to do an heroic deed, for self-sacrifice is always heroic. He went straightway to the hotel where the English gentleman was, and when he had got there remembered that still he did not know the name of Moufflou's owner; but the people of the hotel knew him as Rosina Calabucci's son, and guessed what he wanted, and said the man who had lost the poodle was within upstairs and they would tell him.

Tasso waited some half hour with his heart beating sorely against the packet of hundred franc notes. At last he was beckoned upstairs, and there he saw a foreigner with a mild fair face, and a very lovely lady, and a delicate child who was lying on a couch. 'Moufflou! Where is Moufflou?' cried the little child impatiently, as he saw the youth enter.

Tasso took his hat off and stood in the doorway an embrowned, healthy, not ungraceful figure, in his work clothes of rough blue cloth.

'If you please, most illustrious,' he stammered, 'poor Moufflou has come home.'

The child gave a cry of delight; the gentleman and lady one of wonder. Home! All the way from Rome!

'Yes, he has, most illustrious,' said Tasso, gaining courage and eloquence, 'and now I want to beg something of you. We are poor, and I drew a bad number, and it was for that my mother sold Moufflou. For myself, I did not know anything of it, but she thought she would buy my substitute, and of course she could. But Moufflou is come home, and my little brother Lolo, the little boy your most illustrious first saw playing with the poodle, fell ill of the grief of losing Moufflou, and for a month has lain saying nothing sensible, but only calling for the dog, and my old grandfather died of worrying himself mad over the lottery numbers, and Lolo was so near dying that the blessed Host had been brought, and the holy oil had been put on him, when all at once there rushes in Moufflou, skin and bone, and covered with mud, and at the sight of him Lolo comes back to his senses, and that is now ten days ago, and though Lolo is still as weak as a newborn thing, he is always sensible, and takes what we give him to eat, and lies always looking at Moufflou and smiling, and saying, "Moufflou, Moufflou!" and, most illustrious, I know well you have bought the dog, and the law is with you, and by the law you claim it; but I thought perhaps, as Lolo loves him so, you would let us keep the dog, and would take back the thousand francs, and myself I will go and be a soldier, and heaven will take care of them all somehow.'

Then Tasso, having said all this in one breathless, monotonous recitative, took the thousand francs out of his breast pocket and held them out timidly towards the foreign gentleman, who motioned them aside and stood silent.

'Did you understand, Victor?' he said, at last, to his little son.

The child hid his face in his cushions.

'Yes, I did understand something. Let Lolo keep him: Moufflou was not happy with me.'

But he burst out crying as he said it. Moufflou had run away from him. Moufflou had never loved him, for all his sweet cakes and fond caresses and platefuls of delicate savoury meats. Moufflou had run away and found his own road over two hundred miles and more to go back to some little hungry children, who never had enough to eat themselves, and so, certainly, could never give enough to eat to the dog. Poor little boy! He was so rich and so pampered and so powerful, and yet he could never make Moufflou love him!

Tasso, who understood nothing that was said, laid the ten hundred-franc notes down on a table near him.

'If you would take them, most illustrious, and give me back what my mother wrote when she sold Moufflou,' he said timidly, 'I would pray for you night and day, and Lolo would, too. And as for the dog, we will get a puppy and train him for your little *signorino*. They can all do tricks, more or less, for it comes by nature; and as for me, I will go to the army willingly; it is not right to interfere with fate; my old grandfather died mad because he would try to be a rich man, by dreaming about it and pulling destiny by the ears, as if she were a kicking mule; only, I do pray of you, do not take away Moufflou. And to think he trotted all those miles and miles, and you carried him by train, too, and he never could have seen the road, and he had no power of speech to ask——'

Tasso broke down again in his eloquence, and drew the back of his hand across his wet eyelashes.

The English gentleman was not unmoved.

'Poor faithful dog!' he said, with a sigh. 'I am afraid we were very cruel to him, meaning to be kind. No, we will not claim him, and I do not think you should go for a soldier; you seem so good a lad, and your mother must need you. Keep the money, my boy, and in payment you shall train the puppy you talk of, and bring him to my little boy. I will come and see your mother and Lolo tomorrow. All the way from Rome! What wonderful sagacity! What matchless fidelity!'

You can imagine, without any telling of mine, the joy that reigned in Moufflou's home when Tasso returned thither with the money and the good tidings both. His substitute was bought without a day's delay, and Lolo rapidly recovered. As for Moufflou, he could never tell them his troubles, his wanderings, his difficulties, his perils. He could never tell them by what miraculous knowledge he had found his way across Italy, from the gates of Rome to the gates of Florence. But he soon grew plump again, and merry, and his love for Lolo was yet greater than before.

By the winter all the family went to live on an estate near Spezia that the English gentleman had purchased, and there Moufflou was happier than ever. The little English boy is gaining strength in the soft air, and he and Lolo are great friends and play with Moufflou and the poodle puppy half the day upon the sunny terraces and under the green orange boughs. Tasso is one of the gardeners there; he will probably have to serve as a soldier in some category or another, but he is safe for the time, and is happy. Lolo, whose lameness will always exempt him from military service, when he grows to be a man means to be a florist, and a great one. He has learned to read, as the first step on the road of his ambition.

'But oh, Moufflou, how *did* you find your way home?' he asks the dog a hundred times a week.

How indeed!

THE SMALL WOMAN
Michael Hardwick

Only the sound of harsh, ragged breathing and the buzz of flies could be heard in the Chinese prison compound. The sun beat down on the heads of the convicts as they cringed against a wall, staring in silence at the scene before them. On the ground lay several men, their heads and bodies horribly gashed. Over them stood their attacker. A blood-stained axe was in his hand. His eyes glittered with a dangerous light, as he watched the small English woman who confronted him.

Slowly, deliberately, she began to move towards him, hand outstretched.

'Give me the axe,' she said quietly.

The man frowned. 'Give me the axe,' she repeated, her voice firmer.

There was a gasp from the watching convicts as they saw the man move suddenly—then stop, and meekly hold the axe out to her.

The small woman siezed it. From their place of safety, the prison authorities watched her order the convicts to line up and return quietly to their quarters. They obeyed. She was a 'foreign devil', a European missionary whom they distrusted, but nobody else had been brave enough to go into that compound. Her courage that day earned her much 'face'. She was in need of it.

Gladys Aylward had dreamed of China ever since her childhood in the London suburb of Edmonton. She knew that she wanted to spend her life as a missionary, teaching the Chinese people about Christ and his Church. When she left school she had to go into domestic service as a parlour-maid, but as she grew older her ambition strengthened. Eventually, she enrolled as a student in the China Inland Mission School in London.

After three months she was told that her work was not good enough. It was doubted that she would ever be able to speak Chinese. Besides, she was too old for missionary work abroad. She was twenty-six.

Gladys was deeply disappointed. But she had a strong and determined spirit. She decided that she would make her own way to China. She returned to domestic service and began to save for the journey. The cheapest and quickest route at that time was by train, across Europe and Russia on the Trans-Siberian Railway to Tientsin. The fare was £47. 10s.

She must have seemed an eccentric to the booking clerk at the travel agency when she told him that she wanted to reserve a ticket. He pointed out that Russia and China were at war, and that the Trans-Siberian Railway ran right through the battle zone—if it still ran at all at its eastern end. Gladys was undeterred. The clerk shrugged his shoulders, accepted her three pounds deposit and made the reservation. During the following months she paid regular instalments towards her ticket, worked hard at Bible study, and taught herself to preach by standing on a box at Speakers' Corner, Hyde Park, addressing the crowd always gathered there on Sundays. Few bothered to listen, but it was good practice.

Her perseverance was rewarded. She learned of a missionary in China, an old lady named Jeannie Lawson, who was looking for a younger woman to assist her. Gladys wrote to her at once, and was accepted.

On 18 October 1930, she left London on the first stage of the long and often difficult journey across half the world. Because of the Eastern war, Gladys found herself stranded in Vladivostok. She had little money left and the Russian authorities were on the point of forcing her to work in a factory when she found a friendly young Japanese captain who offered her a free lift to Japan in his ship. It was a roundabout route to China, but she was helped along by missionaries and put aboard another ship which took her to her original destination, Tientsin.

The journey was not over yet, though. Mrs Lawson's mission was in a town in the northern province of Shansi, a wild, mountainous area difficult to cross and swarming with bandits. To avoid attracting their attention, Gladys abandoned her European clothes and travelled as a Chinese, in quilted jacket and trousers. It took her a month—by train, bus, and finally mule—to reach the high-walled town of Yangcheng.

The mission was very small and there were few converts. The people of the town were superstitious and unfriendly and treated the 'foreign devils' with open dislike. Soon after her arrival Gladys saw a man publicly beheaded in the town square. She realized that everything was going to be far harder than she had ever imagined, but she was determined to succeed and began teaching herself the local dialect.

To attract more converts to the mission, she and Mrs Lawson opened a small inn to cater for the men who led the endless mule trains across the mountains. They called it The Inn of Eight Happinesses. After their guests had been fed it became the custom for them to sit around the fire listening to stories from the Bible. The inn began to be a success, and some of the muleteers became Christian converts.

But it was not to last long. Mrs Lawson died after a bad fall, and Gladys was left to carry on alone. Funds were running out. Then, just as things seemed very bleak, help arrived in the unlikely guise of the Mandarin, or chief official, of Yangcheng. The Central Chinese Government had recently banned the ancient custom of binding the feet of baby girls in order to stunt the growth—small feet are considered beautiful by the Chinese. The Mandarin required a 'Foot Inspector' to travel around the villages to see that the new law was obeyed. He wished the appointment to be held by a woman with normal feet, to set an example.

Gladys Aylward became the Mandarin's official Foot Inspector. She combined her tours of inspection with Bible story-telling, as she had at The Inn of Eight Happinesses. Before long there was a growing band of Christian converts attending the mission in Yangcheng. The town authorities regarded this with suspicion. When one of the convicts in the local prison went berserk with an axe, and the soldiers refused to tackle him, the authorities decided to test Gladys. After all, had she not often said that her God protected from harm those who loved him?

Following her success in the prison incident, Gladys decided to work on behalf of the convicts. She was able to secure better living conditions for them. The Governor's friend, a Christian convert, was allowed to preach to them. The grateful convicts gave Gladys a name —Ai-weh-deh, meaning The Virtuous One. She was a foreign devil no longer.

It was through her work as Foot Inspector that she adopted the first of her five children. On one of her tours a woman offered to sell her a small child, a girl, and therefore useless to the woman's family. Gladys was outraged that such traffic was allowed to flourish unchecked. The child was obviously starving. The only thing she could do was to accept the offer. She bought the little girl and named her Ninepence—the price she had cost.

In 1936, when she had been in China six years, Gladys Aylward became a Chinese citizen. Two years later she found herself in the horror of the Japanese invasion.

With Japanese troops gradually occupying the province of Shansi, and treating the people with barbaric cruelty, Yangcheng received its first warning of their approach when planes bombed and machine-gunned the town. Gladys took some of the women and children into the hills for safety. When she returned, it was to a town of the dead. Everyone who had not fled had been massacred. Gladys helped to organize the burials, then left to start a makeshift hospital at a town on the other side of the mountains. On one of her return trips to Yang-cheng she had the proud satisfaction of learning that her erstwhile employer, the Mandarin, wished to become a Christian.

Life was very rough during this period. The Japanese were every-where, killing, destroying, looting, maiming. They attacked the mission at Tsehchow where Gladys was organizing the care of orphaned and refugee children, and beat her up badly when she tried to defend some of the girls from the soldiers. Another time her life was saved from bullets by the quilted jacket which had long since become her habitual wear.

'Do not wish me out of this or in any way seek to get me out,' she wrote to her family in England; 'for I will not be got out while this trial is on. These are my people; God has given them to me, and I will live or die with them for Him and His Glory.'

With her small band of converts she survived terrible acts of carnage, and time after time she organized relief work in towns that had suffered at the enemy's hands. After one raid she was forced to shelter for three weeks in a mountain cave. Her work inevitably brought her to the notice of the Japanese. A price was put on her head—one hundred dollars for 'The Small Woman known as Ai-weh-deh'.

Gladys knew that her time was up in Shansi Province. With the children in her care—almost one hundred of them—she decided to set out for a camp for refugee orphans, far away across the mountains and beyond the great Yellow River. It was a daunting mission, but some of her children were in their teens and would be able to help to look after the little ones. She believed they could make it.

In March 1940 they set out. During the first stage of their journey they were helped by Chinese Nationalist soldiers, but there came a time when they were alone on the mountains—cold, hungry and exhausted. After twelve days they reached the wide, fast-flowing Yellow River. Luckily, they found more soliders willing to ferry them across. But because all traffic on the river was prohibited by the local authorities, Gladys found herself under arrest when she reached the opposite bank. There were several uncomfortable, uncertain hours before she was allowed to continue the journey.

For four days she and the children were able to travel by train. When a bridge was blown up, destroying the track, they had to start walking again. Many of them had no shoes. Sharp stones cut through the rags tied around their feet, so the older children took it in turns to carry the little ones. To keep up their spirits, Gladys encouraged them to sing as they walked, and for hours on end the sound of their voices marked the slow progress through the mountains. After four more days they reached the plain, and were able to get a ride on a coal train.

It was now April. The month-long journey was over, and the children were safe. But the strain and utter exhaustion had proved too much for their leader. She collapsed and was seriously ill for some time. On her recovery she settled with her five adopted children in the westerly province of Chengtu, where she taught English. When the children had grown up she worked in a leper colony.

Gladys Aylward returned to England in 1950, after twenty years. The results of her wartime injuries required hospital treatment of a kind not then available in China.

She spent her last years in England, dying in 1970. Few people had heard of her in her native country, and Gladys saw no reason why she should be singled out for attention. After all, she had only done her duty. 'Nothing very exciting happened,' she replied, when first asked about her long years in China.

THE RESCUE OF LORNA DOONE

R. D. Blackmore

John Ridd had first seen Lorna Doone when as a boy he was returning home from Blundell's School; one of the Doones was carrying the little girl flung across his saddlebow. The Doones were a band of fierce and hated outlaws living in Glen Doone, and it was they who had murdered John's father. John, bent on revenge, finds his way into the Doone valley, and there meets Lorna. They continue to see each other secretly as they grow up and fall in love. When Lorna tells John one day that she is to be starved until she consents to marry Carver Doone, he decides the time has come to take her away from her captors.

To my great delight, I found the weather, not often friendly to lovers, and lately seeming so hostile, had in the most important matter done me a signal service. For when I had promised to take my love from the power of those wretches, the only way of escape apparent lay through the main Doone-gate. For though I might climb the cliffs myself, especially with the snow to aid me, I durst not try to fetch Lorna up them, even if she were not half-starved, as well as partly frozen; and as for Gwenny's door, as we called it (that is to say, the little entrance from the wooded hollow), it was snowed up long ago to the level of the hills around. Therefore I was at my wit's end, how to get them out; the passage by the Doone-gate being long, and dark, and difficult, and leading to such a weary circuit among the snowy moors and hills.

But now, being homeward-bound by the shortest possible track, I slipped along between the bonfire and the boundary cliffs, where I found a caved way of snow behind a sort of avalanche: so that if the Doones had been keeping watch (which they were not doing, but revelling) they could scarcely have discovered me. And when I came to my old ascent, where I had often scaled the cliff and made across the mountains, it struck me that I would just have a look at my first and painful entrance, to wit, the water-slide. I never for a moment imagined that this could help me now; for I never had dared to descend it, even in the finest weather; still I had a curiosity to know what my old friend was like, with so much snow upon him. But, to my very great surprise, there was scarcely any snow there at all, though plenty curling high over head from the cliff, like bolsters over it. Probably the sweeping of the north-east wind up the narrow chasm had kept the showers from blocking it, although the water had no power under the bitter grip of frost. All my water-slide was now less a slide than a path of ice; furrowed where the waters ran over fluted ridges; seamed where wind had tossed and combed them, even while congealing; and crossed with little steps wherever the freezing torrent lingered. And here and there the ice was fibred with the trail of sludge-weed, slanting from the side, and matted, so as to make resting-place.

Lo, it was easy track and channel, as if for the very purpose made, down which I could guide my sledge, with Lorna sitting in it. There were only two things to be feared; one, lest the rolls of snow above should fall in and bury us; the other lest we should rush too fast, and so be carried headlong into the black whirlpool at the bottom, the middle of which was still unfrozen, and looking more horrible by the contrast. Against this danger I made provision by fixing a stout bar across; but of the other we must take our chance, and trust ourselves to providence.

I hastened home at my utmost speed, and told my mother for God's sake to keep the house up till my return, and to have plenty of fire blazing, and plenty of water boiling, and food enough hot for a dozen people, and the best bed aired with the warming-pan. Dear mother smiled softly at my excitement, though her own was not much less, I am sure, and enhanced by sore anxiety. Then I gave very strict directions to Annie, and praised her a little, and kissed her; and I even endeavoured to flatter Eliza, lest she should be disagreeable.

After this I took some brandy, both within and about me; the former because I had sharp work to do; and the latter in fear of whatever might happen, in such great cold, to my comrades. Also I carried some other provisions, grieving much at their coldness; and then I went to the upper linhay, and took our new light pony-sled, which had been made almost as much for pleasure as for business; though God only knows how our girls could have found any pleasure in bumping along so. On the snow, however, it ran as sweetly as if it had been made for it; yet I durst not take the pony with it; in the first place, because his hoofs would break through the ever-shifting surface of the light and piling snow; and secondly, because those ponies, coming from the forest, have a dreadful trick of neighing, and most of all in frosty weather.

Therefore I girded my own body with a dozen turns of hay-rope, twisting both the ends in under at the bottom of my breast, and winding the hay on the skew a little, that the hemp thong might not slip between, and so cut me in the drawing. I put a good piece of spare rope in the sled, and the cross-seat with the back to it, which was stuffed with our own wool, as well as two or three fur coats: and then just as I was starting, out came Annie, in spite of the cold, panting for fear of missing me, and with nothing on her head, but a lanthorn in one hand.

'Oh, John, here is the most wonderful thing! Mother has never shown it before; and I can't think how she could make up her mind. She had gotten it in a great well of a cupboard, with camphor, and spirits, and lavender. Lizzie says it is a most magnificent sealskin cloak, worth fifty pounds, or a farthing.'

'At any rate it is soft and warm,' said I, very calmly flinging it into the bottom of the sled. 'Tell mother I will put it over Lorna's feet.'

'Lorna's feet! Oh, you great fool,' cried Annie, for the first time reviling me; 'over her shoulders; and be proud, you very stupid John.'

'It is not good enough for her feet,' I answered, with strong emphasis; 'but don't tell mother I said so, Annie. Only thank her very kindly.'

With that I drew my traces hard, and set my ashen staff into the snow, and struck out with my best foot foremost (the best one at snow-shoes, I mean), and the sled came after me as lightly as a dog might follow; and Annie with the lanthorn seemed to be left behind and waiting, like a pretty lamp-post.

The full moon rose as bright behind me as a patin of pure silver, casting on the snow long shadows of the few things left above, burned rock, and shaggy foreland, and the labouring trees. In the great white desolation, distance was a mocking vision: hills looked nigh, and valleys far; when hills were far and valleys nigh. And the misty breath of frost, piercing through the ribs of rock, striking to the pith of trees, creeping to the heart of man, lay along the hollow places, like a serpent sloughing.

Even as my own gaunt shadow (travestied as if I were the moonlight's daddy-long-legs) went before me down the slope; even I, the shadow's master, who had tried in vain to cough, when coughing brought good liquorice, felt a pressure on my bosom, and a husking in my throat.

However, I went on quietly, and at a very tidy speed; being only too thankful that the snow had ceased, and no wind as yet arisen. And from the ring of low white vapour girding all the verge of sky, and from the rosy blue above, and the shafts of starlight set upon a quivering bow, as well as from the moon itself and the light behind it, having learned the signs of frost from its bitter twinges, I knew that we should have a night as keen as ever England felt. Nevertheless, I had work enough to keep me warm if I managed it. The question was, could I contrive to save my darling from it?

Daring not to risk my sled by any fall from the valley-cliffs, I dragged it very carefully up the steep incline of ice, through the narrow chasm, and so to the very brink and verge where first I had seen my Lorna, in the fishing days of boyhood. As then I had a trident fork, for sticking of the loaches, so now I had a strong ash stake, to lay across from rock to rock, and break the speed of descending. With this I moored the sled quite safe, at the very lip of the chasm, where all was now substantial ice, green and black in the moonlight; and then I set off up the valley, skirting along one side of it.

The stack-fire still was burning strongly, but with more of heat than blaze; and many of the younger Doones were playing on the verge of it, the children making rings of fire, and their mothers watching them. All the grave and reverend warriors, having heard of rheumatism, were inside of log and stone, in the two lowest houses, with enough of candles burning to make our list of sheep come short.

All these I passed, without the smallest risk of difficulty, walking up the channel of drift which I spoke of once before. And then I crossed, with more care, and to the door of Lorna's house, and made the sign, and listened, after taking my snow-shoes off.

But no one came, as I expected, neither could I espy a light. And I seemed to hear a faint low sound, like the moaning of the snow-wind. Then I knocked again more loudly, with a knocking at my heart; and receiving no answer, set all my power at once against the door. In a moment it flew inwards, and I glided along the passage with my feet still slippery. There in Lorna's room I saw, by the moonlight flowing in, a sight which drove me beyond sense.

Lorna was behind a chair, crouching in the corner, with her hands up, and a crucifix, or something that looked like it. In the middle of the room lay Gwenny Carfax, stupid, yet with one hand clutching the ankle of a struggling man. Another man stood above my Lorna, trying to draw the chair away. In a moment I had him round the waist, and he went out of the window with a mighty crash of glass; luckily for him that window had no bars like some of them. Then I took the other man by the neck; and he could not plead for mercy. I bore him out of the house as lightly as I would bear a baby, yet squeezing his throat a little more than I fain would do to an infant. By the bright moonlight I saw that I carried Marwood de Whichehalse. For his father's sake I spared him, and because he had been my schoolfellow: but with every muscle of my body strung with indignation, I cast him, like a skittle, from me into a snowdrift, which closed over him. Then I looked for the other fellow, tossed through Lorna's window; and found him lying stunned and bleeding, neither able to groan yet. Charleworth Doone, if his gushing blood did not much mislead me.

It was no time to linger now: I fastened my shoes in a moment, and caught up my own darling with her head upon my shoulder, where she whispered faintly; and telling Gwenny to follow me, or else I would come back for her, if she could not walk the snow, I ran the whole distance to my sled, caring not who might follow me. Then by the time I had set up Lorna, beautiful and smiling, with the sealskin cloak all over her, sturdy Gwenny came along, having trudged in the track of my snow-shoes, although with two bags on her back. I set her in beside her mistress, to support her, and keep warm; and then with one look back at the glen, which had been so long my home of heart, I hung behind the sled, and launched it down the steep and dangerous way.

Though the cliffs were black above us, and the road unseen in front, and a great white grave of snow might at a single word come down, Lorna was as calm and happy as an infant in its bed. She knew that I was with her; and when I told her not to speak, she touched my hand in silence. Gwenny was in a much greater fright, having never seen such a thing before, neither knowing what it is to yield to pure love's confidence. I could hardly keep her quiet, without making a noise myself.

I cast him, like a skittle, into a snowdrift . . .

With my staff from rock to rock, and my weight thrown backward, I broke the sled's too rapid way, and brought my grown love safely out, by the self-same road which first had led me to her girlish fancy, and my boyish slavery.

Unpursued, yet looking back as if some one must be after us, we skirted round the black whirling pool, and gained the meadows beyond it. Here there was hard collar work, the track being all uphill and rough; and Gwenny wanted to jump out, to lighten the sled and to push behind. But I would not hear of it; because it was now so deadly cold, and I feared that Lorna might get frozen, without having Gwenny to keep her warm. And after all, it was the sweetest labour I had ever known in all my life, to be sure that I was pulling Lorna, and pulling her to our own farmhouse.

Gwenny's nose was touched with frost, before we had gone much further, because she would not keep it quiet and snug beneath the seal-skin. And here I had to stop in the moonlight (which was very dangerous) and rub it with a clove of snow, as Eliza had taught me; and Gwenny scolding all the time, as if myself had frozen it. Lorna was now so far oppressed with all the troubles of the evening, and the joy that followed them, as well as by the piercing cold and difficulty of breathing, that she lay quite motionless, like fairest wax in the moonlight—when we stole a glance at her, beneath the dark folds of the cloak; and I thought that she was falling into the heavy snow-sleep, whence there is no awaking.

Therefore I drew my traces tight, and set my whole strength to the business; and we slipped along at a merry pace, although with many joltings, which must have sent my darling out into the cold snow-drifts, but for the short strong arm of Gwenny. And so in about an hour's time, in spite of many hindrances, we came home to the old courtyard, and all the dogs saluted us. My heart was quivering, and my cheeks as hot as the Doones' bonfire, with wondering both what Lorna would think of our farmyard, and what my mother would think of her. Upon the former subject my anxiety was wasted, for Lorna neither saw a thing, nor even opened her heavy eyes. And as to what mother would think of her, she was certain not to think at all, until she had cried over her.

And so indeed it came to pass. Even at this length of time, I can hardly tell it, although so bright before my mind, because it moves my heart so. The sled was at the open door, with only Lorna in it: for Gwenny Carfax had jumped out, and hung back in the clearing, giving any reason rather than the only true one—that she would not be intruding. At the door were all our people; first of course Betty Muxworthy, teaching me how to draw the sled, as if she had been born in it, and flourishing with a great broom, wherever a speck of snow lay. Then dear Annie, and old Molly (who was very quiet, and counted almost for nobody), and behind them mother, looking as if she wanted to come first, but doubted how the manners lay. In the distance Lizzie stood, fearful of encouraging, but unable to keep out of it.

Betty was going to poke her broom right in under the sealskin cloak, where Lorna lay unconscious, and where her precious breath hung frozen, like a silver cobweb; but I caught up Betty's broom, and flung it clean away over the corn chamber; and then I put the others by, and fetched my mother forward.

'You shall see her first,' I said; 'is she not your daughter? Hold the light there, Annie.'

Dear mother's hands were quick and trembling, as she opened the shining folds; and there she saw my Lorna sleeping, with her black hair all dishevelled, and she bent and kissed her forehead, and only said, 'God bless her, John!' And then she was taken with violent weeping, and I was forced to hold her.

'Us may tich of her now, I rackon,' said Betty in her most jealous way: 'Annie, tak her by the head, and I'll tak her by the toesen. No taime to stand here like girt gawks. Don'ee tak on zo, missus. Ther be vainer vish in the zea—Lor, but her be a booty!'

With this, they carried her into the house, Betty chattering all the while, and going on now about Lorna's hands, and the others crowding round her, so that I thought I was not wanted among so many women, and should only get the worst of it, and perhaps do harm to my darling. Therefore I went and brought Gwenny in, and gave her a potful of bacon and peas, and an iron spoon to eat it with, which she did right heartily.

Then I asked her how she could have been such a fool as to let those two vile fellows enter the house where Lorna was; and she accounted for it so naturally, that I could only blame myself. For my agreement had been to give one loud knock (if you happen to remember) and after that two little knocks. Well, these two drunken rogues had come; and one, being very drunk indeed, had given a great thump; and then nothing more to do with it; and the other, being three-quarters drunk, had followed his leader (as one might say) but feebly, and making two of it. Whereupon up jumped Lorna, and declared that her John was there.

All this Gwenny told me shortly, between the whiles of eating, and even while she licked the spoon: and then there came a message for me, that my love was sensible, and was seeking all around for me. Then I told Gwenny to hold her tongue (whatever she did, among us), and not to trust to women's words; and she told me they all were liars, as she had found out long ago; and the only thing to believe in was an honest man, when found. Thereupon I could have kissed her, as a sort of tribute, liking to be appreciated; yet the peas upon her lips made me think about it; and thought is fatal to action. So I went to see my dear.

That sight I shall not forget; till my dying head falls back, and my breast can lift no more. I know not whether I were then more blessed, or harrowed by it. For in the settle was my Lorna, propped with pillows round her, and her clear hands spread sometimes to the blazing fireplace. In her eyes no knowledge was of any thing around her, neither in her neck the sense of leaning towards any thing. Only both her lovely hands were entreating something, to spare her or to love her; and the lines of supplication quivered in her sad white face.

'All go away except my mother,' I said very quietly, but so that I would be obeyed; and everybody knew it. Then mother came to me alone; and she said, 'The frost is in her brain: I have heard of this before, John.' 'Mother, I will have it out,' was all that I could answer her; 'leave her to me altogether: only you sit there and watch.' For I felt that Lorna knew me, and no other soul but me; and that if not interfered with, she would soon come home to me. Therefore I sat gently by her, leaving nature, as it were, to her own good time and will. And presently the glance that watched me, as at distance and in doubt, began to flutter and to brighten, and to deepen into kindness, then to beam with trust and love, and then with gathering tears to falter, and in shame to turn away. But the small entreating hands found their way, as if by instinct, to my great protecting palms; and trembled there, and rested there.

For a little while we lingered thus, neither wishing to move away, neither caring to look beyond the presence of the other; both alike so full of hope, and comfort, and true happiness; if only the world would let us be. And then a little sob disturbed us, and mother tried to make believe that she was only coughing. But Lorna, guessing who she was, jumped up so very rashly that she almost set her frock on fire from the great ash-log; and away she ran to the old oak chair, where mother was by the clock-case pretending to be knitting, and she took the work from mother's hands, and laid them both upon her head, kneeling humbly, and looking up.

'God bless you, my fair mistress!' said mother, bending nearer, and then as Lorna's gaze prevailed, 'God bless you, my sweet child!'

And so she went to mother's heart, by the very nearest road, even as she had come to mine; I mean the road of pity, smoothed by grace, and youth, and gentleness.

A TERRIBLY STRANGE BED

William Wilkie Collins

Shortly after my education at college was finished I happened to be staying in Paris with an English friend. We were both young men then, and lived, I am afraid, rather a wild life in the delightful city of our sojourn. One night we were idling about the neighbourhood of the Palais Royal, doubtful to what amusement we should next betake ourselves. My friend proposed a visit to Frascati's; but his suggestion was not to my taste. I knew Frascati's, as the French saying is, by heart; had lost and won plenty of five-franc pieces there, merely for amusement's sake, until it was amusement no longer, and was thoroughly tired, in fact, of all the ghastly respectabilities of such a social anomaly as a respectable gambling-house.

'For heaven's sake,' said I to my friend, 'let us go somewhere where we can see a little genuine, blackguard, poverty-stricken gaming, with no false gingerbread glitter thrown over it at all. Let us get away from fashionable Frascati's, to a house where they don't mind letting in a man with a ragged coat, or a man with no coat, ragged or otherwise.'

'Very well,' said my friend, 'we needn't go out of the Palais Royal to find the sort of company you want. Here's the place just before us, as blackguard a place, by all report, as you could possibly wish to see.' In another minute we arrived at the door and entered the house.

When we got upstairs, and had left our hats and sticks with the door-keeper, we were admitted into the chief gambling-room. We did not find many people assembled there. But, few as the men were who looked up at us on our entrance, they were all types—lamentably true types—of their respective classes.

We had come to see blackguards; but these men were something worse. There is a comic side, more or less appreciable, in all 'black-guardism'—here there was nothing but tragedy—mute, weird tragedy. The quiet in the room was horrible. The thin, haggard, long-haired young man, whose sunken eyes fiercely watched the turning up of the cards, never spoke; the flabby, fat-faced, pimply player, who pricked his piece of pasteboard perseveringly to register how often black won and how often red—never spoke; the dirty, wrinkled old man, with the vulture eyes and the darned greatcoat, who had lost his last sou, and still looked on desperately after he could play no longer—never spoke. Even the voice of the croupier sounded as if it were strangely dulled and thickened in the atmosphere of the room.

I had entered the place to laugh, but the spectacle before me was something to weep over. I soon found it necessary to take refuge in excitement from the depression of spirits which was fast stealing on me. Unfortunately I sought the nearest excitement by going to the table and beginning to play. Still more unfortunately, as the event will show, I won—won prodigiously, won incredibly; won at such a rate that the regular players at the table crowded round me; and, staring at my stakes with hungry, superstitious eyes, whispered to one another that the English stranger was going to break the bank.

The game was *rouge-et-noir*. I had played at it in every city in Europe, without, however, the care or the wish to study the 'theory of chances' —that philosopher's stone of all gamblers! And a gambler, in the strict sense of the word, I had never been.

But on this occasion it was very different—now, for the first time in my life, I felt what the passion for play really was. My success first be-wildered, and then, in the most literal meaning of the word, intoxi-cated me. Incredible as it may appear, it is nevertheless true, that I only lost when I attempted to estimate chances, and played according to

112

previous calculation. If I left everything to luck, and staked without any care or consideration, I was sure to win—to win in the face of every recognized probability in favour of the bank. At first, some of the men present ventured their money safely enough on my colour; but I speedily increased my stakes to sums which they dared not risk. One after another they left off playing, and breathlessly looked on at my game.

Still, time after time, I staked higher and higher, and still won. The excitement in the room rose to fever pitch. The silence was interrupted by a deep-muttered chorus of oaths and exclamations in different languages every time the gold was shovelled across to my side of the table—even the imperturbable croupier dashed his rake on the floor in a fury of astonishment at my success. But one man present preserved his self-possession, and that man was my friend. He came to my side, and, whispering in English, begged me to leave the place, satisfied with what I had already gained. I must do him the justice to say that he repeated his warnings and entreaties several times, and only left me and went away after I had rejected his advice (I was to all intents and purposes gambling-drunk) in terms which rendered it impossible for him to address me again that night.

Shortly after he had gone a hoarse voice behind me cried, 'Permit me, my dear sir!—permit me to restore to their proper place two Napoleons which you have dropped. Wonderful luck, sir! I pledge you my word of honour, as an old soldier, in the course of my long experience in this sort of thing, I never saw such luck as yours!—never! Go on, sir—*Sacré mille bombes!* Go on boldly, and break the bank!'

I turned round and saw, nodding and smiling at me with inveterate civility, a tall man, dressed in a frogged and braided coat.

If I had been in my senses I should have considered him, personally, as being rather a suspicious specimen of an old soldier. He had goggling bloodshot eyes, mangy mustachios, and a broken nose. His voice betrayed a barrack-room intonation of the worst order, and he had the dirtiest pair of hands I ever saw—even in France. These little personal peculiarities exercised, however, no repelling influence on me. In the mad excitement, the reckless triumph of that moment, I was ready to 'fraternize' with anybody who encouraged me in my game. I accepted the old soldier's offered pinch of snuff, clapped him on the back, and swore he was the most honest fellow in the world, the most glorious relic of the Grand Army that I had ever met with. 'Go on!' cried my military friend, snapping his fingers in ecstasy. 'Go on, and win! Break the bank —*Mille tonnerres!* my gallant English comrade, break the bank!'

And I *did* go on—went on at such a rate that in another quarter of an hour the croupier called out, 'Gentlemen! the bank has discontinued for tonight.' All the notes and all the gold in that 'bank' now lay in a heap under my hands; the whole floating capital of the gambling-house was waiting to pour into my pockets!

'Tie up the money in your pocket-handkerchief, my worthy sir,' said the old soldier, as I wildly plunged my hands into my heap of gold. 'Tie it up, as we used to tie up a bit of dinner in the Grand Army; your winnings are too heavy for any breeches pockets that ever were sewed. There, that's it! Shovel them in, notes and all! And now, as an ancient grenadier, as an ex-brave of the French Army, what remains for me to do! I ask what? Simply this: to entreat my valued English friend to drink a bottle of champagne with me, and toast the goddess fortune in foaming goblets before we part!'

'Excellent ex-brave! Convivial ancient grenadier! Champagne by all means! An English cheer for an old soldier!'

'Bravo! the Englishman; the amiable, gracious Englishman, in whose veins circulates the vivacious blood of France! Another glass? Ah,— the bottle is empty! Never mind! *Vive le vin!* I, the old soldier, order another bottle!'

'No, no, ex-brave; never—ancient grenadier! *Your* bottle last time, *my* bottle this. Behold it! Toast away! The French Army!—The great Napoleon!—The present company! The croupier! The honest croupier's wife and daughters—if he has any! The ladies generally! Everybody in the world!'

By this time the second bottle of champagne was emptied. I felt as if I had been drinking liquid fire—my brain seemed all aflame. No excess in wine had ever had this effect on me before in my life. Was it the result of a stimulant acting upon my system when I was in a highly excited state? Was my stomach in a particularly disordered condition? Or was the champagne amazingly strong?

'Ex-brave of the French Army!' cried I, in a mad state of exhilaration, '*I* am on fire! how are *you*? You have set me on fire! Do you hear, my hero of Austerlitz? Let us have a third bottle to put the flame out!'

The old soldier wagged his head, rolled his goggle eyes, until I expected to see them slip out of their sockets; placed his dirty forefinger by the side of his broken nose, solemnly ejaculated, 'Coffee!' and immediately ran off into an inner room.

The word pronounced by the eccentric veteran seemed to have a magical effect on the rest of the company present. With one accord they all rose to depart. Probably they had expected to profit by my intoxication; but finding that my new friend was benevolently bent on preventing me from getting dead drunk, had now abandoned all hope of thriving pleasantly on my winnings. Whatever their motive might be, at any rate they went away in a body. When the old soldier returned and sat down again opposite to me at the table, we had the room to ourselves. I could see the croupier, in a sort of vestibule which opened out of it, eating his supper in solitude. The silence was now deeper than ever.

A sudden change, too, had come over the 'ex-brave'. He assumed a portentously solemn look, and when he spoke to me again his speech was ornamented by no oaths, enforced by no finger-snapping, enlivened by no apostrophes or exclamations.

'Listen, my dear sir,' said he, in mysteriously confidential tones, 'listen to an old soldier's advice. I have been to the mistress of the house —a very charming woman, with a genius for cookery!—to impress on her the necessity of making us some particularly strong and good coffee. You must drink this coffee in order to get rid of your little amiable exaltation of spirits before you think of going home—you *must*, my good and gracious friend! With all that money to take home tonight, it is a sacred duty to yourself to have your wits about you. You are known to be a winner to an enormous extent by several gentlemen present tonight, who, in a certain point of view, are very worthy and excellent fellows; but they are mortal men, my dear, sir, and they have their amiable weaknesses! Need I say more? Ah, no, no! you understand me! Now, this is what you must do. Send for a cabriolet when you feel quite well again, draw up all the windows when you get into it, and tell the driver to take you home only through the large and well-lit thoroughfares. Do this, and you and your money will be safe. Do this, and tomorrow you will thank an old soldier for giving you a word of honest advice.'

Just as the ex-brave ended his oration in very lagubrious tones, the coffee came in, ready poured out in two cups. My attentive friend handed me one of the cups with a bow. I was parched with thirst, and drank it off at a draught. Almost instantly afterwards I was seized with a fit of giddiness, and felt more completely intoxicated than ever. The room whirled round and round furiously; the old soldier seemed to be regularly bobbing up and down before me like the piston of a steam-engine. I was half deafened by a violent singing in my ears; a feeling of utter bewilderment, helplessness, idiocy overcame me. I rose from my chair, holding on by the table to keep my balance, and stammered out that I felt dreadfully unwell, so unwell that I did not know how I was to get home.

'My dear friend,' answered the old soldier—and even his voice seemed to be bobbing up and down as he spoke—'my dear friend, it would be madness to go home in *your* state; you would be sure to lose your money; you might be robbed and murdered with the greatest ease. *I* am going to sleep here: *you* sleep here, too—they make up capital beds in this house—take one; sleep off the effects of the wine, and go home safely with your winnings tomorrow—tomorrow, in broad daylight.'

I had but two ideas left: one, that I must never let go hold of my handkerchief full of money; the other, that I must lie down somewhere immediately and fall off into a comfortable sleep. So I agreed to the proposal about the bed, and took the offered arm of the old soldier, carrying my money with my disengaged hand. Preceded by the croupier, we passed along some passages and up a flight of stairs into the bedroom which I was to occupy. The ex-brave shook me warmly by the hand, proposed that we should breakfast together, and then, fol-lowed by the croupier, left me for the night.

I ran to the wash-stand, drank some of the water in my jug, poured the rest out, and plunged my face into it, then sat down in a chair and tried to compose myself. I soon felt better. The change for my lungs from the stinking atmosphere of the gambling-room to the cool air of the apartment I now occupied; the almost equally refreshing change for my eyes from the glaring gaslights of the salon to the dim, quiet flicker of one bedroom candle, aided wonderfully the restorative effects of cold water. The giddiness left me, and I began to feel a little like a reasonable being again. My first thought was of the risk of sleeping all night in a gambling-house; my second, of the still greater risk of trying to get out after the house was closed, and of going home alone at night, through the streets of Paris, with a large sum of money about me. I had slept in worse places than this on my travels; so I determined to lock, bolt, and barricade my door, and take my chance till the next morning.

Accordingly, I secured myself against all intrusion, looked under the bed and into the cupboard, tried the fastening of the window, and then, satisfied that I had taken every proper precaution, pulled off my upper clothing, put my light, which was a dim one, on the hearth among a feathery litter of wood ashes, and got into bed, with the handkerchief full of money under my pillow.

I soon felt not only that I could not go to sleep, but that I could not even close my eyes. I was wide awake, and in a high fever. Every nerve in my body trembled—every one of my senses seemed to be pre-ternaturally sharpened.

What could I do? I had no book to read. I raised myself on my elbow, and looked about the room, which was brightened by a lovely moon-light pouring straight through the window—to see if it contained any pictures or ornaments that I could at all clearly distinguish.

There was, first, the bed I was lying in; a four-post bed, of all things in the world to meet with in Paris!—yes, a thorough clumsy British four-poster, with the regular top lined with chintz—the regular fringed valance all round—the regular stifling unwholesome curtains, which I remembered having mechanically drawn back againt the posts without particularly noticing the bed when I first got into the room. Then there was the marble-topped wash-stand, from which the water I had spilt, in my hurry to pour it out, was still dripping, slowly and more slowly, on to the brick floor. Then two small chairs.

Then the window—an unusually large window. Then a dark old picture, which the feeble candle dimly showed me. It was the picture of a fellow in a high Spanish hat, crowned with a plume of towering feathers. A swarthy, sinister ruffian, looking upward, shading his eyes with his hand, and looking intently upward—it might be at some tall gallows at which he was going to be hanged. At any rate, he had the appearance of thoroughly deserving it.

This picture put a kind of constraint upon me to look upward too—

117

at the top of the bed. It was a gloomy and not an interesting object, and I looked back at the picture. I counted the feathers in the man's hat—they stood out in relief—three white, two green. I observed the crown of his hat, which was of a conical shape, according to the fashion supposed to have been favoured by Guy Fawkes. I counted the feathers again—three white, two green.

While I still lingered over this very improving and intellectual employment, my thoughts insensibly began to wander. The moonlight shining into the room reminded me of a certain moonlight night in England—the night after a picnic party in a Welsh valley. Every incident of the drive homeward, through lovely scenery, which the moonlight made lovelier than ever, came back to me, though I had never given the picnic a thought for years; though, if I had *tried* to recollect it, I could certainly have recalled little or nothing of that scene long past.

I was still thinking of the picnic—of our merriment on the drive home—of the sentimental young lady who *would* quote *Childe Harold* because it was moonlight. I was absorbed by these past scenes and past amusements, when, in an instant, the thread on which my memories hung snapped asunder: my attention immediately came back to present things more vividly than ever, and I found myself, I neither knew why nor wherefore, looking hard at the picture again.

Looking for what?

Good God! the man had pulled his hat down on his brows!—No! the hat itself was gone! Where was the conical crown? Where the feathers—three white, two green? Not there! In place of the hat and feathers, what dusky object was it that now hid his forehead, his eyes, his shading hand?

Was the bed moving?

I turned on my back and looked up. Was I mad? Drunk? Dreaming? Giddy again? Or was the top of the bed really moving down—sinking slowly, regularly, silently, horribly, right down throughout the whole of its length and breadth—right down upon me as I lay underneath?

My blood seemed to stand still. A deadly paralysing coldness stole all over me as I turned my head round on the pillow and determined to test whether the bed-top was really moving or not by keeping my eye on the man in the picture.

The next look in that direction was enough. The dull, black, frowsy outline of the valance above me was within an inch of being parallel with his waist. I still looked breathlessly. And steadily, and slowly—very slowly—I saw the figure, and the line of frame below the figure, vanish as the valance moved down before it.

I am, constitutionally, anything but timid. I have been on more than one occasion in peril of my life, and have not lost my self-possession for an instant; but when the conviction first settled on my mind that the bed-top was really moving, was steadily and continuously sinking down upon me, I looked up shuddering, helpless, panic-stricken, beneath the hideous machinery for murder, which was advancing closer and closer to suffocate me where I lay.

I looked up, motionless, speechless, breathless. The candle, fully spent, went out; but the moonlight still brightened the room. Down and down, without pausing and without sounding, came the bed-top, and still my panic-terror seemed to bind me faster and faster to the mattress on which I lay—down and down it sank, till the dusty odour from the lining of the canopy came stealing into my nostrils.

At that final moment the instinct of self-preservation startled me out of my trance and I moved at last. There was just room for me to roll myself sideways off the bed. As I dropped noiselessly to the floor the edge of the murderous canopy touched me on the shoulder.

Without stopping to draw my breath, without wiping the cold sweat from my face, I rose instantly on my knees to watch the bed-top. I was literally spellbound by it. If I had heard footsteps behind me, I could not have turned round; if a means of escape had been miraculously provided for me, I could not have moved to take advantage of it. The whole life in me was, at that moment, concentrated in my eyes.

It descended—the whole canopy, with the fringe round it, came down—down—close down, so close that there was not room now to squeeze my finger between the bed-top and the bed. I felt at the sides, and discovered that what had appeared to me from beneath to be the ordinary light canopy of a four-post bed was in reality a thick, broad mattress, the substance of which was concealed by the valance and its fringe. I looked up and saw the four posts rising hideously bare. In the middle of the bed-top was a huge wooden screw that had evidently worked it down through a hole in the ceiling, just as ordinary presses are worked down on the substance selected for compression.

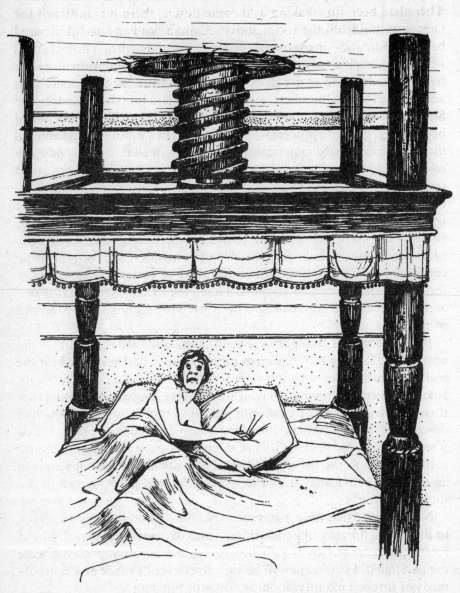

I looked up beneath the hideous machinery for murder, which was advancing closer and closer to suffocate me where I lay.

The frightful apparatus moved without making the faintest noise. There had been no creaking as it came down; there was now not the faintest sound from the room above. Amid a dead and awful silence I beheld before me—in the nineteenth century, and in the civilized capital of France—such a machine for secret murder by suffocation as might have existed in the worst days of the Inquisition, in the lonely inns among the Hartz Mountains, in the mysterious tribunals of Westphalia! Still, as I looked on it I could not move, I could hardly breathe, but I began to recover the power of thinking, and in a moment I discovered the murderous conspiracy framed against me in all its horror. My cup of coffee had been drugged, and drugged too strongly. I had been saved from being smothered by having taken an overdose of some narcotic. How I had chafed and fretted at the fever-fit which had preserved my life by keeping me awake! How recklessly I had confided myself to the two wretches who had led me into this room, determined, for the sake of my winnings, to kill me in my sleep by the surest and most horrible contrivance for secretly accomplishing my destruction! How many men, winners like me, had slept, as I had proposed to sleep, in that bed and had never been seen or heard of more! I shuddered at the bare idea of it.

But ere long all thought was again suspended by the sight of the murderous canopy moving once more. After it had remained on the bed—as nearly as I could guess—about ten minutes, it began to move up again. The villains who worked it from above evidently believed that their purpose was now accomplished. Slowly and silently, as it had descended, that horrible bed-top rose towards its former place. When it reached the upper extremities of the four posts, it reached the ceiling too. Neither hole nor screw could be seen; the bed became in appearance an ordinary bed again—the canopy an ordinary canopy—even to the most suspicious eyes.

Now, for the first time, I was able to move—to rise from my knees— to dress myself in my upper clothing—and to consider of how I should escape. If I betrayed, by the smallest noise, that the attempt to suffocate me had failed, I was certain to be murdered. Had I made any noise already? I listened intently, looking towards the door.

No! No footsteps in the passage outside—no sound of a tread, light or heavy, in the room above—absolute silence everywhere. Besides locking and bolting my door I had moved an old wooden chest against it, which I had found under the bed. To remove this chest (my blood ran cold as I thought of what its contents might be!) without making some disturbance was impossible; and, moreover, to think of escaping through the house, now barred up for the night, was sheer insanity. Only one chance was left me—the window. I stole to it on tiptoe.

My bedroom was on the first floor, above an *entresol*, and looked into the back street. I raised my hand to open the window, knowing that on that action hung, by the merest hair's-breadth, my chance of safety. They keep vigilant watch in a house of murder. If any part of the frame cracked, if the hinge creaked, I was a lost man! It must have occupied me at least five minutes, reckoning by time—five *hours*, reckoning by suspense—to open that window. I succeeded in doing it silently—in doing it with all the dexterity of a house-breaker—and then looked down into the street. To leap the distance beneath me would be almost certain destruction! Next, I looked round at the sides of the house. Down the left side ran the thick water-pipe—it passed close by the outer edge of the window. The moment I saw the pipe I knew I was saved. My breath came and went freely for the first time since I had seen the canopy of the bed moving down upon me!

To some men the means of escape which I had discovered might have seemed difficult and dangerous enough—to *me* the prospect of slipping down the pipe into the street did not suggest even a thought of peril. I had always been accustomed, by the practice of gymnastics, to keep up my schoolboy powers as a daring and expert climber, and knew that my head, hands, and feet would serve me faithfully in any hazards of ascent or descent. I had already got one leg over the window-sill when I remembered the handkerchief filled with money under my pillow. I could well have afforded to leave it behind me, but I was revengefully determined that the miscreants of the gambling-house should miss their plunder as well as their victim.

So I went back to the bed and tied the heavy handkerchief at my back by my cravat. Just as I had made it tight and fixed it in a comfortable place, I thought I heard a sound of breathing outside the door. The chill feeling of horror ran through me again as I listened. No! dead silence still in the passage—I had heard the night air blowing softly into the room. The next moment I was on the window-sill—and the next I had a firm grip on the water-pipe with my hands and knees.

I slid down into the street easily and quietly, as I thought I should, and immediately set off at the top of my speed to a branch Prefecture of Police, which I knew was situated in the immediate neighbourhood. A Sub-prefect and several picked men among his subordinates happened to be up, maturing, I believe, some scheme for discovering the perpetrator of a mysterious murder which all Paris was talking of just then. When I began my story, in a breathless hurry and in very bad French, I could see that the Sub-prefect suspected me of being a drunken Englishman who had robbed somebody; but he soon altered his opinion as I went on, and before I had anything like concluded, he shoved all the papers before him into a drawer, put on his hat, supplied me with another (for I was bare-headed), ordered a file of soldiers, desired his expert followers to get ready all sorts of tools for breaking open doors and ripping up brick-flooring, and took my arm in the most friendly and familiar manner possible to lead me with him out of the house. I will venture to say that when the Sub-prefect was a little boy, and was taken for the first time to the play, he was not half as much pleased as he was now at the job in prospect for him at the gambling-house!

Away we went through the streets, the Sub-prefect cross-examining and congratulating me in the same breath as we marched at the head of our formidable posse. Sentinels were placed at the back and front of the house the moment we got to it; a tremendous battery of knocks was directed against the door; a light appeared at a window; I was told to conceal myself behind the police—then came more knocks, and a cry of 'Open in the name of the law!' At that terrible summons bolts and locks gave way before an invisible hand, and the moment after the Sub-prefect was in the passage, confronting a waiter half-dressed and ghastly pale. This was the short dialogue which immediately took place:

'We want to see the Englishman who is sleeping in this house.'

'He went away hours ago.'

'He did no such thing. His friend went away; *he* remained. Show us to his bedroom!'

'I swear to you, Monsieur le Sous-prefect, he is not here! He——'

'I swear to you, Monsieur le Garçon, he is. He slept here—he didn't find your bed comfortable—he came to us to complain of it—here he is among my men—and here am I ready to look for a flea or two in his bedstead. Renaudin! (calling to one of the subordinates and pointing to the waiter) collar that man and tie his hands behind him. Now, then, gentlemen, let us walk upstairs!'

Every man and woman in the house was secured—the 'old soldier' the first. Then I identified the bed in which I had slept, and then we went into the room above.

No object that was at all extraordinary appeared in any part of it. The Sub-prefect looked round the place, commanded everybody to be silent, stamped twice on the floor, called for a candle, looked attentively at the spot he had stamped on, and ordered the flooring there to be carefully taken up. This was done in no time. Lights were produced, and we saw a deep raftered cavity between the floor of this room and the ceiling of the room beneath. Through this cavity there ran perpendicularly a sort of case of iron thickly greased, and inside the case appeared the screw which communicated with the bed-top below. Extra lengths of screw, freshly oiled; levers covered with felt; all the complete upper works of a heavy press—constructed with infernal ingenuity so as to join the fixtures below, and when taken to pieces again to go into the smallest possible compass—were next discovered and pulled out on the floor. After some little difficulty the Sub-prefect succeeded in putting the machinery together, and, leaving his men to work it, descended with me to the bedroom. The smothering canopy was then lowered, but not so noiselessly as I had seen it lowered. When I mentioned this to the Sub-prefect, his answer, simple as it was, had a terrible significance. 'My men,' said he, 'are working down the bed-top for the first time— the men whose money you won were in better practice.'

We left the house in the sole possession of two police agents—every one of the inmates being removed to prison on the spot. The Sub-prefect, after taking down my statement in his office, returned with me to my hotel to get my passport. 'Do you think,' I asked as I gave it to him, 'that any men have really been smothered in that bed as they tried to smother *me*?'

'I have seen dozens of drowned men laid out at the morgue,' answered the Sub-prefect, 'in whose pocket-books were found letters stating that they had committed suicide in the Seine, because they had lost everything at the gaming-table. Do I know how many of those men entered the same gambling-house that *you* entered, won as *you* won, took that bed as *you* took it, slept in it, were smothered in it, and were privately thrown into the river with a letter of explanation written by the murderers and placed in their pocket-books? No man can say how many or how few have suffered the fate from which you have escaped. The people of the gambling-house kept their bedstead machinery a secret from *us*—even from the police! The dead kept the rest of the secret for them. Good-night, or rather good-morning, Monsieur.'

One good result was produced by my adventure: it cured me of ever again trying *rouge-et-noir* as an amusement. The sight of a green cloth, with packs of cards and heaps of money on it, will henceforth be forever associated in my mind with the sight of a bed-canopy descending to suffocate me in the silence and darkness of the night.

THE MOONLIT ROAD
Ambrose Bierce

Statement of Joel Hetman, Jr.

I am the most unfortunate of men. Rich, respected, fairly well educated and of sound health—with many other advantages usually valued by those having them and coveted by those who have them not—I sometimes think that I should be less unhappy if they had been denied me, for then the contrast between my outer and my inner life would not be continually demanding a painful attention. In the stress of privation and the need of effort I might sometimes forget the sombre secret ever baffling the conjecture that it compels.

I am the only child of Joel and Julia Hetman. The one was a well-to-do country gentleman, the other a beautiful and accomplished woman to whom he was passionately attached with what I now know to have been a jealous and exacting devotion. The family home was a few miles from Nashville, Tennessee, a large, irregularly built dwelling of no particular order of architecture, a little way off the road, in a park of trees and shrubbery.

At the time of which I write I was nineteen years old, a student at Yale University. One day I received a telegram from my father of such urgency that in compliance with its unexplained demand I left at once for home. At the railway station in Nashville a distant relative awaited me to apprise me of the reason for my recall: my mother had been barbarously murdered—why and by whom none could conjecture, but the circumstances were these:

My father had gone to Nashville, intending to return the next afternoon. Something prevented his accomplishing the business in hand, so he returned on the same night, arriving just before the dawn. In his testimony before the coroner he explained that having no latch-key and not caring to disturb the sleeping servants, he had, with no clearly defined intention, gone round to the rear of the house. As he turned an angle of the building, he heard a sound as of a door gently closed, and saw in the darkness, indistinctly, the figure of a man, which instantly disappeared among the trees of the lawn. A hasty pursuit and brief search of the grounds in the belief that the trespasser was someone secretly visiting a servant proving fruitless, he entered at the unlocked door and mounted the stairs to my mother's chamber. Its door was open, and stepping into black darkness he fell headlong over some heavy object on the floor. I may spare myself the details; it was my poor mother, dead of strangulation by human hands!

Nothing had been taken from the house, the servants had heard no sound, and excepting those terrible fingermarks upon the dead woman's throat—dear God! that I might forget them!—no trace of the assassin was ever found.

I gave up my studies and remained with my father, who, naturally, was greatly changed. Always of a sedate, taciturn disposition, he now fell into a so deep dejection that nothing could hold his attention, yet anything—a footfall, the sudden closing of a door—aroused in him a fitful interest; one might have called it an apprehension. At any small surprise of the senses he would start visibly and sometimes turn pale, then relapse into a melancholy apathy deeper than before. I suppose he was what is called a nervous wreck. As to me, I was younger then than now—there is much in that. Youth is Gilead, in which is balm for every wound. Ah, that I might again dwell in that enchanted land! Unacquainted with grief, I knew not how to appraise my bereavement; I could not rightly estimate the strength of the stroke.

One night, a few months after the dreadful event, my father and I walked home from the city. The full moon was about three hours above the eastern horizon; the entire countryside had the solemn stillness of a summer night; our footfalls and the ceaseless song of the katydids were the only sound, aloof. Black shadows of bordering trees lay athwart the road, which, in the short reaches between, gleamed a ghostly white. As we approached the gate to our dwelling, whose front was in shadow, and in which no light shone, my father suddenly stopped and clutched my arm, saying, hardly above his breath:

'God! God! What is that?'

'I hear nothing,' I replied.

'But see—see!' he said, pointing along the road, directly ahead.

I said: 'Nothing is there. Come, father, let us go in—you are ill.'

He had released my arm and was standing rigid and motionless in the centre of the illuminated roadway, staring like one bereft of sense. His face in the moonlight showed a pallor and fixity inexpressibly distressing. I pulled gently at his sleeve, but he had forgotten my existence. Presently he began to retire backward, step by step, never for an instant removing his eyes from what he saw, or thought he saw. I turned half round to follow, but stood irresolute. I do not recall any feeling of fear, unless a sudden chill was its physical manifestation. It seemed as if an icy wind had touched my face and enfolded my body from head to foot; I could feel the stir of it in my hair.

At that moment my attention was drawn to a light that suddenly streamed from an upper window of the house: one of the servants, awakened by what mysterious premonition of evil who can say, and in obedience to an impulse that she was never able to name, had lit a lamp. When I turned to look for my father he was gone, and in all the years that have passed no whisper of his fate has come across the borderland of conjecture from the realm of the unknown.

Statement of Caspar Grattan

Today I am said to live; tomorrow, here in this room, will lie a senseless shape of clay that all too long was I. If anyone lift the cloth from the face of that unpleasant thing it will be in gratification of a mere morbid curiosity. Some, doubtless, will go further and inquire, 'Who was he?' In this writing I supply the only answer that I am able to make—Caspar Grattan. Surely, that should be enough. The name has served my small

He was standing rigid and motionless in the centre of the illuminated roadway . . .

need for more than twenty years of a life of unknown length. True, I gave it to myself, but lacking another I had the right. In this world one must have a name; it prevents confusion, even when it does not establish identity. Some, though, are known by numbers, which also seem inadequate distinctions.

One day, for illustration, I was passing along a street of a city, far from here, when I met two men in uniform, one of whom, half pausing and looking curiously into my face, said to his companion, 'That man looks like 767.' Something in the number seemed familiar and horrible. Moved by an uncontrollable impulse, I sprang into a side-street and ran until I fell exhausted in a country lane.

I have never forgotten that number, and always it comes to memory attended by gibbering obscenity, peals of joyless laughter, the clang of iron doors. So I say a name, even if self-bestowed, is better than a number. In the register of the potter's field I shall soon have both. What wealth!

Of him who shall find this paper I must beg a little consideration. It is not the history of my life; the knowledge to write that is denied me. This is only a record of broken and apparently unrelated memories, some of them as distinct and sequent as brilliant beads upon a thread, others remote and strange, having the character of crimson dreams with interspaces blank and black—witch-fires glowing still and red in a great desolation.

Standing upon the shore of eternity, I turn for a last look landward over the course by which I came. There are twenty years of footprints fairly distant, the impressions of bleeding feet. They lead through poverty and pain, devious and unsure, as of one staggering beneath a burden—'Remote, unfriended, melancholy, slow.'

Ah, the poet's prophecy of me—how admirable, how dreadfully admirable!

Backward beyond the beginning of this *via dolorosa*—this epic of suffering with episodes of sin—I see nothing clearly; it comes out of a cloud. I know that it spans only twenty years, yet I am an old man.

One does not remember one's birth—one has to be told. But with me it was different; life came to me full-handed and endowed me with all my faculties and powers. Of a previous existence I know no more than others, for all have stammering intimations that may be memories and may be dreams. I know only that my first consciousness was of maturity in body and mind—a consciousness accepted without surprise or conjecture. I merely found myself walking in a forest, half-clad, footsore, unutterably weary and hungry. Seeing a farmhouse, I approached and asked for food, which was given me by one who inquired my name. I did not know, yet knew that all had names. Greatly embarrassed, I retreated, and night coming on, lay down in the forest and slept.

The next day I entered a large town which I shall not name. Nor shall I recount further incidents of the life that is now to end—a life of wandering, always and everywhere haunted by an overmastering sense of crime in punishment of wrong and of terror in punishment of crime. Let me see if I can reduce it to narrative.

I seem once to have lived near a great city, a prosperous planter, married to a woman whom I loved and distrusted. We had, it sometime seems, one child, a youth of brilliant parts and promise. He is at all times a vague figure, never clearly drawn, frequently altogether out of the picture.

One luckless evening it occurred to me to test my wife's fidelity in a vulgar, commonplace way familiar to everyone who has acquaintance with the literature of fact and fiction. I went to the city, telling my wife that I should be absent until the following afternoon. But I returned before daybreak and went to the rear of the house, proposing to enter by a door with which I had secretly so tampered that it would seem to lock, yet not actually fasten. As I approached it, I heard it gently open and close, and saw a man steal away into the darkness. With murder in my heart, I sprang after him, but he had vanished without even the bad luck of identification. Sometimes now I cannot even persuade myself that it was a human being.

Crazed with jealousy and rage, blind and bestial with all the elemental passions of insulted manhood, I entered the house and sprang up the stairs to the door of my wife's chamber. It was closed, but having tampered with its lock also, I easily entered, and despite the black darkness soon stood by the side of her bed. My groping hands told me that although disarranged it was unoccupied.

'She is below,' I thought, 'and terrified by my entrance has evaded me in the darkness of the hall.'

With the purpose of seeking her I turned to leave the room, but took a wrong direction—the right one! My foot struck her, cowering in a corner of the room. Instantly my hands were at her throat, stifling a shriek, my knees were upon her struggling body; and there in the darkness, without a word of accusation or reproach, I strangled her till she died!

There ends the dream. I have related it in the past tense, but the present would be the fitter form, for again and again the sombre tragedy re-enacts itself in my consciousness—over and over I lay the plan, I suffer the confirmation, I redress the wrong. Then all is blank; and afterwards the rains beat against the grimy window-panes, or the snows fall upon my scant attire, the wheels rattle in the squalid streets where my life lies in poverty and mean employment. If there is ever sunshine I do not recall it; if there are birds they do not sing.

There is another dream, another vision of the night. I stand among the shadows in a moonlit road. I am aware of another presence, but whose I cannot rightly determine. In the shadows of a great dwelling I catch the gleam of white garments; then the figure of a woman confronts me in the road—my murdered wife! There is death in the face; there are marks upon the throat. The eyes are fixed on mine with an infinite gravity which is not reproach, nor hate, nor menace, nor anything less terrible than recognition. Before this awful apparition I retreat in terror—a terror that is upon me as I write. I can no longer rightly shape the words. See! They——

Now I am calm, but truly there is no more to tell; the incident ends where it began—in darkness and in doubt.

Yes, I am again in control of myself: 'the captain of my soul'. But that is not respite; it is another stage and phase of expiation. My penance, constant in degree, is mutable in kind: one of its variants is tranquillity. After all, it is only a life-sentence. 'To hell for life'—that is a foolish penalty: the culprit chooses the duration of his punishment. Today my term expires.

To each and all, the peace that was not mine.

Statement of the Late Julia Hetman, through the Medium Bayrolles

I had retired early and fallen almost immediately into a peaceful sleep, from which I awoke with that indefinable sense of peril which is, I think, a common experience in that other, earlier life. Of its unmeaning character, too, I was entirely persuaded, yet that did not banish it. My husband, Joel Hetman, was away from home; the servants slept in another part of the house. But these were familiar conditions; they had never before distressed me. Nevertheless, the strange terror grew so insupportable that conquering my reluctance to move I sat up and lit the lamp at my bedside. Contrary to my expectation this gave me no relief; the light seemed rather an added danger, for I reflected that it would shine out under the door, disclosing my presence to whatever evil thing might lurk outside. You that are still in the flesh, subject to horrors of the imagination, think what a monstrous fear that must be which seeks in darkness security from malevolent existences of the night. That is to spring to close quarters with an unseen enemy—the strategy of despair!

Extinguishing the lamp I pulled the bedclothing about my head and lay trembling and silent, unable to shriek, forgetful to pray. In this pitiable state I must have lain for what you call hours—with us there are no hours, there is no time.

At last it came—a soft, irregular sound of footfalls on the stairs! They were slow, hesitant, uncertain, as of something that did not see its way; to my disordered reason all the more terrifying for that, as the approach of some blind and mindless malevolence to which there is no appeal. I even thought that I must have left the hall lamp burning and the groping of this creature proved it a monster of the night. This was foolish and inconsistent with my previous dread of the light, but what would you have? Fear has no brains; it is an idiot. The dismal witness that it bears and the cowardly counsel that it whispers are unrelated. We know this well, we who have passed into the realm of terror, who skulk in eternal dusk among the scenes of our former lives, invisible even to ourselves, and one another, yet hiding forlorn in lonely places; yearning for speech with our loved ones, yet dumb, and as fearful of them as they of us. Sometimes the disability is removed, the law suspended: by the deathless power of love or hate we break the spell—we are seen by those whom we would warn, console, or punish. What form we seem to them to bear we know not; we know only that we terrify even those whom we most wish to comfort, and from whom we most crave tenderness and sympathy.

Forgive, I pray you, this inconsequent digression by what was once a woman. You who consult us in this imperfect way—you do not understand. You ask foolish questions about things unknown and things forbidden. Much that we know and could impart in our speech is meaningless in yours. We must communicate with you through a stammering intelligence in that small fraction of our language that you yourselves can speak. You think that we are of another world. No, we have knowledge of no world but yours, though for us it holds no sunlight, no warmth, no music, no laughter, no song of birds, nor any companionship. O God! what a thing it is to be a ghost, cowering and shivering in an altered world, a prey to apprehension and despair!

No, I did not die of fright: the thing turned and went away. I heard it go down the stairs, hurriedly, I thought, as if itself in sudden fear. Then I rose to call for help. Hardly had my shaking hand found the door-knob when—merciful heaven!—I heard it returning. Its footfalls as it remounted the stairs were rapid, heavy and loud; they shook the house. I fled to an angle of the wall and crouched upon the floor. I tried to pray. I tried to call the name of my dear husband. Then I heard the door thrown open. There was an interval of unconsciousness, and when I revived I felt a strangling clutch upon my throat—felt my arms feebly beating against something that bore me backward—felt my tongue thrusting itself from between my teeth! And then I passed into this life.

No, I have no knowledge of what it was. The sum of what we knew at death is the measure of what we know afterward of all that went before. Of this existence we know many things, but no new light falls upon any page of that; in memory is written all of it that we can read. Here are no heights of truth overlooking the confused landscape of that dubitable domain. We still dwell in the Valley of the Shadow, lurk in its desolate places, peering from brambles and thickets at its mad, malign inhabitants. How should we have new knowledge of that fading past?

What I am about to relate happened on a night. We know when it is night, for then you retire to your houses and we can venture from our places of concealment to move unafraid about our old homes, to look in at the windows, even to enter and gaze upon your faces as you sleep. I had lingered long near the dwelling where I had been so cruelly changed to what I am, as we do while any that we love or hate remain. Vainly I had sought some method of manifestation, some way to make my continued existence and my great love and poignant pity understood by my husband and son. Always if they slept they would wake, or if in my desperation I dared approach them when they were awake, would turn toward me the terrible eyes of the living, frightening me by the glances that I sought from the purpose that I held.

On this night I had searched for them without success, fearing to find them; they were nowhere in the house, nor about the moonlit dawn. For, although the sun is lost to us for ever, the moon, full-orbed or slender, remains to us. Sometimes it shines by night, sometimes by day, but always it rises and sets, as in that other life.

I left the lawn and moved in the white light and silence along the road, aimless and sorrowing. Suddenly I heard the voice of my poor husband in exclamations of astonishment, with that of my son in reassurance and dissuasion; and there by the shadow of a group of trees they stood—near, so near! Their faces were toward me, the eyes of the elder man fixed upon mine! He saw me—at last, at last, he saw me! In the consciousness of that, my terror fled as a cruel dream. The death-spell was broken: Love had conquered law! Mad with exultation I shouted—I *must* have shouted, 'He sees, he sees: he will understand!' Then, controlling myself, I moved forward, smiling and consciously beautiful, to offer myself to his arms, to comfort him with endearments, and, with my son's hand in mine, to speak words that should restore the broken bonds between the living and the dead.

Alas! alas! his face went white with fear, his eyes were as those of a hunted animal. He backed away from me, as I advanced, and at last turned and fled into the wood—whither, it is not given to me to know.

To my poor boy, left doubly desolate, I have never been able to impart a sense of my presence. Soon he, too, must pass to this Life Invisible and be lost to me for ever.

THE WHITE-RUFFED VIXEN

H. Mortimer Batten

It was not fox-hunting country, so when the shepherd came in with the news that he had found a litter of cubs in the open heather, and that his dog had worried all but one, he was handsomely tipped by his employer. The shepherd carried the sole survivor under his arm, and while he told his story in the yard of the farm steading, old Don, his dog, did sentry go round and about, keeping an officious eye fixed on the woolly mite, lest it might even yet escape. The cub had been spared purely because it wore about its neck a ruff of snowy whiteness.

'I thought maybe he'd be worth keeping,' said the shepherd at the conclusion of his story. 'He was the best of the bunch, and I never before saw one like him.'

'Och,' replied the tenant, 'I've no time for the little varmint! If you want to keep him, take him home. Maybe he'll be worth rearing.'

At this juncture Joey stepped forward. He had been an almost unnoticed spectator hitherto, but now he put in his word. 'Then if you don't want him, Mr Keel, may I have him?' he asked, stretching out his hands to take the cub from the doubtful mercy of the shepherd.

In view of the fact that Joey was the landlord's son, his request was not likely to be turned down, yet Mr Keel did not jump at it.

'Ay, laddie,' he said rather reluctantly, 'you may keep him if you'll feed him, but if he starts killing chickens, we'll have to be quit of him. What do you intend to do with him when you go home?'

To this Joey could find no immediate answer. He did not like to think too much about 'going home', for he was not yet ready to leave this paradise of farm life for the dusty, half-forgotten pavements of his home city, and the chill corridors of school life. So he said, 'I don't know,' but he did know very well that he wanted to take the bright-eyed cub into his care, if only to shield it from a similar fate to that which had befallen its brothers and sisters.

'Let the laddie take it,' put in the shepherd, clinching the matter by handing the cub over to Joey. 'He'll bite you, maybe, laddie, but he'll dae nae harm wi' his milk teeth.'

So the cub did bite Joey several times during the first few seconds, but the youngster held gamely to his adopted charge, and the next matter to be settled was the point of accommodation. The shepherd, who was a kindly man, stayed to lend a hand with this. An old kennel was rolled out from the cobwebs and hayseeds of an outhouse, complete with chain and collar. They placed it in a corner of the yard by the white gate, and filled the kennel with new straw. The collar was drawn tightly round the neck of the little captive—the shepherd saw to that—and so the final imprisonment of the child of the wild was completed.

'Give him plenty of new milk,' said the shepherd. 'Otherwise feed him the same as you feed a dog, and he'll tak' nae harm.'

Once, in the half-forgotten past, Joey had been ill, so his parents had sent him into the hills for a whole term from school in the hope that his legs would regain their rotundity, and the colour return to his cheeks. Truly he was all right now, after four months in the mountain air, and that evening, by way of a treat, since his holiday was drawing to a close, the tenant took him to a local fair in the farm Ford. So it was close upon midnight ere they returned to the steading. Joey with visions of kilted highlanders wide flung in the fantastic light, but nearing the white gate they beheld something which eclipsed the events of the evening. First, two green points of light were reflecting the head-lamps of the old car; then as they drew nearer they discerned the outline of a fox, an adult fox, standing on the wall top immediately above the place where the cub was imprisoned. Caught in the act of trespass—if such it were—she stood stock still watching their approach till the car was within ten yards of her, then, as though the spell were suddenly broken, she made a vertical leap for the roof of an outhouse, over which she vanished.

'Well, I never!' exclaimed Mr Keel. 'That's the mother. You bet your boots it's the mother!'

Joey did not see any special reason why he should bet his boots on anything, for, after all, it seemed to him quite a natural thing that the poor bereaved mother should visit her captive cub; but when he had thought about it a little, he began to see that it was indeed rather wonderful. The shepherd had killed the cubs five miles away, and on the upwind side, so she could not have followed the body scent of the cub so far. She must have followed the man, either by watching him through the heather, or by scent, thus tracking him down to the place where the last survivor of her brood was a prisoner.

All this Joey puzzled out as he lay in bed, and he wondered what really *had* happened up there in the bleak heights, where the curlews called and the grey crows ranged the heather. Doubtless the vixen had watched the shepherd's first approach—watched with desperate anxiety, unable to divert the pending tragedy. She must have known that it *would* be a tragedy, for the feud between man and fox, and man's dogs and the wild foxes of the heather, is all but as old as the hills. Had she seen what happened when her first fears were realized, and if so—what then? What had she done when the man and his dog were gone, leaving five little mangled corpses stretched on the silver sand? Had she steered clear of the horrible place, or had she crept up and seen—all that there was to see? And having seen, had she realized that the white-ruffed cub was missing from those who never again could know her caresses?

Joey reasoned it out that probably she had not thought so far as that. A dreadful calamity had befallen her, and so, with the closing of the friendly shadows, she had followed the man's trail into the valley, and found the white-ruffed cub a prisoner at the door of man's very stronghold. How she must hate man and his dogs! But at any rate, it was very, very brave of her to come thus to the farm steading with its lights and its sounds, and the murderer, Don, on guard.

When Joey went out next morning, he noticed two things. First of all old Don's food bowl was full of dirt, and on the ground nearby were

the claw marks of the creature which had scraped the dirt into the bowl.
Old Don bristled and rumbled as he sniffed the ground, and strange to
say, nothing would induce him after that morning to take his food
from that bowl. Secondly, Joey saw that all round the little kennel in
which the cub was a prisoner, holes had been scratched in the hard
ground. For the space of several feet it looked as though a motor plough
had been at work, and it did not seem likely that so small a cub could
have been so active through the night. The shepherd cleared the air.

'That', he said, 'was the vixen. She's been trying to bury the chain,
finding that it prevented her from carrying the cub away.'

Joey's holiday, I say, was drawing near its close, and the midday post
brought him letters from home. His mother hoped that *this* term—how
he hated that 'this'—he would really do his best to make up for lost time,
for he was sadly behind other boys of his age. He must now put pleasures
aside and devote himself undividedly to work, but—sometimes I
wonder if his mother was not blind to the mind of a boy who loved
very dearly the open air, or surely she would have written him differently? She would have told him that the world could not rob him of
that boundless freedom he loved.

Yes, go he must, but what of his cub? Only a few days now remained
to him, and he could not take the little captive back to the city. He
would rather leave her here in her own countryside.

That evening he took the grass-grown hill road to his favourite place
where he might think it over. As he sat there, thinking, and the wood-
cocks pin-wheeled overhead, as the far-off hills faded into an eternity of
indigo, and the soft grey mists crept up the little glen, a shadow stole
from the hazel thicket almost at his feet. Joey did not start. He had become too much of a master of woodcraft for that, and so the shadow
came slowly on towards him. It was a fox, trotting with lolling tongue,
her nose to the ground. She passed within twenty feet of where he sat,
heading towards the valley, where the homestead lights were already
twinkling. Then suddenly her head flashed in his direction. For a second
he met her amber eyes, then she was gone.

But Joey knew that he had seen again the mother of the captive cub,
for she wore about her neck a collar of pure white!

It was that same night that the thing happened. Joey had been in bed
quite a long time when he was roused by a piercing scream, followed

The fox passed within a few feet of where Joey sat . . .

by the barking of old Don. His bedroom window overlooked the yard, so he jumped up and peered out, certain that the scream he had heard was that of his cub, or of the vixen. It was brilliant moonlight, but though each feature of the yard below stood out clearly he could see nothing to account for the cry. Evidently the cub was inside the kennel, and if the vixen had paid a visit, she was surely gone now, for old Don was walking about in officious possession of the yard. Possibly the vixen had come back, and failing to free the cub, she had screamed that vicious desperate scream of hatred at the sleeping Don.

It rang in Joey's ears till he went to sleep, and many months after— nay, many years—he could recall its cadences; but next morning, when he went out, the sequel awaited him. Near to the kennel, in fact alongside it, was the nine-foot wall which ran from the white gate to the farm buildings, and on the opposite side of this wall, suspended by its collar, hung the fox cub. It was very still and very cold, and what had happened was quite clear. The vixen had come back, and taking the cub in her jaws—forgetful of the chain, which neither she nor her offspring would ever understand—she had leapt to the wall-top with her little charge,

140

and dropped to earth beyond. But the chain was too short—too short! It had jerked her baby from her jaws in mid-leap, leaving him suspended by the neck. Thus she had died; but even then, hoping against hope, she had returned. For on the ground below lay a dead blackbird she had brought for her.

It was Mr Keel who took the cub in his hands and loosened the collar from its neck, and even he had not the heart to laugh, though as a matter of fact he was glad that the difficulty had solved itself. He handed the limp little body over. 'Take her away, Joey,' he said, 'Bury her deep.'

So Joey took her away to bury her. He thought he would bury her out on the hill somewhere, to which her own free race belonged, so away he went up the little valley, with its twisted birch trees and its ferns and its laughing waters far below. There was a lump in his throat, and he did not like to look at the little woolly thing which had died so tragically—a victim of her own poor mother's devotion, yet withal the victim of man.

He sat himself down on the same rock and spread the dead infant of the wild at his feet. He was not afraid of looking at it now—now that there was no one about, no one to see what might have been an unmanly act, though when he grew to be a man, he knew that there would have been nothing unmanly in it. He looked and thought and wondered, and as he looked, he could have sworn that he saw the fur moving about the white ruff. For a full five minutes he sat, then suddenly the dead cub raised its head and stared at him. Joey did not stir. He seemed to be bound hand and foot. He saw the cub rise wearily to its woolly legs, and with a last distrustful glance in his direction, it began to trot away down the steep slope. It had not gone fifty paces when he saw the last strange thing of this strange little drama which had come into his life with the falling of the curtain on that great summer dream. He saw the white-ruffed vixen come out of the near thicket, and dash at the cub as though she would destroy her, rolling her roughly over and over. She obtained a hold of the little creature's body, and then, for fully a second, she stood, staring into Joey's face, then she turned about, and vanished among the hazels with her cub.

So Joey went home, happy that he had at any rate given to one of the wild things that he loved the freedom which could not be his.

THE MUMMY'S FOOT

Théophile Gautier

I had entered, in an idle mood, the shop of one of those curiosity-venders, who are called *marchands de bric-à-brac* in that Parisian slang which is so perfectly unintelligible elsewhere in France.

You have doubtless glanced occasionally through the windows of some of these shops, which have become so numerous now that it is fashionable to buy antiquated furniture.

There is one thing there which clings alike to the shop of the dealer in old iron, the wareroom of the tapestry-maker, the laboratory of the chemist, and the studio of the painter—in all those gloomy dens where a furtive daylight filters in through the window-shutters, the most manifestly ancient thing is dust; the cobwebs are more authentic than the gimp laces; and the old pear-tree furniture on exhibition is actually younger than the mahogany which arrived but yesterday from America.

The warehouse of my *bric-à-brac* dealer was a veritable Capharnaum; all ages and all nations seemed to have made their rendezvous there; an Etruscan lamp of red clay stood upon a Boule cabinet, with ebony panels, brightly striped by lines of inlaid brass; a duchess of the court of

Louis XV nonchalantly extended her fawn-like feet under a massive table of the time of Louis XIII with heavy spiral supports of oak, and carven designs of chimeras and foliage intermingled.

Upon the shelves of several sideboards glittered immense Japanese dishes with red and blue designs relieved by gilded hatching; side by side with enamelled works by Bernard Palissy, representing serpents, frogs, and lizards in relief.

From disembowelled cabinets escaped cascades of silver-lustrous Chinese silks and waves of tinsel, which an oblique sunbeam shot through with luminous beads; while portraits of every era, in frames more or less tarnished, smiled through their yellow varnish.

The dealer followed me closely through the tortuous way contrived between the piles of furniture; warding off with his hand the hazardous sweep of my coat-skirts; watching my elbows with the uneasy attention of an antiquarian and a money-lender.

'Will you not buy something from me today, sir? Here is a Malay dagger with a blade undulating like flame: look at those grooves contrived for the blood to run along, those teeth set backwards so as to tear out the entrails in withdrawing the weapon—it is a fine character of ferocious arm, and will look well in your collection: this two-handed sword is very beautiful—it is the work of Josepe de la Hera; and this *coliche-marde*, with its perforated guard—what a superb specimen!'

'No; I have quite enough weapons and instruments of carnage. I want a small figure, something which will suit me as a paper-weight; for I cannot endure those trumpery bronzes which the stationers sell, and which may be found on everybody's desk.'

The old gnome foraged among his ancient wares, and finally arranged before me some antique bronzes—so-called, at least; fragments of malachite; little Hindu or Chinese idols—a kind of poussah toys in jade-stone, representing the incarnations of Brahma or Vishnu, and wonderfully appropriate to the very undivine office of holding papers and letters in place.

I was hesitating between a porcelain dragon, all clustered with warts —its mouth formidable with bristling tusks and ranges of teeth—and an abominable little Mexican fetish, representing the god Zitziliputzili, when I caught sight of a charming foot, which I at first took for a fragment of some antique Venus.

'That foot will be my choice,' I said to the merchant, who regarded me with an ironical air, and held out the object desired that I might examine it more fully.

I was surprised at its lightness; it was not a foot of metal, but in sooth a foot of flesh—an embalmed foot—a mummy's foot; on examining it still more closely the very grain of the skin, and the almost imperceptible lines impressed upon it by the texture of the bandages, became perceptible. The toes were slender and delicate, and terminated by perfectly formed nails, pure and transparent as agates; the great toe, slightly separated from the rest, afforded a happy contrast, in the antique style, to the position of the other toes, and lent it an aerial lightness—the grace of a bird's foot; the sole, scarcely streaked by a few almost imperceptible cross lines, afforded evidence that it had never touched the bare ground, and had only come in contact with the finest matting of Nile rushes, and the softest carpets of panther skin.

'Aha!—you want the foot of the Princess Hermonthis,' exclaimed the merchant, with a strange giggle, fixing his owlish eyes upon me, 'for a paper-weight! An original idea!—artistic idea! Old Pharaoh would certainly have been surprised had someone told him that the foot of his adored daughter would be used for a paper-weight after he had had a mountain of granite hollowed out as a receptacle for the triple coffin, painted and gilded—covered with hieroglyphics and beautiful paintings of the Judgment of Souls,' continued the queer little merchant, half audibly, as though talking to himself.

'How much will you charge me for this mummy fragment?'

'Ah, the highest price I can get, for it is a superb piece. If I had the match of it you could not have it for less than five hundred francs; the daughter of a Pharaoh! Nothing is more rare.'

'Assuredly that is not a common article; but, still, how much do you want?'

'Five louis for the foot of the Princess Hermonthis! That is very little, very little indeed; 'tis an authentic foot,' muttered the merchant, shaking his head, and imparting a peculiar rotary motion to his eyes.

He poured the gold coins into a sort of mediaeval alms-purse hanging at his belt, repeating, 'The foot of the Princess Hermonthis, to be used for a paper-weight!'

Then turning his phosphorescent eyes upon me, he exclaimed in a voice strident as the crying of a cat which has swallowed a fish-bone, 'Old Pharaoh will not be well pleased; he loved his daughter—the dear man!'

'You speak as if you were a contemporary of his: you are old enough, goodness knows! But you do not date back to the pyramids of Egypt,' I answered, laughingly, from the threshold.

I went home, delighted with my acquisition.

With the idea of putting it to profitable use as soon as possible, I placed the foot of the divine Princess Hermonthis upon a heap of papers scribbled over with verses.

Well satisfied with this embellishment, I went out with the gravity and pride becoming one who feels that he has the advantage over all the passers-by whom he elbows, of possessing a piece of the Princess Hermonthis, daughter of Pharaoh.

Happily I met some friends, whose presence distracted me in my infatuation with this new acquisition: I went to dinner with them; for I could not very well have dined with myself.

When I came back that evening, with my brain slightly confused by a few glasses of wine, a vague whiff of Oriental perfume delicately titillated my senses. The heat of the room had warmed the natron, bitumen, and myrrh in which the *paraschistes*, who cut open the bodies of the dead, had bathed the corpse of the princess; it was a perfume at once sweet and penetrating—a perfume that four thousand years had not been able to dissipate.

The dream of Egypt was eternity: her odours have the solidity of granite, and endure as long.

I soon drank deeply from the black cup of sleep: for a few hours all remained opaque to me; oblivion and nothingness inundated me with their sombre waves.

Yet light gradually dawned upon the darkness of my mind; dreams commenced to touch me softly in their silent flight.

The eyes of my soul were opened; and I beheld my chamber as it actually was; I might have believed myself awake, but for a vague consciousness which assured me that I slept, and that something fantastic was about to take place.

The odour of the myrrh had augmented in intensity; and I felt a slight headache, which I very naturally attributed to several glasses of champagne that we had drunk to the unknown gods and our future fortunes.

I peered through my room with a feeling of expectation which I saw nothing to justify: every article of furniture was in its proper place; the lamp, softly shaded by its globe of ground crystal, burned upon its bracket; the water-colour sketches shone under their Bohemian glass; the curtains hung down languidly; everything wore an aspect of tranquil slumber.

After a few moments, however, all this calm interior appeared to become disturbed. The woodwork cracked stealthily; the ash-covered log suddenly emitted a jet of blue flame; and the discs of the pateras seemed like great metallic eyes, watching, like myself, for the things which were about to happen.

My eyes accidentally fell upon the desk where I had placed the foot of the Princess Hermonthis.

Instead of remaining quiet—as befitted a foot which had been embalmed for four thousand years—it commenced to act in a nervous manner, contracted itself, and leaped over the papers like a startled frog; one would have imagined that it had suddenly been brought into contact with a galvanic battery: I could distinctly hear the dry sound made by its little heel, hard as the hoof of a gazelle.

I became rather discontented with my acquisition, inasmuch as I wished my paper-weights to be of a stationery disposition, and thought it very unnatural that feet should walk about without legs; and I commenced to experience a feeling closely akin to fear.

Suddenly I saw the folds of my bed-curtain stir; and heard a bumping sound, like that caused by some person hopping on one foot across the floor. I must confess I became alternately hot and cold; that I felt a strange wind chill my back; and that my suddenly rising hair caused my nightcap to execute a leap of several yards.

The bed-curtains opened and I beheld the strangest figure imaginable before me.

It was a young girl of a very deep coffee-brown complexion, possessing the purest Egyptian type of perfect beauty: her eyes were almond-shaped and oblique, with eyebrows so black that they seemed blue; her nose was exquisitely chiselled, almost Greek in its delicacy of outline; and she might indeed have been taken for a Corinthian statue of bronze, but for the prominence of her cheek-bones and the slightly

*The bed-curtains opened and I beheld the strangest figure imaginable before
me . . . possessing the purest beauty.*

African fullness of her lips, which compelled one to recognize her as belonging beyond all doubt to the hieroglyphic race which dwelt upon the banks of the Nile.

Her arms, slender and spindle-shaped, like those of very young girls, were encircled by a peculiar kind of metal bands and bracelets of glass beads; her hair was all twisted into little cords; and she wore upon her bosom a little idol-figure of green paste, bearing a whip with seven lashes, which proved it to be an image of Isis: her brow was adorned with a shining plate of gold; and a few traces of paint relieved the coppery tint of her cheeks.

As for her costume, it was very odd indeed.

Fancy a loin-cloth or skirt all formed of little strips of material bedizened with red and black hieroglyphics, stiffened with bitumen, and apparently belonging to a freshly unbandaged mummy.

In one of those sudden flights of thought so common in dreams I heard the hoarse falsetto of the bric-à-brac dealer, repeating like a monotonous refrain the phrase he had uttered in his shop with so enigmatical an intonation:

'Old Pharaoh will not be well pleased: he loved his daughter, the dear man!'

One strange circumstance, which was not at all calculated to restore my equanimity, was that the apparition had but one foot; the other was broken off at the ankle!

She approached the table where the foot was starting and fidgeting about more than ever, and there supported herself upon the edge of the desk. I saw her eyes fill with pearly-gleaming tears.

Although she had not as yet spoken, I fully comprehended the thoughts which agitated her: she looked at her foot—for it was indeed her own—with an exquisitely graceful expression of sadness; but the foot leaped and ran hither and thither, as though impelled on steel springs.

Twice or thrice she extended her hand to seize it, but could not succeed.

Then commenced between the Princess Hermonthis and her foot—which appeared to be endowed with a special life of its own—a very fantastic dialogue in a most ancient Coptic tongue, such as might have been spoken thirty centuries ago in the syrinxes of the land of Ser:

148

luckily, I understood Coptic perfectly well that night.

The Princess Hermonthis cried, in a voice sweet and vibrant as the tones of a crystal bell:

'Well, my dear little foot, you always flee from me; yet I always took good care of you. I bathed you with perfumed water in a bowl of alabaster; I smoothed your heel with pumice-stone mixed with palm oil; your nails were cut with golden scissors and polished with a hippopotamus tooth . . .'

The foot replied, in a pouting and chagrined tone:

'You know well that I do not belong to myself any longer. I have been bought and paid for; the old merchant knew what he was about; he bore you a grudge for having refused to espouse him. This is an ill turn which he has done you. Have you five pieces of gold for my ransom?'

'Alas, no! My jewels, my rings, my purses of gold and silver, they were all stolen from me,' answered the Princess Hermonthis, with a sob.

'Princess,' I then exclaimed, 'I never retained anybody's foot unjustly; even though you have not got the five louis which it cost me, I present it to you gladly. I should feel unutterably wretched to think that I were the cause of so amiable a person as the Princess Hermonthis being lame.'

I delivered this discourse in a royally gallant, troubadour tone, which must have astonished the beautiful Egyptian girl.

She turned a look of deepest gratitude upon me; and her eyes shone with bluish gleams of light.

She took her foot—which surrendered itself willingly this time—like a woman about to put on her little shoe, and adjusted it to her leg with much skill.

This operation over, she took a few steps about the room, as though to assure herself that she was really no longer lame.

'Ah, how pleased my father will be!—he who was so unhappy because of my mutilation, and who from the moment of my birth set a whole nation at work to hollow me out a tomb so deep that he might preserve me intact until that last day, when souls must be weighed in the balance of Amenthi! Come with me to my father; he will receive you kindly, for you have given me back my foot.'

I thought this proposition natural enough. I arrayed myself in a dress-

149

ing-gown of large-flowered pattern, which lent me a very Pharaonic aspect; hurriedly put on a pair of Turkish slippers, and informed the Princess Hermonthis that I was ready to follow her.

Before starting, Hermonthis took from her neck the little idol of green paste, and laid it on the scattered sheets of paper which covered the table.

'It is only fair,' she observed smilingly, 'that I should replace your paper-weight.'

She gave me her hand, which felt soft and cold, like the skin of a serpent; and we departed.

We passed for some time with the velocity of an arrow through a fluid and greyish expanse, in which half-formed silhouettes flitted swiftly by us, to right and left.

For an instant we saw only sky and sea.

A few moments later obelisks commenced to tower in the distance: pylons and vast flights of steps guarded by sphinxes became clearly outlined against the horizon.

We had reached our destination.

The princess conducted me to the mountain of rose-coloured granite, in the face of which appeared an opening so narrow and low that it would have been difficult to distinguish it from the fissures in the rock, had not its location been marked by two stones wrought with sculptures.

Hermonthis kindled a torch, and led the way before me.

We traversed corridors hewn through the living rock: their walls, covered with hieroglyphics and paintings of allegorical processions, might well have occupied thousands of arms for thousands of years in their formation.

At last we found ourselves in a hall so vast, so enormous, so immeasurable, that the eye could not reach its limits; files of monstrous columns stretched far out of sight on every side, between which twinkled livid stars of yellowish flame—points of light which revealed further depths incalculable in the darkness beyond.

The Princess Hermonthis still held my hand, and graciously saluted the mummies of her acquaintance.

My eyes became accustomed to the dim twilight, and objects became discernible.

I beheld the kings of the subterranean races seated upon thrones—grand old men, though dry, withered, wrinkled like parchment, and blackened with naphtha and bitumen—all wearing *pshents* of gold, and breastplates and gorgets glittering with precious stones; their eyes immovably fixed like the eyes of sphinxes, and their long beards whitened by the snow of centuries.

After permitting me to gaze upon this bewildering spectacle a few moments, the Princess Hermonthis presented me to her father Pharaoh, who favoured me with a most gracious nod.

'I have found my foot again!—I have found my foot!' cried the Princess, clapping her little hands together with every sign of frantic joy: 'it was this gentleman who restored it to me.'

The races of Kemi, the races of Nahasi—all the black, bronzed, and copper-coloured nations repeated in chorus:

'The Princess Hermonthis has found her foot again!'

Even Xixouthros himself was visibly affected.

He raised his heavy eyelids, stroked his moustache with his fingers, and turned upon me a glance weighty with centuries.

'By Oms, the dog of Hell, and Tmei, daughter of the Sun and of Truth! This is a brave and worthy lad!' exclaimed Pharaoh, pointing to me with his sceptre, which was terminated with a lotus-flower.

'What recompense do you desire?'

Filled with that daring inspired by dreams in which nothing seems impossible, I asked him for the hand of the Princess Hermonthis—the hand seemed to me a very proper antithetic recompense for the foot.

Pharaoh opened wide his great eyes of glass in astonishment at my witty request.

'What country do you come from, and what is your age?'

'I am a Frenchman; and I am twenty-seven years old, venerable Pharaoh.'

'Twenty-seven years old! And he wishes to espouse the Princess Hermonthis, who is thirty centuries old!' cried out at once all the Thrones and all the Circles of Nations.

Only Hermonthis herself did not seem to think my request unreasonable.

'If you were even only two thousand years old,' replied the ancient King, 'I would willingly give you the Princess; but the disproportion is too great; and, besides, we must give our daughters husbands who will last well: you do not know how to preserve yourselves any longer; even those who died only fifteen centuries ago are already no more than a handful of dust. Behold! my flesh is solid as basalt, my bones are bars of steel!

'I shall be present on the last day of the world, with the same body and the same features which I had during my lifetime: my daughter Hermonthis will last longer than a statue of bronze.

'Then the last particles of your dust will have been scattered abroad by the winds; and even Isis herself, who was able to find the atoms of Osiris, would scarce be able to recompose your being.

'See how vigorous I yet remain, and how mighty is my grasp,' he added, shaking my hand in the English fashion with a strength that buried my rings in the flesh of my fingers.

He squeezed me so hard that I awoke, and found my friend Alfred shaking me by the arm to make me get up.

'O you everlasting sleeper!—must I have you carried out into the middle of the street, and fireworks exploded in your ears? It is after noon; don't you recollect your promise to take me with you to see M. Aguado's Spanish pictures?'

'God! I forgot all, all about it,' I answered, dressing myself hurriedly; 'we will go there at once; I have the permit lying on my desk.'

I started to find it—but fancy my astonishment when I beheld, instead of the mummy's foot I had purchased the evening before, the little green paste idol left in its place by the Princess Hermonthis!

MY SHIP IS SO SMALL

Ann Davison

Ann Davison was impelled by a tragedy to cross the Atlantic single-handed. She and her husband, Frank, had decided to sail round the world. In a 70-foot ketch, they set off without adequate preparation in the hope of increasing the value of their boat and thereby paying off the debts they had incurred. Cruel weather wrecked their craft and Frank Davison succumbed to cold and exposure.

His widow writes: 'It was not in any spirit of defiance, or revenge, or expiation, or vindication, that I chose to return to a way of life that had barely begun before ending so disastrously . . . I knew I would, I had to. If I could navigate a ship across the ocean on my own, it might be that I would be well on the way to learning how to live.'

Despite terror and hardship, she sailed to Canary and thence to Dominica; after which she made a leisurely, but still exciting, cruise to Nassau, Miami and New York.

The actual realization of a dream is neither better nor worse than imagined. It is entirely different. Before setting out, I thought I had no illusions about the voyage or sailing alone. I expected to be lonely. I expected to be frightened. What I did not expect was the positive panic of emotion that swamped me at the outset of the voyage. I was so lonely that whenever a ship appeared I could not take my eyes off her until she vanished. Once I turned and followed a trawler for nearly an hour, although she was apparently bound for Iceland, because I could not bear the friendless vista of an empty sea. Loneliness does not come from the physical state of being on one's own so much as from fear, the same old fear that stems from ignorance; and having thrust myself out into the unknown with only myself to rely on, I had reverted at once to the primitive. A child with a bogey round every corner. I was not only afraid of the wind and the sea, I was afraid of the ship. I was afraid of reefing the sails, or putting them up or changing them in any way. I was afraid of stopping the engine, and having stopped it, afraid of starting it again.

The numbness with which I set out wore off very slowly, and the first few days passed in a frightened haze upon which the entries in my log book throw very little light. These entries were mostly recording of times, a sort of notch-cutting to mark the passing of hours. It is inconceivable that I did not eat for five days, but there is no mention of my having done so, and I cannot recall a single meal, not even a cup of coffee. Fortunately I was not seasick, but I had guarded against *that* contingency by repeated doses of Drammamine, a very effective protection against seasickness, the only snag being that it is inclined to make one drowsy. Neither do I remember actually going to sleep during those first few days, though I must have done so. I do remember feeling so tired that my only ambition was to fold up and sleep for a week.

The second night out is identifiable in my memory because of fog. Nothing particularly horrific occurred, except that a steamer loomed up astern and scared me even more witless, quite unnecessarily, as she sheered off to starboard and disappeared into the murk, wailing like a lost soul. The rest of the night was spent in clammy discomfort in the cockpit, expecting to be run down any moment.

The course I was trying to steer was sou'westerly, but this was hampered by a head wind, so I made in a general southerly direction, plotting estimated positions by dead reckoning on the chart. I made several attempts to take sights with the sextant, and found it a very difficult proposition in real life, infinitely more difficult than taking a sight from the high cliffs of Devon with a friend standing by with a stop-watch. The high cliffs of Devon stay put on their nice firm underpinnings, but the deck of a lively little vessel offers a poor support for an inexperienced sight-taker. I concluded it was an impossible undertaking and unreasonable of anyone to think otherwise.

On the fourth day out the log read 230 miles. By then it seemed I had spent a lifetime at sea, and there was another 700 miles to go to Madeira. How embarrassing it would be if Madeira failed to turn up at the appointed time. There was, so far as I could see, very little reason why it should. And what would one do then? Turn right? Or left? Or keep straight on? Or accost a passing vessel, 'Have you seen Madeira lately?'

Then, as if a kindly fate had interposed to keep me from getting too discouraged, the following night granted a few hours of sheer magic. One of those rare glorious experiences that lift you right out of the commonplace (though God knows there is little of the commonplace about being at sea single-handed) on to Olympian heights of delight. The wind had backed right round to the north-east, and *Felicity Ann* was flying before it, her boom way out and impatient of restraint. Her mainsail, taut and straining, was silhouetted against the night sky. And the night sky was a black velvet backcloth for countless glittering stars. Wavelets tumbled in a foam of phosphorescence spilling a thousand bright jewels on the sea. A comet spanned the heavens, leaving a broad white wake across the sky even as the ship sped over the waves leaving a broad white wake on the water. All the loneliness and fears were forgotten, dissolved into nothing by an ecstasy of being so pure, so complete, that nothing else mattered or existed. There was no past, no future, only the participation of a brilliant present. An exquisite distillation of the meaning of life.

Then the kind fate went off duty. Before dawn it was blowing all hell and I was staring in horror at the mounting waves. I reefed the main and, when that was not enough, took it in altogether and changed the staysails for the storm jib. The dawn was scowling and bleak, overhung with a canopy of low cloud. Later, the wind eased a little but left a heavy cross sea for the ship to wallow in. I was in no mood for another bout with the sails, so started the engine and plugged on towards the never-never land of Madeira.

Then the ship began to behave strangely. So much was obvious even to me. She seemed sluggish, rising to the seas with an effort, quite unlike her usual buoyancy, and she rolled with a slow deliberation as if waterlogged. I slid back the hatch and looked into the cabin. She was waterlogged. The cabin was awash, with water way up over the floorboards and slopping from side to side, leaving an oily tidemark on the woodwork. Both bilge pumps were jammed solid when I tried to use them. Anyone else would have pulled up the floorboards, baled the ship out, cleared the pumps, found out why the water was coming in, and taken steps to stop it. I did none of these things. They never occurred to me. I was too stupid with fatigue, too tense and too tired from an excess of experience to think constructively. I was confused, and wanted to stop and take stock of the situation. I wanted to be still and free from the incessant motion; I wanted, most desperately, to sleep. The ship was half full of water which I was unable to get out by the obvious methods, therefore I must find somewhere where I could start thinking again under normal conditions. I looked at the chart and decided to make for Brest, the nearest port, about seventy or eighty miles away if my reckoning was correct.

Later on in the morning the clouds lifted and broke apart, the sun shone and my outlook improved enormously until the colour of the water changed to light green. This was disturbing, as it was different and therefore probably dangerous. Everything was suspect at that stage of my seagoing, which no amount of reassurance from the charts and reckoning could allay.

I passed two fishing-boats, very gay and colourful and French, neither of them fishing, but lying to, rolling heavily, evidently waiting for the tide or weather. The fishermen, as colourful as their boats, leant over the side and watched my progress with interest. Some of them waved and I waved back, much heartened by the sight of real live people. Then it occurred to me it would be sensible to ask for a position check, so I turned back to the nearest ship, a bright blue, broad-beamed trawler called *Fends les Vagues* ('Wave-cleaver') which seemed a pretty appropriate choice under the circumstances. I motored round and round her trying to convey in basic French and Indian sign language what I wanted. '*Où est Brest?*' I shouted, that being the nearest I could get to expressing my needs. Fishermen crowded the bulwarks, looking eager, interested, and absolutely blank. I expressed these needs several times on both sides of the fishing-boat, up wind and down wind, but succeeded only in throwing the entire crew into a fever of excitement as they threshed from side to side across the deck trying to keep me in sight.

I motored round to the stern of the vessel and read the port of registry. Douarnenez. All right then: '*Où est Douarnenez?*' I tried, with no better result, and regretted, not for the first nor by any means the last time in my life, having started something that was proving difficult to continue and impossible to stop. And I would have gone on my way, but a handsome young man wearing a dashing cap and chewing on a cigarette-end and looking as if he had stepped straight out of a French movie, authoritatively waved me alongside, a manoeuvre I accomplished with a masterly and quite unexpected precision. Several agile men leapt down on to *Felicity Ann* and held her off with a dramatic show of strength and dexterity. '*Venez abord, Madame,*' invited the handsome young skipper courteously, and, completely fascinated by the turn of events, I climbed up on the trawler, a fairly athletic feat, and appreciated as such by the onlookers, as the two boats were rolling wildly and inharmoniously.

'*Et maintenant,*' said the skipper politely, '*qu'est-ce que vous désirez, Madame . . ?*'

It was eleven o'clock in the morning when after three weeks there, I sailed out of Douarnenez on 10 June, down the long arm to the open sea, and it was not until a quarter-past six that evening that we cleared Armen Buoy and the curious popples and overfalls outside the Bay. Two hours later I stopped the engine, reefed down and changed the jib and hove to for the night. *Felicity Ann* hove to better reefed down; with full canvas she was inclined to sail on; but also I was not very happy yet about altering sail in the dark and as there was a smartish north-easterly breeze blowing by then I was not taking any chances. Playing jibs on the pitching foredeck was my undoing, however. I had omitted to take any Drammamine and was horribly seasick all night, but by next morning had recovered and got under way, feeling a little wan but firing on all cylinders.

The Bay of Biscay did not live up to its evil reputation, and on the whole we made good time, crossing the Bay, some 300 miles, in five days. This is only an average of sixty miles a day, but a single-hander has really only half a day to sail in as he has to navigate, eat, and sleep some time. There was a following wind, pretty fresh, most of the time, and there were torrential downpours of rain. Low black clouds dragged across the sky, and heavy grey seas humped up and grumbled after us. I did not care for the weather, but it might have been very much worse. I sailed during the day and hove to each night around eight or nine o'clock to sleep, waking at intervals to look out and see if anything was coming. Ships were many and manifest during the night and in the morning, but unaccountably disappeared during the afternoon.

I was not nearly so lonely this time, a little more knowledgeable, a little less scared, not so tired but still apprehensive and disinclined to take anything on trust. I still grasped the tiller as if holding the ship together by main force.

The radio was not operating, for reasons best known to itself, and I was unable to take any sights that made sense, through sheer lack of skill, it must be admitted; so navigation was purely by dead reckoning, and I wondered what sort of landfall we would make. I was aiming for the north-west corner of Spain—a little east of it, actually, so as not to miss it altogether and go sailing on and on into the Atlantic. On the night of 15 June a number of insects appeared aboard: flies, moths, and a hunting wasp. I wondered what she thought she was doing out there. A pigeon flew round the ship, took its bearings and flew off. The colour of the sea changed to dark green and all the signs pointed to land near by. The following evening the mountains of Spain stood up stark and clear in the failing light. Lights blinked their signals from the shore, but I could not make them match up with the lights shown on the chart. At first I thought we had made landfall much further east than intended, and was much put out until I recognized the light of Cap Vilano, and then was so pleased at being where I wanted that I washed out any notion of going in to Corunna and decided to carry on for Vigo.

There was no sleep that night. We had joined the main road and the traffic was thick. Motoring, for there was no wind to speak of, down towards Cape Finisterre in company with a vast concourse of shipping, I felt absurdly important at being such a little ship among all the big ones; for there were vessels on their way to and from the Mediterranean, Africa, Panama, South and Central America; liners, tankers, freighters, tramps, and . . . one small sloop.

About three o'clock in the morning a little breeze sprang up and I went below to switch off the engine. This has a short routine if done properly. You throttle back, unscrew the primer valve and remove the cap and put a rag over it; the engine blows back as it stops and clears its throat, so to speak, and the operation makes for easier starting by keeping the primer clear, otherwise it gums up and you develop biceps swinging the engine to not much purpose. It is not a long operation, yet when I came out again into the cockpit the ship was enveloped in thick fog, and the world had shrunk to a radius of a few yards. Knowing the amount of shipping in the vicinity I was very alarmed. I could hear them hooting all around.

158

On such occasions it is well to keep busy and not dwell too much on the situation. I lit every oil lamp aboard and hung them from strategic points about the ship, lit the cabin light so that it shone through the ports, fixed a flashlight so that the beam illuminated the mainsail, and hoped that the general glow might be noticed if anything came too close. A pretty thin hope, but, if nothing else, the lights imparted a certain cheer—to me.

Through some oversight there was neither bell nor hooter aboard, and no way of making a noise other than beating the bottom of the frying pan, which made a most inadequate little sound, although I did my best, and the frying pan was never any good for omelettes afterwards.

The breeze had faded out altogether with the descent of fog and, as it seemed highly desirable to be mobile, I started the motor again. Then, with a bunch of flares Georges had given me in case of such an emergency, I returned to the cockpit to steal quietly on course at quarter throttle, listening with ears like antennae to the warnings of invisible ships.

One in particular seemed to be coming nearer. A big ship with a deep bass voice like those of the 'Queens'. I held my breath. It *was* coming nearer. Each hoot was louder than the last, and I could hear a throbbing . . . It was like being under a stick of bombs during the war—would the next one be on or over? I stood up in the cockpit. Suddenly the blast of her hooter nearly blew us out of the water. The whole atmosphere vibrated. I ripped off the top of a flare, nearly blinding myself with its purple brilliance, kicked the throttle wide open, and *Felicity Ann* leapt from under a roar and a swoosh.

We might just as well have leapt into it, but I could no more have stopped my flight reaction than I could have stopped the progress of the ship. Her next blast came from further away, but I could hardly hear it for the blood beating in my ears, I was so scared. We romped over a monstrous wake and with ears flat back skittered westwards across the shipping lane with the sole purpose of getting away from it as quickly as possible. For two hours we raced on, and then suddenly shot out of the fog, leaving it behind us like a wall to the eastward. By then it was dawn. I put out the lights, stopped the engine, and flopped on the cabin-sole, dead to the world . . .

The person that first said 'pride goeth before a fall' must have tried to reef down in a strong northerly. The winds waited until we got nicely out to sea and some forty miles on our way to Gibraltar and then, just on nightfall, said, 'There she is!' and came tearing along full of vigour and rumbustiousness, at which my new-found confidence retired to let 'old man caution' take over again, and I turned up into wind to shorten sail. *FA* at once went into her demented seesaw act, and I crawled forrard to change jibs feeling uncommonly like an apprentice lion-tamer about to attempt the subjugation of a singularly angry lion, for, heavens, how that sail can hate. It throbs with a rage that shakes the ship and lashes out with canvas, sheets and shackles, making a terrible noise, the embodiment of unbridled ferocity, while its wet and windy supporters on the sidelines scream derision and hurl great dollops of spray.

By the time I had taken in the staysail and hanked on the storm jib I was soaked, battered, and worn out.

Reefing the mainsail does not present any problems with roller reefing providing it is tackled in a proper manner, but make one false move on a ship and the resultant hurrah's nest is horrible to behold. And worse to rectify.

I didn't get the sister-hooks on the topping-lift—a tackle that takes the weight of the boom when you lower the sail—properly hooked on to the shackle on the collar at the end of the boom, so that the collar jammed and revolved with the boom instead of allowing the boom to revolve inside it, and in no time flat the mainsheet was wound round the boom, round the mainsail, and for reasons best known to itself, round the boom gallows as well. The tangle-up had the Laocoön making daisy-chains by comparison. I was forward, of course, winding the reefing gear, paying out the main halyard, easing the mainsail down, and holding on, a simple operation calling for only four hands. When I saw what was happening I rushed aft, forgetting to belay the main halyard, which promptly flew out to sea and then wrapped itself round the upper crosstrees. So then I scrambled back and forth, scrabbling at the lash-up in a frenzy, swearing all I knew and a lot I didn't and achieving absolutely nothing at all, until *FA* lost patience and gave me one easy lesson in how to keep your head by nearly removing mine. She swung a classic haymaker with her boom and dropped me neatly into the cockpit.

After a while I got up and sat on the seat. *FA* had returned to her seesaw routine, rocking up and down, spitting spray and grumbling : 'Why the stampede? There's all the time in the world. If only you thought what you were going to do before you did it, you would save yourself so much trouble.'

Maybe she did not say it. Maybe the crack on my head just made me think she did. But I learnt something all the same.

We ran all night under reefed main and storm jib, but by seven o'clock the following morning the north winds were blowing in earnest and I had to take the mainsail in altogether and run under storm jib only. The seas were high, grey, and impressive. They came up under the ship and lifted her until all the world was spread about beneath, then they rushed on and left her to sink back into a canyon of tall, toppling waters. Stray bits of advice from quay men came percolating back from fitting-out days: 'Never let her run too fast, she's too fine aft.' Never let her run too fast. What is too fast? A big sea curled over and broke on the quarter-deck. That was enough for me. I can take a hint. Out went the sea-anchor. It was amazing the difference it made. *FA* might have been set in concrete. The anchor warp thrummed with the strain. Then I dropped the jib and *FA*, who had been riding by the stern, came round and lay broadside on to the sea. I did not like this, but did not know what to do about it then, so went below and left *FA* to look after herself. She knew so much better than I.

The cabin was wonderfully reassuring. It was hard to believe there was so much unpleasantness going on outside, except for the noise. The scream of the wind, the roar of the sea, the hiss of a big wave, the *thrrrrup* of spray on deck, occasionally a crash when she took it green. Then the cabin would go dark, and I would look up from my book and see water solid through the portholes as though looking into an aquarium, and I would turn several pages without a notion of what I was reading.

It was quite a wind. Within the next twenty-four hours no less than four steamers hove to and hooted at us, all set for a big rescue operation. I used to slide back the hatch and wave with a false nonchalance, and dive below before too much sea got into the ship. I hated to see them go, but was inestimably comforted by their concern.

We lost the sea-anchor; it fridged through its own fastenings at the end of the warp. I reckoned we made a sou'westerly drift of about

161

twenty-four miles in that blow, which eased to the merest breath after a couple of days and worked its way through east to south, leaving a lumpy and confused sea to contend with. I started the engine, because it is aggravating to hang about to no purpose, and so found the clutch was suffering from a surfeit of sea water and had frozen in gear, which made starting rather hard work. The southerly wind freshened and a shark swam round the ship, which was somehow rather dispiriting, and I was very tired. Then we had a day of flat calm to recover in, but this was immediately followed by a northerly wind that blew with even greater ferocity than before.

We lay to a warp for two days. During the nights I had to keep constant watch for ships, as none of the oil lamps would stay alight in those conditions and there was not a hope of our being seen. A small ship does not even show up on the radar screen. It was frankly terrifying, but a high pitch of fear cannot be sustained for long—it turns to a state of apathetic resignation. All the same I wore myself out worrying. I worried about the gear; whether there was anything I could or should do; if there was a ship bearing down . . . they were very close by the

We climbed out of the way as the big freighter slid by . . .

time you could see them in those seas . . . ; and the more I fretted the wearier I got, and the wearier I got the more I worried.

The windage of the mast and the rigging was enough in that wind to lay the ship over, and she had a curious way of jiggling, rocking herself very quickly, until she was hit by a big sea, then she would remain perfectly still for a moment as if shocked—you can't do this to me—and then she would pull herself together and start rocking again. When this happened the Primus gimbals, swinging clear out of the galley over the floor of the cabin, would groan *oooh . . . oooh* in the most pathetic and appropriate manner. They should have been oiled and made groan-proof, but were so amusing in a rather unfunny situation that I left them alone to state the case for me vicariously, and then it wasn't necessary. A monster sea caught the ship and threw her on her beam ends. One never quite knows what happens on these occasions. The sound of the wave breaking was like an explosion, and it felt as if *FA* was trying to do a barrel roll. Everything on the starboard side of the cabin broke loose and crashed over to port. Cups, plates, books, charts, navigation instruments, pepper, salt, soap, detergents hurtled

through the air. The entire galley, Primus stove, gimbals and all, came out by the roots. Kettles, bowls, and pans tumbled about in frantic confusion. Something hit the compass and smashed it. Water poured through the sliding hatch as if it was wide open.

As soon as *FA* came up for air I looked out to see if anything was left on deck. The cockpit was filled to the coamings and the whole ship was dripping as if she had just been fished up from the bottom of the sea, but otherwise everything was as it should be, nothing had parted or been carried away, or gone ping. I helped the self-drainers drain the cockpit by baling with a bucket, and then worked like a maniac in the cabin trying to restore order, as if doing so could prevent another big sea hitting us.

Actually it did moderate after that, and about midday the clouds broke apart and bright sunshine shone down upon the water. A heartening feature; disaster never seems quite so imminent when the sun shines.

The following day we pottered along uncomfortably in a high sea that did not have enough wind to support it. I reckoned we were off Cape St Vincent by evening, and was surprisingly rewarded by the flash of its light at nightfall. We had been ten days at sea, and had covered most of the distance from Vigo at a fast drift. The wind freshened during the night again, and there were so many ships about I fidgeted and could not sleep and started the next day's work limp and nervous. We rounded the Cape and altered course for the Straits of Gibraltar, navigating by the hand-bearing compass as the other was out of commission. The sea was lumpy and confused and our progress was slow.

I hove to at six o'clock, worn out and discouraged by the small advance made for the energy expended. A steamer hove to near by and looked at us questioningly, but I waved reassuringly as usual, and she went on her way to leave us to get through another restless and uncomfortable night. It blew with gale force, and although the seas were nothing like as high as before, they were short and fast with plenty of weight in them, which made them harder to take than the bigger seas. I barely had the strength to get under way the following day, one of peculiar emptiness. The sky was hard and absolutely cloudless. There were no birds and no ships to be seen. Land was out of sight. The sea did not sparkle, it was dull and angry and leaden for all the clarity of atmosphere. I looked in the water, but even the ship seemed to be.

hibernating. One little cloud would have been welcome. Lonely, weary, and acutely depressed, I cast about in the lockers for something to eat, not having done so for a couple of days.

Cold food in bad weather is singularly unappetizing, but since the stove had gone out of action there had been no alternative. I found a tin of plum cake which I had forgotten, one slice of which held the magic of recuperation, and I was heartened enough to experiment with a self-steering device I thought I had invented. I had not, and was compelled to continue steering. The wind was nearly west by now, on the port quarter, and at nine-thirty I hove to and turned in, oblivious and uncaring of ships, seas, or anything else, and passed out cold until eleven o'clock the next morning, when I woke refreshed and slightly guilty, to find gorgeous motoring weather with only the merest suggestion of air from the west. The respite did not last long, however, the weather turned squally, then the wind went into the east and blew half a gale, and so it went on, day after day, and it seemed as though I had never known and never would know anything but a life of dismal, damp endurance.

One night we were nearly run down. The seas were fierce, and we were lying to without any canvas, when suddenly a steamer appeared on the crest of a wave, a triangle of lights, port, starboard, and masthead, coming straight for us. No time to get sail up, no time to prime the engine. I swung the starting handle with strength borrowed from fear, and the engine started. We climbed out of the way as the big freighter slid by to disappear as quickly as she came, hidden by the seas.

After that there was no more sleep.

The following night the loom of a light appeared on the horizon sky ahead, and I took it to be the one I was expecting to see on the Spanish coast at the entrance to the Straits of Gibraltar. It was not possible to time the light and check it, as most of the time it was obscured by waves. None the less, I altered course to go through the Straits and plugged on all through the night, only to find we were plugging our way smack on to the African coast somewhere down by Larache in the morning. I could have kicked myself. The light had been Cape Spartel. For a moment I was almost of a mind to carry on to Casablanca, but having said I was going to Gibraltar, to Gibraltar I was going if it took the rest of my life.

We thumped north along the African coast under motor and a sweltering sun. There was no wind at all and the sea was smooth and oily; there was a thick pink haze, and I sat at the tiller, sweating and burning, acutely discomforted by the violent change of conditions. The clutch was slipping badly, so it was 8 p.m. by the time we reached Cape Spartel, and I was dizzy with fatigue, having been at the helm without sleep or respite for forty-eight hours; and there had been little enough sleep or respite before then either. Life now simply resolved itself into one of imperative urges, and the most impressive urge of all was sleep. I wanted oblivion with every fibre of my being. And here we were right at the entrance to the Straits, where ships were crowding through like sheep at a gate. One might as well pull up in the middle of Broadway for a quiet nap.

Extreme fatigue does strange things. As in a dream I became aware of two other people aboard, and as in a dream it seemed perfectly natural that they should be there. One of them sat on the coachroof and the other came aft holding on to the boom quiescent in its gallows. 'Okay,' he said, 'you kip down. We'll keep watch.' Obediently I went below and slept till morning.

Stretching and yawning and still weary, I climbed into the cockpit in the light of day. 'Thank you,' I said. 'That was good . . .' but they had gone. Never had the cockpit looked so empty . . .

THE MAN WHO COULD WORK MIRACLES

H. G. Wells

It is doubtful whether the gift was innate. For my own part, I think it came to him suddenly. Indeed, until he was thirty he was a sceptic, and did not believe in miraculous powers. And here, since it is the most convenient place, I must mention that he was a little man, and had eyes of a hot brown, very erect red hair, a moustache with ends that he twisted up, and freckles. His name was George McWhirter Fotheringay—not the sort of name by any means to lead to any expectation of miracles—and he was clerk at Gomshott's. He was greatly addicted to assertive argument. It was while he was asserting the impossibility of miracles that he had his first intimation of his extraordinary powers. This particular argument was being held in the bar of the Long Dragon, and Toddy Beamish was conducting the opposition by a monotonous but effective 'So *you* say', that drove Mr Fotheringay to the very limit of his patience.

There were present, besides these two, a very dusty cyclist, landlord Cox, and Miss Maybridge, the perfectly respectable and rather portly barmaid of the Dragon. Miss Maybridge was standing with her back to Mr Fotheringay, washing glasses; the others were watching him, more or less amused by the present ineffectiveness of the assertive method. Goaded by the Torres Vedras tactics of Mr Beamish, Mr Fotheringay determined to make an unusual rhetorical effort. 'Looky here, Mr Beamish,' said Mr Fotheringay. 'Let us clearly understand what a miracle is. It's something contrariwise to the course of nature done by power of will, something what couldn't happen without being specially willed.'

'So *you* say,' said Mr Beamish, repulsing him.

Mr Fotheringay appealed to the cyclist, who had hitherto been a silent auditor, and received his assent—given with a hesitating cough and a glance at Mr Beamish. The landlord would express no opinion, and Mr Fotheringay, returning to Mr Beamish, received the unexpected concession of a qualified assent to his definition of a miracle.

'For instance,' said Mr Fotheringay, greatly encouraged. 'Here would be a miracle. That lamp, in the natural course of nature, couldn't burn like that upsy-down, could it, Beamish?'

'*You* say it couldn't,' said Beamish.

'And you?' said Fotheringay. 'You don't mean to say—eh?'

'No,' said Beamish reluctantly. 'No, it couldn't.'

'Very well,' said Mr Fotheringay. 'Then here comes someone, as it might be me, along here, and stands as it might be here, and says to that lamp, as I might do, collecting all my will—"Turn upsy-down without breaking, and go on burning steady," and——Hullo!'

It was enough to make anyone say 'Hullo!' The impossible, the incredible, was visible to them all. The lamp hung inverted in the air, burning quietly with its flame pointing down. It was as solid, as indisputable as ever a lamp was, the prosaic common lamp of the Long Dragon bar.

Mr Fotheringay stood with an extended forefinger and the knitted brows of one anticipating a catastrophic smash. The cyclist, who was sitting next to the lamp, ducked and jumped across the bar. Everybody jumped, more or less. Miss Maybridge turned and screamed. For nearly three seconds the lamp remained still. A faint cry of mental distress came from Mr Fotheringay. 'I can't keep it up,' he said, 'any longer.' He staggered back, and the inverted lamp suddenly flared, fell against the corner of the bar, smashed upon the floor, and went out.

It was lucky it had a metal receiver, or the whole place would have been in a blaze. Mr Cox was the first to speak, and his remark, shorn of needless excrescences, was to the effect that Fotheringay was a fool. Fotheringay was beyond disputing even so fundamental a proposition as that! He was astonished beyond measure at the thing that had occurred. The subsequent conversation threw absolutely no light on the matter so far as Fotheringay was concerned; the general opinion not only followed Mr Cox very closely but very vehemently. Everyone accused Fotheringay of a silly trick, and presented him to himself as a foolish destroyer of comfort and security. His mind was in a tornado of perplexity, he was himself inclined to agree with them, and he made a remarkably ineffectual opposition to the proposal of his departure.

He went home flushed and heated, coat-collar crumpled, eyes smarting and ears red. He watched each of the ten street-lamps nervously as he passed it. It was only when he found himself alone in his little bedroom in Church Row that he was able to grapple seriously with his memories of the occurrence, and ask, 'What on earth happened?'

He had removed his coat and boots, and was sitting on the bed with his hands in his pockets repeating the text of his defence for the seventeenth time, '*I* didn't want the confounded thing to upset,' when it occurred to him that at the precise moment he had said the commanding words he had inadvertently willed the thing he said, and that when he had seen the lamp in the air he had felt that it depended on him to maintain it there without being clear how this was to be done. He had not a particularly complex mind, or he might have stuck for a time at that 'inadvertently willed', embracing, as it does, the abstrusest problems of voluntary action; but as it was, the idea came to him with a quite acceptable haziness. And from that, following, as I must admit, no clea logical path, he came to the test of experiment.

He pointed resolutely to his candle and collected his mind, though he felt he did a foolish thing. 'Be raised up,' he said. But in a second that feeling vanished. The candle was raised, hung in the air one giddy moment, and as Mr Fotheringay gasped, fell with a smash on his toilet-table, leaving him in darkness save for the expiring glow of its wick.

For a time Mr Fotheringay sat in the darkness, perfectly still. 'It did happen, after all,' he said. 'And 'ow I'm to explain it I *don't* know.' He sighed heavily, and began feeling in his pockets for a match. He could find none, and he rose and groped about the toilet-table. 'I wish I had a match,' he said. He resorted to his coat, and there were none there, and then it dawned upon him that miracles were possible even with matches. He extended a hand and scowled at it in the dark. 'Let there be a match in that hand,' he said. He felt some light object fall across his palm, and his fingers closed upon a match.

After several ineffectual attempts to light this, he discovered it was a safety-match. He threw it down, and then it occurred to him that he might have willed it lit. He did, and perceived it burning in the midst of his toilet-table mat. He caught it up hastily, and it went out. His perception of possibilities enlarged, and he felt for and replaced the candle in its candlestick. 'Here! *You* be lit,' said Mr Fotheringay, and forthwith the candle was flaring, and he saw a little black hole in the toilet-cover with a wisp of smoke rising from it. For a time he stared from this to the little flame and back, and then looked up and met his own gaze in the looking-glass. By this he communed with himself in silence for a time.

'How about miracles now?' said Mr Fotheringay at last, addressing his reflection.

The subsequent meditations of Mr Fotheringay were of a severe but confused description. So far as he could see, it was a case of pure willing with him. The nature of his first experiences disinclined him for any further experiments except of the most cautious type. But he lifted a sheet of paper, and turned a glass of water pink and then green, and he created a snail, which he miraculously annihilated, and got himself a miraculous new toothbrush. Sometime in the small hours he had reached the fact that his will-power must be of a particularly rare and pungent quality, a fact of which he had certainly had inklings before, but no certain assurance. The scare and perplexity of his first discovery was now qualified by pride in this evidence of singularity and by vague intimations of advantage. He became aware that the church clock was striking one, and as it did not occur to him that his daily duties at Gomshott's might be miraculously dispensed with, he resumed undressing, in order to get to bed without further delay. As he struggled to get his shirt over his head, he was struck with a brilliant idea. 'Let me be in bed,' he said, and found himself so. 'Undressed,' he stipulated; and, finding the sheets cold, added hastily, 'and in my nightshirt—no, in a nice soft woollen nightshirt. Ah!' he said with immense enjoyment. 'And now let me be comfortably asleep . . .'

He awoke at his usual hour and was pensive all through breakfast-time, wondering whether his overnight experience might not be a particularly vivid dream. At length his mind turned again to cautious experiments. For instance, he had three eggs for breakfast; two his landlady had supplied, good, but shoppy, and one was a delicious fresh goose-egg, laid, cooked, and served by his extraordinary will. He hurried off to Gomshott's in a state of profound but carefully concealed excitement, and only remembered the shell of the third egg when his landlady spoke of it that night. All day he could do no work because of this astonishing new self-knowledge, but this caused him no inconvenience, because he made up for it miraculously in his last ten minutes.

As the day wore on his state of mind passed from wonder to elation, albeit the circumstances of his dismissal from the Long Dragon were still disagreeable to recall, and a garbled account of the matter that had reached his colleagues led to some badinage. It was evident he must be careful how he lifted breakable articles, but in other ways his gift promised more and more as he turned it over in his mind. He intended among other things to increase his personal property by unostentatious acts of creation. He called into existence a pair of very splendid diamond studs, and hastily annihilated them again as young Gomshott came across the counting-house to his desk. He was afraid young Gomshott might wonder how he had come by them. He saw quite clearly the gift required caution and watchfulness in its exercise, but so far as he could judge the difficulties attending its mastery would be no greater than those he had already faced in the study of cycling. It was that analogy, perhaps, quite as much as the feeling that he would be unwelcome in the Long Dragon, that drove him out after supper into the lane beyond the gas-works, to rehearse a few miracles in private.

There was possibly a certain want of originality in his attempts, for apart from his will-power Mr Fotheringay was not a very exceptional man. The miracle of Moses' rod came to his mind, but the night was dark and unfavourable to the proper control of large miraculous snakes. Then he recollected the story of 'Tannhäuser' that he had read in the back of the Philharmonic programme. That seemed to him singularly attractive and harmless. He struck his walking-stick—a very nice Poona-Penang lawyer—into the turf that edged the footpath, and commanded the dry wood to blossom. The air was immediately full of the scent of roses, and by means of a match he saw for himself that this beautiful miracle was indeed accomplished. His satisfaction was ended by advancing footsteps. Afraid of a premature discovery of his powers, he addressed the blossoming stick hastily: 'Go back.' What he meant was 'Change back'; but of course he was confused. The stick receded at a considerable velocity, and incontinently came a cry of anger and a bad word from the approaching person. 'Who are you throwing brambles at, you fool?' cried a voice. 'That got me on the shin.'

'I'm sorry, old chap,' said Mr Fotheringay, and then realizing the awkward nature of the explanation, caught nervously at his moustache. He saw Winch, one of the three Immering constables, advancing.

'What d'yer mean by it?' asked the constable. 'Hullo! It's you, is it? The gent that broke the lamp at the Long Dragon!'

'I don't mean anything by it,' said Mr Fotheringay. 'Nothing at all.'

'What d'yer do it for then?'

'Oh, bother!' said Mr Fotheringay.

'Bother indeed! D'yer know that stick hurt? What d'yer do it for, eh?'

For the moment Mr Fotheringay could not think what he had done it for. His silence seemed to irritate Mr Winch. 'You've been assaulting the police, young man, this time. That's what *you* done.'

'Look here, Mr Winch,' said Mr Fotheringay, annoyed and confused. 'I'm very sorry. The fact is——'

'Well?'

He could think of no way but the truth. 'I was working a miracle.' He tried to speak in an off-hand way, but try as he would he couldn't.

'Working a——! 'Ere, don't you talk rot. Working a miracle, indeed! Miracle! Well, that's downright funny! Why, you's the chap that don't believe in miracles . . . Fact is, this is another of your silly conjuring tricks—that's what this is. Now, I tell you——'

But Mr Fotheringay never heard what Mr Winch was going to tell him. He realized he had given himself away, flung his valuable secret to all the winds of heaven. A violent gust of irritation swept him to action. He turned on the constable swiftly and fiercely. 'Here,' he said, 'I've had enough of this, I have! I'll show you a silly conjuring trick, I will! Go to Hades! Go, now!'

He was alone!

Mr Fotheringay performed no more miracles that night, nor did he trouble to see what had become of his flowering stick. He returned to the town, scared and very quiet, and went to his bedroom. 'Lord!' he said, 'it's a powerful gift—an extremely powerful gift. I didn't hardly mean as much as that. Not really . . . I wonder what Hades is like!'

He sat on the bed taking off his boots. Struck by a happy thought he transferred the constable to San Francisco, and without any more interference with normal causation went soberly to bed. In the night he dreamt of the anger of Winch.

The next day Mr Fotheringay heard two interesting items of news. Someone had planted a most beautiful climbing rose against the elder Mr Gomshott's private house in the Lullaborough Road, and the river as far as Rawling's Mill was to be dragged for Constable Winch.

Mr Fotheringay was abstracted and thoughtful all that day, and performed no miracles except certain provisions for Winch, and the miracle of completing his day's work with punctual perfection in spite of all the bee-swarm of thoughts that hummed through his mind. And the extraordinary abstraction and meekness of his manner was remarked by several people, and made a matter for jesting. For the most part he was thinking of Winch.

On Sunday evening he went to chapel, and oddly enough, Mr Maydig, who took a certain interest in occult matters, preached about 'things that are not lawful'. Mr Fotheringay was not a regular chapel-goer, but the system of assertive scepticism, to which I have already alluded, was now very much shaken. The tenor of the sermon threw an entirely new light on these novel gifts, and he suddenly decided to consult Mr Maydig immediately after the service. So soon as that was determined, he found himself wondering why he had not done so before.

Mr Maydig, a lean, excitable man with quite remarkably long wrists and neck, was gratified at a request for a private conversation from a young man whose carelessness in religious matters was a subject for general remark in the town. After a few necessary delays, he conducted him to the study of the Manse, which was contiguous to the chapel, seated him comfortably, and, standing in front of a cheerful fire—his legs threw a Rhodian arch of shadow on the opposite wall—requested Mr Fotheringay to state his business.

At first Mr Fotheringay was a little abashed, and found some difficulty

173

in opening the matter. 'You will scarcely believe me, Mr Maydig, I am afraid'—and so forth for some time. He tried a question at last, and asked Mr Maydig his opinion of miracles.

Mr Maydig was still saying 'Well' in an extremely judicial tone, when Mr Fotheringay interrupted again: 'You don't believe, I suppose, that some common sort of person—like myself, for instance—as it might be sitting here now, might have some sort of twist inside him that made him able to do things by his will.'

'It's possible,' said Mr Maydig. 'Something of the sort is possible.'

'If I might make free with something here, I think I might show you by a sort of experiment,' said Mr Fotheringay. 'Now, take that tobacco-jar on the table, for instance. What I want to know is whether what I am going to do with it is a miracle or not. Just half a minute, Mr Maydig, please.'

He knitted his brows, pointed to the tobacco-jar and said: 'Be a bowl of vi'lets.'

The tobacco-jar did as it was ordered.

Mr Maydig started violently at the change, and stood looking from the miracle-worker to the bowl of flowers. He said nothing. Presently he ventured to lean over the table and smell the violets; they were fresh-picked and very fine ones. Then he stared at Mr Fotheringay again.

'How did you do that?' he asked.

Mr Fotheringay pulled his moustache. 'Just told it—and there you are. Is that a miracle, or is it black art, or what is it? And what do you think's the matter with me? That's what I want to ask.'

'It's a most extraordinary occurrence.'

'And this day last week I knew no more that I could do things like that than you did. It came quite sudden. It's something odd about my will, I suppose, and that's as far as I can see.'

'Is *that*—the only thing? Could you do other things besides that?'

'Lord, yes!' said Mr Fotheringay. 'Just anything.' He thought, and suddenly recalled a conjuring entertainment he had seen. 'Here!' He pointed. 'Change into a bowl of fish—no, not that—change into a glass bowl full of water with goldfish swimming in it. That's better. You see that, Mr Maydig?'

'It's astonishing. It's incredible. You are either a most extraordinary . . . But no——'

'Stop there!' said Mr Fotheringay, and the pigeon hung motionless in the air.

175

'I could change it into anything,' said Mr Fotheringay. 'Just anything. Here! be a pigeon, will you?'

In another moment a blue pigeon was fluttering round the room and making Mr Maydig duck every time it came near him. 'Stop there, will you,' said Mr Fotheringay; and the pigeon hung motionless in the air. 'I could change it back to a bowl of flowers,' he said, and after replacing the pigeon on the table worked that miracle. 'I expect you will want your pipe in a bit,' he said, and restored the tobacco-jar.

Mr Maydig had followed all these later changes in a sort of ejaculatory silence. He stared at Mr Fotheringay and, in a very gingerly manner, picked up the tobacco-jar, examined it, replaced it on the table. '*Well!*' was the only expression of his feelings.

'Now, after that it's easier to explain what I came about,' said Mr Fotheringay; and proceeded to a lengthy and involved narrative of his strange experience, beginning with the affair of the lamp in the Long Dragon and complicated by persistent allusions to Winch. As he went on, the transient pride Mr Maydig's consternation had caused passed away; he became the very ordinary Mr Fotheringay of everyday again. Mr Maydig listened intently, the tobacco-jar in his hand, and his bearing changed also with the course of the narrative. Presently, while Mr Fotheringay was dealing with the miracle of the third egg, the minister interrupted with a fluttering extended hand——

'It is possible,' he said. 'It is credible. It is amazing, of course, but it reconciles a number of difficulties. The power to work miracles is a gift —a peculiar quality like genius or second sight—hitherto it has come very rarely and to exceptional people. But in this case . . . I have always wondered at the miracles of Mahomet, and at yogis' miracles, and the miracles of Madame Blavatsky. But, of course! Yes, it is simply a gift! It carries out so beautifully the arguments of that great thinker'—Mr Maydig's voice sank—'his Grace the Duke of Argyll. Here we plumb some profounder law—deeper than the ordinary laws of nature. Yes— yes. Go on. Go on!'

Mr Fotheringay proceeded to tell of his misadventure with Winch, and Mr Maydig, no longer overawed or scared, began to jerk his limbs about and interject astonishment. 'It's this what troubled me most,' proceeded Mr Fotheringay; 'it's this I'm most mightily in want of advice for; of course he's at San Francisco—wherever San Francisco may be—

but of course it's awkward for both of us, as you'll see, Mr Maydig. I don't see how he can understand what has happened, and I dare say he's scared and exasperated something tremendous, and trying to get at me. I dare say he keeps on starting off to come here. I send him back, by a miracle, every few hours, when I think of it. And of course, that's a thing he won't be able to understand, and it's bound to annoy him; and, of course, if he takes a ticket every time it will cost him a lot of money. I done the best I could for him, but of course it's difficult for him to put himself in my place. I thought afterwards that his clothes might have got scorched, you know—if Hades is all it's supposed to be—before I shifted him. In that case I suppose they'd have locked him up in San Francisco. Of course I willed him a new suit of clothes on him directly I thought of it. But, you see, I'm already in a deuce of a tangle——'

Mr Maydig looked serious. 'I see you are in a tangle. Yes, it's a difficult position. How you are to end it . . .' He became diffuse and inconclusive.

'However, we'll leave Winch for a little and discuss the larger question. I don't think this is a case of the black art or anything of the sort. I don't think there is any taint of criminality about it at all, Mr Fotheringay—none whatever, unless you are suppressing material facts. No, it's miracles—pure miracles—miracles, if I may say so, of the very highest class.'

He began to pace the hearthrug and gesticulate, while Mr Fotheringay sat with his arm on the table and his head on his arm, looking worried. 'I don't see how I'm to manage about Winch,' he said.

'A gift of working miracles—apparently a very powerful gift,' said Mr Maydig, 'will find a way about Winch—never fear. My dear sir, you are a most important man—a man of the most astonishing possibilities. As evidence, for example! And in other ways, the things you may do . . .'

'Yes, *I've* thought of a thing or two,' said Mr Fotheringay. 'But—some of the things came a bit twisty. You saw that fish at first? Wrong sort of bowl and wrong sort of fish. And I thought I'd ask someone.'

'A proper course,' said Mr Maydig, 'a very proper course—altogether the proper course.' He stopped and looked at Mr Fotheringay. 'It's practically an unlimited gift. Let us test your powers, for instance.

If they really *are* . . . If they really are all they seem to be.'

And so, incredible as it may seem, in the study of the little house behind the Congregational Chapel, on the evening of Sunday, 10 November 1896, Mr Fotheringay, egged on and inspired by Mr Maydig, began to work miracles. The reader's attention is specially and definitely called to the date. He will object, probably has already objected that certain points in this story are improbable, that if any things of the sort already described had indeed occurred, they would have been in all the papers a year ago. The details immediately following he will find particularly hard to accept, because among other things they involve the conclusion that he or she, the reader in question, must have been killed in a violent and unprecedented manner more than a year ago.

Now a miracle is nothing if not improbable, and as a matter of fact the reader *was* killed in a violent and unprecedented manner a year ago. In the subsequent course of this story that will become perfectly clear and credible, as every right-minded and reasonable reader will admit. But this is not the place for the end of the story, being but little beyond the hither side of the middle. And at first the miracles worked by Mr Fotheringay were timid little miracles—little things with the cups and parlour fitments, as feeble as the miracles of Theosophists, and, feeble as they were, they were received with awe by his collaborator. He would have preferred to settle the Winch business out of hand, but Mr Maydig would not let him. But after they had worked a dozen of these domestic trivialities, their sense of power grew, their imagination began to show signs of stimulation, and their ambition enlarged. Their first larger enterprise was due to hunger and the negligence of Mrs Minchin, Mr Maydig's housekeeper. The meal to which the minister conducted Mr Fotheringay was certainly ill-laid and uninviting as refreshment for two industrious miracle-workers; but they were seated, and Mr Maydig was descanting in sorrow rather than in anger upon his housekeeper's shortcomings, before it occurred to Mr Fotheringay that an opportunity lay before him. 'Don't you think, Mr Maydig,' he said, 'if it isn't a liberty, I——'

'My dear Mr Fotheringay! Of course! No—I didn't think.'

Mr Fotheringay waved his hand. 'What shall we have?' he said, in a large, inclusive spirit, and, at Mr Maydig's order, revised the supper very thoroughly. 'As for me,' he said, eyeing Mr Maydig's selection,

'I am always particularly fond of a tankard of stout and a nice Welsh rarebit, and I'll order that. I ain't much given to Burgundy,' and forthwith stout and Welsh rarebit promptly appeared at his command. They sat long at their supper, talking like equals, as Mr Fotheringay presently perceived with a glow of surprise and gratification, of all the miracles they would presently do. 'And, by the by, Mr Maydig,' said Mr Fotheringay, 'I might perhaps be able to help you—in a domestic way.'

'Don't quite follow,' said Mr Maydig, pouring out a glass of miraculous old Burgundy.

Mr Fotheringay helped himself to a second Welsh rarebit out of vacancy, and took a mouthful. 'I was thinking,' he said, 'I might be able (*chum chum*) to work (*chum chum*) a miracle with Mrs Minchin (*chum chum*)—make her a better woman.'

Mr Maydig put down the glass and looked doubtful. 'She's——she strongly objects to interference, you know, Mr Fotheringay. And—as a matter of fact—it's well past eleven and she's probably in bed and asleep. Do you think, on the whole——'

Mr Fotheringay considered these objections. 'I don't see that it shouldn't be done in her sleep.'

For a time Mr Maydig opposed the idea, and then he yielded. Mr Fotheringay issued his orders, and a little less at their ease, perhaps, the two gentlemen proceeded with their repast. Mr Maydig was enlarging on the changes he might expect in his housekeeper next day, with an optimism that seemed even to Mr Fotheringay's senses a little forced and hectic, when a series of confused noises from upstairs began. Their eyes exchanged interrogations, and Mr Maydig left the room hastily. Mr Fotheringay heard him calling up to his housekeeper and then his footsteps going softly up to her.

In a minute or so the minister returned, his step light, his face radiant. 'Wonderful!' he said, 'and touching! Most touching!'

He began pacing the hearthrug. 'A repentance—a most touching repentance—through the crack of the door. Poor woman! A most wonderful change! She had got up. She must have got up at once. She had got up out of her sleep to smash a private bottle of brandy in her box. And to confess it too! . . . But this gives us—it opens—a most amazing vista of possibilities. If we can work this miraculous change in *her* . . .'

179

'The thing's unlimited seemingly,' said Mr Fotheringay. 'And about Mr Winch——'

'Altogether unlimited.' And from the hearthrug Mr Maydig, waving the Winch difficulty aside, unfolded a series of wonderful proposals—proposals he invented as he went along.

Now what those proposals were does not concern the essentials of this story. Suffice it that they were designed in a spirit of infinite benevolence, the sort of benevolence that used to be called post-prandial. Suffice it, too, that the problem of Winch remained unsolved. Nor is it necessary to describe how far that series got to its fulfilment. There were astonishing changes. The small hours found Mr Maydig and Mr Fotheringay careering across the chilly market-square under the still moon, in a sort of ecstasy of thaumaturgy, Mr Maydig all flap and gesture, Mr Fotheringay short and bristling, and no longer abashed at his greatness. They had reformed every drunkard in the parliamentary division, changed all the beer and alcohol to water (Mr Maydig had overruled Mr Fotheringay on this point), they had, further, greatly improved the railway communication of the place, drained Flinders' swamp, improved the soil of One Tree Hill, and cured the vicar's wart. And they were going to see what could be done with the injured pier at South Bridge. 'The place,' gasped Mr Maydig, 'won't be the same place tomorrow! How surprised and thankful everyone will be!' And just at that moment the church clock struck three.

'I say,' said Mr Fotheringay, 'that's three o'clock! I must be getting back. I've got to be at business by eight. And besides, Mrs Wimms——'

'We're only beginning,' said Mr Maydig, full of the sweetness of unlimited power. 'We're only beginning. Think of all the good we're doing. When people wake——'

'But——' said Mr Fotheringay.

Mr Maydig gripped his arm suddenly. His eyes were bright and wild. 'My dear chap,' he said, 'there's no hurry. Look'—he pointed to the moon at the zenith—'Joshua!'

'Joshua?' said Mr Fotheringay.

'Joshua,' said Mr Maydig. 'Why not? Stop it.'

Mr Fotheringay looked at the moon.

'That's a bit tall,' he said after a pause.

'Why not?' said Mr Maydig. 'Of course it doesn't stop. You stop

180

the rotation of the earth, you know. Time stops. It isn't as if we were doing harm.'

'H'm!' said Mr Fotheringay. 'Well,' He sighed. 'I'll try. Here——'

He buttoned up his jacket and addressed himself to the habitable globe, with as good an assumption of confidence as lay in his power. 'Jest stop rotating, will you,' said Mr Fotheringay.

Incontinently he was flying head over heels through the air at the rate of dozens of miles a minute. In spite of the innumerable circles he was describing per second, he thought; for thought is wonderful— sometimes as sluggish as flowing pitch, sometimes as instantaneous as light. He thought in a second, and willed. 'Let me come down safe and sound. Whatever else happens, let me down safe and sound.'

He willed it only just in time, for his clothes, heated by his rapid flight through the air, were already beginning to singe. He came down with a forcible but by no means injurious bump in what appeared to be a mound of fresh-turned earth. A large mass of metal and masonry, extraordinarily like the clock-tower in the middle of the market-square, hit the earth near him, ricochetted over him, and flew into stonework, bricks, and masonry, like a bursting bomb. A hurtling cow hit one of the larger blocks and smashed like an egg. There was a crash that made all the most violent crashes of his past life seem like the sound of falling dust, and this was followed by a descending series of lesser crashes. A vast wind roared throughout earth and heaven, so that he could scarcely lift his head to look. For a while he was too breathless and astonished even to see where he was or what had happened. And his first movement was to feel his head and reassure himself that his streaming hair was still his own.

'Lord!' gasped Mr Fotheringay, scarce able to speak for the gale. 'I've had a squeak! What's gone wrong? Storms and thunder. And only a minute ago a fine night. It's Maydig set me on to this sort of thing. *What* a wind! If I go on fooling in this way I'm bound to have a thundering accident!

'Where's Maydig?'

'What a confounded mess everything's in!'

He looked about him so far as his flapping jacket would permit. The appearance of things was really extremely strange. 'The sky's all right anyhow,' said Mr Fotheringay. 'And that's about all that is all right.

And even there it looks like a terrific gale coming up. But there's the moon overhead. Just as it was just now. Bright as midday. But as for the rest—— Where's the village? Where's—where's anything? And what on earth set this wind a-blowing! *I* didn't order no wind.'

Mr Fotheringay struggled to get to his feet in vain, and after one failure, remained on all fours, holding on. He surveyed the moonlit world to leeward, with the tails of his jacket streaming over his head. 'There's something seriously wrong,' said Mr Fotheringay. 'And what it is—goodness knows.'

Far and wide nothing was visible in the white glare through the haze of dust that drove before a screaming gale but tumbled masses of earth and heaps of inchoate ruins, no trees, no houses, no familiar shapes, only a wilderness of disorder vanishing at last into the darkness beneath the whirling columns and streamers, the lightnings and thunderings of a swiftly rising storm. Near him in the livid glare was something that might once have been an elm-tree, a smashed mass of splinters, shivered from boughs to base, and further a twisted mass of iron girders—only too evidently the viaduct—rose out of the piled confusion.

You see, when Mr Fotheringay had arrested the rotation of the solid globe, he had made no stipulation concerning the trifling movables upon its surface. And the earth spins so fast that the surface at its equator is travelling at rather more than a thousand miles an hour, and in these latitudes at more than half that pace. So that the village, and Mr Maydig, and Mr Fotheringay, and everybody and everything had been jerked violently forward at about nine miles per second—that is to say, much more violently than if they had been fired out of a cannon. And every human being, every living creature, every house, and every tree—all the world as we know it—had been so jerked and smashed and utterly destroyed. That was all.

These things Mr Fotheringay did not, of course, fully appreciate. But he perceived that his miracle had miscarried, and with that a great disgust of miracles came upon him. He was in darkness now, for the clouds had swept together and blotted out his momentary glimpse of the moon, and the air was full of fitful struggling tortured wraiths of hail. A great roaring of wind and waters filled earth and sky, and, peering under his hand through the dust and sleet to windward, he saw by the play of the lightnings a vast wall of water pouring towards him.

'Maydig!' screamed Mr Fotheringay's feeble voice amid the elemental uproar. 'Here!—Maydig!'

'Stop!' cried Mr Fotheringay to the advancing water. 'Oh, for
goodness' sake, stop!'

'Just a moment,' said Mr Fotheringay to the lightnings and thunder.
'Stop jest a moment while I collect my thoughts . . . And now what
shall I do?' he said. 'What *shall* I do? Lord! I wish Maydig was about.'

'I know,' said Mr Fotheringay. 'And for goodness' sake let's have it
right *this time.*'

He remained on all fours, leaning against the wind, very intent to
have everything right.

'Ah!' he said. 'Let nothing what I'm going to order happen until I
say "Off!" . . . Lord! I wish I'd thought of that before!'

He lifted his little voice against the whirlwind, shouting louder and
louder in the vain desire to hear himself speak. 'Now then!—here
goes! Mind about that what I said just now. In the first place, when all
I've got to say is done, let me lose my miraculous power, let my will
become just like anybody else's will, and all these dangerous miracles
be stopped. I don't like them. I'd rather I didn't work 'em. Ever so
much. That's the first thing. And the second is—let me be back just
before the miracles begin; let everything be just as it was before that
blessed lamp turned up. It's a big job, but it's the last. Have you got it?
No more miracles, everything as it was—me back in the Long Dragon
just before I drank my half-pint. That's it! Yes.'

He dug his fingers into the mould, closed his eyes, and said 'Off!'

Everything became perfectly still. He perceived that he was standing
erect.

'So *you* say,' said a voice.

He opened his eyes. He was in the bar of the Long Dragon, arguing
about miracles with Toddy Beamish. He had a vague sense of some
great thing forgotten that instantaneously passed. You see, except for
the loss of his miraculous powers, everything was back as it had been;
his mind and memory therefore were now just as they had been at the
time when this story began. So that he knew absolutely nothing of all
that is told here, knows nothing of all that is told here to this day. And
among other things, of course, he still did not believe in miracles.

'I tell you that miracles, properly speaking, can't possibly happen,'

183

he said, 'whatever you like to hold. And I'm prepared to prove it up to the hilt.'

'That's what *you* think,' said Toddy Beamish, and 'Prove it if you can.'

'Looky here, Mr Beamish,' said Mr Fotheringay. 'Let us clearly understand what a miracle is. It's something contrariwise to the course of nature done by power of will . . .'

MY FIRST FLIGHT IN A STORM CLOUD

Hanna Reitsch

*Hanna Reitsch, just over five feet tall, will probably always be Ger-
many's most famous woman pilot, so skilful and so dedicated that in
the Second World War it was she rather than male pilots who was
chosen to test-fly the prototype of a rocket plane, the Me 163, and a
piloted version of the V1, known in Britain as the 'buzz-bomb' or
'doodle-bug'. But before the war, encouraged by gliding pioneer Wolf
Hirth, she had also become a record-breaking glider pilot when scarcely
in her twenties—as this chapter from her autobiography relates.*

May, 1933. Home again to Hirschberg for the holidays—the countryside still wrapped in the splendour of spring, the peaks of the Riesengebirge still in their snowy mantles. Everywhere on trees and bushes
the buds are beginning to burst and the air is sweetly soft and warm.
Wonderful weather for gliding! As I walk through the sun-drenched
streets of Hirschberg, I am yearning to soar up into the blue, gleaming
sky, veiled only here and there by a happy-seeming cloud of purest
white.

Suddenly, as though in answer to my wish, there is a screech of brakes
and a car jerks to a stop beside me. A well-known voice speaks a greeting
in my ear—Wolf Hirth! He and his wife are going to Grunau for a
short flight to take some cine films of Hirschberg from the air, and I may
come with them to be towed up in the 'Grunau-Baby', the very latest
type of training glider—just as I am, in my light summer dress, with
short stockings and sandals! But what does it matter? There is hardly a
cloud in the sky, there will be very little bumpiness, though perhaps
somewhere I shall be able to find a faint up-wind.

An hour later, I am sitting in the cabin of my glider, without goggles or helmet, the parachute harness buckled straight over my frock.

Wolf Hirth tells me to try flying blind, by instruments only and, as far as possible, not let my eyes stray outside the cabin.

In the evenings I had spent with Wolf Hirth I had learnt that a pilot is deprived of his vision not only at night but also when flying through cloud.

Up-winds are usually to be found under cumulus cloud, and even stronger up-winds are encountered inside the cloud itself, particularly in storm clouds. In the latter, the wind can reach a vertical speed of 130 to 160 feet per second and any aircraft caught in it is pulled upward with gigantic force. Such violent turbulence can be a danger to any type of plane, particularly when accompanied by thunder storms, hail or icing-up. Moreover, when in cloud, an airman is unable to determine the attitude of his plane in relation to the horizon, the human organs of equilibrium being inadequate to convey to us our 'absolute position in space'.

I had learnt that in cloud his instruments are the pilot's most important aid. In those days the chief of these was the turn-and-slip indicator. Theoretically I had often practised blind-flying, using a well known and simple aid. I drew on separate pieces of cardboard about playing-card size all the combinations of readings—there are nine in all—which the turn-and-slip indicator and the cross-level could show for different positions of the aircraft. I made a habit of carrying these cards with me pulling one out in a spare moment to test my knowledge, thus:

Indicator right—cross-level central:

a normal right-handed turn.

Indicator right—cross-level left:

a flat, skidding turn with not enough bank.

At first, when faced with a card, I had to think for the answer and as long as this was necessary, I considered myself unfit to cope with an emergency. Thought, I argued to myself, has a habit of 'cutting-out' in moments of danger and therefore an immediate, purely mechanical reaction is essential if the right action is to be taken in time. So I continued my daily practice with the cards until I could translate completely automatically the instrument readings on each into the movements required to control the plane.

As Wolf Hirth towed me up in my glider, I therefore felt quite confident that I should be able to fly 'blind' without getting into difficulties.

At about 1,200 feet, Wolf gave me the signal to cast off and as soon as I had done so, I began to lose height, gliding softly and swiftly down without the faintest breath of an up-current anywhere. Now I was no more than 250 feet up and was fast nearing the earth.

I was already looking for a suitable spot to land when suddenly the glider began to quiver. What did this mean—up-current or down-current? Then I saw that the pointer of the Variometer stood a little over zero at 'climb'.

I now began to circle, maintaining my height and even increasing it a little. Then, once more, I suddenly dropped. I searched round for the up-current and found, instead, a different one, much stronger. Again I climbed, this time very fast. The Variometer started at $1\frac{1}{2}$ feet per second, then rose to 3, then 6, then 9 feet per second, and still it went on rising, faster and faster. I had never experienced this kind of thing before.

I went on circling up and up till, before I knew what was happening, I had risen a further 1,500 feet, in about two-and-a-half minutes.

And now, quite involuntarily, my eyes turned from the instruments to the sky. Immediately overhead stood a gigantic black cloud: it must have formed only in the last few minutes. A more practised eye would, of course, have discovered it long ago, but I had acted strictly according to Wolf Hirth's instructions and had kept my gaze riveted the whole time on my instruments, so as not to be tempted to judge the attitude of the plane by the horizon.

At any rate, the sight of this dark monster filled me with glee. Here, at last, was the opportunity of an experience I had been longing for, to fly through a cloud. Without an inkling of the real danger of my situation, I was still absolutely confident, pinning my faith on my knowledge of the instruments, and had not Wolf Hirth himself told me that as long as he has that knowledge, a pilot can come to no harm?

So, surging ever higher, here I sit, 3,000 feet, and higher still to 3,600 feet—and now, I break in at the base of the cloud, the first dark wisps brush past me and I take a farewell look at the solid world. I have just time to see a last tiny fragment before a thick white veil suddenly drops, shutting me tightly in, alone with my cloudy company . . .

With eager concentration, I rivet my gaze on the instruments. Afraid? No, not in the least! I am as confident as confident can be—more confident than I shall ever be in any sort of a cloud again.

And still I am climbing, faster and faster, at twenty feet a second now. Is the cloud, perhaps, slowly approaching the peaks of the Riesengebirge, there to deposit me on the Schneekoppe, the topmost peak of all? A second's thought, and I am reassured. My own height is now 5,500 feet, but the Schneekoppe is only 5,200 feet—so all is well and I am out of danger. I take a deep breath of relief, little suspecting what is yet to come . . .

And then—a million drum-sticks suddenly descend on the glider's wings and start up, in frenzied staccato, an ear-splitting, hellish tattoo, till I am dissolved and submerged in fear. Through the windows of the cabin, which are already icing up, I can see the storm-cloud spewing out rain and hail. I take some time to bring my fear under control, but when I have repeated to myself often enough that this, after all, is a perfectly normal natural phenomenon and can see as well from the evidence of my instruments that the plane is in the correct attitude of flight, I become calmer again.

Soon, indeed, the drumming ceases, but in the conflicting air currents the wings are alternately lifted and depressed and, thrown about from corner to corner of my cabin, I have a hard struggle to make my instruments continue reading as the text-book says they should. And all the while, the glider is still climbing—8,500 feet, 9,100, 9,750 feet above the earth.

What I now see, I simply cannot bring myself to believe—the instruments seem to be sticking. They still move, but more and more slowly till, finally, they cease to move at all and not all my blows and buffets will bring them to life again. They are stuck, because they are frozen solid.

I try to hold the control column in the normal position, but it is a hopeless task, for—what is the normal position? With my instruments useless, I cannot tell . . . Now there is nothing left that I can do.

. . . There is a new sound, a kind of high-pitched whistle, now loud, now soft. As soon as it stops, I know I must put the nose down quickly, for that will be the moment when the plane has reached the stall. But now, as I suddenly pitch forward, helpless in my harness, and the blood shoots painfully into my head, I know that the moment has already passed.

188

MY FIRST FLIGHT IN A STORM CLOUD

The plane must be diving vertically and have swung over almost on to its back.

Then it swings forward again and plunges down at immense speed in a headlong dive.

I heave at the stick and heave and go on heaving (quite unaware that I am performing a series of involuntary loops)—and again I suddenly find myself hanging in my harness, while the glider arrows down, shrieking . . .

The mica window of the cabin has long ago frosted over and now, rather than be shut in any longer, powerless and alone, I break a hole in it with my fist. At least I shall be able to see.

Now I am shivering, all over, in every tissue of my body, and my bare hands turn blue as, nearly 10,000 feet above the earth, in my summer frock, I sit, basking in rain, hail and snow, my streaming hair tossed like seaweed in a storm.

The plane no longer answers to the controls and, in any case, is probably better left now to its own devices. So, hoping faintly that its inherent stability may suffice to avert disaster, I abandon the stick. As I do so, no longer the pilot now, but a passenger, I feel the fear inside me suddenly lift and creep a pace nearer my heart.

The tempest has now mounted to an inferno. Helpless as a shuttle, I am thrown ceaselessly to and fro in the cockpit, unable to stretch my feet to the control pedals, unable even to clench my teeth now the gale has wedged open my jaws.

. . . And the glider is climbing again—already, my eyes are straining out of their sockets. Soon, I know, the blood will spurt from my temples . . . And the fear lifts on its haunches for another spring. My brain is drained almost empty, the last shreds of thought flit through it, like leaves across an autumn sky.

How long to go before she breaks up, till I can bale out? Wolf Hirth, Hirth—what did he say? 'Everyone knows fear sometime—if alone, then talk to yourself, aloud—loud—' 'HANNA-A——!' I scream, 'Ya! Ya-a! Coward! Hang on, can't you, cowa-ar——!'

Listen! I thought I heard a voice—yes, there! Very faint, thin, but a human voice—a miracle . . .

For a few minutes, I feel warmer—I think they are minutes for I have lost all count of time. Then, as in choral crescendo the winds wrap

Rather than be shut in any longer, powerless and alone, I broke a hole in the window with my fist.

roaring round the plane, the fear within me starts again to snarl—
'*HANNA-A-A*——', it hesitates, then, in one savage leap, it pounces—
and the jaws of terror close.

Quite suddenly, it has become lighter and now it is getting lighter
still. I raise my eyes—no sky to be seen! But what I do see is earth, dark
brown earth—above me! I see it when I look up—and when I look
down, clouds, white streamers, stringing along in line. Now I know that
I am flying upside-down.

Mechanically, I seize the control column, and the situation is reversed.
Under me, the earth, with far away and just discernible, the snow-white
peaks of the Riesengebirge; above me, the white clouds, breaking up,
and higher yet, drawing slowly away, the towering pillar of the storm-
cloud. As it goes, it spews out a multitude of greying wisps as, a few
minutes ago, it spewed me out, head-first, into space.

Once more in the blessed light, I am feeling no more terror or pain as
slowly, softly, I glide on the silver-grey wings of my bird, thought-free
and free of all feeling save that of profound gratitude.

We are floating down towards the glittering white ridge of the
Riesengebirge. I can already distinguish the mountain huts and the little
black dots of the skiers, turning homeward at close of day. Here, on the
Schneekoppe, I will make my landing, where there are people to help.

It was already late afternoon when I touched down beside the hotel-
restaurant on the Schneekoppe; the daylight was beginning to fade and
the skiers had all vanished from the slopes. So I was able, undisturbed,
to make fast the glider, piling snow on the wing-tips to prevent the
wind from carrying her away. As I did so, I saw how the wings had
been holed in countless places by the hail-stones.

My plane and I would somehow have to get back to Hirschberg that
very evening and that meant I would have to telephone to Wolf Hirth
so that he could fly over and drop me a starting rope.

Bedraggled and sopping wet, I went into the hotel, encountering
many suspicious glances as I waited for my call to come through.
Around me, all was gusty fellowship and good cheer, the guests chattering and laughing in an atmosphere blue with tobacco smoke and laced
with the aroma of freshly ground coffee. But of these surroundings I
was barely conscious, hearing only the ebb and flow of laughter and

191

voices and, somewhere in the background, a zither's fragmentary sound. If only my call would come through!

And then someone saw the 'Grunau-Baby'. Immediately, there was a wild stampede among the guests, all thronging to the windows to see the incomprehensible with their own eyes. I went with them, as if it were no concern of mine. I found a fat, middle-aged man beside me, almost sweating with emotion.

'Fräulein,' he stammered, 'I tell you, it has descended just—just like the Incarnate One. It certainly wa-wasn't standing there five minutes ago . . .'

He could get no further, for at that moment his wife tugged him by the coat and drew him away. He ought not to have gone talking to such a ragamuffin, I heard her say, as she marched him angrily to the door . . .

The rest was lost, for I was now called to the telephone.

'Hanna!' Wolf Hirth shouted. 'Where in God's name are you?' I hardly had time to answer before a torrent of words roared into my ear, leaving me completely numbed and thinking only that, somehow, I must be in the storm-cloud again. Seconds later, I realized what he had been saying. The Schneekoppe lay in the neutral zone adjoining the Czechoslovak frontier and in landing an aircraft there without permission, I had committed an offence which would probably entail the withdrawal of my flying permit.

I put down the receiver in utter despair. Never more certainly than at this moment, I knew, as every real flier must, that flying was my whole life—I could not live without it.

Once they had got over the shock of my appearance, they did everything they could at the hotel to cheer me up. In desperation, they even put on a special film-show for me. But it was no good. No good until I was told that Wolf Hirth wanted me on the telephone again urgently. This time he spoke very briefly. He told me to get ready for the take-off, collect as many people as possible in a great circle outside the hotel and wait till he flew over and dropped the starting-rope, in about half-an-hour.

In a flash, my gloom dispersed and I was filled with jubilation. The hotel guests willingly did as I asked them and spread out, marking a great circle on the snow-field. Though it was now almost dark and the cold was intense, no one complained and all waited tensely expectant, straining to catch the first faint throb of an aircraft. Within the half-hour Wolf Hirth flew over, dropped a package in the circle we had marked out for him, roared up over our heads and receded once more into the night.

Now I had the starting-rope and a flag with a message attached telling me how to take off and what arrangements were being made for the landing. They were going to collect as many cars as possible in the valley below and flood-light a landing-ground for me.

From among the hotel guests I now picked two teams, each of ten men, to stand at each end of the starting-rope. They were told what they had to do and first we practised without connecting the glider, so that they could get accustomed to the various words of command and learn to run with the rope at speed towards the edge of the precipice without giving way to the impulse to slow up. Otherwise, the take-off would, quite literally, be a flop. When all were proficient, I climbed into the glider, buckled my parachute harness and gave the signal to go.

Meanwhile, Wolf Hirth, with Edmund Schneider, the designer of the 'Grunau-Baby', had been circling above us in his plane, like an anxious clucking hen whose chick has gone exploring on its own—and after dark, at that!

Never in my life have I had a better take-off. The teams put so much energy into their task that the glider soared up with terrific impetus and the next moment was hovering over the mountain side. Below me, I could just make out the dim, receding shapes of woods and fields and, here and there, a village, beckoning with a cluster of lights, while overhead there stretched a velvet, darkening expanse, pricked through, one by one, by the glittering sword-points of the stars.

Above me flew Wolf Hirth, his small machine showing black against the sky. He was showing the identification lights required by international convention—green on the starboard wing, red on the port, one white light at the nose and another at the tail.

I had hoped to be able to reach the airfield at Hirschberg, as I soon found that it would be quite impossible to pick out the small illuminated patch of landing-ground from among the lights of the villages in the valley. But first I had to fly over a medium-sized hill and, the glider fast losing height, I decided the safer course would be to land as soon as I could.

I search round anxiously and catch sight of what looks like an open field. But in the gathering darkness, I cannot be sure. It would be easy not to see small clumps of trees, even a house. But I will try it. I put the glider down right at the edge of the field, she bumps a little, then slithers to a stop. At last, I am on brown earth again.

For a while, I feel no desire to move and sit in drowsy bliss, the tension slowly ebbing from my mind. Wolf Hirth is happy, too; I can see and hear it as, having thus far hovered protectively overhead, he suddenly roars up his engine, dips his wings, then curves away and, quickly gaining speed, flies off—to arrange, I hope, for a car to fetch me.

I listen to his engine as it roars, hums, throbs and finally sinks away in the distance.

And now there is silence, everywhere. Earth and sky seem wrapped in sleep. My glider-bird slumbers, too, gleaming softly against the stars. Beautiful bird that out-flew the four winds, braved the tempest, shot heavenward, searching out the sky—soaring higher, as I am soon to learn, than any glider-plane has ever flown before.

A MIDNIGHT BRIDAL

Halliwell Sutcliffe

Maurice St Quain rode out from Edinburgh town—rode as a man rides on whom the world's cares sit lightly. Seen by the light of the moon, the stars, the oil lamps that creaked fretfully the length of the Canongate, he showed a square, big-headed, well-knit fellow; and his clothes were London-made.

'Damme, what a night!' he muttered as the keen wind blew through him and about. 'For an east wind and a raw air, commend me to this same capital of Scotland.'

He rode far out from the smoky lamps of the town, and was nearing a small and lonesome loch that lay on the left hand of his road, when a figure, bent and cloaked, stepped out into the moonlit road. A hand was laid upon his bridle, and at the moment a wild blast of wind swept back the cloak, revealing a woman's face—old, worn and wrinkled beyond belief. For a full moment she stood there, saying no word, but looking at his face, his wearing-gear, the appointments of his horse. Nor did he break the silence; this figure, coming from the dreary night, seemed rather a spirit's than a woman's, and time and place alike combined to overlay the man's undoubted courage.

'Aye, the Lord is guid,' murmured the old woman at last. 'Didna I pray for sic a callant to come riding by the loch-side?'

'What is it, mother?' asked St Quain, finding his voice again.

'I sent up many a prayer, an' ye have come.'

St Quain laughed—laughed as the Scots themselves are wont to do, with hardship and a sound of dryness in the throat. ''Tis the first time, to my knowledge, that I have come in answer to any woman's prayer, unless she chanced to be young and buxom. Come, mother, can I serve you? And if so, how? For time is pressing with me.'

'An' isna time pressing wi' the bonnie bairn—the bit lassie I nursed on my ain knee? There's a tryst for ye the nicht, an' ye'll no fail to keep it.'

'A tryst? Why, yes; but how should you know of it?'

Again she eyed him for awhile in silence; then, 'The hour is no just one for yon kind o' love,' said she. 'There's death will be the grooms-man if ye winna come wi' me.'

Maurice St Quain began to shiver, what with the wind that chilled his body and this queer speech that chilled his soul.

'What would you?' he said.

'Ye maun let me hold your bridle an' guide ye to the muckle house above the loch'—pointing a shrivelled finger, as she spoke, across the moonlit lake. 'Ye maun ask naething as to aething, for there's little time, I'm thinking if the lassie's to be kept from out a bridal shroud.'

Slowly it was borne in upon him that there was a life to be saved—a young girl's life. Not all the night wind could frost his chivalry; not all the love trysts in the world could turn him from a clear errand of mercy such as this.

'I'll go with you,' he said.

The woman clutched his bridle, muttered a blessing, so it seemed, and strode off along a grass-grown bridle-track with the step of one who had fewer years to carry. Down by the loch-side they went, with a mist of spray in their faces; up the further side of the steep they journeyed, and in at a rude gateway. The moon shone fair upon a rugged, loose-built house, and from an upper chamber came the light of many candles.

'Get ye doon,' murmured the old nurse. 'I'll lead your beastie to the stable, if ye'll bide a wee.'

He waited, as if under orders from his superior officer; and the wind shrilled about the walls; and the waters of the loch went lapping, lapping up the reedy beach.

'Com wi' me,' the same voice murmured at his ear, while yet he was in the midst of wonder and of vague affright.

He followed her across the courtyard, and up a flight of steps, and into a great hall. And now, for the first time, he ventured to draw breath. Without, there was the wind, the moonlight and the witchery; within all seemed to have a usual air about it—the air of a house whose master is well-found in this world's goods. A manservant was putting logs upon the great fire on the hearth-place; a hound, long-nosed, long-bodied, dozed beside the blaze; the very nurse herself, who had shown as some weird creature of the night, grew to the likeness of a woman as she doffed her cloak. She crossed to the board that held the middle of the floor, and poured a goblet of wine, and brought it to the strangely bidden guest.

'And, aye, she's bonnie,' she murmured, with a sort of hard encouragement. 'Ye needna look as if 'twere pain to save the lassie's life.'

St Quain gulped down his wine, and felt the red of it go tingling through him. The old nurse watched him curiously, and something like a smile was on her face as she noted once again the big comeliness, the air of consequence, that hung about this Englishman.

'My lady waits ye, and the meenister,' she said.

He could make nothing of it. Who was my lady? And the minister— surely he would not be there unless the maid were on the point of death; and if she were so near the end, what service could a stranger render her? The house, moreover, did not seem like one that entertained old death as visitor; for serving-men, with careless faces, free from any trace of woe, were moving in and out of the grim hall, making ready against supper-time. Again, what did it mean, he asked himself.

'Perchance there is a supper party,' he said, with sudden inspiration, 'and a guest has failed you?'

The old nurse was plucking at his sleeve impatiently. 'There'll be one guest o' the twa come into hall the nicht,' she muttered. 'One o' the twa —and the other's death, I'm telling ye.'

He followed her, with quickened breath. They mounted a broad stair of oak, and crossed a landing hung round about with trophies of the case and battlefield.

The nurse flung open a door on the right hand, and St Quain found himself in a well-lit parlour. A spinet stood at the far end, and round the hearth was grouped a company of three. The first, a lean greybeard, habited in black, was talking to a stately matron; the third member of the group sat on the other side of the hearth, and twined and untwined her white fingers restlessly.

All the gallantry in Maurice St Quain, all the tenderness and passion, came headlong to the front as he looked at that third figure. There was witchery in the pale face; he had known no other like her, though he had wandered through many countries with an eye wide open for such matters.

'My prayer went bonnily, my lady,' the old nurse said. 'I met him on the road doon by the loch, an', tho' he's Southron, he's no that ill to look at.'

My lady checked her. 'Your errand here must seem a strange one, sir,' she said. 'It will seem stranger when you hear the nature of it.'

He scarcely heard her; for his glance was on the lassie seated at the far side of the hearth, and he was thinking how gladly he would have journeyed half through England to win a sight of her.

'Your name, sir, is——?' went on my lady.

'St Quain, at your service.'

'A gentleman of quality, if I mistake not?'

'Nephew to Lord St Quain,' he answered drily.

'Then, sir, I must ask your patience while I tell you how it comes that we entertain a guest so unexpected—and so welcome,' she added, with a cold politeness that was almost insolence.

'We are the Lockerbies of Loch,' went on my lady, with the air of one who has said enough to compel both homage and surprise.

St Quain, indeed, felt no little surprise, for the Lockerbies were famed for their poverty, their pride, and the beauty of their women. He understood now my lady's bearing, and resented it not at all; for no Lockerbie that he had heard or read of had thought to find his equal.

'I am honoured by any summons from Lady Lockerbie,' he said.

My lady glanced shrewdly at him; it seemed she liked his quick address, and liked the fashion of his face and figure.

'There is a curse upon our house,' she went on, with a note of fear beneath her coldness.

'I have heard of it.'

'Who has not? You know the danger, then, that overhangs our daughters?'

In a flash he saw the meaning of it all, and his firse sense was one of wonder that an old superstition could die so hard. Was it not the year of grace 1750? And could it be that four folk gathered here together—one a minister, the others women of pluck and sense—were following this Jack-o'-Lanthorn legend with implicit faith? He caught the minister's eye, and the man of prayer began to shift his feet uneasily.

'Such matters are idle; they are snares of Belial,' he said; 'yet the curse has never failed through three long centuries.'

'Legend and history bear out your tale, sir,' said St Quain, and he paused in doubt.

The pause was broken by a sudden, eager cry from the lassie who was the head and fount of all this trouble.

'It is idle, sir,' she said, with a swift glance at St Quain. 'Scots lassies do not die of legends, and so I tell them.'

Yet under her gaiety, too, there was a note of fear. And under her gaiety, likewise, there was a something that told St Quain the truth he hungered for. Mystery or no—hasty wedlock or no—it was plain that in her denial of the need there was a confession that he had already found some place in her regard.

My lady came and laid a hand on the girl's shoulder; and all her pride was gone. 'Janet,' she said tenderly, 'I have but you, and the curse is stronger than we are.'

'But, mother, you are asking'—the colour swept across her face and left it pale again—'you are asking this gentleman to—to give his life for mine.'

'What folly, child!'

'He will be bound to me—to me, whom he did not know a half-hour since. What will his life be worth to him afterwards?'

It was St Quain who spoke now. 'My life will be worth little to me if I lose you,' he said.

And the old nurse, standing in the shadows, rubbed her lean hands together. Southron or no, he spoke as women like to hear a lover speak.

There was an awkward silence, broken on the sudden by a deep whirr from the eight-day clock that stood beside the hearth. All turned to the dial-face; all listened while the ten strokes were struck, sonorous and deliberate. The girl herself began to tremble, for the legends of her race were strong on her, and two more hours might see her wedded to a grimmer bridegroom than St Quain.

'Haste ye, haste ye,' crooned the old nurse. 'It's gey ill to play wi' time as ye are doing.'

The minister was grey of face, and now and then he muttered a prayer. And then there came a wailing from without, as if in answer to the deep voice of the clock—a wailing that drifted round the courtyard, and down the slope, and across the lapping waters of the loch.

'Cannot ye hear?' the old nurse cried.

'It is the wind—the wind, woman,' said the minister fretfully.

'Oh, an' it's the wind, say ye? Well, I've heard it twice in a long life, an' I dinna like its voice.' She looked at her young mistress, 'For the love of heaven, dearie, save yoursel',' she said.

St Quain could scarce remember afterwards what chanced. He was aware of wind and rain against the window panes, of the loud ticking of the clock, of Janet's hand in his. He recalled vaguely that the minister had talked and prayed above them, and that his heart beat high as he named the girl his wife. But what he did remember in after years was the great sob of relief that came from Lady Lockerbie; it was plain that she looked on her daughter as one returned almost from the grave.

When next he felt himself awake, Lady Lockerbie's voice was in his ears, and the pride that was almost insult had come back to it.

'We owe you more of explanation than we have given,' she said, taking him aside. 'Why, you will ask, knowing as we did the danger that hunger over us, why did we leave all to the last moment?'

St Quain's air was full of quiet gaiety. 'I ask for no explanation,' he said. 'I have won your daughter, and I count it the happiest evening of my life.'

'Yet you will wonder by and by, and I must tell you. My daughter was to have been married this morning to an old lover of hers; everything was in readiness, and he—he was killed in a duel yesternight. The news reached us at daybreak, and we have spent the day in fear so horrible that you could not credit it.'

'There was a fate in it,' said St Quain—and, indeed, he felt as much; 'and if I bring your daughter one-half the happiness I have won——'

'Our pride must suffer,' put in my lady; 'the Lockerbies have never yet needed to go abroad in search of an alliance—to seek it in the public road. I fear, sir, your thoughts of us must be something of the strangest.'

Plain as was my lady's attitude—of gratitude all chilled by Scottish pride—her daughter's was different altogether. Half-shy she was, not knowing how this trim-built gallant felt toward her; but the pressure of her hand upon his arm was friendly, warm, confiding almost.

'I shall love wild nights henceforward,' he whispered in her ear. 'The wind and the rain have brought me—you!'

It seemed that she had suffered from deep feeling long repressed; for on the sudden she looked him in the face, and let a dangerous light come into her grey eyes. 'I was to have married Bruce of Muirtown,' she murmured, 'and, oh, how I hated him. Better have died, I think, than go through life with him.'

They were in the hall by this time, and the minister was bowing Lady Lockerbie into her chair.

'Why should such a destiny as ours hang over us?' the girl murmured. The fear, suspense and shame that she had undergone lay heavy still upon her, and she shivered as she spoke.

'The legend says, if I remember rightly, it was because some long-dead Lockerbie did bitter wrong to his neighbour's daughter.'

'You know our story well, it seems.'

'I have lived much in Scotland, and its tales are dear to me.'

'Yet where is the justice of it? All this was centuries ago, and I——'

'And you have pride and all the other legacies to bear. He did grievous wrong to this girl, did he not—your ancestor? And she drowned herself upon her eighteenth birthday; and the mother came to him as he sat in the hall, and cursed him, saying that no maid of his should pass her eighteenth year.'

She nodded gravely, and turned to shudder at the wind-beats that rocked the very walls. 'And we have escaped—all but two of our race—by making maidens wives before they reached the fatal age.'

Lady Lockerbie frowned at them from her seat at the table-head. 'Mr St Quain,' she said, in measured tones, 'I must offer you a lodging for the night. Tomorrow, if it suits you, I should wish you to ride into England, to warn your friends of this alliance, and to make all preparations for a second marriage in due form.'

St Quain laughed outright. The wine and the witchery and the sweetness of it all had got into his blood. 'I ask for no second marriage,' he said. 'Happiness is happiness—and I have found it here tonight.'

Lady Lockerbie looked coldly at her son-in-law.

'I think,' she said, 'that happiness has very little to do with this matter. We are an old race, sir—indeed, you come of an old race yourself, so far as England goes—and I should wish to treat with your father as to settlements, and——'

St Quain felt a dull pain at his heart. He had loved his father well. 'My father died,' he said gravely, 'four years ago—at Culloden.'

Had he unsheathed his sword at the supper-table, the effect of this quiet speech could not have been more dire.

'Died at Culloden?' echoed Lady Lockerbie, clutching the table with restless fingers. 'On which side, sir, did he fight?'

'Why, for the King.'

'The King? Which King—our own Stuart, or the Usurper?'

'For King George. We have been loyal subjects always.'

The minister began to mutter vaguely to himself. He knew not what might follow this rash confession of St Quain's.

'*Loyalty*, sir?' cried my lady, in a voice of bitter scorn. 'We Lockerbies do not play with words, as you would seem to do. I lost my husband at Culloden—and your father fought against him, so it seems.'

'I can but regret,' said St Quain slowly. 'Yet it would be a poor thing, surely, for the children to cherish enmity because the fathers were brave men and fought for different causes.'

'It takes all rights from you, so far as my daughter is concerned.'

St Quain felt the girl on his right hand move closer to him, with a sort of instinctive denial.

'You have saved her life, sir,' went on my lady, in the same cold, even tones; 'you have done us a service, and we thank you for it—but you must never have speech or sight of her again.'

It was St Quain's turn now. He rose to his full height, and Janet, looking up at him, could not keep back that glow of pride and tenderness which had swept over her at his first coming.

'Lady Lockerbie,' he said, 'I have won my wife, and I shall take her home with me as soon as she has made her preparations. I care little for King George or Charlie Stuart—but I love *her* as I never thought that a man could love a woman.'

'You do not understand,' put in my lady. 'Culloden was worse than Flodden even; the memory of it is with us day and night. We *hate* you English folk.'

'Janet,' said St Quain, and he laughed as he turned to the girl—'Janet, what say·you? Granted I was unhappy in my English birth—and, faith, I had little choice about the matter!—are you willing to fare out with me and trust to my sword-arm and my honour?'

The Lockerbie pride took diverse forms, and my lady had no exclusive share in it. The girl rose, too, and put a warm hand into her lover's. 'I will go with you,' she said, 'and—I shall go fearlessly.'

Again there was a troubled silence, broken this time by a loud rattling at the door.

'The wind, my lady,' murmured the grey minister, who seemed more uneasy than the rest.

'Open, open!' came a shout from the other side of the door.

'God help us, 'tis Bruce's voice!' murmured Lady Lockerbie. 'Bruce —and we thought him dead!'

'The nicht is full of the wee bit ghosties,' murmured the old nurse, standing behind her lady's chair. 'He, too, I'm thinking, couldna rest quiet i' his quiet bed, while the English-born stepped into his dead shoon.'

Again the girl moved nearer to St Quain, and slipped her hand into his own under cover of the board. 'It is Bruce's voice,' she whispered. 'Bruce of Muirtown, and I fear him so!'

'Fear him, with me beside you?'

'Yes, for he has loved me since I was a child. Oh, he's not bad, not bad at all! But he is fierce, and I do not love him, and—and I would this trouble had not been brought on you.'

St Quain's heart leaped high. Her last thought was for him, despite her own dread of Bruce; the pressure of her hand was sure and wifely.

'See, child,' he whispered, 'do you love me? May I act as if you were my wife in truth as well as in the letter?'

The pressure of her hand alone replied; and then the sound of knocking at the door grew louder, unmistakable. The old nurse went to open, and let in a storm of wind and rain that half-blinded those within. And when at last their eyes grew clearer, they saw a big fellow, with blue eyes and rain-wet hair of yellow, standing, like a storm-sprite, his eyes fixed upon my lady's daughter.

'I feared to be too late,' he cried. 'It wants but an hour to midnight, and——'

He paused, and clutched his heart as if in pain. And now they noticed that his left arm was bandaged, and that a kerchief was wrapped about his brow.

'They—they said that you were dead,' my lady stammered. 'Say, Bruce of Muirtown, is't your ghost?'

'My ghost?' he echoed. 'Nay, but 'twas like to be. I was wounded, and fell into a sort of trance through loss of blood; and when I woke there was a voice that called to me—your voice, Janet—and I rode out through the storm.'

A sudden pity fell upon them. His eyes dwelt hungrily upon the girl, and it was clear that only love had given him strength to ride so far.

'She is married already,' whispered my lady.

He looked more like a fiend than any fleshly man, as he paused to understand his misery. 'Married? To whom?' he thundered.

St Quain bowed quietly. 'To me, sir, an hour gone,' he said.

Bruce of Muirtown began to mutter like a man deranged; then asked the minister if this were true.

'They are fast as the Kirk can make them,' said the grey man of peace.

Again there was a silence; then Bruce laughed harshly, and lifted a glass from the table, and flung the contents full in his rival's face.

'We'll fight upon it, sir, and she shall be a widow before tomorrow breaks.'

St Quain felt a rush of shame come over him—shame, not for his wine-stained face, but for the weakness of this man who had challenged him to combat.

'I regret, sir,' he stammered, wiping his cheeks and brow, 'that you are only strong enough to offer insult—not to atone for it.'

Bruce of Muirtown turned his hungry eyes away—turned them from the lass he worshipped, and let them rest upon St Quain.

'I am recovered,' he said, with a heaviness of voice that belied him; 'I will fight you in the meadows by the loch tonight.'

'Nay, for I refuse,' St Quain answered quietly. 'I do not fight with wounded men.'

Bruce lifted a wine glass from the table and flung the contents in his rival's face.

Janet, for her part, wondered at his self-command; for already she had grown to love him, and no love-ridden woman doubts her lover's courage. But Lady Lockerbie was of different mould, and her voice was cold as the raving wind without when she turned toward St Quain.

'In Scotland, sir, *men* answer insult with the sword,' she said.

St Quain drew back, with something near to horror. For the first time he understood this woman—understood the depth of her prejudice and her pride. She had been glad to save her daughter's life; she was more glad to think that Bruce of Muirtown had returned to cut the bridal-knot with one sharp stroke of his sword.

And yet the man was weak through loss of blood and long riding under rough skies. How could he fight with him?

' 'Tis not the first time we have daunted Englishmen,' said Bruce, with a mocking laugh. 'See how he pales beneath the wine-stains—and all because he sees a hand go down toward a sword-hilt.'

St Quain was mortal, though brave and tender-hearted. 'You fasten a quarrel on me,' he said. 'Well and good—but these ladies should know nothing of it.'

'Ay, ay, they should, seeing that one of them is my promised wife. And, gad, sir,' he added, in a white heat of passion, 'if you dally further, I'll thrash you in their presence.'

St Quain could do no more. He lifted his wife's hand and kissed it; he bowed, as a courtier might have done, to Lady Lockerbie.

'I am ready, sir, and the moon is full tonight,' he said.

The black-robed minister stepped forward. 'Gentlemen, gentle-men——' he began.

'It is too late,' said Bruce of Muirtown.

'Too late,' echoed St Quain, turning, as he left the hall, to find his wife's eyes fixed on his, with a tenderness in them beyond belief.

'Yet think, sir,' said the minister, his hand on St Quain's arm. 'A duel is at all times a godless enterprise; but when your adversary is sick——'

'True,' said St Quain quietly. 'In England we do not fight with such as Mr Bruce here, but it seems that in Scotland the matter shows far otherwise.'

'In Scotland men fight for a right cause, whether they be sick or well,' said Lady Lockerbie sharply.

St Quain bowed low to her. He was beginning to understand how pride—Scottish pride—may oust all womanhood.

'You will fight?' said Bruce of Muirtown eagerly, as he gulped down a measure of red wine.

'You leave me no option, sir,' answered St Quain.

Together they went out into the windy night, he and the man whose left arm carried bandages; and even now, amid the stress of weather and of feeling, he wondered that the prospect of sword-play could be so bracing to a wounded man.

'There will be none to watch us,' muttered Bruce. 'The minister is pledged to peace, and we can scarcely ask the women-folk to act as seconds.'

'Where is the ground?' said St Quain shortly.

'Rather, what is your weapon? You are the challenged party.'

'Swords,' said the other, after a scarce perceptible pause.

The clouds had left the moon by this time, and the wind was dying into fitful moans and gusts as they went out into the grim courtyard and forward to the meadow-lands beyond. From time to time Bruce halted in his walk, but always recovered and went forward with an air so hard and desperate that St Quain felt chilled and awestruck. He could love and hate, this thwarted lover, and spared himself as little, so it seemed, as he spared man or woman when his heart was set upon a matter.

They marked their ground, and once again St Quain drew back.

'You are ill, sir, and I am ashamed,' he said. 'Will you not wait awhile, and send your friend to me in proper form?'

'And let you snatch *my wife* from me? I think not, sir. Either you fight me now, or I have you kicked into the high road by the serving-men.'

St Quain drew his sword. 'I am ready,' he said, in a voice as hard as Bruce's own.

His enemy's attack was overwhelming at the first; Bruce, it was plain, distrusted his own staying-power, and his onslaught, like himself, was rash, impetuous, regardless of all laws. St Quain, recovering after the first surprise, played a quiet, watchful blade; he made no effort of any sort to thrust, but parried each wild stroke with a studied ease that brought the other's blood to fever pitch.

Time after time Bruce strove to beat the other down; and then a mist came before his eyes; and after that he felt his sword go up, and up, and up, toward the grey moon, and a heaviness, as of death, came over him.

He awoke to find St Quain bending over him—bending over him with a strange, almost womanish, solicitude.

'You fought—you fought well, sir,' murmured Bruce.

But shame was strong upon St Quain. True, he had striven to avoid the combat; yet it was terrible to fight, as he had done, with one so weak.

'Can you stand?' he said. 'If so, I'll help you to the house; your bandages have slipped, and the blood is trickling.'

'Where did you prick me?' said Bruce of Muirtown faintly.

'Prick you? Nowhere. I robbed you of your sword, and then you fell into a swoon. I am English, sir, but I am not the coward you would wish.'

Bruce rose stiffly from the wet, moon-bright grass, and passed a hand across his brow. 'I played the bully awhile since,' he stammered; 'I raved and swore, and challenged you to fight; but them—God help me, I had lost a wife.'

St Quain would listen to no more. He linked his arm in Bruce's. 'And I have gained one,' he said softly. 'Surely, sir, you will grant feelings to us English, though we're of a different race.'

Dizzy as he was, sick of heart and brain and fortune, Bruce could not but warm to the manliness, the straightforward wish to give and take which marked his rival's manner. It was his turn now to feel shame; and, in love or war, in pride or shame, it had never been his way to do anything by halves.

'St Quain,' he said, stammering even as he spoke for weakness' sake, 'you are a man—and I regret that insult more than any other deed of my wild life.'

'Then quit regrets, for I have forgotten all. Good God, does not Janet make a good excuse for any folly!'

They had reached the door by this time, and Bruce of Muirtown leaned a heavy hand upon his arm.

'And the girl,' he muttered. 'Will she go with you, do you think?'

'Yes, though her mother says she shall not.'

'And why?'

'I named Culloden in her hearing, and she learned that my father had fought upon the English side.'

Despite his weakness, despite his old sense of loss and his new sense of repentance, Bruce laughed aloud. 'Even for a Scot, she dwells too much upon Culloden,' he said. 'You had better have robbed her plate-chest than mention what you did. The serving-folk are of a like mind, too; you'll have trouble, if you wish to take your bride.'

'I'll take her, if all Scotland says I shall not.'

Like most wildings, Bruce of Muirtown had a heart. He had shown it once tonight, when he could find room for honest admiration of a rival—a rival who had robbed him of a mistress, and who had given him back a forfeit life.

'St Quain,' he said, still standing on the wind side of the oaken door, 'I'll play no dog-in-the-manger part. She's yours, and you shall win her yet.'

They passed into the hall, where Lady Lockerbie was seated alone in front of the great fire. She looked up eagerly as they came in, and her face was white as Bruce's own, soon as she saw them standing there—St Quain in health, his adversary leaning heavily on his arm.

'You—you are hurt, Bruce,' she stammered.

'No,' he said, 'except so far as I was hurt before. Mr St Quain has worsted me, and given me my life. I hope that he will count me his friend henceforward.'

My lady rose. There was a sort of madness in her face—the madness of long hatred indulged in overmuch. She seemed to gain in stature and in coldness.

'His father fought against my husband,' she said. 'He is English; he can be nothing to any Lockerbie.'

'He chances to be husband to a Lockerbie,' put in St Quain drily, 'and he means to claim his right.'

Taller yet she seemed to grow, and her grey eyes deepened, and her voice, no longer cold, was full of passion.

'My daughter is in safety, sir. She would have followed you, to interrupt this duel which has ended so unhappily; but I prevented it.'

'I will find her,' said St Quain doggedly, 'if I spend a twelve-month in the search.'

'And I will help you,' put in Bruce of Muirtown.

My lady looked from one to the other. 'What is this talk of friendliness, Bruce? This stranger has robbed you—robbed you.'

'Nay, it is I who would have robbed him; and I, no less than Janet, owe my life to him.'

Obeying a sudden impulse, Bruce took my lady to one side and talked to her. St Quain could hear nothing of what passed; but he guessed that his own cause was being pleaded by one who had so lately wished to kill him. And by and by Lady Lockerbie returned, and held her hand out with some show of warmth.

'I cannot pretend to welcome the match,' she said, 'but I am old, and weary, and I cannot but see that lives may well be ruined. Will you—will you treat her well?'

Her voice broke at the last; and St Quain saw down into the tenderness that lay beneath her pride.

'I will treat her well,' he answered huskily.

My lady turned to a manservant who stood by the door. 'Prepare the bridal chamber,' she said.

And St Quain looked out upon the loch, the moonlight, and the peaceful sky. And only the whimpering wind was left to recall the storm that had brought a wife to him.

BETTER LET BLAME' WELL ALONE

Mark Twain

Huckleberry Finn is living with the Widow Douglas, who has custody of him, and is slowly adapting to a life of schoolwork and regular habits. However, his drunken father reappears and is granted custody of the boy by a new judge. Huck makes his escape, and stages it so that it seems he has been murdered. On Jackson Island in the Mississippi he meets Jim, the Widow Douglas's Negro, who has run away because he thinks the widow's sister is about to sell him. They link their fortunes, and continue together down the Mississippi.

It must 'a' been close on to one o'clock when we got below the island at last, and the raft did seem to go mighty slowly. If a boat was to come along we was going to take to the canoe and break for the Illinois shore; and it was well a boat didn't come, for we hadn't ever thought to put the gun in the canoe, or a fishing line, or anything to eat. We was in ruther too much of a sweat to think of so many things. It warn't good judgment to put *everything* on the raft.

If the men went to the island I just expect they found the campfire I built, and watched it all night for Jim to come. Anyways, they stayed away from us, and if my building the fire never fooled them it warn't no fault of mine. I played it as low-down on them as I could.

When the first streak of day began to show we tied up to a towhead in a bend on the Illinois side, and hacked off cottonwood branches with the hatchet, and covered up the raft with them so she looked like there had been a cave-in in the bank there. A towhead is a sand-bar that has cottonwoods on it as thick as harrow teeth.

We had mountains on the Missouri shore and heavy timber on the Illinois side, and the channel was down the Missouri shore at that place, so we warn't afraid of anybody running across us. We laid there all day, and watched the rafts and steamboats spin down the Missouri shore, and up-bound steamboats fight the big river in the middle. I told Jim all about the time I had jabbering with that woman; and Jim said she was a smart one, and if she was to start after us herself *she* wouldn't set down and watch a campfire—no, sir, she'd fetch a dog. Well, I said, why couldn't she tell her husband to fetch a dog? Jim said he bet she did think of it by the time the men was ready to start, and he believed they must 'a' gone uptown to get a dog and so they lost all that time, or else we wouldn't be here on a towhead sixteen or seventeen mile below the village—no, indeedy, we would be in that same town again. So I said I didn't care what was the reason they didn't get us as long as they didn't.

When it was beginning to come on dark we poked our heads out of the cottonwood thicket, and looked up and down and across; nothing in sight; so Jim took up some of the top planks of the raft and built a snug wigwam to get under in blazing weather and rainy, and to keep the things dry. Jim made a floor for the wigwam, and raised it a foot or more above the level of the raft, so now the blankets and all the traps was out of reach of steamboat waves. Right in the middle of the wigwam we made a layer of dirt about five or six inches deep with a frame around it for to hold it to its place; this was to build a fire on in sloppy weather or chilly; the wigwam would keep it from being seen. We made an extra steering oar, too, because one of the others might get broke on a snag or something. We fixed up a short forked stick to hang the old lantern on, because we must always light the lantern whenever we see a steamboat coming downstream, to keep from getting run over; but we wouldn't have to light it for upstream boats unless we see we was in what they call a 'crossing'; for the river was pretty high yet, very low banks being still a little under water; so upbound boats didn't always run the channel, but hunted easy water.

This second night we run between seven and eight hours, with a current that was making over four mile an hour. We catched fish and talked, and we took a swim now and then to keep off sleepiness. It was kind of solemn, drifting down the big, still river, laying on our backs looking up at the stars, and we didn't ever feel like talking loud, and it warn't often that we laughed—only a little kind of a low chuckle.

We had mighty good weather as a general thing, and nothing ever happened to us at all—that night, nor the next, nor the next.

Every night we passed towns, some of them away up on black hillsides nothing but just a shiny bed of lights; not a house could you see. The fifth night we passed St Louis, and it was like the whole world lit up. In St Petersburg they used to say there was twenty or thirty thousand people in St Louis, but I never believed it till I see that wonderful spread of lights at two o'clock that still night. There warn't a sound there; everybody was asleep.

Every night now I used to slip ashore toward ten o'clock at some little village, and buy ten or fifteen cents' worth of meal or bacon or other stuff to eat; and sometimes I lifted a chicken that warn't roosting comfortable, and took him along. Pap always said take a chicken when you get a chance, because if you don't want him yourself you can easy find somebody that does, and a good deed ain't ever forgot. I never see Pap when he didn't want the chicken himself, but that is what he used to say, anyway.

Mornings before daylight I slipped into cornfields and borrowed a watermelon, or a mushmelon, or a punkin, or some new corn, or things of that kind. Pap always said it warn't no harm to borrow things if you was meaning to pay them back sometime; but the widow said it warn't anything but a soft name for stealing, and no decent body would do it. Jim said he reckoned the widow was partly right and Pap was partly right; so the best way would be for us to pick out two or three things from the list and say we wouldn't borrow them any more—then he reckoned it wouldn't be no harm to borrow the others. So we talked it over all one night, drifting along down the river, trying to make up our minds whether to drop the water-melons, or the cantaloups, or the musk-melons, or what. But toward daylight we got it all settled satisfactory, and concluded to drop crab-apples and p'simmons. We warn't feeling just right before that, but it was all comfortable now. I was glad the way it come out, too, because crab-apples ain't ever good and the p'simmons wouldn't be ripe for two or three months yet.

We shot a waterfowl now and then that got up too early in the morning or didn't go to bed early enough in the evening. Take it all round, we lived pretty high.

The fifth night below St Louis we had a big storm after midnight,

213

with a power of thunder and lightning, and the rain poured down in a solid sheet. We stayed in the wigwam and let the raft take care of itself. When the lightning glared out we could see a big straight river ahead, and high, rocky bluffs on both sides. By and by says I, 'Hel-*lo*, Jim, looky yonder!' It was a steamboat that had killed herself on a rock. We was drifting straight down for her. The lightning showed her very distinct. She was leaning over, with part of her upper deck above water, and you could see every little chimbly guy clean and clear, and a chair by the big bell, with an old slouch hat hanging on the back of it, when the flashes come.

Well, it being away in the night and stormy, and all so mysterious-like, I felt just the way any other boy would 'a' felt when I seen that wreck laying there so mournful and lonesome in the middle of the river. I wanted to get aboard of her and slink around a little, and see what there was there. So I says:

'Le's land on her, Jim.'

But Jim was dead against it at first. He says:

'I doan' want to go fool'n' 'long er no wrack. We's doin' blame' well, en we better let blame' well alone, as de good book says. Like as not dey's a watchman on dat wrack.'

'Watchman your grandmother,' I says; 'there ain't nothing to watch but the texas and the pilothouse; and do you reckon anybody's going to resk his life for a texas and a pilothouse such a night as this, when it's likely to break up and wash off down the river any minute?' Jim couldn't say nothing to that, so he didn't try. 'And besides,' I says, 'we might borrow something worth having out of the captain's stateroom. See-gars, *I* bet you—and cost five cents apiece, solid cash. Steamboat captains is always rich, and get sixty dollars a month, and *they* don't care a cent what a thing costs, you know, long as they want it. Stick a candle in your pocket; I can't rest, Jim, till we give her a rummaging. Do you reckon Tom Sawyer would ever go by this thing? Not for pie, he wouldn't. He'd call it an adventure—that's what he'd call it; and he'd land on that wreck if it was his last act. And wouldn't he throw style into it?—wouldn't he spread himself, nor nothing? Why, you'd think it was Christopher C'lumbus discovering Kingdom Come. I wish Tom Sawyer *was* here.'

Jim he grumbled a little, but give in. He said we mustn't talk any more than we could help, and then talk mighty low. The lightning showed us the wreck again just in time, and we fetched the starboard derrick, and made fast there.

The deck was high out here. We went sneaking down the slope of it to labboard, in the dark, towards the texas, feeling our way slow with our feet, and spreading our hands out to fend off the guys, for it was so dark we couldn't see no sign of them. Pretty soon we struck the forward end of the skylight, and clumb on to it; and the next step fetched us in front of the captain's door, which was open, and by Jimminy, away down through the texas hall we see a light! and all in the same second we seem to hear low voices in yonder!

Jim whispered and said he was feeling powerful sick, and told me to come along. I says, all right, and was going to start for the raft; but just then I heard a voice wail out and say:

'Oh, please don't, boys; I swear I won't ever tell!'

Another voice said, pretty loud:

'It's a lie, Jim Turner. You've acted this way before. You always want more'n your share of the truck, and you've always got it, too, because you've swore 't if you didn't you'd tell. But this time you've said it jest one time too many. You're the meanest, treacherousest hound in this country.'

By this time Jim was gone for the raft. I was just a-biling with curiosity; and I says to myself, Tom Sawyer wouldn't back out now, and so I won't either; I'm a-going to see what's going on here. So I dropped on my hands and knees in the little passage, and crept aft in the dark till there warn't but one stateroom betwixt me and the cross hall of the texas. Then in there I see a man stretched on the floor and tied hand and foot, and two men standing over him, and one of them had a dim lantern in his hand, and the other one had a pistol. This one kept pointing the pistol at the man's head on the floor, and saying:

'I'd *like* to! And I orter, too—a mean skunk!'

The man on the floor would shrivel up and say, 'Oh, please don't, Bill; I hain't ever goin' to tell.'

And every time he said that the man with the lantern would laugh and say:

''Deed you *ain't!* You never said no truer thing 'n that, you bet you.' And once he said: 'Hear him beg! and yit if we hadn't got the best of

'In there I see a man stretched on the floor tied, hand and foot, and two men standing over him.'

him and tied him he'd 'a' killed us both. And what *for*? Jist for noth'n'. Jist because we stood on our *rights*—that's what for. But I lay you ain't a-goin' to threaten nobody any more, Jim Turner. Put *up* that pistol, Bill.'

Bill says:

'I don't want to, Jake Packard. I'm for killin' him—and didn't he kill old Hatfield jist the same way—and don't he deserve it?'

'But I don't *want* him killed, and I've got my reasons for it.'

'Bless yo' heart for them words, Jake Packard! I'll never forgit you long's I live!' says the man on the floor, sort of blubbering.

Packard didn't take no notice of that, but hung up his lantern on a nail and started toward where I was, there in the dark, and motioned Bill to come. I crawfished as fast as I could about two yards, but the boat slanted so that I couldn't make very good time; so to keep from getting run over and catched I crawled into a stateroom on the upper side. The man came a-pawing along in the dark, and when Packard got to my stateroom, he says:

'Here—come in here.'

And in he come, and Bill after him. But before they got in I was up in the upper berth, cornered, and sorry I come. Then they stood there, with their hands on the ledge of the berth, and talked. I couldn't see them, but I could tell where they was by the whisky they'd been having. I was glad I didn't drink whisky; but it would't made much difference anyway, because most of the time they couldn't 'a' treed me because I didn't breathe. I was too scared. And, besides, a body *couldn't* breathe and hear such talk. They talked low and earnest. Bill wanted to kill Turner. He says:

'He's said he'll tell, and he will. If we was to give both our shares to him *now* it wouldn't make no difference after the row and the way we've served him. Shore's you're born, he'll turn state's evidence; now you hear *me*. I'm for putting him out of his troubles.'

'So'm I,' says Packard, very quiet.

'Blame it, I'd sorter begun to think you wasn't. Well, then, that's all right. Le's go and do it.'

'Hold on a minute; I hain't had my say yit. You listen to me. Shooting's good, but there's quieter ways if the things *got* to be done. But what *I* say is this: it ain't good sense to go court'n' around after a halter if you can git at what you're up to in some way that's jist as good and at the same time don't bring you into no resks. Ain't that so?'

'You bet it is. But how you goin' to manage it this time?'

'Well, my idea is this: we'll rustle around and gather up whatever pickin's we've overlooked in the staterooms, and shove for shore and hide the truck. Then we'll wait. Now I say it ain't a-goin' to be more'n two hours befo' this wrack breaks up and washes off down the river. See? He'll be drownded, and won't have nobody to blame for it but his own self. I reckon that's a considerable sight better 'n killin' of him. I'm unfavourable to killin' a man as long as you can git aroun' it; it ain't good sense, it ain't good morals. Ain't I right?'

'Yes, I reck'n you are. But s'pose she *don't* break up and wash off?'

'Well, we can wait the two hours anyway and see, can't we?'

'All right, then; come along.'

So they started, and I lit out, all in a cold sweat, and scrambled forward. It was dark as pitch there; but I said, in a kind of a coarse whisper, 'Jim!' and he answered up, right at my elbow, with a sort of a moan, and I says:

'Quick, Jim, it ain't no time for fooling around and moaning; there's a gang of murderers in yonder, and if we don't hunt up their boat and set her drifting down the river so these fellows can't get away from the wreck there's one of 'em going to be in a bad fix. But if we find their boat we can put *all* of 'em in a bad fix—for the sheriff'll get 'em. Quick —hurry! I'll hunt the labboard side, you hunt the stabboard. You start at the raft, and——'

'Oh, my lordy, lordy! *Raf'*? Dey ain' no raf' no mo'; she done broke loose en gone!—en here we is!'

Well, I catched my breath and 'most fainted. Shut up on a wreck with such a gang as that! But it warn't no time to be sentimentering. We'd *got* to find that boat now—had to have it for ourselves. So we went a-quaking and shaking down the stabboard side, and slow work it was, too—seemed a week before we got to the stern. No sign of a boat. Jim said he didn't believe he could go any farther—so scared he hadn't hardly any strength left, he said. But I said, come on, if we get left on this wreck we are in a fix, sure. So on we prowled again. We struck for the stern of the texas, and found it, and then scrabbled along forwards on the skylight, hanging on from shutter to shutter, for the edge of the skylight was in the water. When we got pretty close to the cross-hall door there was the skiff, sure enough! I could just barely see her. I felt ever so thankful. In another second I would 'a' been aboard of her, but just then the door opened. One of the men stuck his head out only about a couple of foot from me, and I thought I was gone; but he jerked it in again, and says:

'Heave that blame lantern out o' sight, Bill!'

He flung a bag of something into the boat, and then got in himself and set down. It was Packard. Then Bill *he* come out and got in. Packard says, in a low voice:

'All ready—shove off!'

I couldn't hardly hang on to the shutters, I was so weak. But Bill says:

'Hold on—'d you go through him?'

'No. Didn't you?'

'No. So he's got his share o' the cash yet.'

'Well, then, come along; no use to take truck and leave money.'

'Say, won't he suspicion what we're up to?'

'Maybe he won't. But we got to have it anyway. Come along.'

So they got out and went in.

The door slammed to because it was on the careened side; and in a half second I was in the boat, and Jim come tumbling after me. I out with my knife and cut the rope, and away we went!

We didn't touch an oar, and we didn't speak nor whisper, nor hardly even breathe. We went gliding swift along, dead silent, past the tip of the paddlebox, and past the sterm; then in a second or two more we was a hundred yards below the wreck, and the darkness soaked her up, every last sign of her, and we was safe, and knowed it.

When we was three or four hundred yards downstream we see the lantern show like a little spark at the texas door for a second, and we knowed by that that the rascals had missed their boat, and was beginning to understand that they was in just as much trouble now as Jim Turner was.

Then Jim manned the oars, and we took out after our raft. Now was the first time that I begun to worry about the men—I reckon I hadn't had time to before. I begun to think how dreadful it was, even for murderers, to be in such a fix. I says to myself, there ain't no telling but I might come to be a murderer myself yet, and then how would I like it? So says I to Jim:

'The first light we see we'll land a hundred yards below it or above it, in a place where it's a good hiding place for you and the skiff, and then I'll go and fix up some kind of a yarn, and get somebody to go for that gang and get them out of their scrape, so they can be hung when their time comes.'

THE TAMING OF PERCY

Gerald Durrell

As a young man in 1950 the famous naturalist Gerald Durrell went to British Guiana (modern Guyana, in northern South America) to bring back for zoological gardens in Britain a living collection of the birds, mammals, reptiles and fish that inhabit that country. In this extract from his book Three Singles to Adventure *he is exploring the creek lands to the north-west with two companions, Ivan and Bob, and a local guide, Kahn, who has become rather tiresome with stories of his prowess as a hunter.*

At the end of the valley the creek waters dutifully re-entered their appointed bed and flowed through a section of thickly wooded countryside. The trees grew closer and closer, until we were travelling in green twilight under a tunnel of branches and shimmering leaves, on water that was as black as ebony, touched in places with silver smears of light where there were gaps in the branches overhead. Suddenly a bird flew from a tree opposite to us and sped up the dim tunnel, to alight on the trunk of another tree that was spotlighted with sunshine. It was a great black woodpecker with a long, curling wine-red crest and an ivory-coloured beak.

As it clung to the bark, peering at us, it was joined by its mate, and together they started to scuttle up and down the tree trunk, tapping it importantly with their beaks and listening with their heads on one side. occasionally they would utter a short burst of shrill, metallic laughter, tittering weirdly over some private joke between themselves. They looked like a couple of mad, red-headed doctors, sounding the chest of the great tree and giggling delightedly over the diseases they found, the worm-holes, the tubercular patches of dry rot, and the army of larvae steadily eating their hosts to pieces. The woodpeckers thought it a rich jest.

They were exotic, fantastic-looking birds, and I was determined to try and add some of them to our collection. I pointed them out to Ivan.

'What do they call those, Ivan?'

'Carpenter birds, sir.'

'We must try and get some.'

'I will get you some,' said Mr Kahn. 'Don't you worry, Chief, I will get you anything you want.'

I watched the woodpeckers as they flew from tree to tree, but they were eventually lost to sight in the tangled forest. I hoped that Mr Kahn was right, but I doubted it.

Towards evening we were nearing our destination, an Amerindian village with a tiny mission school, hidden away among the backwaters of the creek lands. We left the main creek and entered an even narrower tributary, and here the growth of aquatic plants was so thick that it covered the water from bank to bank. This green lawn was studded with hundreds of miniature flowers in mauve, yellow and pink, each thimble-sized bloom growing on a stem half an inch high. It seemed when I sat in the bows that the boat was drifting smoothly up some weed-grown drive, for only the ripples of our wash undulating the plants as we passed gave indication of the water beneath. We followed this enchanting path for miles as it twisted through woodland and grassfields, and eventually it led us to a small white beach fringed with palm trees. We could see a few shacks, half hidden among the trees, and a cluster of canoes lying on the clean sand.

As we switched off the engine and drifted shorewards a host of chattering, laughing Amerindian children ran down to meet us, all stark naked, their bodies glistening in the sun. Following them came a tall African who, as soon as we landed, introduced himself as the schoolmaster. He led us, surrounded by the noisy, laughing children, up the white beach to one of the huts, and then he left us, promising to return when we had unpacked and settled down. Our ears had got used to hearing the throb of the boat's engine all day, so the peace and quiet of that little hut among the palms was delightfully soothing. We unpacked and ate a meal in a contented silence; even Mr Kahn seemed to be affected by the place, and remained unusually quiet.

221

Presently the schoolmaster returned, and with him was one of his small Amerindian pupils.

'This boy wants to know if you will buy this,' said the schoolmaster.

'This' turned out to be a baby crab-eating raccoon, a tiny ball of fluff with sparkling eyes, that looked just like a chow puppy. There was no trace of the mournful expression that it was to wear in later life; instead it was full of good spirits, rolling and gambolling and pretending to bite with its tiny milk teeth, waving its bushy tail like a flag. Even if I had not wanted him I would have found it difficult to resist buying such a charming creature. I felt that he was too young to share a cage with the adult, so I set to work and built him a special one of his own; we installed him in this, his tummy bulging with the meal of milk and fish I had given him, and he curled up in a pile of dry grass, belched triumphantly and then went to sleep.

The schoolmaster suggested that we should attend his class the next morning and show the children pictures of the various animals we wanted. He said that he knew many of his pupils had pets that they would be willing to part with. He also promised to find us some good hunters who would take us out into the creeks in search of specimens.

So the next morning Bob and I attended the school and explained to forty young Amerindians why we had come there, what animals we wanted and the prices we were willing to pay. With great enthusiasm they all promised to bring their pets that afternoon, all, that is, except one small boy, who looked very worried and conversed rapidly with the schoolmaster in a whisper.

'He says,' explained the master, 'he has a very fine animal, but it is too big for him to bring by canoe.'

'What sort of animal is it?'

'He says it is a wild pig.'

I turned to Bob.

'Could you go and fetch it in the boat this afternoon, d'you think?'

Bob sighed.

'I suppose so,' he said, 'as long as it's well tied up.'

That afternoon Bob set off in the boat, accompanied by the little Amerindian boy, to bring back the peccary. I had impressed upon him to buy any other worthwhile specimens he might see in the Amerindian village, and so I awaited his return hopefully. Shortly after the boat had left the first children arrived, carrying their pets, and soon I was deeply engrossed in the thrilling and exciting job of buying specimens, surrounded on all sides by grinning Amerindians and a weird assortment of animals.

Perhaps the commonest ones were agoutis, golden-brown creatures with long, slim legs and rabbit-like faces. They are really not very intelligent creatures, and are so nervous that they have hysterics if you so much as breathe in their direction. Then there were pacas, plump as young pigs, chocolate-coloured beasts decorated with longitudinal lines of cream-coloured blotches. Four or five squirrel and capuchin monkeys capered and chattered on the end of long strings, scrambling up and down the children's bodies as if they were so many bushes.

Many of the children produced young boa-constrictors, beautifully coloured in pink and silver and fawn, coiled round their owners' waists or wrists. They may seem a rather unusual choice of pet for a child, but the Amerindians don't seem to suffer from the European's ridiculous fear of snakes. They keep the boas in their huts and allow the reptiles the run of the place; in return the snake discharges the function usually fulfilled by a cat in more civilized communities, that is to say it keeps the place free from rats, mice and other edible vermin. I cannot think of a better arrangement, for not only is the boa a better ratter than a cat could ever be, but it is much more decorative and beautiful to look at; to have one draped over the beams of your house in the graceful manner that only snakes can achieve would be as good as having a rare and lovely tapestry for decoration, with the individual advantage that your decoration works for its living.

Just as I had finished with the last of the children there came a wild, ringing laugh and one of the red-headed woodpeckers swooped across the clearing and disappeared into the forest.

'Ah!' I yelped, pointing, 'I want one of those.'

The children could not understand my words, but my gesture combined with my pleading, imploring expression told them what they wanted to know. They all burst into roars of laughter, stamping and spluttering and nodding their heads, and I began to feel more hopeful of getting a specimen of the woodpecker. When the Amerindians had gone I set to work to build cages for the varied assortment of wildlife I had bought. It was a long job, and by the time I had finished I could

The slats flew off the box and the enraged pig hauled himself out . . .

hear in the distance the faint chugging of the returning boat, so I walked down the beach to meet Bob and the peccary.

As the boat came into view I could see Bob and Ivan on the flat roof, sitting back to back on a large box, with strained expression on their faces. The boat nosed into the shallows, and Bob glared at me from his seat on the box.

'Did you get it?' I enquired hopefully.

'Yes, thank you,' said Bob, 'and we've been trying to keep it in this blasted box ever since we left the village. Apparently it doesn't like being shut up. I thought it was meant to be tame. In fact I *remember* you telling me it was a tame one. That was the only reason I agreed to go and fetch it.'

'Well, the boy said it was tame.'

'The boy, bless him, was mistaken,' said Bob coldly; 'the brute appears to be suffering from claustrophobia.'

Gingerly we carried the box from the boat to the beach.

'You'd better watch out,' warned Bob, 'it's already got some of the slats loose on top.'

As he spoke the peccary leapt inside the box and hit the top like a sledge-hammer; the slats flew off like rockets, and the next minute a bristling and enraged pig had hauled himself out and was galloping up the beach, snorting savagely.

'There!' said Bob, 'I knew that would happen.'

Halfway up the beach the peccary met a small group of Amerindians. He rushed among them, squealing with rage, trying to bite their legs; his sharp, half-inch tusks clicked together at each bite. The Amerindians fled back to the village, hotly pursued by the pig, who was in turn being chased by Ivan and myself. When we reached the huts the inhabitants appeared to have vanished, and the peccary was having a quick snack off some mess he had found under a palm tree. We had rounded the corner of a hut and come upon him rather unexpectedly, but he did not hestitate for a minute. Leaving his meal he charged straight towards us with champing mouth, uttering a bloodcurdling squeal. The next few moments were crowded, with the peccary twirling round and round, chopping and squealing, while Ivan and I leapt madly about with the speed and precision of a well-trained *corps de ballet*. At last the pig decided that we were too agile for him, and he retreated into a gap between two of the huts and stood there grunting derisively at us.

'You go round and guard the other end, Ivan,' I panted. 'I'll see he doesn't get away this side.'

Ivan disappeared round the other side of the huts, and I saw Mr Kahn waddling over the sand towards me. I was filled with an unholy glee.

'Mr Kahn,' I called. 'Can you come and help for a minute?'

'Surely, Chief,' he said, beaming. 'What you want?'

'Just stand here and guard this opening, will you? There's a peccary in there and I don't want him to get out. I'll be back in a second.'

Leaving Mr Kahn peering doubtfully at the peccary, I rushed over to our hut and unearthed a thick canvas bag, which I wrapped carefully round my left hand. Thus armed I returned to the scene of the fray. To my delight I was just in time to see Mr Kahn panting flatfootedly round the palm trees with the peccary close behind. To my disappointment the pig stopped chasing Mr Kahn as soon as he saw me and retreated once more between the huts.

'Golly!' said Mr Kahn. 'That pig's plenty fierce, Chief.'

He sat down in the shade and fanned himself with a large red handkerchief, while I squeezed my way between the huts and moved slowly towards the peccary. He stood quite still, watching me, champing his jaws occasionally and giving subdued grunts. He let me get within six feet of him, and then he charged. As he reached me I grabbed the bristly scruff of his neck with my right hand and plunged my left, encased in canvas, straight into his mouth. He champed his jaws desperately, but his tusks made no impression through the canvas. I shifted my grip, got my arm firmly round his fat body and lifted him off the ground. As soon as he felt himself hoisted into the air his confidence seemed to evaporate, he stopped biting my hand and started squeaking in the most plaintive manner, kicking out with his fat little hind legs. I carried him over to our hut and deposited him in a box that was strong enough to hold him.

Soon he had his snout buried in a dish full of chopped bananas and milk and was snorting and squelching with satisfaction. Never again did he show off and try to be the Terror of the Jungle; in fact he became absurdly tame. A glimpse of his feeding dish would send him into squealing transports of delight, a frightful song that would only end when his nose was deep in the dish and his mouth full of food. He adored being scratched, and if you continued this treatment for long enough he would heel over and fall flat on his side, lying motionless, with his eyes tighly closed and giving tiny grunts of pleasure. We christened him Percy, and even Bob grew quite fond of him, though I suspect that the chief reason for this was that he had seen him chasing Mr Kahn round the palm trees.

SPECTRE LOVERS

Joseph Sheridan le Fanu

There lived some fifteen years since, in a small and ruinous house little better than a hovel, an old woman who was reported to have considerably exceeded her eightieth year, and who rejoiced in the name of Alice, or popularly, Ally Moran. Her society was not much courted, for she was neither rich, nor, as the reader may suppose, beautiful. In addition to a lean cur and a cat she had one human companion, her grandson, Peter Brien, whom, with laudable good nature, she had supported from the period of his orphanage down to that of my story which finds him in his twentieth year.

Peter was a good-natured slob of a fellow, much more addicted to wrestling, dancing, and love-making than to hard work, and fonder of whisky punch than good advice. His grandmother had a high opinion of his accomplishments, which indeed was but natural, and also of his genius, for Peter had of late years begun to apply his mind to politics; and as it was plain that he had a mortal hatred of honest labour, his grandmother predicted, like a true fortune-teller, that he was born to marry an heiress, and Peter himself (who had no mind to forego his freedom even on such terms) that he was destined to find a pot of gold.

Upon one point both agreed, that being unfitted by the peculiar bias of his genius for work, he was to acquire the immense fortune to which his merits entitled him by means of a pure run of good luck. This solution of Peter's future had the double effect of reconciling both himself and his grandmother to his idle courses, and also of maintaining that even flow of hilarious spirits which made him everywhere welcome, and which was in truth the natural result of his consciousness of approaching affluence.

It happened one night that Peter had enjoyed himself to a very late hour with two or three choice spirits near Palmerstown. They had talked politics and love, sung songs, and told stories, and, above all, had swallowed, in the chastened disguise of punch, at least a pint of good whisky, every man.

It was considerably past one o'clock when Peter bid his companions good-bye, with a sigh and a hiccough, and lighting his pipe set forth on his solitary homeward way.

The bridge of Chapelizod was pretty nearly the midway point of his night march, and from one cause or another his progress was rather slow, and it was past two o'clock by the time he found himself leaning over its old battlements, and looking up the river, over whose winding current and wooded banks the soft moonlight was falling.

The cold breeze that blew lightly down the stream was grateful to him. It cooled his throbbing head, and he drank it in at his hot lips. The scene, too, had, without his being well sensible of it, a secret fascination. The village was sunk in the profoundest slumber, not a mortal stirring, not a sound afloat, a soft haze covered it all, and the fairy moonlight hovered over the entire landscape.

In a state between rumination and rapture, Peter continued to lean over the battlements of the old bridge, and as he did so he saw, or fancied he saw, emerging one after another along the river-bank in the little gardens and enclosures in the rear of the street of Chapelizod, the queerest little white-washed huts and cabins he had ever seen there before. They had not been there that evening when he passed the bridge on the way to his merry tryst. But the most remarkable thing about it was the odd way in which these quaint little cabins showed themselves.

First he saw one or two of them just with the corner of his eye, and when he looked full at them, strange to say, they faded away and disappeared. Then another and another came in view, but all in the same coy way, just appearing and gone again before he could well fix his gaze upon them; in a little while, however, they began to bear a fuller gaze, and he found, as it seemed to himself, that he was able to by an effort of attention to fix the vision for a longer and a longer time, and when they waxed faint and nearly vanished he had the power of recalling them into light and substance, until at last their vacillating indistinctness became less and less, and they assumed a permanent place in the moonlit landscape.

'Be the hokey,' said Peter, lost in amazement, and dropping his pipe into the river unconsciously, 'them is the quarist bits iv mud cabins I ever seen, growing up like musharoons in the dew of an evening, and poppin' up here and down again there, and up again in another place, like so many white rabbits in a warren; and there they stand at last as firm and fast as if they were there from the deluge; bedad it's enough to make a man a'most believe in the fairies.'

This latter was a large concession from Peter, who was a bit of a freethinker, and spoke contemptuously in his ordinary conversation of that class of agencies.

Having treated himself to a long last stare at these mysterious fabrics, Peter prepared to pursue his homeward way; having crossed the bridge and passed the mill, he arrived at the corner of the main street of the little town, and casting a careless look up the Dublin road, his eye was arrested by a most unexpected spectacle.

There was no other than a column of foot-soldiers, marching with perfect regularity towards the village, and headed by an officer on horseback. They were at the far side of the turnpike, which was closed; but much to his perplexity he perceived that they marched on through it without appearing to sustain the least check from that barrier.

On they came at a slow march; and what was most singular in the matter was, that they were drawing several cannons along with them; some held ropes, others spoked the wheels, and others again marched in front of the guns and behind them, with muskets shouldered, giving a stately character of parade and regularity to this, as it seemed to Peter, most unmilitary procedure.

It was owing either to some temporary defect in Peter's vision, or to some illusion attendant upon mist and moonlight, or perhaps to some other cause, that the whole procession had a certain waving and va-poury character which perplexed and tasked his eyes not a little. It was like the pictured pageant of a phantasmagoria reflected upon smoke. It was as if every breath disturbed it; sometimes it was blurred, sometimes obliterated; now here, now there. Sometimes, while the upper part was quite distinct, the legs of the column would nearly fade away or vanish outright, and then again they would come out into clear relief, marching on with measured tread, while the cocked hats and shoulders grew, as it were, transparent, and all but disappeared.

Notwithstanding these strange optical fluctuations, however, the column continued steadily to advance. Peter crossed the street from the corner near the old bridge, running on tip-toe, and with his body stopped to avoid observation, and took up a position upon the raised footpath in the shadow of the houses, where, as the soldiers kept the middle of the road, he calculated that he might, himself undetected, see them distinctly enough as they passed.

'What the div——, what on airth,' he muttered, checking the irreligious ejaculation with which he was about to start, for certain queer misgivings were hovering about his heart, notwithstanding the artificial courage of the whisky bottle. 'What on airth is the manin' of all this? Is it the French that's landed at last to give us a hand and help us in airnest to this blessed repale? If it is not them, I simply ask who the div——, I mane who on airth are they, for such sogers as them I never seen before in my born days?'

By this time the foremost of them were quite near, and truth to say they were the queerest soldiers he had ever seen in the course of his life. They wore long gaiters and leather breeches, three-cornered hats bound with silver lace, long blue coats with scarlet facings and linings, which latter were sewn by a fastening which held together the two opposite corners of the skirt behind; and in front the breasts were in like manner connected at a single point, where and below which they sloped back, disclosing a long-flapped waistcoat of snowy whiteness; they had very large, long cross-belts, and wore enormous pouches of white leather hung extraordinarily low, and on each of which a little silver star was glittering.

But what struck him as most grotesque and outlandish in their costume was their extraordinary display of shirt-frill in front, and of ruffle

231

about their wrists, and the stranger manner in which their hair was frizzled out and powdered under their hats, and clubbed up into great rolls behind. But one of the party was mounted. He rode a tall white horse, with high action and arching neck; he had a snow-white feather in this three-cornered hat, and his coat was shimmering all over with a profusion of silver lace. From these circumstances Peter concluded that he must be the commander of the detachment, and examined him attentively as he passed. He was a slight, tall man, whose legs did not half fill his leather breeches, and he appeared to be at the wrong side of sixty. He had a shrunken, weather-beaten, mulberry-coloured face, carried a large black patch over one eye, and turned neither to the right nor to the left, but rode on at the head of his men, with a grim, military inflexibility.

The countenances of these soldiers, officers as well as men, seemed all full of trouble, and, so to speak, scared and wild. He watched in vain for a single contented or comely face. They had, one and all, a melancholy and hang-dog look; and as they passed by, Peter fancied that the air grew cold.

He had seated himself upon a stone bench, from which, staring with all his might, he gazed upon the grotesque and noiseless procession as it filed by him. Noiseless it was; he could neither hear the jingle of accoutrements, the tread of feet, nor the rumble of the wheels; and when the old colonel turned his horse a little, and made as though he were giving the word of command, and a trumpeter, with a swollen blue nose and white feather fringe round his hat, who was walking beside him, turned about and put his bugle to his lips, still Peter heard nothing, although it was plain the sound had reached the soldiers, for they instantly changed their front to three abreast.

'Botheration!' muttered Peter, 'is it deaf I'm growing?'

But that could not be, for he heard the sighing of the breeze and the rush of the neighbouring Liffey plain enough.

'Well,' said he, in the same cautious key, 'by the piper, this bangs Banagher fairly! It's either the French Army that's in it, come to take the town iv Chapelizod by surprise, an' makin' no noise for feard iv wakenin' the inhabitants; or else it's—it's—what it's—somethin' else. But, tundher-an-ouns, what's gone wrong wid Fitzpatrick's shop across the way?'

The brown dingy stone building at the opposite side of the street looked newer and cleaner than he had been used to see it; the front door of it stood open, and a sentry in the same grotesque uniform, with shouldered musket, was pacing noiselessly to and fro before it. At the angle of this building, in like manner, a wide gate (of which Peter had no recollection whatever) stood open, before which, also, a similar sentry was gliding and into this gateway the whole column gradually passed, and Peter finally lost sight of it.

'I'm not asleep; I'm not dhramin',' said he, rubbing his eyes, and stamping slightly on the pavement, to assure himself that he was wide awake. 'It is a quare business, whatever it is; an' it's not alone that, but everything about the town looks strange to me. There's Tresham's house new painted, bedad, an' them flowers in the windies! An' Delaney's house, too, that had not a whole pane of glass in it this morning, and scarce a slate on the roof of it! It is not possible it's that it's dhrunk I am. Sure there's the big tree, and not a leaf of it changed since I passed, and the stars overhead, all right. I don't think it is in my eyes it is.'

And so looking about him, and every moment finding or fancying new food for wonder, he walked along the pavement, intending, without further delay, to make his way home.

But his adventures for the night were not concluded. He had nearly reached the angle of the short lane that leads up to the church, when for the first time he perceived that an officer, in the uniform he had just seen, was walking before, only a few yards in advance of him.

The officer was walking along at an easy, swinging gait, and carried his sword under his arm, and was looking down on the pavement with an air of reverie.

In the very fact that he seemed unconscious of Peter's presence, and disposed to keep his reflection to himself, there was something reassuring. Besides, the reader must please to remember that our hero had a sufficient quantity of good punch before his adventure commenced, and was thus fortified against those qualms and terrors under which, in a more reasonable state of mind, he might not impossibly have sunk.

The idea of the French invasion revived in full power in Peter's fuddled imagination, as he pursued the nonchalant swagger of the officer.

'Be the powers iv Molly Kelly, I'll ax him what it is,' said Peter, with a sudden accession of rashness. 'He may tell me or not, as he plases, but he can't be offinded, anyhow.'

With this reflection having inspired himself, Peter cleared his voice and begun:

'Captain!' said he, 'I ax your pardon, an' maybe you'd be so condescindin' to my ignorance as to tell me, if it's plasin' to yer honour, whether your honour is not a Frenchman, if it's plasin' to you.'

This he asked, not thinking that, had it been as he suspected, not one word of his question in all probability would have been intelligible to the person he addressed. He was, however, understood, for the officer answered him in English, at the same time slackening his pace and moving a little to the side of the pathway, as if to invite his interrogator to take his place beside him.

'No; I am an Irishman,' he answered.

'I humbly thank your honour,' said Peter, drawing nearer—for the affability and the nativity of the officer encouraged him—'but maybe your honour is in the sarvice of the King of France?'

'I serve the same king as you do,' he answered, with a sorrowful significance which Peter did not comprehend at the time; and, interrogating in turn, he asked, 'But what calls you forth at this hour of the day?'

'The day, your honour!—the night, you mane.'

'It was always our way to turn night into day, and we keep to it still,' remarked the soldier. 'But no matter, come up here to my house; I have a job for you, if you wish to earn some money easily. I live here.'

As he said this, he beckoned authoritatively to Peter, who followed almost mechanically at his heels, and they turned up a little lane near the old Roman Catholic chapel, at the end of which stood, in Peter's time, the ruins of a tall, stone-built house.

Like everything else in the town, it had suffered a metamorphosis. The stained and ragged walls were now erect, perfect, and covered with pebble-dash; window-panes glittered coldly in every window; the green hall-door had a bright knocker on it. Peter did not know whether to believe his previous or his present impressions: seeing is believing, and Peter could not dispute the reality of the scene. All the records of his memory seemed but the images of a tipsy dream. In a trance of astonishment and perplexity, therefore, he submitted himself to the chances of his adventure.

The door opened, the officer beckoned with a melancholy air of authority to Peter, and entered. Our hero followed him into a sort of hall, which was very dark, but he was guided by the steps of the soldier, and, in silence, they ascended the stairs. The moonlight, which shone in at the lobbies, showed an old, dark wainscoting, and a heavy, oak banister. They passed by closed doors at different landing-places, but all was dark and silent as, indeed, became that late hour of the night.

Now they ascended to the topmost floor. The captain paused for a minute at the nearest door, and, with a heavy groan, pushing it open, entered the room. Peter remained at the threshold. A slight female form in a sort of loose, white robe, and with a great deal of dark hair hanging loosely about her, was standing in the middle of the floor with her back towards them.

The soldier stopped short before he reached her, and said, in a voice of great anguish, 'Still the same, sweet bird—sweet bird! Still the same.' Whereupon, she turned suddenly, and threw her arms about the neck of the officer, with a gesture of fondness and despair, and her frame was agitated as if by a burst of sobs. He held her close to his breast in silence; and honest Peter felt a strange terror creep over him, as he witnessed these mysterious sorrows and endearments.

'Tonight, tonight—and then ten years more—ten long years—another ten years.'

The officer and the lady seemed to speak these words together; her voice mingled with his in a musical and fearful wail, like a distant summer wind, in the dead hour of night wandering through ruins. Then he heard the officer say, alone in a voice of anguish:

'Upon me be it all, for ever, sweet birdie, upon me.'

And again they seemed to mourn together in the same soft and desolate wail, like sounds of grief heard from a great distance.

Peter was thrilled with horror, but he was also under a strange fascination, and an intense and dreadful curiosity held him fast.

The moon was shining obliquely into the room, and through the window Peter saw the familiar slopes of the Park, sleeping mistily under its shimmer. He could also see the furniture of the room with tolerable distinctness—the old balloon-backed chairs, a four-post bed in a sort of recess, and a rack against the wall, from which hung some military clothes and accoutrements; and the sight of all these homely

235

objects reassured him somewhat and he could not help feeling unspeakably curious to see the face of the girl whose long hair was streaming over the officer's epaulet.

Peter, accordingly, coughed, at first slightly, and afterward more loudly, to recall her from her reverie of grief, and, apparently, he succeeded; for she turned round, as did her companion, and both, standing hand in hand, gazed upon him fixedly. He thought he had never seen such large, strange eyes in all his life; and their gaze seemed to chill the very air around him, and arrest the pulses of his heart. An eternity of misery and remorse was in the shadowy faces that looked upon him.

If Peter had taken less whisky by a single thimbleful, it is probable that he would have lost heart altogether before these figures, which seemed every moment to assume a more marked and fearful, though hardly definable, contrast to ordinary human shapes.

'What is it you want with me?' he stammered.

'To bring my lost treasure to the churchyard,' replied the lady, in a silvery voice of more than mortal desolation.

The word 'treasure' revived the resolution of Peter, although a cold sweat was covering him, and his hair was bristling with horror; he believed, however, that he was on the brink of fortune, if he could but command nerve to brave the interview to its close.

'And where,' he gasped, 'is it hid—where will I find it?'

They both pointed to the sill of the window, through which the moon was shining at the far end of the room, and the soldier said:

'Under that stone.'

Peter drew a long breath, and wiped the cold dew from his face, preparatory to passing to the window, where he expected to secure the reward of his protracted errors. But looking steadfastly at the window, he saw the faint image of a new-born child sitting upon the sill in the moonlight, with its little arms stretched toward him, and a smile so heavenly as he never beheld before.

At sight of this, strange to say, his heart entirely failed him, he looked on the figures that stood near, and beheld them gazing on the infantine form with a smile so guilty and distorted, that he felt as if he were entering alive among the scenery of hell, and, shuddering, he cried in an irrepressible agony of horror:

'I'll have nothing to say with you, and nothing to do with you; I

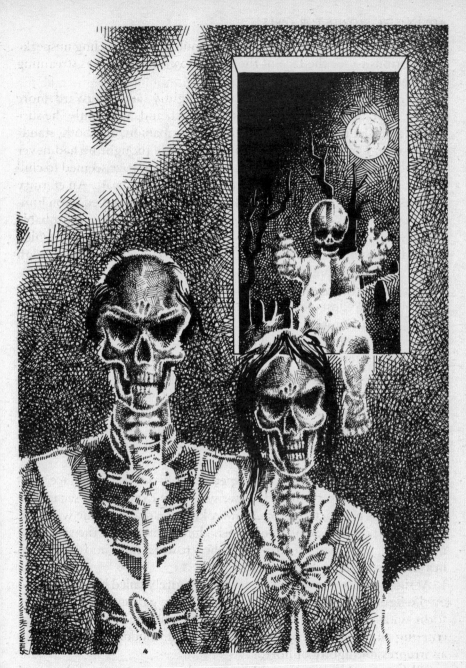

He saw the faint image of a new-born child.

don't know what yez are or what yez want iv me, but let me go this minute, every one of yez, in the name of God.'

With these words there came a strange rumbling and sighing about Peter's ears; he lost sight of everything, and felt that peculiar and not unpleasant sensation of falling softly, that sometimes supervenes in sleep, ending in a dull shock. After that he had neither dream nor consciousness till he wakened, chill and stiff, stretched between two piles of old rubbish, among the black and roofless walls of the ruined house. We need hardly mention that the village had put on its wonted air of neglect and decay, or that Peter looked around him in vain for traces of those novelties which had so puzzled and distracted him upon the previous night.

'Ay, ay,' said his grandmother, removing her pipe, as he ended his description of the view from the bridge, 'sure enough I remember myself, when I was a slip of a girl, these little white cabins among the gardens by the river-side. The artillery sogers that was married, or had not room in the barracks, used to be in them, but they're all gone long ago.'

'The Lord be merciful to us!' she resumed, when he had described the military procession, 'it's often I seen the regiment marchin' into the town, just as you saw it last night, acushla. Oh, voch, but it makes my heart sore to think iv them days; they were pleasant times, sure enough; but is not it terrible, avick, to think it's what it was the ghost of the rigiment you seen? The Lord betune us an' harm, for it was nothing else, as sure as I'm sittin' here.'

When he mentioned the peculiar figure of the old officer who rode at the head of the regiment:

'That,' said the old crone, dogmatically, 'was ould Colonel Grimshaw, the Lord preserve us! He's buried in the churchard iv Chapelizod, and well I remember him, when I was a young thing, an' a cross ould floggin' fellow he was wid the men, an' a devil's boy among the girls— rest his soul!'

'Amen!' said Peter; 'it's often I read his tombstone myself; but he's a long time dead.'

'Sure, I tell you he died when I was no more nor a slip iv a girl—the Lord betune us and harm!'

'I'm afeard it is what I'm not long for this world myself, afther seeing such a sight as that,' said Peter fearfully.

'Nonsense, avourneen,' retorted his grandmother, indignantly, though she had herself misgivings on the subject; 'sure there was Phil Doolan, the ferryman, that seen black Ann Scanlan in his own boat, and what harm ever kem of it?'

Peter proceeded with his narrative, but when he came to the description of the house, in which his adventure had had so sinister a conclusion, the old woman was at fault.

'I know the house and the ould walls well, an' I can remember the time there was a roof on it, and the doors an' windows in it, but it had a bad name about being haunted, but by who, or for what, I forget intirely.'

'Did you ever hear was there gold or silver there?' he inquired.

'No, no, avick, don't be thinking about the likes; take a fool's advice, and never go next or near them ugly black walls again the longest day you have to live; an' I'd take my davy, it's what it's the same word the priest himself I'd be afther sayin' to you if you wor to ax his raverence consarnin' it, for it's plain to be seen it was nothing good you seen there, and there's neither luck nor grace about it.'

Peter's adventure made no little noise in the neighbourhood, as the reader may well suppose; and a few evenings after it, being on an errand to old Major Vandeleur, who lived in a snug old-fashioned house, close by the river, under a perfect bower of ancient trees, he was called on to relate the story in the parlour.

The Major was, as I have said, an old man; he was small, lean, and upright, with a mahogany complexion, and a wooden inflexibility of face; he was a man, besides, of few words, and if he was old, it follows plainly that his mother was older still. Nobody could guess or tell how old, but it was admitted that her own generation had long passed away, and that she had not a competitor left. She had French blood in her veins, and although she did not retain her charms quite so well as Ninon de l'Enclos, she was in full possession of all her mental activity, and talked quite enough for herself and the Major.

'So, Peter,' she said, 'you have seen the dear old Royal Irish again in the streets of Chapelizod. Make him a tumbler of punch, Frank; and Peter, sit down, and while you take it let us have the story.'

Peter accordingly, seated near the door, with a tumbler of the nectarian stimulant steaming beside him, proceeded with marvellous courage, considering they had no light but the uncertain glare of the fire, to relate with minute particularity his awful adventure. The old lady listened at first with a smile of good-natured incredulity; her cross-examination touching the drinking-bout at Palmerstown had been teasing, but as the narrative proceeded she became attentive, and at length absorbed, and once or twice she uttered ejaculations of pity or awe. When it was over, the old lady looked with a somewhat sad and stern abstraction on the table, patting her cat assiduously meanwhile, and then suddenly looking upon her son, the Major, she said:

'Frank, as sure as I live, he has seen the wicked Captain Devereux.'

The major uttered an inarticulate expression of wonder.

'The house was precisely that he had described. I have told you the story often, as I heard it from your dear grandmother, about the poor young lady he ruined, and the dreadful suspicion about the little baby. She, poor thing, died in that house heartbroken, and you know he was shot shortly after in a duel.'

This was the only light that Peter ever received respecting his adventure. It was supposed, however, that he still clung to the hope that treasure of some sort was hidden about the old house, for he was often seen lurking about its walls, and at last his fate overtook him, poor fellow, in the pursuit; for climbing near the summit one day, his holding gave way, and he fell upon the hard uneven ground, fracturing a leg and a rib, and after a short interval died; he, like the other heroes of these true tales, lies buried in the little churchyard of Chapelizod.

JOAN OF ARC
Mollie Hardwick

The slim, dark-haired girl lifted her head with a puzzled frown on her almost boyish face, and looked everywhere around. She was quite alone in the garden, and yet she could hear a voice—as clearly as though someone were standing right beside her.

She listened more intently. There it was again! She had heard it before, telling her then that her mother wanted her to go indoors; but when she had obeyed she found that she had not been summoned at all.

Where could the voice be coming from? Perhaps she had been working too long in the sun and was getting dizzy from the heat? She dropped the hoe she had been using and walked towards the shade of her father's farmhouse. The disembodied voice followed her, a soothing, peaceful, melodic sound repeating her name over and over—'Joan . . . Joan . . .'

The girl was Joan of Arc, and she was now thirteen years old. She had lived all her life in the village of Domrémy, in the province of Lorraine in eastern France. Although her father was quite a prosperous farmer she could not read or write; but she could cook and sew and spin, and help in the fields. She was strong-minded and intelligent, and differed from the other village children in that instead of playing games she liked to sit alone in the peace of the little church.

Joan soon grew used to hearing the strange voice. Sometimes there seemed to be others, and all had the same message: that she must be good, take care of herself, and attend church regularly. She decided they must be angels speaking to her, and began to wonder if she had been specially chosen to fulfil an ancient prophesy she knew of—that France would one day be saved by a girl from Lorraine.

At this time, 1425, France had been at war with England for years. Large areas of the country were occupied by English soldiers. Villages were continually being raided and destroyed, causing widespread misery and suffering. The more Joan listened to her 'voices', as she called them, the more she became convinced that she was the girl destined to save France.

No one believed her when she first told her family and friends. And when strange visions started appearing to her no one believed her account of them, either. This was when she was sixteen. They were misty and indistinct at first, she said, but later she recognized one of the figures as the Archangel Michael. He was dressed in a suit of gleaming armour, and beside him stood the two patron saints of Lorraine, St Margaret and St Catherine.

Joan's family could not decide whether she was ill, or trying to frighten them with such fanciful stories—particularly when, one day, she told them that her voices had given her a new message. She had been chosen by God to drive the English from France, to lead the army to victory and secure the throne for the Dauphin—the title borne by the eldest son of the kings of France. This one, Charles, had actually succeeded to the throne in 1416, when he was only thirteen, but the war with England and civil strife in the provinces had so far prevented his coronation as Charles VII.

'Daughter of God,' Joan claimed she had been told, 'go to the town of Vaucouleurs and seek out the commander, Robert de Baudricourt. He will provide you with soldiers to take you to the Dauphin.'

Joan was now seventeen years old, a small girl, only five feet two inches tall, but strong and healthy and quite used to walking the distance it took to reach the neighbouring town of Vaucouleurs. Here she enlisted the help of an uncle and, through him, arranged an interview with Robert de Baudricourt. In her patched red dress she stood before the powerful commander and told him her story. At first he was furious at having his valuable time wasted with such 'nonsense'. He said her father should box her ears to knock a little sense into her.

Undeterred, Joan persisted in her request for his help, and her obvious sincerity impressed the tough, professional soldier. He began to wonder whether she might not, after all, be telling the truth. This was an age of deep superstition and credulity, when people believed in all kinds of miracles and wonders. If Joan really had been sent by God to save France, reasoned de Baudricourt, it would be wrong to hinder her. Besides, the army had just suffered another defeat and morale among the soldiers was very low. The message brought by this simple country girl might put fresh heart into them.

So, just as her voices had told her, Joan set out to see the Dauphin with an escort provided by the commander. She had changed her appearance for the journey: in place of the red gown she wore trousers and shirt, and her dark hair had been cropped short, so that she looked even more like a boy.

'God told me to wear a man's clothing because I am to carry a man's weapons. If I am dressed as a man among men, they will treat me as one of themselves and thus I will be able to preserve my chastity, both of spirit and body.'

The journey was a long and dangerous one, covering more than two hundred miles across battle territory. Joan's destination was the city of Chinon, near Tours, where the Dauphin had set up his court. Charles was a sickly, timid young man who relied heavily on the advice of his counsellors, only rousing himself by fits and starts. But he was extremely pious, and very superstitious, and when he learned of Joan's arrival in Chinon and the purpose of her journey he was only too ready to grant her an audience.

But to test her, he disguised himself as a courtier while another man took his place on the throne. It is part of the legend surrounding Joan of Arc that when she arrived in the audience chamber—a slight, travel-stained figure in contrast with the jewel-encrusted noblemen surrounding her—she turned from the throne and immediately singled out the Dauphin. Kneeling before him she cried out, 'Sire, I have been sent by God to bring help to the kingdom and to tell you that you are the true heir to France!'

243

Charles believed her. His counsellors advised him to be cautious until they had questioned this strange girl, but in the end they too were convinced. Joan told them that her first task was to drive the English from the besieged city of Orléans. Two months earlier, in February 1429, the enemy had encircled it, and if they succeeded in capturing it the whole of southern France would be soon overrun. Joan was placed at the head of an army of three thousand men. By this time rumour of her mission, of her voices and visions of saints, had spread among the soldiers. They hailed her as the saviour of France, calling her *La Pucelle*—The Maid.

Before beginning the expedition she sent a message to the English, ordering them to withdraw from the towns they had captured. 'If you do not,' she warned, 'know that I am military leader and wherever I find your soldiers I shall chase them out of France whether they wish to go or not.'

There was no reply. The English leaders could not believe that a mere girl of seventeen could be appointed head of an army—unless she had used witchcraft to enchant the Dauphin and his counsellors. They had already heard how she had apparently been led to the lost sword of the

She rode at the head of the army towards Orléans and the English soldiers . . .

244

old French hero, Charles Martel, discovered where Joan said it would be, buried behind the altar of a small church. When her battle steed, one of the massively powerful horses used at that time, had reared up and refused to let her mount, she led him to the market cross and the horse had quietened immediately.

To the English these stories sounded like sorcery. The French soldiers were inspired by them and their devotion to The Maid deepened with each fresh account of her power. To them she appeared 'a thing wholly divine' as she rode at the head of the army towards Orléans. The Dauphin had presented her with a suit of white armour, over which she wore a surcoat of scarlet and silver, and at her side fluttered her personal banner embroidered with the figure of Christ.

The army commanders were not so easily impressed. They were still smarting from the humiliation of having to take orders from a mere girl, and plotted to sabotage her plans by leading her to the wrong side of the River Loire. The soldiers could not cross over because the wind was blowing against them; yet no sooner had Joan arrived than it changed direction and the entire army was able to reach the city. The

French saw this as yet another sign of her holy power; the English interpreted it as further proof of diabolical witchcraft.

The battle to drive the enemy from Orléans lasted over two days of bitter fighting. Wherever the fray was thickest Joan's banner could be seen as she encouraged her soldiers forward. They fought with such ferocity that the English were finally forced to retreat. Her victory was regarded as nothing less than a miracle, and the legends about her redoubled. A white dove carrying a crown of gold was said to have alighted on her banner; angelic warriors were seen galloping across the sky; divine signs were rumoured to have been observed at the moment of her birth.

The English called her 'disciple and bloodhound of the Devil' and 'the fiend of France'. Their hatred and fear of her increased even more after she won a further resounding victory against them at Patay and captured some of their leading knights. Within a short time they had been driven from all the towns they had taken in the Loire district, and were forced to retreat to Paris.

Joan was now able to fulfil her promise to place the Dauphin on the throne. She rode at his side on the long journey to Rheims, and stood by the high altar in the cathedral as he knelt to receive the crown and be declared Charles VII of France. Her job was done, her mission completed. Her father had come to fetch her, and now she could go home.

But it was not to be. The new king still wanted her to lead his forces, and reluctantly Joan had to obey him. But she no longer heard voices, no longer saw visions of the saints. Although during the months that followed she took part in many skirmishes against the English, her inspiration seemed to have gone. She was beginning to show signs of fatigue. An attempt to drive the English out of Paris failed miserably. As she lay wounded by an arrow, her soldiers scattering before the overwhelming forces of the enemy, she felt intuitively that it would not be long before she was taken prisoner. Her intuition was right.

In May 1430, during an attack on Compiègne, Joan was captured by soldiers of the Duke of Burgundy, an ally of the English. In exchange for ten thousand livres she was handed over to her enemies to stand trial for witchcraft and heresy. She was taken to the English-held city of Rouen, where, during a long and arduous interrogation, she was treated with great cruelty by her captors. She was not allowed to attend

Mass, and was kept chained to a wooden stake in an underground cell.

At the end of March 1431, Joan was found guilty of the charges made against her. She was condemned to be burned to death. Her king, Charles VII, for whom her inspired deeds had won his throne, did nothing to intercede for her. She was only nineteen years old when, on 30 May, she died agonizingly at the stake in the market-place of Rouen. As the flames were lit around her an English soldier thrust a rough wooden cross into her hands. When it was all over, her ashes were thrown into the River Seine.

In 1456 Pope Calixtus III formally pronounced Joan to be innocent of all the charges made against her. In 1920 she was canonized as St Joan of Arc and became the national saint of France. Each year, on the anniversary of her death, young girls in white garments strew flowers on the waters of the Seine at Rouen, at the spot where her ashes were scattered so unceremoniously by her enemies.

Whatever the truth of her seemingly mystic gifts, her story has always served as the inspiration for French patriotism. She did not win that long war—the Hundred Years War—but her countrymen gained new heart from her example and fought at last as one nation, undivided by old feuds and jealousies. To Napoleon and others since she has been the symbol of France's ability to survive threat and even defeat.

ATTACK ON THE TAKAO

Commander John Kerans

'Start her up!' said Lieutenant Ian Fraser, almost as conversationally as though he had said: 'Pass the sugar, please.' Except that he didn't say please because he was giving an order and except that he didn't really feel so remarkably casual because they were just setting out on a suicide mission.

'They' comprised Sub-Lieutenant W. J. 'Kiwi' Smith, a New Zealander, who was a particular friend of Fraser's, Leading Seaman J. J. 'Mick' Magennis, a burly Irishman, and Engine Room Artificer Charles Reed, a quiet, dedicated young man who could be relied upon to stay calm in the most desperate situation. And they were likely to be faced with just such a situation because their current mission was to penetrate Japanese-occupied Singapore Harbour in a midget submarine and blow up the 10,000-ton battle-cruiser *Takao*!

It was late July 1945. The Japanese had been smashed by the British in Burma, and the destruction of the formidable *Takao* had to be effected in readiness for the coming attack on Malaya and Singapore. The *XE-3*, as the tiny submarine was designated, was less than fifty feet long, no more than six feet in diameter. It had just been towed 1,400 miles by

248

the British submarine *Stygian*, for it was capable of making only short voyages—very short one-way trips, was what some Royal Navy men predicted. It had been specially constructed for the hair-raising task of creeping through mine curtains, passing sound locators, slipping past close-patrolling destroyers, anti-submarine boats and searching aircraft. Throughout the long tow from the base at Labuan Island, near Borneo, the men now in the *XE-3* had been passengers in the *Stygian*. The toy-like *XE-3*, stringing along behind at the end of a thin steel cable, had been manned by a 'ferrying' crew so that the fighting crew could keep fresh for the hazards ahead.

The change-round had been effected forty miles out to sea from Singapore. In the sort of silence that prompts men to talk in whispers a rubber dinghy had left the *Stygian* and Fraser, Smith, Magennis and Reed had paddled over to the *XE-3*. They had crossed the wide silver pathway the great lantern of a moon had spread down across the flat calm sea, had changed places with the ferry crew ('Rather you than me, chum, any day!' one of them had murmured) and said their farewells. They were ready to go into action. The compact diesel engine throbbed into life, and they were under way.

In the constricted space available to the crew Fraser, the captain, sat slightly above the others. The three roughly equal sections into which the *XE-3* was divided contained ballast and trim tanks forward, batteries for running submerged amidships, reserve fuel for the diesel and various necessary stores. Cramped crew quarters were just under the forward escape-hatch and airlock. There sat Magennis, with the charts, Reed just behind him, Fraser up at the periscope, and then Smith operating the engine controls, hydroplanes and pump. Into the compartment immediately behind Smith were packed the main ballast tank, the fresh-water tank, a diminutive hot-plate for cooking and the air-cooler and pumping plant. There was no room for their powerful explosive charges to be carried within the submarine so they were attached each side of the deck on the hull outside.

The *XE-3* was not the sort of submarine that destroyed its victims from a distance with torpedoes. Mick Magennis was there to do what a torpedo usually did. He was their frogman, their spearhead. Once they had located and gone right up against their target, Magennis would attach time-fused explosive charges so devastating they would rip out

249

its bottom. A man of tremendous physical strength and a prodigious swimmer, he was fearless and determined, a splendid man to have on such a desperate mission. The cool courage of young Reed, coxswain of the midget sub, was also the right sort for the job. As for 'Kiwi' Smith, there was not much Fraser did not know about him and his absolute reliability and level-headedness, which was why he had chosen him. The four men comprised a splendidly-balanced team, precisely what was needed if such a hazardous operation were to stand any chance of success.

The *XE-3* cruised steadily through the moon glitter towards Singapore, her diesel throbbing quietly, a filmy wake fanning out behind her. Fraser was not too happy about the moon but knew it could work both ways; it was likely to help him see an enemy warship before the enemy could spot him. He was standing up in the conning tower, his powerful nightglasses searching the way ahead. The chart Intelligence had produced showed that the first minefield of Singapore's outer defences should come up before them after one hour's sailing. Fraser knew he would then be glad of the moonlight. Although he had been warned of the location of some of the minefields, there were some that had not been charted. Nearer the great harbour these would be more numerous, and so would the patrolling anti-submarine vessels.

Before the *XE-3* could penetrate to the inner harbour where the *Takao* lay, they would also have to slide beneath, or in some way pass, a series of widely-spread anti-submarine nets. Beyond, the harbour itself would surely be busy with all manner of vessels, any one of which might spot their periscope as they came up to observe. If they remained submerged, they would still be liable to be seen, a dark shape against the pale bottom, as they negotiated the shallower parts of the harbour. Moreover, with blind navigation there were the attendant perils of running into sandbanks, into minefields, or fouling anti-submarine nets. One way or another, it did not seem to be an operation with a lot of future in it! The plan was that the attack should be made in broad daylight, however, and Fraser and his crew had worked out the moves and gone over them again and again. They did at least have an accurate, detailed chart of Singapore Harbour's natural features and mud-banks, and these they had memorized.

They entered the first minefield with cold-blooded deliberation.

Every so often Fraser sighted the ugly, horned shape of a mine wallowing just below the surface and directed Reed to steer past it. The exact pattern and density of the minefield was impossible to gauge, so it was a case of feeling their way all the time. Never for a moment could vigilance be relaxed. Shortly before three a.m. Fraser had to take a chance—a Japanese tanker with an armed escort appeared ahead and there was nothing for it but to dive. They gave the enemy ship half an hour to get clear and then surfaced again. Fraser opened the conning tower and looked out.

Although he was horrified at what he saw his even tones did not betray it. 'Just take us down again a little bit, will you Kiwi?' he said with studied politeness. 'We seem to be resting right against the spikes of a mine.' The three men inside held their breath for agonizing seconds as the little submarine gently subsided a few feet down, clear of the mine. The hush was broken by Fraser, who grinned and said: 'It's okay. It didn't go off.'

The agony of the minefield continued for nearly three hours, and then they were clear. Luck seemed to be with them and they knew they could not have too much of it. It made them feel better to think they were lucky.

The dawn was suddenly upon them in all the startling beauty of the East and the sun began to climb visibly to heat the new day. A little flock of flying fish arose from the rosy sea, passed close to the submarine like strange, flickering birds, and as abruptly vanished into the water. It was so peaceful and warm and friendly it was hard to realize every minute of this gentle cruising took them steadily towards terrible danger. A blur on the horizon swelled and became substantial, until it was identifiable as land. Then it became land with a city upon it, and soon the great port of Singapore was right before them. The sun shimmered on the white buildings, bathed docks and waterfront and trees in its brilliance; it did not look like a place of such peril, where so much stark cruelty existed.

It was 10.30 that morning before anything occurred to disrupt the peace. Then the stubby, menacing shape of an armed Japanese trawler loomed. Fraser knew that this was the vessel guarding the gateway through the first anti-submarine net. 'Take us down,' he ordered softly. The XE-3 submerged, slanted down to the bottom. 'We'll stay here for a bit, it's time to rest anyway,' Fraser said. They munched biscuits for breakfast, not one of them having a hearty appetite under the circumstances.

Magennis began to move about quietly, laying out his frogman suit and equipment ready for action. 'I should think it's about time I started net-cutting, isn't it, sir?' the big Irishman queried. 'I reckon it is,' replied Fraser.

The first of their frightening dangers was confronting them. They had been warned the Japanese might have wired their anti-submarine nets so that alarms would stridently proclaim the presence of any interloper attempting to sneak through. Would what Magennis was about to do swiftly bring down upon them a holocaust of depth-charges and bombs, set the sea churning with hunting vessels and the air throbbing with searching planes? The tense silence in which each man thought about this was broken by Fraser. 'It would probably be a good idea to wait for a ship, sneak right up to the gate behind it, and then slip under the guardship,' he said. 'There'd be no need for Mick to get out then.'

Kiwi Smith consulted his chart. 'It's a bit shallow,' he observed. 'I make it to be thirty-five feet deep with a light sandy bottom.' They looked at each other; they all knew that under such conditions the submarine could be quite clearly visible to any searching vessel or plane above. But they also knew the most audacious plan very often succeeded just because the enemy would not be expecting it. 'Say, now, if any of you can see any real reason why we shouldn't do that,' Fraser said. The others, tight little grins on their lips, shook their heads without speaking, so Fraser ordered quietly: 'Action stations. Mick, tell me the moment anything is overhead.'

For some minutes there was complete silence as they lay waiting. Then, 'There's a good-sized ship above us, sir, heading into the harbour,' came Magennis' soft, urgent report. 'Up to periscope depth,' ordered Fraser evenly. With the tell-tale protrusion of their periscope above the flat, glittering sea for the eyes of any keen watcher to pick out, they hovered just beneath the surface. The silence intensified as Fraser moved his body slightly one way, then the other, scanning the sparkling world above. 'Down to thirty feet,' he ordered. 'The guard trawler is dead overhead!'

XE-3 dropped gently down until the gauge showed thirty feet; she began to slide silently forward. Each man concentrated on his immediate duties as though trying to keep his mind from picturing the scene, a scene in which they featured so prominently—a moving merchant ship with them just below and behind, a spreading submarine net dead ahead of them, and an armed trawler, depth-charges ready on its decks and its lookouts scanning around, dead above them. Over all, a blazing sun, its brilliant rays penetrating to the bottom of the shallow sea, its dancing light reflected from the sandy bottom to make the midget sub stand out like an identification silhouette . . .

'Let's bump the bottom Kiwi,' Fraser suddenly broke the silence. Smith tipped the hydroplanes and they gently subsided. There came the faint jar of contact with the sea floor. The depth gauge now stood at thirty-seven feet. Fraser considered for a moment, then said: 'Bring her up just a few feet and don't worry if we do bump again. We'll bump our way along the bottom until we're through.' And so they did. Directly under the dark shadow of the guardship, from which the almond eyes of Japanese searchers should have been watching for submarines, the little *XE-3* slipped through. Every breathless second the four men expected the shock of the first underwater explosion that would set off a cataclysm around them. But there was nothing, not even the sound of engines anywhere above, to indicate that a search was being made.

Cautiously the little submarine rose towards the surface; the periscope was inched up until it emerged making hardly a ripple. 'We're inside all right!' exclaimed Fraser, peering intently. 'Down to twenty feet.' Again *XE-3* gently subsided and began to creep forward into the crowded harbour. From now on they knew they would be constantly passed over by ships and in danger of discovery by anyone aboard who might casually glance down into the sea and observe their suspicious dark shadow against the sandy sea floor. Even greater would be the danger of discovery when they occasionally near-surfaced, as they must do, to make a visual check of their whereabouts through the periscope. Added to this, there was the difficulty of sighting their target through the bustle of shipping, both large and small, in the harbour basin. The men remained silent, each contemplating his own particular job as they pushed on steadily into Singapore Harbour.

Fraser took *XE-3* deliberately into the main shipping channel; there

253

they were sure of maximum depth and freedom from underwater obstruction. The chief disadvantage, of course, was that when they rose to observe there would be maximum danger of discovery. For an hour they crept forward, proceeding by the dead reckoning they had learned and practised so assiduously for just such an occasion. Dozens of times they had sneaked into Singapore Harbour in theory—now they were doing it in practice. So far it had been just like all the dummy runs. But it couldn't last, they knew. 'Periscope depth', ordered Fraser quietly once again. As the small eye of the periscope again rippled the surface to open up the outside world to them, Fraser took a fix. 'Give me a course to reach position BB and alter course at exactly 11.37,' he said. There was silence while Smith made a calculation and then : 'New course 285 just as charted,' he reported triumphantly. So far their dead reckoning had been immaculate.

Quietly, but purposefully, they pressed on, deeper into the stronghold of the enemy. Then : 'Launch dead ahead !' Fraser called breathlessly from the periscope. 'It's about two cable lengths off and making straight for us. Flood Q thirty feet.' They slanted down once more but kept going. Inevitably they all felt tense, but did not show it except in their eyes and the set lines of their mouths.

Shortly before midday Fraser brought XE-3 up again to check visually. After silent seconds of peering through the periscope he suddenly said excitedly : 'There's the Takao. She's right where she's supposed to be !' The tension vanished in a surge of excitement. So many things could have happened to deny them their prey, such as the great cruiser leaving the harbour on a mission or changing its berth, but nothing like that had happened. In the blazing sunshine the Takao lay at anchor just where she should be, her upstanding complicated superstructure a distinct recognition feature. She was formidably armed they knew with eight eight-inch guns, eight five-inch guns, eight forty-seven millimetre cannons and eight twenty-one inch torpedo tubes. She also carried four reconnaissance seaplanes. But none of this armament would avail the Takao if XE-3's mission were successfully completed.

Precisely at 2 p.m. Fraser ordered the little sub up and its periscope probed out above the surface. 'Down! Down fast!' rapped Fraser, raising his voice with real urgency for the first time. He had looked straight into a Japanese liberty boat crammed with sailors the moment the periscope had emerged! It was inconceivable that none of these men had sighted the tell-tale antenna of the submarine above the gently undulating sea. *XE-3* dived straight to the bottom, met it with a shuddering jolt and lay still.

'Stop motors!' Fraser said tersely.

No one spoke. They just crouched there holding themselves in readiness for the nerve-shattering shock waves from bursting depth-charges. But none came.

After a while Fraser said: 'Well, I just can't imagine how nobody saw us, but they don't seem to have done. We had better get on with it then. I just had a glimpse of what I think was the *Takao* directly behind that liberty boat so we will push on dead ahead. I don't think I'll take any more looks now.'

Estimating they were nearly up to the *Takao*, Fraser decided to work the submarine slowly forward along the bottom until they rammed the steel wall of the great ship's keel. He ordered the motor to be started and to tick over at the lowest possible speed while they felt their way blindly towards their quarry. 'After about sixty yards we'll stop if we haven't bumped,' Fraser said. And to Magennis: 'It will be up to you then Mick to go out, look around and tell us exactly where we are.' Magennis drew his frogman's outfit towards him in readiness as *XE-3* shivered and gently bumped forward. All of them tensed for the final jar of contact with the *Takao*. When at the end of sixty yards it still had not come Fraser ordered: 'Stop motors.' To Magennis he said: 'When you get outside, if you can see the *Takao*, lead us on to it by giving two raps on our hull with your wrench for port and three for starboard.' Even as the mighty Magennis grinned at the prospect of action the submarine bumped and lurched. 'We're there!' exclaimed Reed triumphantly. 'Start motor; ahead slow,' Fraser ordered.

Magennis, continuing to shrug himself slowly into his black skin-tight costume, began to wriggle his toes into the flippers. Even though he was not needed as an underwater guide he had work to do—plenty of it, and dangerous in the extreme. There came another scraping bump as *XE-3* rubbed her snub nose against the harsh underwater mass of the cruiser. The fact of the two bumps meant the little submarine must have bounced back about a dozen feet from the first impact. 'You know what that means,' said Fraser quietly. 'Our grappling antenna isn't working.' They looked at each other in dismay. The success of this crucial phase of the attack depended on the sub sticking limpet-like against its mighty victim while Magennis detached the heavy warhead and fixed it against the *Takao*'s keel. It was beyond the strength of even Magennis to drag it twelve feet or so underwater from the submarine to the cruiser and they had only the one frogman suit to execute that particular operation.

'What's to do then?' queried Magennis. 'I'll have a go if you like.' But Fraser, frowning, replied: 'Let's see if we can think this one out.' They sat silently in the narrow steel tube that was their war vessel, the air they breathed shallowly becoming increasingly foul.

The problem they pondered was this: fixed to the outside of the submarine's hull, from which Magennis would detach it with his wrench, was the big explosive-packed warhead which was their main weapon of destruction. There were also a number of limpet mines. *XE-3* should, on bumping, have been held instantly against the cruiser's hull by the automatic action of the antenna. The warhead would then have been pressed close against the keel, only requiring Magennis to fix it firmly. With its time-fuse set to give the submarine a reasonable chance to get well clear it would rip out the *Takao*'s bottom when it exploded. If it were detonated close by, and not against the keel, it would do no more than damage the vessel. The limpet mines Magennis could certainly carry one at a time to fix to the cruiser, and they would do considerable damage, but only by the close detonation of the big warhead could they be sure of fulfilling their mission.

'The tide is on the ebb now,' said Fraser after a while. 'That means that the *Takao* will come down nearer the bottom. There is no doubt about our having to get the warhead right against her, so I propose to move in under her. When she comes down we shall be wedged between her and the bottom of the harbour. That will mean the warhead is nearly there and Magennis should be able to manage the rest.' Fraser coolly looked from one to the other as he said this. Then he added: 'Of course, there is the danger of us getting stuck as the tide ebbs and being crushed by the *Takao*, but that is something we shall have to risk. Does anyone have any objections?' He looked again slowly and deliberately at his companions but each met his eyes evenly. There were no objections. Even though they knew there was practically no hope if the huge cruiser crushed their eggshell submarine, even though they knew that a miraculous escape from such a fate must result in capture by the Japanese, there were no objections.

'Then we'll do just that,' announced Fraser firmly. At 2.40 p.m., therefore, *XE-3* wriggled herself into the soft mud directly beneath the *Takao*. When they tried to back out they couldn't so they knew they had trapped themselves as intended between cruiser and sea bed! 'We're in position now,' said Fraser with satisfaction. 'Right, Magennis, get to work!' The big Irishman, looking like some weird undersea monster in his black frogman's outfit, grinned widely and climbed the iron ladder. It seemed unlikely that his bulk could be crammed into the airlock chamber but it was and he flooded the chamber in readiness to pass on out into the sea. As the last soft gurgle of inrushing water died Magennis pushed strongly against the hatchway through which he would emerge. It did not move. Magennis pushed again, this time exerting a rush of sudden strength. It jerked open a few inches, then stuck. Cursing violently, breathing hard, Magennis collected his great strength and put it all into one vast angry push. Again the hatch cover refused to move. It dawned on the panting Magennis at this moment what had happened—the 10,000-ton mass of the *Takao* was pressing down on *XE-3*, holding the hatch-cover down!

For ten minutes Mick Magennis hurled his giant strength against the cover, furiously pitting himself against the gargantuan weight that was frustrating him. Dimly aware of his struggles, but unable to do anything to aid him, the other three men sat anxiously silent in the submarine below. Magennis slumped back, gulping foul air in shuddering spasms. To be baulked in this way when they had come so far was infuriating.

When he had recovered somewhat he took a closer look at the hatch-cover; it did seem to be nearly a quarter open. Could he possibly squeeze his huge square-shouldered frame through? There was one thing he could do. He deflated his aqualung, exhaled completely to reduce his deep chest to the very minimum, then jammed his body into the narrow opening. He wriggled and pushed, tortured by the need to breathe but holding his breath nevertheless. What if he stuck half way and slowly drowned? What if he should get through but lose consciousness and float up to give the whole thing away? What if he did get out, but couldn't get back? Magennis gave one last desperate heave—and was through. He rested against the hull, then gave a gentle rap with his wrench to signal to the others. They relaxed, relieved of their growing anxiety.

After his efforts to get clear Magennis found the fixing of the warhead to the *Takao* a comparatively simple affair. He patted it affectionately when the deed was done. As he did so he chilled with horror on seeing a stream of air bubbles climbing strongly from his frogman's suit. He must have torn it in his struggle through the hatchway! His imagination saw the bubbles at their journey's end, as they would be seen by a lookout on the great cruiser above. How could the enemy fail to spot such a give-away trail? But the big Irishman was of the temperament which considered troubles only when they had actually arrived. He shrugged his thoughts away and pushed on with the job.

He moved to where the limpet mines were housed on *XE-3*'s deck, detached two and then, holding one in each hand, flickered his legs to drive him through the water along the cruiser's massive length. He stopped at the point where he intended to attach the mines.

When he went to perform the comparatively simple act of sticking the mines against the *Takao*'s keel, they would not hold. Naval Intelligence had forgotten that the Japanese built their warships' keels differently from those of the average European navy; instead of a straight flat surface on which the mines would fasten there was a rounded one giving no sure anchorage! The limpets just would not stick!

Magennis looked for an alternative method of attaching his mines and soon found one. There were numbers of great barnacles encrusting much of the *Takao*'s keel, and by breaking some of these away he could probably create a surface to which the mines would cling. He had no tools to lever off the rugged shells so he used his bare hands. As he scrabbled and tugged he cut and tore his hands until they bled, but did not slacken his efforts. One at a time he affixed the limpet mines, three on each side, fifteen feet between them. As he completed each fixing he banged once on the submarine's hull, to keep those inside informed of his progress. The half-hour this took him was the longest half-hour of his life.

By the time he had fixed the last limpet Mick Magennis, despite his great strength, was all in. The rent in his frogman's suit had steadily seeped water so that it was now almost full. He had swallowed a lot of sea-water and was overcome with nausea. Such had been his expenditure of effort, both physical and mental, that a deadly weariness was settling on him. 'I'll never make it back,' he told himself dully. 'I'll just lie down here and die.' But by will-power alone he got back and by will-power alone he forced up the stiff hatchway and wriggled painfully in. He closed the cover, opened the draining cock, and felt himself passing into unconsciousness. But he still retained a vital thread of sensibility which permitted him to go through all the necessary actions. He opened the lower hatch and slumped into his place in the crew's compartment. He was barely aware of the other three peeling off his clammy suit.

Magennis was brought back sharply when Reed applied iodine to his shredded, bleeding hands. With an oath he sat up and looked around. 'We aren't still here are we?' he asked. 'We won't be for long, Mick, don't you worry,' said Fraser gently, patting his shoulder to signify the admiration of all of them. Then Fraser called softly: 'Start motor. Full astern.' Thanks to Magennis all the powerful explosive charges were correctly in place, their time mechanisms were in control, in due course they would explode with a terrible devastation. The motor murmured, swelled, roared—but *XE-3* did not move an inch.

'Hell! We're stuck!' exclaimed Reed.

Indeed, they were. Wedged between the mighty *Takao* and the harbour bottom. Trapped within a few yards of what would be the centre of a tremendous explosion.

'Full ahead!' Fraser ordered. But the submarine moved not one inch forward. 'Full astern!' he ordered. But it moved not one inch back. Again and again, time and again, he repeated those orders but the racing engines moved them not at all. Would the Japanese just above them hear those racing engines? At first the four men thought of this and only of this, but after a time they wondered also: was the ebbing tide lowering the *Takao*'s 10,000 tons pitilessly to crush their hull like an eggshell? Such thoughts were in all of their minds as they sat silent, blank-faced at their posts. Only Fraser's voice tense, strained, but never panicking, was heard. 'Full ahead!—Full astern!—Pump!—Blow out!' One after the other, interminably in monotonous sequence, the little submarine was put through the mechanical processes which might ease

259

He opened the hatch and slumped into his place.

it out of its desperate plight.

Suddenly it jerked free like a cork out of a bottle. It careered violently towards the surface.

'Down!' shouted Fraser. 'Down!' Instantly each man reacted. The little submarine was brought under control, dipped its nose, came to rest on the bottom again. 'Stop motors,' said Fraser. Once more *XE-3* lay motionless, silent under the shadow of the great cruiser it had sought to destroy. Each one knew what the other was listening for without asking—the throb of motors, the churning of propellers, the detonation and shock of depth-charges and bombs. How could the Japanese have failed to see that continuous stream of bubbles that had gone up from Magennis, that column of water which must have spurted twenty feet or more as *XE-3* plunged clear? Still nothing happened.

'Time we got out of here,' said Fraser after a while. Once again the submarine throbbed and gathered way. Then: 'I can't hold trim, Sir!' called Smith. 'There's something stuck outside which is throwing us off. We shall be forced to the surface any minute!' Magennis remembered the empty limpet mine container was still on the deck outside. There was a special lever to release it, which Fraser now operated. But though he jerked it again and again the container would not budge. Fraser ordered the motor stopped. *XE-3* settled once more on the bottom. They were in no more than fifteen feet of transparent water. Above and all around were warships, merchant ships, patrol craft and ferry boats, hundreds of Japanese eyes some of which surely must spot them. Without a word Fraser pulled Magennis' discarded black rubber suit towards him, began to work himself into it. At first the others could not imagine what he was going to do or why. Then it dawned on Magennis and his jaw tightened. 'Oh no you don't!' he exclaimed. 'I'm the one who does that. You can't go!'

'*You* certainly can't,' replied Fraser doggedly. He was in the frogman's suit now and it flapped around him in folds because Magennis was so much bigger. '*You* can't go!' Magennis replied, belligerent now. 'I bet you can't even swim. You certainly won't know what to do if you get out there!' Fraser motioned him away. 'Of course I can do it,' he said. But the quick Irish blood of Magennis was up; he was angry that his skipper should seek to face dangers for which he himself had been specially trained. 'Get out of my suit!' he said bluntly, with no suggestion of the usual 'sir'. Before Fraser could do anything more about it, the big Irishman pulled the black rubber suit down off him. Then Fraser grinned and made no further effort to restrain him.

Swiftly the Irishman wriggled into the suit, seized the wrench and moved towards the hatch. 'Good luck, Mick,' said Fraser, and Magennis disappeared into the airlock chamber. They heard the soft gurgle again and the scrape of the frogman's departure. Moments later the submarine was filled with the clangour of iron upon iron as Magennis hammered with the wrench with all his might at the mine container.

In the midst of the enemy, *XE-3*'s presence was now being proclaimed with ringing blows that *must* have been heard far and wide for water does little to damp down sound waves. The three men in the submarine could feel the sweat of apprehension trickling down their spines as Magennis hammered away. Then he stopped.

There came just one sharp rap on the hull—mission completed!

Could they get away before the anger of their enemies fell upon them? They sensed the hatch lifting and falling, the airlock draining out as Magennis returned. Then he tumbled down among them, gasping, wild-eyed, his torn hands running blood. Tenderly they laid him out on the floor, eased off his dripping black suit and dabbed at his raw hands. 'Full ahead,' said Fraser. At the controls, Reed headed *XE-3* for home.

With the same mine curtains to negotiate, just as much shipping above, the same patrol vessels guarding the entrance, their return journey had to be made just as carefully. This time, however, it was even more necessary they kept up to their schedule, for a furious hornet's nest of searching ships and planes would erupt as soon as the great explosion rocked and destroyed the *Takao*.

XE-3 made it, stage by stage, systematically, stealthily, each man coolly playing his part. They were well out to sea at 9.30 that night when a thunderous explosion overwhelmed the *Takao* lifting her great bulk bodily, tearing a vast gash sixty feet by thirty feet in her bottom. It wrecked delicate direction equipment, blew many Japanese to eternity. The great cruiser settled down on to the floor of the harbour, out of the war for good.

In due course, for their cold-blooded bravery, Fraser and Magennis were each awarded the Victoria Cross, and Reed and Smith the Distinguished Service Cross.

RESCUE OPERATION

Desmond Varaday

All too often it has been man who has caused tragedy and destruction in the world of nature. But nature has her own tragedies, and sometimes man comes to the rescue, as in this instance.

There is a wonderland of wild bush country in the triangle of the Shashi and Limpopo rivers—a broad wedge which forms the east border of the Bechuanaland Protectorate where I was warden of a private reserve. This fifty square miles of territory is a wildlife paradise, with roaming herds of elephant, led by venerable old bulls with almost two hundred pounds of ivory in their huge tusks; eland, kudu, and impala mix with troops of zebra and wildebeest, while the great hunting-cats live here in luxury on nature's fully stocked larder.

Dangers await the unwary, and often the four-footed hunters become the hunted too—as on that late afternoon at the Limpopo when I was taking water-level readings on marked poles near the shore.

An almost imperceptible furrow on the water's surface gave the signal. The movement was directly ahead near a pole in deeper water, and could only have been caused by the tail of a crocodile. This was no unusual occurrence, for nearly all of Africa's waters house crocodiles, but in this case I hastily withdrew to the bank, for by the way the murky water churned under that furrow, it was clear that a huge reptile lurked there, a menace to any creature at the water's edge.

The crocodile reared up, dropping the cheetah . . .

While I made the requisite notes on the readings, some thirty yards upwind a magnificent cheetah stepped out of cover, testing the wind with high-held shiny nose. Satisfied, it walked obliquely down to where I had been only a few minutes earlier.

Then as the cheetah slowly lapped up water, it found itself looking into the glassy yellow-green eyes of the huge crocodile, which had been approaching the shore since it had first seen me. The cheetah uttered a sharp bird-like cry of surprise.

For one instant the flat nose and the eyes of the reptile looked like any of the numerous small rocks pitting the water's surface; in the next, there was a terrible commotion as the crocodile sped through the narrow space of shallows separating it from its intended victim. The great wide mouth opened in a loathsome caricature of a smile, and then the jagged teeth clamped together over the cheetah's head. The victim never had a chance.

The water boiled during the momentary tug of war. The hapless hunting-cat fought desperately to free itself. But the attacker was dragging it into the water, where it could hold its prize until it drowned.

I lifted my .375 Magnum H. & H. sporting rifle and fired a snap shot at the reptile's head. The crocodile was submerged only a few inches below the surface. Water splashed at the impact and I clearly heard the 'flup' of the bullet striking and then the whine of a ricochet.

The monster reared up, dropping the cheetah, and fell backwards into the water with a resounding crack. But it seemed to be dazed only temporarily, for it made its way off rapidly. By the chain fastened to its right armpit, I recognized Mulembe, the sacred crocodile of the Ba-Kwena tribe, who, several decades before, used to come out of the water in response to the call of his worshippers to be fed and honoured. Long since, however, the tribe had become civilized, leaving Mulembe to provide his own fare.

After the shot, I reloaded at once and ran across the sand to see if I could help the cheetah. It was lying in the shallows—dead. Its head had been terribly mauled by those powerful jaws. I noticed with regret that the cheetah was a nursing mother; her teats were swollen with milk. She had hoped, it seemed, to drink a sundowner before returning to feed her family. Her death was just one of many unrecorded tragedies daily enacted in the wild bushlands of Africa.

Since cheetahs are clannish animals, living and hunting in pairs or families, it was likely that the male would automatically take on the task of feeding the cubs if the mother failed to return to the nursery. The only question was whether the cubs were old enough to feed on what the father could provide. I was curious to find out.

The report of my shot brought Freddie, my Tswana tracker, to the spot. He carried the cheetah's carcase to our Land-Rover. I was not happy to have it on hand, for cheetahs are royal game—protected by law—and to have its pelt around my quarters could have led to unfair conclusions. But then I realized that its head injuries would be visible, and so I had the pelt pegged out to dry in the camp. That was the action which led to our finding the cubs.

On the second night after the tragedy, I awoke to the sound of a plaintive miaow, a cheetah call. Rex, my fox terrier bitch who had recently had a litter, lifted her head and gave a low growl. The cheetah's cry had come from close by. I suspected it was the male calling its dead mate, for these large hunting-cats are very shy and normally avoid a camp.

I must have dropped off to sleep again, because I was awakened now by the eerie moaning wails of hyenas: '*Aar-u-ee, aar-u-eee*' they complained. The hideous cries came nearer and nearer the camp. After several minutes of quiet a sudden burst of savage snarling, growls, and cat-like spitting rent the night air. In half a minute it was over. All was silent. But not for long. There came a fresh outburst—this time wilder.

Taking my flashlight and my rifle I went out, Rex following. There was a wild rush of shadowy forms; eyes shone green in the flashlight beam; then came the crazy laughter-like howl of disturbed hyenas: '*Ti-tatata, tita-tatata.*'

A yellowish body dashed through the grass and out of sight. It was a large cheetah: there was no mistaking its long-legged bound and long thick tail. Rex rushed into the scrub to scare away the hyenas who appeared intent on stealing the dead cheetah's pelt, which the male had apparently been defending.

At sunrise we read the spoors—the newsprint of the bush—and saw that the cheetah had come upon the scent of his missing mate, approached the camp while calling to her, and at lack of response had come into the camp and found her pegged-out pelt. In the meantime hyenas had also come on the scent.

Two or three hungry hyenas together often become daring, as these had. Many a time they had passed through camp at night snatching away biltong (sun-dried meat), fleshy oddments and supper left-overs, bones and even old skins. This time there was a fierce guardian to keep them from the drying pelt.

In the scuffle the cheetah had obviously received a bite, for on his spoor we found drops of blood. Freddie (an expert in bush-craft), Rex and I followed the spoor on foot. We must have gone nearly five miles into gradually thinning bush, losing the spoor, then finding it again, before we came upon a wide depression in the ground. It was densely covered with tall green grass. In the middle of the depression stood a solitary marula tree. Freddie indicated the tree with his eye. We stood and listened—to the unmistakable squeals of hungry cubs. This was the cheetah's lair.

A 'koto-koto'—yellow-billed hornbill—was sitting on one of the high branches. When we moved forward, it gave the alarm. I saw the father cheetah slink away from the lair to draw us off the track of the cubs. At the same instant the koto-koto winged off, protesting loudly at our intrusion.

The long grass, fallen leaves and dead branches under the marula tree did not afford a hiding place for a pair of grown cheetahs, but the cubs were so well hidden by a branch that, but for Rex, we would probably not have found them. They must have heard the fall of our steps, for they lay still and silent—a litter of three.

A few feet away on a clear patch there were small mounds of chewed meat, evidently regorged by the father. None of the mounds appeared to have been touched. For lack of teats and mother's milk, the parent instinctively did what he thought the next best thing. But such food was for cubs many weeks older than these.

I realized that although the father was trying, he would be unable to save the cubs, and so I decided to take them. By their size and unspotted tawny grey-coloured fur, we judged them to be no more than a couple of weeks old. They had not received nourishment now for over two days, and as I picked up two of them it was obvious that they were famished, for they were as light as bundles of feathers.

I made Rex lie down beside the cubs, and I put the three starved orphans to her teats. As soon as the cubs began to swarm on her, nuzzling her underside hungrily, Rex lifted her lips in a warning snarl. I stroked her and cajoled, and at length my words and possibly her motherly instinct got the better of her repulsion for the strange litter. She let the cubs suckle. For a while noisy feeding was heard.

One of the three, the only female cub, appeared to be the liveliest and fiercest of them all. She had emptied a teat and high-handedly fought one and then the other of her brothers for possession of the remaining milk faucets. She succeeded in getting them, too. I had to laugh at her antics, and, despite her sex, there and then named her Cheeky Charlie. Freddie shook his head in disapproval of the name.

While we carried the cubs back to camp, I wondered whether Rex was sufficiently equipped to cope with three additional boarders. Her two healthy pups were always ravenous and there was possibly not enough milk for the newcomers.

Once home, Rex refused absolutely to accept the duties of foster mother. So I had to adopt them and care for the orphans. I groomed them by brushing out their matted fur and wiping them over with a warm, damp cloth. We fed the brood every two hours on powdered milk mixed with water and administered with an eyedropper. It was a long and tedious performance, because we had only one dropper. By the time I had completed the round, the first one was almost due for another feed. It was a full-time job.

To remedy the unavoidable running stomachs, I mixed finely powdered charcoal with the milk and added a pinch of bismuth. Diarrhoea, however, got the upper hand. I then resorted to chlorodine, the taste of which did not quite make feeding an unqualified success.

Cheeky Charlie had the 'I want to live' instinct and the stronger constitution of a female. She took to the artificial nourishment and, in a way, flourished. Her brothers barely existed and began to look dehydrated and scruffy. I had fears for their survival.

In fact, from the very first day I had doubts about the smaller of the two. After a few days, while feeding him I found that the milk was coming back through his nostrils. On examining his mouth I noticed that he had something like a cleft palate which diverted much of every pull of food to his nose. In the second week he died.

Rex still determinedly refused to assist with the feeding. At night she would stealthily remove her pups from the basket, leaving squeaking cheetah cubs to huddle together for communal warmth. When this warmth proved insufficient, the cubs protested loudly, waking me. I gave Rex a dark look but she always pretended a deep sleep, though I knew she was shamming. Eventually there was nothing to do but to take the cubs into bed with me. One at a time I popped them under the blanket and pushed them down to my feet. When they were snug I would try to continue the broken night's rest. They remained quiet and slept, pressed against my feet. The nights were getting colder.

Food was the all-important commodity for my fluffy pair, and they made their demands known as long as they were awake. Freddie shared the duties of feeding because I could no longer cope alone. One day, he took one of the cubs out of the basket and stood holding it in his arm while putting the feeder, a lemonade bottle fitted with a rubber teat, to the cub's mouth. The hungry little thing lunged forward and slipped from Freddie's grasp, falling with a dull thud on the hard floor. Its tender young body was internally injured, and after that it refused all food. In spite of our efforts to nurse it back to health, it faded away. Both Freddie and I were very upset at the loss of the cub.

I have never heard of cheetahs breeding in captivity and it seemed that even those born in the wilds were difficult to rear.

Now the only survivor was the female: still as lively and demanding as on the first day. She accepted the feeding device as naturally as though it were the real thing, wrapping her tongue around the teat and holding the bottle with forepaws, purring and suckling contentedly on it long after it was empty, like an old man sucking a pipe. She allowed only me to feed her, spitting and striking out at all who came near her.

I suppose the name Cheeky Charlie would have remained hers had not a primitive, dishevelled specimen—a detribalized Bushman—arrived at my camp to seek employment as a game scout. I was busy feeding the little cub when Freddie escorted the man to me. As no African is more cunning in the craft of tracking than a Bushman, I engaged him. The way Piet looked at the cub convinced me immediately that he was a keen animal-lover and had a passion for handling wild game. Respectfully he asked permission to stroke the cub: this I granted.

269

But Piet had hardly reached out to stroke the cub's head when she spat at him so fiercely and loudly that he instinctively withdrew his hand. He laughed at the savagery of the small unspotted fur-ball, and also at his own fright. 'Ow!' he exclaimed. 'This is Gara-Yaka, mother of the monsters and the ghosts that walk by night!'

And from then on she was called Gara-Yaka. In a short while her ears became so attuned to the sound of this name that she answered to no other.

Somehow Rex had become less harsh to the lone cub. She even permitted the cheetah to share the family basket. I was surprised to find Gara-Yaka also sharing Rex's milk with the pups, but she condescended to accept this belated hospitality only during the daytime. The nights she still spent with me, smuggled under the bedclothes, occasionally coming up for air.

Soon she was running and gambolling around with the pups, an absolute picture of health and happiness, scratching at fleas as vigorously as the dogs did. She had learned how to ask to be picked up: she would stretch her long arms, place them on me, and look until I gathered her up.

At three months Gara-Yaka was big. She appropriated the dog basket, using it as her daytime apartment. She was always quick to mete out punishment to the dogs if they ventured too near the comfortable basket.

My pet was by now a cuddlesome, feline beauty, with long gangling dog legs. She was a strange mixture of dog and cat. Polka dots were becoming clearly defined on her tawny, golden side. The fur on her rounded belly was creamy, the texture of swan's-down.

As on grown cheetahs, Gara-Yaka's head was her most typical feature. The lyre-shaped black lines were already fully marked on her cheeky face, starting at the inner corner of her eyes and ending at her upper lip, where, like badly applied make-up, the 'tear-stain' became smudged and lost in the growing whiskers. She was still quite fluffy, and her loose coat was well padded with puppy fat. By the day she grew more affectionate.

At about this time she began serious bouts of hide-and-seek with her stepbrothers. It was mostly she who stalked. Instinct gave her the know-how. The game usually ended with a rush and a charge in which the

270

pups were caught at a hopeless disadvantage. They rolled over with stumbling clumsiness. But there were times when they came on Gara-Yaka unexpectedly, and this scared her. I noticed that she was easily frightened. On these occasions, she would rise to her full height, get up on her toes, arch her back, and stretch her tail out stiff, its hairs bristling like a bottle brush, and then hop sideways, stiff-legged. Then she would get even with the pups by spitting at them and cuffing them repeatedly. At times when they charged her she raced up a tree like a cat, still with that wild look in her eyes.

This appeared to be the age for ratifying established relationships. She spat and growled at all Bantu except Freddie and Piet, whom she accepted as part and parcel of the camp.

To all intents and purposes I was still Mama, and this was confirmed daily when she clambered into my lap while I was relaxing. She would creep up to my chest and lie there, purring in a strange, deep, throaty gurgle and 'making puddings'—kneading me with her semi-retractile claws. Then the real caressing would begin: she would rub her face against my cheeks and gaze into my eyes. In bright sunlight her large eyes shone like polished jasper.

Her attitude towards Rex became very frivolous, and gradually she looked upon the mother dog as an equal. In spite of the dog's cool superiority and occasional chastisement—in what seemed to be a last effort on Rex's part to establish her waning authority—the cheetah accepted no such discipline.

When Gara-Yaka was with the dogs, she considered herself one of them, even trying to behave like them. She learned everything and did everything the dogs could do, except bark. Her voice remained that of a big cat.

Then there were times when Gara-Yaka behaved like a human baby, especially when she lay on my chest. She made no secret of her own belief that I was still Mother, and that she lived only to love me. I had noticed this very deep affection among wild cheetahs, who, at the finish of a meal, with much ado, lick each other's face clean and then lie sleeping with arms and legs entwined like human lovers.

My cheetah did this to her foster brothers, who, although visibly disliking this sort of familiarity, put up with it for the sake of peace, while lifting their lips in a warning grimace. Gara-Yaka would have one or the other pup by the throat and gently but firmly squeeze her jaws together to force the pup to accept whatever she was meting out. The happy family circle would then break up with much squealing and howling on the part of the dogs. At this, Gara-Yaka would be thoroughly fed up with the unsporting attitude of the pups and come and join me. She was obviously self-willed and independent, her wild heritage showing through her every act.

Wherever I went, she came too. I had no choice, for she would follow anyway. The moment she opened her eyes in the morning, she would greet me with an affectionate whistle-like miaow. She shared my tea, lapping out of my saucer, but if I was too slow pouring hers first, she would firmly but politely remind me of my negligence by placing her paw on the tray, almost upsetting it. Even when the saucer was empty, she made quite sure that no dregs were left: she held it firm while she ran her tongue over it looking for the last drop, tea-leaves and all.

Eventually, Gara-Yaka was weaned from her liquid diet to solids. At the first attempt I chopped the meat finely for her. To my consternation she would not even look at it. Taking a leaf from her father's book, I chewed raw liver for her, but achieved similar results. The raw offal tasted horrible, but anything for a good cause!

Patiently I dipped my finger into the chewed bloody mess and smeared it across her lips. Surprisingly she took my finger in her mouth and sucked off the blood. This manoeuvre, repeated three or four times, comprised the meal. Later I purposely dropped minced liver on the floor. She picked up the small lumps, and from then on she took to raw meat almost eagerly. Her survival as a carnivore was thus assured.

Gara-Yaka's happy relationship with the game warden continued, and half-tame, half-wild, she grew up in the reserve and eventually mated and became a mother.

THE LEFT-HANDED SWORD

E. Nesbit

His name was Hugh de Vere Coningsby Drelincourt, and he lived with his mother in a queer red-roofed house incoherently built up against the corner of the old castle that stands on the edge of the hill looking out over the marshes. Once the castle and the broad lands about it had all belonged to the Drelincourts, and they had kept great state there. But they had been loyal to King Charles, and much went then. Later Hugh's father had spent what was left on lawyers, gaining nothing. And now only the castle itself was left, and some few poor fields. His mother was Lady Drelincourt by rights, and he himself, since his father was dead, was Sir Hugh, but there was no money to keep up the title, so she called herself plain Mrs Drelincourt, and he was just Hugh.

They lived very simply and kept cows and pigs, and Hugh did lessons with his mother and was very happy. There was no money to send him to school, but he minded that less than his mother did. It was a pleasant little house, and all the furniture in it was old and very beautiful, carved oak and polished apple-wood, and delicate lovely glass and china. But there was often only bread and cheese to put on the china plates, and cold water from the well in the castle courtyard to fill the Venice glasses.

There were relics too—an old silver bowl with raised roses round the brim, and a miniature or two, and a little sword that some boy Drelincourt had worn many many years ago. This sword Hugh had for his very own, and it hung over the mantelpiece in his bedroom. And the sword had been made for a left-handed little boy, because all the Drelincourts are left-handed.

Hugh used to wander about the old place, climb the old walls, and explore the old passages, always dreaming of the days when the castle was noisy with men-at-arms, and gay with knights and ladies.

Now the wild grasses and wallflowers grew in the rugged tops of the walls, and the ways to the dungeons were choked with fern and bramble. And there was no sound but the cooing of pigeons and the hum of wild bees in the thyme that grew over the mounds beyond the moat.

'You spend all your time dreaming,' his mother used to say, as she sat darning his stockings or mending his jackets, 'and the castle comes through all your clothes.'

'It comes through all everything,' Hugh would say. 'I wish I could see it as it was in the old days.'

'You never will,' said his mother, 'and isn't it beautiful enough as it is? We've got a lovely home, my son, and we've got each other.'

Then he would hug her and she would hug him, and he would try to pay more attention to his lessons, and not so much to the castle.

He loved his mother very much, and did many things to please her —lessons and errands and work about the house; and once when she was ill, and a silly woman from the village came in to do the housework, he mounted guard on the stairs all day, so that the woman should not disturb his mother with silly questions about where the soda was kept, and what dusters she was to use.

So now he tried to think less of the castle; but for all his trying the castle filled his life with dreams. He explored it and explored, till he thought he knew every inch of it.

One wall of Hugh's bedroom was just the thick, uneven stones of the old castle wall, against which the house was built. They were grey with time, and the mortar was crumbling from between them; the fires he had in the room in the winter, when he had colds, dried the mortar and made it crumble more than ever. There was an arch in this wall that had been filled up, in forgotten days, with heavy masonry. Hugh used to watch that arch, and wish it was a door that he could get through. He could not find the other side, though he had searched long and well.

'I expect it was only a cupboard,' his mother said, as she peeled the potatoes or made the puddings; 'I wouldn't worry about it if I were you.'

Hugh did not worry about it, but he never forgot it. And when the next winter he had one of those bad colds that made his mother so anxious, and caused him to be tormented with linseed poultices and water-gruel and cough-mixture and elder-flower tea, he had plenty of time to think, and he thought of the arch, and of nothing else.

And one night, when his mother had gone to bed, tired out with taking all sorts of care of him, he could not sleep, and he got out of bed and fingered the stones inside the arch as he had so often done before, to see if any one of them was loose. Before, none ever had been— but now . . . oh, joy! one was loose. The fire had dried the old mortar to mere dust that fell away as Hugh's fingers pulled at the stone— weakly, because his cold had really been a very severe one. He put out all the strength he could, however, and pulled and tugged and twisted, and shifted the stone, till it was quite loose in its place, and with the help of the poker he prised it out, and with difficulty put it on the floor.

He expected to seek a dark hole, through which a cold wind would blow; but no cold wind blew, and curiously enough, the hole was not dark. There was a faint grey light, like the light of daylight in a room with a small window.

Breathless and eager, he pulled out another stone. Then his heart gave a jump and stood still. For he heard something moving on the other side of the arch—not the wind or rustling leaves or creaking tree-boughs, but something *alive*. He was quite as brave as most boys, and, though his heart was going like a clock when you have wound it up, and forgotten to put on the pendulum, had the courage to call out:

'Hullo! who's there?'

'Me,' said a voice on the other side of the arch. 'Who are you?'

'Who are you, if it comes to that?' Hugh asked cautiously.

'Sir Hugh de Drelincourt,' said the voice from the hole in the wall.

'Bud thad's *by* dabe,' said Hugh with the cold in his head; and as he spoke another stone disappeared, and the hole was larger. Now in silence two pairs of hands worked at loosening the stones from the crumbling mortar.

'Ibe cobing through,' said Hugh suddenly; 'the hole's big edough.'

And he caught the little sword from the wall, and he set his knee on the bottom of the hole and through he went.

Through into a little room whose narrow window showed the blue daylit sky—a room with not much in it but a bed, a carved stool, and a boy of his own age, dressed in the kind of dress you see in the pictures of the little sons of Charles I.

'Why, you're me!' the strange boy said, and flung his arms round him. And Hugh felt that he spoke the truth. Then a sudden fear caught at him; he threw off the other boy, and turned to go back quickly into his own room, with the dancing firelight and the cough-mixture and the elder-flower tea.

And then a greater fear wiped out the first, as a great wave might wash out a tear-mark on the sea-sand. For the hole in the wall was no more there. All the wall was unbroken and straight and strongly stony. And the boy who had been so like him was there no longer. And he himself wore the laced breeches, the little handsome silk coat, the silk stockings and buckled shoes of that other boy. And at his side hung his own little left-handed sword.

'Oh, I'm dreaming,' said Hugh. 'That's all right. I wonder what I shall dream next!'

He waited. Nothing happened. Outside the sun shone, and a rainbow-throated pigeon perched in the window preened her bright feathers.

So presently he opened the heavy door and went down a winding stair. At its foot was a door opening on the arched gateway that he knew so well. A serving-man in brown came to him as he passed through the door.

'You lazy young lie-a-bed,' he said, 'my lady has asked for you three times already——'

'Where is my lady?' Hugh asked, without at all knowing that he was going to ask it.

'In her apartments, where any good son would have been with her,' said the serving-man.

'Show me where,' said Hugh.

The serving-man looked at him, and nodded to a group of men in armour who stood in the gatehouse.

' 'Mazed,' he said, touching his forehead, ' 'mazed with the cannons and the shoutings and the danger, and his father cold in the chapel, and . . . Come, lad,' he said, and took Hugh's hand in his.

Hugh found himself led into a long, low room, with a square wooden pattern on the ceiling, pictures along one side, and windows along the other. A lady, with long curls, a low-necked dress, and a lace collar, was stooping over an open chest from which came the gleam of gold and jewels. She rose as his shoes pattered on the floor.

'My son,' she said, and clasped him in her rich-clad arms, and her face, and her embrace, were the embrace and the face of his own mother, who wore blue cotton and washed the dishes in the little red-tiled castle house.

'All is lost,' said the lady, drawing back from the embrace. 'The wicked Roundheads have almost battered in the east wall. Two hours at least our men can keep them out. Your father's at peace, slain while you were asleep. All our wealth—I must hide it for you and for the upkeep of our ancient name. Ralph and Henry will see to it, while you and I read the morning prayers.'

Hugh is quite sure that in that long pleasant gallery, with the morning sun gay in the square garden outside, he and his mother read the prayers, while some serving-men staggered out with chest upon chest of treasure.

'Now,' his mother said, when the prayers were ended, 'all this is in the vault beneath your bed-chamber. We will go there, and I will lie down a little on your bed and rest, for, indeed, I am weary to death. Let no man enter.'

'No man shall enter. I will keep guard,' said Hugh, 'on the stairs without,' and felt proudly for his little sword at his side.

When they had come to that little room he kissed the silk-clad lady that was his mother, and then took up his station on the stairs outside.

And now he began to hear more and more loudly the thunder of artillery, the stamping and breathless shouting of fighting men. He sat there very still, and there was no sound from the chamber where his mother lay.

Long, very long, he waited there, and now there was no thought in him of its being a dream. He *was* Hugh de Drelincourt; the Roundheads were sacking his father's castle; his father lay in the chapel, dead,

The thrust was too fierce . . . .

and his mother slept on the bed inside. He had promised that none should enter. Well, they should not.

And at long last came the clatter of mail on the stairs, and the heavy sound of great boots, and, one above another, heads in round steel caps, and shoulders in leather came round the newel of the little stair.

'A page-in-waiting,' cried the first man; 'where is your lady, my young imp?'

'My lady sleeps,' Hugh found himself saying.

'We have a word for your lady's ears,' said the round-capped man, trying to push past.

'Her ears are not to be soiled by your words,' Hugh was surprised to hear himself say.

'Don't thou crow so loud, my young cockerel,' the man said, 'and stand back, and make room for thy betters.'

The round caps and leather shoulders pushed upward, filling, crowding the staircase.

'Stand back!' they all cried, and the foremost drew a big sword, and pointed it, laughing, at the child.

''Tis thou shalt stand back!' Hugh cried, and drew his own little left-handed blade. A great shout of laughter echoed in the narrow staircase, and someone cried, 'Have a care, Jeremiah, lest he spit thee like a woodcock!'

Hugh looked at the coarse, laughing faces, and saw, without looking at it, the dear quiet face that lay in the room behind him.

'You shall *not* speak to her!' he cried, and thrust furiously with the little sword. The thrust was too fierce. It carried him forward on to the point of that big sword. There was a sharp pain in his side, a roaring in his ears: through it all he heard: 'This for our pains: a dead woman and a little child slain!' Then the roaring overpowered everything—the roaring and the pain, and to the sound of heavy feet that clattered down the stairs he went out of life, clutching to the last the little sword that had been drawn for her.

He was clutching the iron edge of his bed, his throat was parched and stiff, and the pain in his side was a burning pain, almost unbearable. 'Mother!' he called, 'Mother, I've had such a dreadful dream, and my side does hurt so!'

She was there even as he called—alive, living, tenderly caressing him. But not even in the comfort of her living presence, with the warmth of linseed poultices to the side that hurt, of warm lemon drink to the parched throat, could he tell a word of his dream. He has never told it to anyone but me.

'Now let this be a lesson to you, my darling,' his mother said; 'you must *not* climb about in those windy walls and arches, in this sort of weather. You're quite feverish. No wonder you've had bad dreams.'

But the odd thing is that nothing will persuade Hugh that this was only a dream. He says he knows it all happened—and indeed, the history books say so too. Of course, I should not believe that he had gone back into the past, as he says, and seen Drelincourt Castle taken by the Roundheads, but for one curious little fact.

When Hugh got well of his pleurisy, for that was the name the doctors gave to the pain that came from a dream sword-wound in his side, he let his mother have no peace till she sent for Mr Wraight, the builder at Dymchurch, and had all the stones taken out of that arch. And, sure enough, beyond it was a little room with a narrow window and no door. And the builder's men took up the stone floor, because nothing else would satisfy the boy, and sure enough again, there was a deep vault, and in it, piled on top of the other, chests upon chests of silver plate, and gold plate, and money, and jewels, so that now Lady Drelincourt can call herself by that gentle title, and Sir Hugh was able to go to Eton and to Oxford, where I met him, and where he told me this true tale.

And if you say that the mother of Hugh de Drelincourt, who died to defend his mother from the Roundheads, could not have been at all like the mother of little Hugh, who lived in the red-tiled castle house, and drank the elder-flower tea, and loved the left-handed sword that hung over his mantelpiece, I can only say, that mothers are very like mothers here, there, and everywhere else, all the world over, when all is said and done.

WHAT A NIGHT!

Pat Smythe

The three Jays—Jimmy, his sister Jane, Jacqueline plus their friend Billy Noakes—had come up with me from Miserden in the Cotswolds and were at the Horse of the Year Show in the Haringey arena to compete for the Prince Philip Cup for riders under seventeen.

As non-riding captain of the team I knew they were up against tough opposition—all the more reason to avoid snags. But having had my permission to watch Jacky's cousin Darcy test-fly a new jet plane at Northolt during the afternoon, Jimmy, after some hair-raising adventures, had got back only just in time for the start of the competition at five past ten, while earlier in the day the hoof of a pony from another team had landed smack on Jane's right foot. What with Jimmy missing and Jane's badly swollen foot, it had seemed for a time that the Miserden team would have to scratch. But Jane was determined to go on. 'I'm going to get on my pony', she had said, 'and ride into the ring. And I'm not coming out till the competition's over!'

What a night it had been! And there was still the last exciting event to go—the climax to weeks of effort and hopes. I sank into my seat, feeling quite exhausted by the strain of it all and by Jimmy's sudden appearance just when I was sure he would never turn up in time. As the teams paraded, I glanced at the figures I had scribbled down in the margin of my programme. Of the four teams with this one round to go, the leaders had thirty-four points to date, Miserden had thirty-two, the third team had thirty and the other team had only twenty-three. That meant that Miserden, if they maintained the same average—and so did the other teams—would finish second overall. If somehow they could get back three points from the present leaders, they would win the Prince Philip Cup!

There were two enormous 'ifs' and they both pointed at Jane. Jimmy, I knew, was tough, and although he looked as though he had been through some harrowing experiences in the last few hours—judging by his torn and dirty clothes and the scratches on his hands—as long as he was physically sound he had a natural buoyancy that would lift him up in a crisis.

But Jane was the problem. She rode past with head erect, but her face was chalk-white and her lips were compressed. I suspected that she was still in great pain and I wondered whether she would be able to keep going.

The first event was the Grooms' Stakes. The number one in each team had to mount his own pony and then lead the number two's pony round four bending posts to the other end of the arena and hand over to the number two, who would lead the number three's pony back and hand over in turn—and so on until the number four completed the event by riding his own pony and leading the number one's past the finishing post.

This was not too bad for Jane and the others almost made up the yard or two lost by not being able to vault on. In a very tight finish Miserden came second, beating the team that was two points ahead of them by a length or so. Miserden had pulled back a valuable point.

Next came the Sharpshooters' Race. Two riders from each team would be mounted bareback on one pony. One rider from each pair would have to dismount and fling wooden balls at the Aunt Sallies until they were knocked flat. Then the riders had to remount and both pairs would gallop back to the start-line.

The Miserden team had worked it out in practice that the pairings should be Jane and Jimmy on one pony and Jacky and Billy on the other, with the two boys being the sharpshooters because of their superior throwing power. The choosing of this event was a lucky break for our team, for it meant that Jane would stay aboard her pony all the time and conserve her strength. And the luck held. The other teams had one boy apiece but otherwise had to rely on girls to knock down the Aunt Sallies. Whatever one's feelings about the ability of girls to ride better than boys, when it comes to throwing even the most ardent feminist has to admit that boys are usually superior.

So it was this time. Jimmy and Billy slid off the backs of the ponies, ran to the heaps of wooden balls on the arena floor and, with that side-arm flick that girls never seem to be able to manage, they began to fling the balls at the flat wooden targets. The crowd was roaring encouragement to the throwers and chuckling whenever a particularly wide throw sent a ball sailing into the stop-net at the back, thoughtfully provided by the arena party. It took Jimmy and Billy only three or four throws each to send their targets tilting backwards; then they turned, ran back, leap-frogged over their respective pony's quarters and grabbed Jane and Jacky round the waist as the ponies bounded towards the start-line.

Miserden finished a length ahead of the next team and the luckless pair who came last just couldn't hit their Aunt Sallies. The other teams had all finished and still they threw ever more wildly while the audience rocked with laughter. The two girls were brave enough to persevere, for they knew that every point was valuable and minutes later they managed to get the targets down.

The four valuable points they had gained put the Miserden team in the lead with thirty-nine points. One behind came the previous leaders, who had come third in the Sharpshooters' Race, and the next team had thirty-four points. Two more events to go and a one-point lead—a shudder of excitement ran through my limbs. Could they do it? Would Jane's bad foot stand up to the strain? Their present rivals were breathing down their necks, one point away. The crisis was on.

The arena party were marking out a circle with small bushes in wooden boxes and were planting one straight row of posts in the centre. I guessed that the next event was to be Musical Hats. Wide-brimmed straw hats were to be placed on top of the poles and there would be one hat fewer than the number of riders taking part. The riders had to circle round the ring and when the music stopped make a dash to the centre and grab a hat off a pole. The rider left hatless would be eliminated, one hat would then be removed and so on until two riders vied for the last hat. The team points were calculated on a cumulative basis, so that it did not follow that the team supplying the individual winner automatically won the whole event.

Jane was eliminated in the first round, although she usually excelled at this event, being able to keep her head and judge the right distance to the nearest hat when her rivals got flurried with excitement. However, on this occasion her injured foot must have been hurting her just when the music stopped, as she was not concentrating at that moment and was caught at the end of the arena farthest from the hats. Jacky went out before long after tearing half the brim off a hat in her mad rush past. Unluckily for her, another competitor had already gripped it firmly, so Jacky was left waving the brim while her grinning rival donned the rest of the hat.

Jimmy, too, had misfortune and was knocked out soon after. The music seemed to stop and he bolted for the centre, only to find that the band was just breaking into a waltz. While he was still turning back outside the circle, the music really did stop and poor Jimmy was left facing the wrong way in the rush.

By cantering slowly whenever he was facing the band and speeding up whenever he had to turn a corner away from them, Billy was cunning enough to survive to the last two but, when the points were added up, it turned out that Miserden came third over all. Their chief rivals came second and that brought them up to level pegging—with one event to go. The other two teams were no longer in the hunt, the nearer one being four points behind the joint leaders at this stage. And so, in the next three or four minutes, one of them was going to win the Prince Philip Cup.

My throat was dry and my heart seemed to be knocking against my ribs. And then my erratically beating heart sank. I saw the arena party laying out four sacks on the centre line. The final event was to be the Sack Race—and none of the twelve events listed could have been worse from Jane's point of view. Each rider in turn had to dash for the centre line, dismount, climb into a sack and then hobble or hop to the far end, leading his pony. On crossing the far line, he would hand the sack over to the next rider who in turn rode for the centre line, dismounted and hopped the rest of the course; and so on until number four crossed the last line, leading his pony.

Jimmy must have spotted that something was wrong with Jane's foot, for I saw him go into a whispered huddle with Billy and then talk urgently to the other two. Jane shook her head but the others seemed to persuade her. Were they going to withdraw? I wondered. It would be an anti-climax to all their efforts but it might save Jane from further pain. But then I realized that Jimmy and Billy had changed the order. Instead of going second Jane was to go to last. Perhaps they hoped to have built up such a lead when her turn came that she could take things easy. I licked my dry lips and waited.

The starter dropped the handkerchief and the leading riders in the four teams were away. Jimmy had practised a flying getaway on his pony, training it to spring from a standing start like a polo pony. He picked up a yard on their rivals. slid off and, leading his pony at arm's length so that it would not tread on the sack, he hopped up to the far end, gaining another yard in the process. A quick handover and Jacky was away next. She pulled Pickles into a 'four-wheel skid' at the centre line, dismounted, climbed into the sack and went like a dangeroo for the far end. As Jimmy had done, she gained another two yards for the Miserden team and slowly I began to breathe again.

Billy was his usual dependable self—neat, precise and determined not to risk all by losing his head. He reached the centre line, was off in a flash but very deliberately climbed into the sack. I wanted to yell at him to hurry, to get on with it—but I knew in my heart that he was right not to be rushed. He took small, controlled hops but he covered the ground and his pony trotted quietly alongside. The number three of their chief rivals may have picked up a couple of feet, even a yard, but Miserden held the lead.

And now it all hung on Jane. The packed arena was roaring encouragement at the teams and my shout of 'Come on, Jane!' was lost in the din. She grabbed the sack from Billy and shot away from the line. She sprang off her pony at the centre point and I could see her wince as her bad foot hit the ground. She climbed into the sack, a shade clumsily, and now her rival was only two yards behind.

Twenty yards to go to win the Prince Philip Cup—and perhaps twenty hops to do it in. Twenty times her injured foot would come crashing down on the hard ground and a searing pain would shoot up her leg. Just twenty yards and twenty hops—but each one a concentration of agony. Jane started off with one hand holding her pony's mane, so as to take some of the weight off her foot. I had to blink the misty tears from my eyes and concentrate on watching her face. She landed and her mouth screwed up with shock. On she went, gathering her strength and her nerve for each jump, landing awkwardly as she tried to take her weight on her sound left leg, tottering, then capturing her balance and repeating the effort. The pony sensed the excitement and Jane had to leave the support of the mane in order to control its head with the reins.

Twelve yards to go and now her rival was only a foot behind. Three more agonizing hops—and they were dead level. Jane made a supreme effort and for the next five yards she kept abreast. But her face had gone milk-white, her eyes were almost closed and she was swaying like a tired top at the end of its run. Three yards to go and the other number four went ahead. And then, as Jane made her last despairing effort, she pitched headlong. I thought she had fainted and I half-rose in my seat. But somehow she staggered to her feet, took two last hops, then fell across the line. She had come a gallant second, beaten by just a yard.

There was pandemonium in the arena—cheers for the winner and a roar of sympathy for Jane. She quickly recovered and was able to take part in the prize-giving ceremony and the tour of honour that followed.

It was nearly half an hour before I could commiserate with the Jays for the arena went dark, there was a roll on the drums and twin spotlights picked out the four state trumpeters and the drummer from the Royal Horse Guards who heralded the cavalcade which wound up the show. Into the ring came the great horses and riders of this and past years. They assembled in their pride and a strange hush settled over the audience as the well-known voice of Dorian Williams read out that splendid tribute to the horse, written by Ronald Duncan:

'Where in this wide world can man find nobility without pride, friendship without envy or beauty without vanity? Here, where grace is laced with muscle, and strength by gentleness confined.

'He serves without servility, he has fought without enmity. There is nothing so powerful, nothing less violent; there is nothing so quick, nothing more patient.

'England's past has been borne on his back. All our history is his industry. We are his heirs, he our inheritance. Ladies and Gentlemen—the Horse!'

So ended the Horse of the Year Show. On the following morning we started back for the Cotswolds, not at all down-hearted. Though we had not won the Cup the team had proved its worth against the toughest competition in Britain. And next time . . . 'Next time,' said Jane cheerily, 'nobody's pony is going to stamp on *me*, don't you worry!'

THE ESCAPE OF PRINCESS CLEMENTINA

John Buchan

In the year 1718 the Chevalier de St George, or, as some called him, the Old Pretender, after the defeat of his hopes in Scotland, had retired to Rome. At the age of thirty he was still a bachelor, but the unhappiness of his condition was due not to his celibacy but to his misfortunes. The Jacobite campaign of 1715 had proved a disastrous failure; and although he still retained the courtesy title of James III, he was a king without a realm. While the royal exile was twiddling his thumbs in the Italian capital, waiting for a better turn of luck, his friends, seeing that nothing further was to be gained by the pursuit of Mars, sought the aid of Cupid. They laid before the Chevalier the flattering proposal of a marriage with a princess of beauty and race. This move was inspired less by romance than by politics, for a suitable marriage would not only encourage the waning Jacobite hopes, but might also raise up an heir to their cause.

The Chevalier readily concurred in the scheme, and a certain Mr Charles Wogan was dispatched to the various European courts to report on a suitable bride for the Chevalier. Wogan's choice fell on the little Polish Princess Clementina Sobiesky, daughter of James Sobiesky of Poland and Edwige Elizabeth Amelia of the house of Newburgh, and grand-daughter of the famous John Sobiesky, the 'deliverer of Christendom'.

The chronicles of the time are loud in the praises of this lady, her illustrious birth, her qualities of heart and mind, 'her Goodness, Sweetness of Temper, and other Beauties of a valuable character'. She is said to have been 'happy in all the Charms, both of Mind and Body, her Sex can boast of'; 'the Agreeableness of Seventeen and the Solidity of Thirty'. Her accomplishments included Polish, High Dutch, French, Italian, and English, all of which she spoke so well that it was difficult to distinguish which of these languages was the most familiar to her. She was also a young woman of exemplary piety, and therefore a suitable bride for a king in exile. Princess Clementina was only sixteen when the Chevalier and his friends laid siege to her affections.

It was no ordinary business, for there were many hazards and difficulties in the way. The Chevalier had given his consent to the proposed alliance; it was for his friends to see it brought to a successful issue, and the plan of campaign was left entirely in their hands. The bridegroom was a mere pawn—a willing pawn—in the game. The real difficulty was the House of Hanover, the inveterate enemy of the Stuart cause, which was by no means inclined to look with indulgence on the proposed alliance. Although the affair was kept a profound secret, the matter gradually leaked out; and George I of England protested with such vigour to the Emperor on the folly and danger of the impending marriage, threatening among other things to break up the Quadruple Alliance, that Princess Clementina was arrested at Innsbruck with her mother and kept there under strict surveillance.

The Chevalier and his friends were in a quandary. Obviously a man built in the heroic mould was necessary to extricate them from the dilemma. They bethought them of Wogan, who had been recalled from his delicate mission on the pretext that it was impolitic to entrust the matter further to an Irish Catholic. Wogan was well adapted for this sort of adventure. He was, besides being something of a poet, a cavalier and a courtier. He had shared the hard fortunes of the Chevalier in Scotland, and had suffered imprisonment for his devotion to the Stuart cause. Once more the soldier of fortune was called upon to prove his devotion in a cause no less hazardous.

The Pope, who had been taken into the secret, had provided Wogan with a passport in the name of the Comte de Cernes, and forth he fared like a fairy-tale knight to rescue a distressed princess. Never had d'Artagnan and his Musketeers a more difficult task. Wogan duly arrived at Innsbruck in the disguise of a merchant, and obtained an interview with the Princess and her mother, who heartily concurred in the proposed plan of a secret 'elopement'. We next find him at Ohlau in quest of the Prince Sobiesky, the lady's father. Here he met with a rebuff. Prince Sobiesky, a practical man of the world, viewed the whole affair as midsummer madness, and absolutely refused to lend his aid or consent to Wogan's scheme.

Wogan was in a quandary, but he did not lose heart. He had nothing to complain of during his stay with Prince Sobiesky, for he was well lodged and treated with the most flattering attentions, but the real business of the mission hung fire. Still he waited—he had long learned the game of patience—and, being a courtier, was used to waiting.

At length a happy accident turned the scale in his favour. On New Year's Day, Prince Sobiesky, as a mark of his esteem, presented his guest with a magnificent snuff-box, formed of a single turquoise set in gold, a family heirloom, and part of the treasure found by John Sobiesky in the famous scarlet pavilion of Kara Mustapha. Wogan, with a charming gesture, declined the gift on the plea that, although he was sensible of the high honour shown him by the Prince, he could not think of returning to Italy with a present for himself and a refusal for his master. The Prince was so touched that he finally yielded, and furnished Wogan with the necessary instructions to his wife and daughter. Wogan set out once more on his adventures in high spirits, carrying not only the precious instructions, but the snuff-box, which Prince Sobiesky had pressed on him as a parting gift.

The next thing was to establish secret communication with the Princess. This was more easily said than done. The garrulity of Prince Sobiesky, who in his parental agitation had babbled the whole story to a certain German baron, and the suspicions of the Countess de Berg, a noted *intriguante* and spy of the Austrian court, almost brought Wogan's mission to an inglorious end. The baron was brought over at 'considerable expenditure', but the Countess was a more difficult matter. While Wogan was the guest of honour of Prince Sobiesky she had been puzzled at the attentions shown to him, which she argued could be for no good end, and set her spies on his track. Wogan escaped by the skin of his teeth, and only evaded capture by ostentatiously announcing his departure for Prague. Then by a skilful detour he gave his pursuers the slip and posted on to Vienna, where he vainly tried to enlist the sympathy of the Papal Nuncio, Monseigneur Spinola.

Then came a thunderbolt, for suddenly Prince Sobiesky changed his mind. He dispatched an urgent message to Wogan saying that both the Princess and her mother, alarmed at the dangers that encompassed them, had resolved to proceed no further in the business, and that he forthwith cancelled his previous instructions.

Here was a pretty kettle of fish! Wogan was a stout-hearted fellow, but this new blow almost unmanned him. In his dilemma he wrote to the Chevalier and told the whole story, asking him at the same time to send a confidential servant to obtain fresh powers from Prince Sobiesky. The Chevalier promptly dispatched one of his valets, a Florentine called Michael Vezzosi, who, when attached to the Venetian Embassy in London, had been instrumental in aiding the escape of Lord Nithsdale from the Tower. The Chevalier reminded Prince Sobiesky that by his foolish behaviour he was not only needlessly endangering the lives of Wogan and his friends, but adding to the difficulties of the captives at Innsbruck. He also gave the most explicit instructions to Wogan to proceed with the enterprise.

Wogan accordingly set out for Schlettstadt, where he met his three kinsmen, Major Gaydon and Captains Misset and O'Toole, who were to lend their aid in the now difficult mission. Mrs Misset accompanied her husband, together with her maid Jeanneton, but neither of the women was told the real nature of the undertaking. Jeanneton was to play a conspicuous part in the escape of Clementina. Wogan's plan was that the maid should change places with the Princess and generally impersonate her till she had made good her escape. The light-headed girl was told a cock-and-bull story about O'Toole having fallen violently in love with a beautiful heiress, and Wogan played to such a tune on her sense of the romantic that she gleefully entered into the plot of the 'elopement'.

Wogan, however, was not yet out of the wood. So far he had succeeded, but he had now to deal with the whims and caprice of the ladies

291

who had been pressed into the enterprise. Jeanneton, whose importance to the success of the venture was paramount, proved especially trouble-some. First of all she refused point-blank to wear the low-heeled shoes which had been specially ordered for her, so as to reduce her height to conformity with that of the Princess; and not only screamed and swore, but went so far in her tantrums as to knock the shoemaker down. She had once been a camp-follower, and her manners were those of the tented field. It was not until Mrs Misset, in an excess of despair, had thrown herself imploringly at her feet, a ceremony in which the gentle-men of the party were constrained to join, that the maid relented, and the party set forth at last in a ramshackle berline for Innsbruck.

So far so good. At an inn between Nassereith and Innsbruck, while the other members of the party regaled themselves with a banquet of wild boar and sauerkraut, Wogan stole out in the rain to keep an im-portant appointment with a certain M. Châteaudoux, gentleman-usher to the Princess Sobiesky. This gentleman had not Wogan's spirit, and proposed to defer the matter of the escape till the weather had cleared and the roads were in better condition for travel.

Wogan firmly waived aside his objections, and succeeded so well in convincing him that now or never was the time, that at half-past eleven that same night he and the precious Jeanneton made their way in the storm to the *schloss* where the Princess was confined. Fortune smiled on the enterprise, and even the tempest was propitious, for the sentry, heedless of danger on such a night, had sought refuge in the inn.

Meanwhile within the prison walls the Princess Clementina, in order to assist the plan of escape, was playing the part of an invalid. Jeanneton's role was simple: the Princess having regained her freedom, all that the maid had to do was to keep her bed on the plea that her migraines were no better, refusing to see any one but her mother. The secret was well kept; not even the governess was told, lest her grief at the sudden de-parture of the Princess might arouse suspicions.

At midnight, according to plan, Châteaudoux was in readiness, and Jeanneton, clad in a shabby riding-hood and female surtout, was suc-cessfully smuggled into the sleeping chamber of the Princess. Wogan and O'Toole waited at the street corner ready to convoy the Princess to the inn. There was a lengthy farewell scene between the Princess and her mother. The two having wept and embraced each other, Clemen-

Princess Clementina followed Châteaudoux down the winding stairs and out into the night. . .

tina excused herself for her hurried departure on the plea that nothing in heaven or earth must stand in the way between her and her husband. Then she hastily dressed herself in Jeanneton's clothes, and followed Châteaudoux down the winding stairs and out into the night.

The Princess was no longer a captive. The tempest, which had increased, favoured the escape. Once more successfully evading the sentry, they quickly gained the street corner where Wogan and O'Toole were kicking their heels, consumed with fear and anxiety. They reached the inn, drenched to the skin, with but one slight misadventure. Clementina, mistaking a floating wisp of hay for a solid log of wood, slipped and plunged over the ankles into a channel of half-melted snow. At the inn she eagerly swallowed a cup of hot spiced wine and changed her soaking garments. Konski, her mother's page, had followed meanwhile with what the chronicles of the period call 'inside apparel' and a casket containing her jewels, said to be valued at about 150,000 pistoles. The foolish Konski, no doubt scared out of his wits at his share in the adventure, had thrown the precious packet behind the door and taken ignominiously to his heels.

They were now ready for the road. Captain Misset, who had gone out to reconnoitre, having returned with a favourable report, off they started. The inn was silent and shuttered, everybody having retired for the night, including the landlady; so they stole off unobserved. As the ancient coach lumbered past the dismal *schloss* where the Princess had been so recently a prisoner, she could not restrain some natural emotion at the thought of her mother; and then suddenly she discovered the loss of the precious packet. Here was a nice to-do! There was nothing for it but to return to the inn and fetch the packet. O'Toole was entrusted with this anxious mission. By one more stroke of good fortune he succeeded in retrieving it from behind the door where the careless Konski had thrown it, but he had first to prise the door off its hinges.

At sunset the party reached the village of Brenner, where the Princess, who had so far borne up nobly, had a slight attack of the vapours. She was speedily revived, however, by a dose of eau de Carmes, and, having had a meal, soon regained her accustomed gaiety, and began to ply Wogan with all sorts of innocent questions about the manners and customs of the English and his adventures with the Chevalier in Scotland. One by one the party dropped off to sleep, all but Wogan, who as the Master of Ceremonies, managed to keep himself awake by the expedient of taking prodigious pinches of snuff. At last even he, overcome by the ardours of the night, began to show signs of drowsiness. While dropping off to sleep, his snuff-box accidentally slipped from his lap and fell on to the curls of the Princess, who with her head resting against his knees was reposing at the bottom of the carriage.

Verona was still a journey of forty-six hours, and the party were much inconvenienced by the lack of post-horses. To their horror they discovered that they were travelling in the wake of the Princess of Baden and her son, one of the husbands who had been proposed for Clementina, and whom she had been actually bribed to marry! At another stage of the journey the coackman was drunk, and they were saved only by a miracle from being dashed to pieces at the foot of one of the precipitous gorges of the Adige.

They were now approaching the most difficult part of the journey, and it was arranged before they passed the frontier of the Venetian States that O'Toole and Misset should remain behind to intercept any messengers from Innsbruck and guard the retreat. This prescience was amply rewarded. O'Toole had soon the satisfaction of waylaying a courier who had been dispatched in hot pursuit of the fugitive. The fellow was not only put entirely off the scent, but at supper was plied so generously with old brandy he had to be carried drunk to bed. Having relieved him of his documents the cavaliers rode on to rejoin the party in the berline.

One or two trials had still to be overcome. At Trent there was some delay owing to the behaviour of a surly governor who put every obstacle in their way. There was besides the continual fear of Clementina being detected by her Highness of Baden, who had installed herself in state at the inn. The poor little Princess had perforce to remain hidden at the bottom of the coach in the public square until such time as they could obtain fresh relays. The best they could find was a couple of tired screws taken from a neighbouring field. At Roveredo things were even worse, as no horses were to be had at all; and to crown their misfortunes they had not proceeded six miles with their weary beasts when the axle of the ramshackle old berline broke!

But at length they reached the great white wall that denoted the boundary between the Venetian States and the dominions of the

Emperor. At half-past three in the morning they stole across the frontier and solemnly offered up a *Te Deum* for their safe deliverance. They reached Pery with the bells merrily ringing for Mass, and narrowly missed being recognized by the Princess of Baden, who with her son was just entering the church when the berline drew up at the church door.

Verona was reached at dusk, and here for the first time during the three days' journey the Princess had her hair dressed. They came to Bologna on 2 May, where the Princess sent a message to the Cardinal Origo announcing her arrival. The Cardinal speedily repaired to pay his respects, bringing the present of a 'toyley, artificial flowers, and other little things', and the offer of a box at the opera. More welcome and important than the courtesies of the Cardinal was the arrival of Mr Murray, the Chevalier's agent, with messages from his royal master.

The drama of the royal elopement draws to its close. On 9 May Clementina was married by proxy. The little Princess, all agog with excitement, rose at 5 a.m., and having attired herself in a white dress and a pearl necklace went to Mass and received the Holy Communion. The marriage ceremony was performed by an English priest. The Chevalier was represented by Mr Murray, with Wogan as witness, and Prince Sobiesky by the Marquis of Monte-Boularois, a loyal friend of the Stuart cause. The 'powers' of the Chevalier were read publicly on conclusion of the Mass, setting forth his willingness to marry the Princess Clementina Sobiesky, and the ceremony was forthwith performed with the ring which he had sent expressly for the purpose.

The Princess entered Rome on 15 May, amid general rejoicings; and on 2 September a public marriage was celebrated at Montefiascone.

The daring flight and escape of the Princess Clementina caused some sensation at the time, and a medal was struck to commemorate the event. The Chevalier created Wogan a baronet, as well as his three kinsmen, and Wogan had the further distinction of being made a Roman Senator by Pope Clement XI. Jeanneton, who had played her part well, apart from the regrettable incident of the low-heeled shoes, duly escaped from Innsbruck and was sent to Rome as the maid of the Duchess of Parma. Prince Sobiesky was exiled to Passau by the Emperor for his complicity in the business, and was also deprived of a couple of valuable duchies. Wogan, who had always been something of a poet, devoted the remainder of his life to the cultivation of the Muse, his efforts drawing encomiums from so severe a critic as Dean Swift, to whom he had sent a copy of his verses in 'a bag of green velvet embroidered in gold'. He died in 1747.

As for the Princess, her wedded life did not fulfil the romantic promise of its beginnings. Married to a worthy but doleful husband, she never sat on the throne which she had been promised. She was the mother of Prince Charles Edward, and seems to have fallen into delicate health, for in one of his boyish letters, the little Prince promises not to jump or make a noise so as to 'disturb mamma'.

THE DANCING ACADEMY

Charles Dickens

Of all the dancing academies that ever were established, there never was one more popular in its immediate vicinity than Signor Billsmethi's, of the 'King's Theatre'. It was not in Spring Gardens, or Newman Street, or Berners Street, or Gower Street, or Charlotte Street, or Percy Street, or any other of the numerous streets which have been devoted time out of mind to professional people, dispensaries, and boarding-houses; it was not in the West End at all—it rather approximated to the eastern portion of London, being situated in the populous and improving neighbourhood of Gray's Inn Lane.

It was not a dear dancing academy—four-and-sixpence a quarter is decidedly cheap upon the whole. It was *very* select, the number of pupils being strictly limited to seventy-five, and a quarter's payment in advance being rigidly exacted. There was public tuition and private tuition—an assembly-room and a parlour. Signor Billsmethi's family were always thrown in with the parlour, and included in parlour price; that is to say a private pupil had Signor Billsmethi's parlour to dance *in*, and Signor Billsmethi's family to dance *with*; and when he had been broken in in the parlour he ran in couples in the assembly-room.

Such was the dancing academy of Signor Billsmethi when Mr Augustus Cooper, of Fetter Lane, first saw an unstamped advertisement walking leisurely down Holborn Hill, announcing to the world that Signor Billsmethi, of the King's Theatre, intended opening for the season with a grand ball.

Now, Mr Augustus Cooper was in the oil and colour line—just of age with a little money, a little business, and a little mother, who, having managed her husband and his business in his lifetime took to managing her son and *his* business after his decease; and so, somehow or other, he had been cooped up in the little back parlour behind the shop on weekdays, and in a little deal box without a lid (called by courtesy a pew) at Bethel Chapel, on Sundays, and had seen no more of the world than if he had been an infant all his days; whereas Young White, at the gasfitter's over the way, three years younger than him, had been flaring away like winkin'—going to the theatre—supping at harmonic meetings—eating oysters by the barrel—drinking stout by the gallon—even stopping out all night, and coming home as cool in the morning as if nothing had happened. So Mr Augustus Cooper made up his mind that he would not stand it any longer, and had that very morning expressed to his mother a firm determination to be 'blowed' in the event of his not being instantly provided with a street-door key. And he was walking down Holborn Hill, thinking about all these things, and wondering how he could manage to get introduced into genteel society for the first time, when his eyes rested on Signor Billsmethi's announcement, which it immediately struck him was just the very thing he wanted; for he should not only be able to select a genteel circle of acquaintance at once out of the five-and-seventy pupils at four-and-sixpence a quarter, but should qualify himself at the same time to go through a hornpipe in private society, with perfect ease to himself, and great delight to his friends. So he stopped the unstamped advertisement—an animated sandwich, composed of a boy between two boards—and having procured a very small card with the Signor's address indented thereon, walked straight at once to the Signor's house—and very fast he walked too, for fear the list should be filled up, and the five-and-seventy completed before he got there. The Signor was at home, and, what was still more gratifying, he was an Englishman! Such a nice man—and so polite! The list was not full, but it was a most extraordinary circumstance that there was only just one vacancy, and even that one would have been filled up that very morning, only Signor Billsmethi was dissatisfied with the reference, and being very much afraid that the lady wasn't select, wouldn't take her.

'And very much delighted I am, Mr Cooper,' said Signor Billsmethi, 'that I did *not* take her. I assure you, Mr Cooper—I don't say it to flatter you, for I know you're above it—that I consider myself extremely fortunate in having a gentleman of your manners and appearance, sir.'

'I am very glad of it too, sir,' said Augustus Cooper.

'And I hope we shall be better acquainted, sir,' said Signor Billsmethi.

'And I'm sure I hope we shall too, sir,' responded Augustus Cooper. Just then the door opened, and in came a young lady with her hair curled in a crop all over her head, and her shoes tied in sandals all over her legs.

'Don't run away, my dear,' said Signor Billsmethi; for the young lady didn't know Mr Cooper was there when she ran in and was going to run out again in her modesty, all in confusion-like. 'Don't run away, my dear,' said Signor Billsmethi, 'this is Mr Cooper—Mr Cooper, of Fetter Lane. Mr Cooper, my daughter, sir—Miss Billsmethi, sir, who I hope will have the pleasure of dancing many a quadrille, minuet, gavotte, country-dance, fandango, double-hornpipe, and faringaholka-jingo with you, sir. She dances them all, sir; and so shall you sir before you're a quarter older sir.'

And Signor Billsmethi slapped Mr Augustus Cooper on the back as if he had known him a dozen years—so friendly; and Mr Cooper bowed to the young lady, and the young lady curtseyed to him, and Signor Billsmethi said they were as handsome a pair as ever he'd wish to see; upon which the young lady exclaimed, 'Lor, pa!' and blushed as red as Mr Cooper himself—you might have thought they were both standing under a red lamp at a chemist's shop; and before Mr Cooper went away it was settled that he should join the family circle that very night —taking them just as they were—no ceremony nor nonsense of that kind—and learn his positions, in order that he might lose no time and be able to come out at the forthcoming ball.

Well; Mr Augustus Cooper went away to one of the cheap shoe-makers' shops in Holborn, where gentlemen's dress-pumps are seven-and-sixpence, and men's strong walking, just nothing at all, and bought a pair of the regular seven-and-sixpenny, long-quartered, town mades, in which he astonished himself quite as much as his mother, and sallied forth to Signor Billsmethi's. There were four other private pupils in the parlour: two ladies and two gentlemen. Such nice people! Not a bit of pride about them. One of the ladies in particular, who was in training for a Columbine, was remarkably affable, and she and Miss Billsmethi took such an interest in Mr Augustus Cooper, and joked and smiled, and looked so bewitching, that he got quite at home and learnt his steps in no time. After the practising was over, Signor Billsmethi, and Miss Billsmethi, and Master Billsmethi, and a young lady, and the two ladies, and the two gentlemen, danced a quadrille—none of your slipping and sliding about but regular warm work, flying into corners, and diving among chairs, and shooting out at the door—something like dancing! Signor Billsmethi in particular notwithstanding his having a little fiddle to play all the time, was out on the landing every figure, and Master Billsmethi, when everybody else was breathless, danced a horn-pipe with a cane in his hand, and a cheese-plate on his head, to the un-qualified admiration of the whole company.

Then Signor Billsmethi insisted as they were so happy, that they should all stay to supper, and proposed sending Master Billsmethi for the beer and spirits, whereupon the two gentlemen swore, 'strike 'em wulgar if they'd stand that'; and they were just going to quarrel who should pay for it, when Mr Augustus Cooper said he would, if they'd have the kindness to allow him—and they *had* the kindness to allow him; and Master Billsmethi brought the beer in a can, and the rum in a quart-pot. They had a regular night of it; and Miss Billsmethi squeezed Mr Augustus Cooper's hand under the table; and Mr Augustus Cooper returned the squeeze and returned home too, at something to six o'clock in the morning when he was put to bed by main force by the apprentice, after repeatedly expressing an uncontrollable desire to pitch his reverend parent out of the second-floor window, and to throttle the apprentice with his own neck-handkerchief.

Weeks had worn on, and the seven-and-sixpenny town-mades had nearly worn out, when the night arrived for the grand dress-ball at which the whole of the five-and-seventy pupils were to meet together for the first time that season, and to take out some portion of their respective four-and-sixpences in lamp-oil and fiddlers. Mr Augustus

301

Cooper had ordered a new coat for the occasion—a two-pound-tenner from Turnstile. It was his first appearance in public; and after a grand Sicilian shawl-dance by fourteen young ladies in character, he was to open the quadrille department with Miss Bellsmethi herself, with whom he had become quite intimate since his first introduction.

It *was* a night! Everything was admirably arranged. The sandwich-boy took the hats and bonnets at the street-door; there was a turn-up bedstead in the back parlour, on which Miss Billsmethi made tea and coffee for such of the gentlemen as chose to pay for it, and such of the ladies as the gentlemen treated; red port-wine, negus and lemonade were handed round at eighteen pence a head, and, in pursuance of a previous engagement with the public-house at the corner of the street, an extra potboy was laid on for the occasion. In short, nothing could exceed the arrangements, except the company. Such ladies! Such pink silk stockings! Such artificial flowers! Such a number of cabs! No sooner had one cab set down a couple of ladies, than another cab drove up and set down another couple of ladies, and they all knew, not only one another, but the majority of the gentlemen into the bargain, which made it all as pleasant and lively as could be. Signor Billsmethi in black tights, with a large blue bow in his buttonhole, introduced the ladies to such of the gentlemen as were strangers: and the ladies talked away —and laughed they did—it was delightful to see them.

As to the shawl-dance, it was the most exciting thing that ever was beheld; there was such a whisking, and rustling, and fanning, and getting ladies into a tangle with artificial flowers, and then disentangling them again; and as to Mr Augustus Cooper's share in the quadrille, he got through it admirably. He was missing from his partner now and then certainly, and discovered on such occasions to be either dancing with laudable perseverance in another set, or sliding about in perspective, apparently without any definite object; but, generally speaking, they managed to shove him through the figure, until he turned up in the right place. Be this as it may, when he had finished a great many ladies and gentlemen came up and complimented him very much, and said they had never seen a beginner do any thing like it before; and Mr August Cooper was perfectly satisfied with himself, and everybody else into the bargain, and 'stood' considerable quantities of spirits and water, negus, and compounds, for the use and behoof of two or three

Miss Billsmethi betrayed her jealousy by calling the young lady a 'creeter'.

dozen very particular friends, selected from the select circle of five-and-seventy pupils.

Now, whether it was the strength of the compounds, or the beauty of the ladies, or what not, it did so happen that Mr Augustus Cooper encouraged, rather than repelled, the very flattering attentions of a young lady in brown gauze over white calico who had appeared particularly struck with him from the first; and when the encouragements had been prolonged for some time, Miss Billsmethi betrayed her spite and jealousy thereat by calling the young lady in brown gauze a 'creeter', which induced the young lady in brown gauze to retort in certain sentences containing a taunt founded on the payment of four-and-sixpence a quarter, and some indistinct reference to a 'fancy man'; which reference Mr Augustus Cooper, being then and there in a state of considerable bewilderment, expressed his entire concurrence in. Miss Billsmethi, thus renounced, forthwith began screaming in the loudest key of her voice at the rate of fourteen screams a minute; and being unsuccessful, in an onslaught on the eyes and face, first of the lady in gauze and then of Mr Augustus Cooper, called distractedly on the other three-and-seventy pupils to furnish her with oxalic acid for her own private drinking, and the call not being honoured, made another rush at Mr Cooper, and then had her stay-lace cut and was carried off to bed.

Mr Augustus Cooper, not being remarkable for quickness of apprehension, was at a loss to understand what all this meant, till Signor Billsmethi explained it in a most satisfactory manner by stating to the pupils that Mr Augustus Cooper had made and confirmed diverse promises of marriage to his daughter on diverse occasions, and had now basely deserted her; on which the indignation of the pupils became universal and as several chivalrous gentlemen inquired rather pressingly of Mr Augustus Cooper, whether he required anything for his own use, or, in other words, whether he 'wanted anything for himself', he deemed it prudent to make a precipitate retreat.

And the upshot of the matter was, that a lawyer's letter came the next day, and an action was commenced next week; and that Mr Augustus Cooper, after walking twice to the Serpentine for the purpose of drowning himself, and coming twice back without doing it, made a confidant of his mother, who compromised the matter with twenty pounds from the till, which made twenty pounds four shillings and sixpence paid to Signor Billsmethi, exclusive of treats and pumps; and Mr Augustus Cooper went back and lived with his mother, and there he lives to this day; and as he has lost his ambition for society, and never goes into the world, he will never see this account of himself and will never be any the wiser.

THE FIRST LADY OF FLYING

Graeme Cook

By 1928 the Atlantic Ocean had been crossed by air no fewer than ten times, but even so it was still a dangerous undertaking. There were, however, men prepared to take the risk to list their names amongst the pioneers headed by Alcock and Brown. Two such men were Americans Lou Gordon and Wilmer Stultz, who planned to make the crossing in that year.

It occurred to the two men and their friend and aviation enthusiast George Putnam Palmer, a New York publisher, that only *men* had so far flown the Atlantic. What a gimmick and boost for the prestige of American womanhood if they could take a woman along with them. The more they thought about it, the more enthusiastic they became. But there was a problem. Where would they get a young woman willing to risk possible death amid the Atlantic waves?

At once a nationwide search began, led by Palmer, who interviewed a host of willing candidates. Alas, none of them was really suitable. Above all they needed a stable, 'down-to-earth' woman with just the right degree of self-confidence and one who would not panic in an emergency. So far none of the girls Palmer had interviewed had all the necessary qualities. When he had almost exhausted his supply of candidates, he searched his mind for others, running through the list of lady friends he had. It was then that he remembered a young girl teacher and social worker he had known for some time. He decided to get in touch with her and see if she was interested.

Palmer's friend had, he remembered, flown with Frank Hawkes, one of America's famous barn-stormers who performed feats of daring in the air to excited crowds across America. Then, he recalled, she had herself become a pilot but lack of money had forced her to give it up. This girl, he thought, might just be the one he was looking for. Little did he know then that she was to become one of the most famous pilots ever to take to the air. Her name was Amelia Earhart.

So it was that the tall, thirty-year-old girl with the short, unkempt tawny hair walked eagerly into his office, trying desperately not to show too much enthusiasm and excitement. Amelia was attractive in a boyish way with her short hair, her freckled face and open grey eyes. She certainly didn't look her thirty years.

Palmer and Amelia talked at some length about her experience of flying; what she had done, whom she had flown with and the most important question of all—whether or not she would like to fly the Atlantic with Gordon and Stultz. For Amelia the question need never have been asked. It was obvious to Palmer, a particularly good judge of character, that he had found his girl. She was just what he had been looking for. The answer was an emphatic 'yes'. Palmer pointed out the many hazards she was likely to face on such a trip but Amelia merely replied that she would not consider going on the trip if there was not an element of danger. She loved a challenge and regarded life as not worth living without one.

Soon everything was arranged and the long, tiring flight with all its dangers took place. Throughout the flight, the inexhaustible Amelia spent most of her time helping the pilots and bombarding them with hosts of questions about this and that instrument or navigational problem and even about the aircraft's engines.

Although she took no real part in the flying of the aircraft, the very fact that she had actually flown the Atlantic made Amelia world-famous almost overnight. She was asked to go on lecture tours of America, telling of her experiences, and to write articles for newspapers and magazines, all of which brought her in the money she needed to continue her flying.

But there was more to Amelia's wish to become a better pilot than hopes of short-haul trips in America. Spurred on by her Atlantic flight, she determined that one day she would fly the Atlantic again, but this time she would do it alone. At the very suggestion of this, Palmer was staggered. By then his relationship with Amelia had grown into something more than just friendship and he did all in his power to persuade her to forget this foolish venture. But Amelia was made of strong and stubborn stuff. She continued flying until she became a first-class pilot and certainly the match for any man.

As time went by and Amelia gained more and more distinctions by completing long cross-country flights in America, the desire to fulfil her ambition grew. Palmer did all in his power to dissuade her from undertaking the trip, but her resolution won the day and in 1931 she declared that she was ready for the flight. Realizing that he could never stop her, Palmer at last gave her his blessing, doing everything he could to help her. But before committing himself too far, he asked her to marry him. After due consideration, Amelia accepted his proposal of marriage, but not without certain conditions, which she even went to the extent of putting down in writing! He was in no way to interfere with her flying. A 'beaten man', Palmer agreed to her conditions and they were duly married.

The truth of the matter was that Palmer fully understood Amelia's desire for freedom and need for an ever-present challenge. Palmer had won fame for his courage during two Arctic expeditions which he had undertaken, so the lust for adventure was in him, too.

The following year, 1932, Amelia achieved her dream. She flew solo across the Atlantic in only thirteen and a half hours, shattering a world record and becoming the world's first lady of aviation. The trip was not without its difficulties. Like many others before her she had faced abominable weather, howling gales, fierce rain-storms and dense cloud. To make matters worse, her altimeter and petrol gauge had failed, then an exhaust pipe on her Lockheed Monoplane split open and choking fumes and flames crept into the cockpit. Only her superb skill as a pilot and her dogged tenacity brought her through the ordeal.

After her epic flight, the name of Amelia Earhart became a household word. But she determined not to stop there. There were other challenges to overcome, other oceans to cross. She made many more dramatic flights and became an expert on aircraft engines, showing a particular interest in the autogyro, the forerunner of the modern-day helicopter. She actually flew the autogyro on several occasions and gave many technical lectures throughout the country.

Amelia Earhart was, above all, determined to show that aviation was not a world exclusively set aside for men. She did all in her power to encourage other women to take up flying . . . not because she was an ardent advocate of 'women's liberation', but because she wanted other women to experience the thrill of flight as she had done.

In 1935, Amelia once more staggered the world when she flew solo across the Pacific Ocean from Hawaii to California, the first person ever to do so. World records fell to her as the years went by and Amelia kept on with the same resolve she had shown in earlier years. She was aiming for the one achievement which, until then, had eluded her. She wanted to fly right around the world.

This, she promised her husband, would be the last long-distance trip she would make. Amelia could not have foreseen then that what she said would come literally true—but in a tragic way.

The route she was to fly from Oakland, California was to take her across the American continent, down to Brazil, over the South Atlantic to Africa then east across the world, culminating in a flight across the Pacific Ocean. She was to take with her as navigator one of the most skilled in the business, Fred Noonan.

In 1937, Amelia was presented with a brand new twin-engined Lockheed aircraft for her services to aviation. She christened it *Electra*. It was in this aircraft that she planned to make her round-the-world trip. On 1 June 1937, she and Fred Noonan took off from Oakland and the epic adventure began . . .

In spite of adverse conditions much of the way, the trip round the world to the Pacific Ocean went according to plan. It was this vast expanse of ocean that was to prove the final challenge to Amelia Earhart. The weather alone, as they waited to take off from Lae, in New Guinea, seemed to herald disaster. Their next stop in the hops across the Pacific was to be Howland, a tiny coral island over 2,500 miles from Lae. The weather was appalling. From the airstrip which had been hastily cut out

All her skill was required to get the fuel-laden aircraft over the trees.

of the jungle, they experienced the full force of a Pacific storm. It rained incessantly while thunder boomed and lightning streaked the storm-blackened sky.

While she and Fred waited for the storm to abate, Amelia set about checking their flight plan, provisions and safety equipment for the journey. This was to be the longest single lap of the journey and she was taking every precaution. The vital radio was checked along with the rubber dinghy, Very pistol, signalling lamps, iron rations and the many other things that went to make for a safer trip. Nothing had been left to chance. If they were forced down into the sea, they would have all the equipment necessary for survival.

She wrote to her husband: 'The whole width of the world has passed beneath us, except this broad ocean. I shall be glad when we have the hazard of its navigation behind us.'

It was not until the morning of 2 July that the weather brightened and Amelia and Fred could contemplate taking off. The take-off alone presented considerable difficulties for the intrepid flier. The space which had been cleared for a runway was small and further complicated by the towering trees which surrounded it. All Amelia's skill was going to be required to get the fuel-laden aircraft up and over the trees.

The lumbering aircraft trundled along the runway and lifted into the air, barely skimming the tops of the trees then made off into the blue sky dotted with puffy white clouds. The weather for the hop to Howland was reasonable and there seemed to be no problems ahead of them, save for the gargantuan task Fred Noonan had to face in navigating across the vast waste of rolling waves.

The difficulty of navigation was an enormous one but Noonan was equal to the task. He had pioneered the San Francisco–Manila run for Pan-American Airways. If it were humanly possible to navigate across the trackless wastes of ocean, Noonan was the man to do it, and he had planned his route for the last leg of the journey with meticulous care.

A coastguard cutter, the *Itasca*, was riding at anchor off Howland with orders to help guide Amelia's aircraft in to the airstrip. The boat was equipped with high-powered radio equipment and capable of transmitting weather information to the *Electra*. The whole schedule of the operation had been worked out in detail. Commander Thompson, the captain of the cutter, was given explicit instructions which were to be followed to the letter. They read:

'Earhart's call letters are K.H.A.Q.Q. Earhart to broadcast her position on 3105 kilocycles at every 15 and 45 minutes past the hour. *Itasca* to broadcast weather and homing signal on 3105 and 7500 kilocycles on the hour and half-hour.'

The system seemed without fault and incapable of misinterpretation —but problems were to arise. Something happened to the *Electra* with disastrous consequences . . .

In the radio cabin of the *Itasca*, the operator tried in vain to contact *Electra* for seven hours after she had left Lae. No reply came. In desperation, Thompson contacted a radio direction finder unit at Howland to see if they had any more promising news, but he drew a blank. They had not heard a thing.

At one o'clock in the morning of 4 July, Thompson put out a call to the coastguard on the Californian coast indicating that he had heard nothing from Amelia but that he was not unduly concerned because, according to the schedule, they were at that time still 1,000 miles away.

Following the message to the coastguard he broadcast to *Electra* the weather conditions which were 'excellent'. Then he waited . . . and waited . . . but nothing was heard from Amelia until just before three o'clock in the morning, when a faint voice was heard through heavy static on the radio. It was Amelia.

'Encountering headwinds . . . cloudy and overcast.' Then the voice died out. More messages were transmitted from *Electra* but they were so distorted by static that they were almost unintelligible. Then at 6.15 a.m. Howland time came the most coherent message of the night.

'We are about 100 miles out. Please take a bearing on us and report in half an hour. I will transmit in the microphone.' The message was short and clipped . . . too short for the Howland operators to get a proper radio 'fix' on the aircraft.

From then on there was complete silence. In a bid to find the tiny aircraft, the radio direction finder unit swept the sky with its beams, only to encounter utter silence. As far as they were concerned, the *Electra* was lost but they were determined not to give up trying and continued the search. Then came a stroke of luck; Amelia's voice came through with startling clarity at 7.42 . . .

'We must be right on top of you but we can't see you. Our gas is running low and we've only about thirty minutes left. Have been unable to reach you by radio. We are flying at an altitude of 1,000 feet. Please take a bearing.' Then the din of static started up again and Amelia's voice was lost. Shortly afterwards came yet another message . . .

'We are circling but still cannot see you! Go ahead on 7500 kilocycles either now or on the scheduled half-hourly time!'

The *Itasca*, at the duly appointed time, transmitted Amelia's call sign in Morse code in the hope that it would not be affected by static, but it was still impossible to get a bearing. Then Amelia made a transmission . . .

'We are receiving your signals but we are unable to get a minimum. Please take a bearing and answer with voice on 3105.'

Not long after, at 8.45, Amelia was heard for the last time. She said in a weak voice . . .

'We are in a line of position 157-337, repeat 157-337. Will repeat this message now on 6210 kilocycles. We are running north and south. We have only half an hour's fuel left and we cannot see land.'

Amelia Earhart and Fred Noonan were never heard or seen again.

As the minutes ticked by into hours it was obvious to all that they had ditched into the sea. But that did not necessarily mean they were doomed. Everyone hoped that they had survived the crash and were waiting to be picked up in their life-raft. There was still a chance that they were alive.

It must be remembered that the search procedures in the 1930s were not the elaborate ones they are today. There was, however, one ray of hope. The fuel tanks of the *Electra* would be empty and therefore provide considerable buoyancy for the aircraft. If only the crash-landing was successful then there was a fair chance that they might still be alive, if not in the life-raft then waiting on the buoyant wings of the aircraft for rescue. However, a full-scale search by ships and aircraft revealed nothing. In spite of attempts by radio 'hams' all around the Pacific coastline, there was no sign of life from Amelia's radio.

A whole string of suspected calls from K.H.A.Q.Q. were heard or reported as having been heard. The most promising of these was . . .

'We are on a coral reef just below the equator . . . we are okay but a little weak.'

However, none of the reported messages led to anything. Wild rumours about their fate were rife throughout the world but one particularly sinister one came from the island of Saipan, which lies north of Howland Island. Years later someone on the island, while discussing the mysterious disappearance of Amelia Earhart, remembered an incident which occurred in 1937 when a light aircraft carrying a man and a woman crash-landed in the sea just off the island coast. Then another person recalled seeing an aircraft crash-land in the sea and a man and woman emerge from it to be arrested by armed Japanese, who were at that time building an airstrip on the island. This witness saw the couple taken into the woods by the Japanese and there followed two shots. Nothing more was heard of them. Putting two and two together they surmised that the couple were none other than Amelia and Fred Noonan. But this posed a question. Why should the Japanese murder them out of hand? Was it to hide the fact that they were illegally building an airstrip on the island? If word of that got out there would surely be an international incident. It was a horrific possibility.

The rumours grew to alarmist proportions and there were suggestions that both Amelia and Fred Noonan were in fact American spies who had been using the round-the-world trip to cover up their true mission . . . to seek out the islands on which the Japanese were carrying out their unlawful work. There are those who, even now, believe that this was the case. It is said that the Japanese military authorities held a complete dossier on Amelia Earhart. Why would they have such a thing on a female whose sole interest in life was flying? Could it have been that she was a Japanese spy? There are those who believe this version to be true and also believe that the aircraft she was flying did not crash-land but was shot down by American fighters to cover up her duplicity!

Knowing of Amelia's love for adventure and the thrill of a challenge, it is not too difficult to believe that she may have been implicated or engaged in spying on behalf of the Americans, but the very suggestion that she was in any way connected with the Japanese is too ridiculous to be considered. Amelia Earhart was an American in every sense of the word, loyal and abundantly proud of her country.

Was Amelia Earhart spying or was she, as many hold to be true, killed with Fred Noonan when their aircraft crashed into the sea? Perhaps somewhere there is hidden the truth—but it seems unlikely that the mysterious disappearance of the world's greatest woman pilot will ever be solved.

THE TREASURE HUNT

Robert Louis Stevenson

Jim Hawkins, whose father kept the Admiral Benbow Inn, *discovers a map in the sea-chest of old Billy Bones and takes it to Squire Trelawney. It turns out to be a map giving details of the buried treasure of Captain Flint, a pirate with whom Bones has served. Squire Trelawney, taking with him Dr Livesey and Jim, fits out the* Hispaniola *at Bristol to find the treasure. The squire's careless talk, however, attracts the scheming Long John Silver, who persuades Trelawney to enrol him as ship's cook and to crew the schooner with his nominees. The latter are all cut-throats and mutineers, and Silver himself Flint's old quartermaster.*

Immediately on landing at Treasure Island the trouble starts. The squire, the doctor and Jim, together with a few loyal seamen, escape from the ship and shift for themselves on the island.

Jim discovers Ben Gunn, who has been marooned for three years; but returning from a hazardous journey round the island on the Hispaniola, *which he has secured in North Islet, he falls into the hands of Silver and his gang. Silver now has possession of the map through a deal with the doctor, but the lack of success of his plans to this point has put him in danger from his unruly followers. The pirates, taking Jim with them, start on the treasure hunt and stumble across a skeleton.*

Partly from the damping influence of this alarm, partly to rest Silver and the sick folk, the whole party sat down as soon as they had gained the brow of the ascent.

The plateau being somewhat tilted toward the west, this spot on which we had paused commanded a wide prospect on either hand. Before us, over the treetops, we beheld the Cape of the Woods fringed with surf; behind, we not only looked down upon the anchorage and Skeleton Island, but saw—clear across the spit and the eastern lowlands

314

—a great field of open sea upon the east. Sheer above us rose the Spyglass, here dotted with single pines, there black with precipices. There was no sound but that of the distant breakers, mounting from all round, and the chirp of countless insects in the brush. Not a man, not a sail upon the sea; the very largeness of the view increased the sense of solitude.

Silver, as he sat, took certain bearings with his compass.

'There are three "tall trees",' said he, 'about in the right line from Skeleton Island. "Spyglass shoulder", I take it, means that lower p'int there. It's child's play to find the stuff now. I've half a mind to dine first.'

'I don't feel sharp,' growled Morgan. 'Thinkin' o' Flint—I think it were—has done me.'

'Ah, well, my son, you praise your stars he's dead,' said Silver.

'He were an ugly devil,' cried a third pirate, with a shudder; 'that blue in the face, too!'

'That was how the rum took him,' added Merry.

'Blue! well, I reckon he was blue. That's a true word.'

Ever since they had found the skeleton and got upon this train of thought they had spoken lower and lower, and they had almost got to whispering by now, so that the sound of their talk hardly interrupted the silence of the wood. All of a sudden, out of the middle of the trees in front of us, a thin, high, trembling voice struck up the well-known air and words:

'Fifteen men on the dead man's chest—Yo-ho-ho, and a bottle of rum!'

I never have seen men more dreadfully affected than the pirates. The colour went from their six faces like enchantment; some leaped to their feet, some clawed hold of others; Morgan grovelled on the ground.

'It's Flint, by——!' cried Merry.

The song had stopped as suddenly as it began—broken off, you would have said, in the middle of a note, as though someone had laid his hand upon the singer's mouth. Coming so far through the clear, sunny atmosphere among the green treetops, I thought it had sounded airily and sweetly; and the effect on my companions was the stranger.

'Come,' said Silver, struggling with his ashen lips to get the word out, 'this won't do. Stand by to go about. This is a rum start, and I can't name the voice: but it's someone skylarking—someone that's flesh and blood, and you may lay to that.'

His courage had come back as he spoke, and some of the colour to his face along with it. Already the others had begun to lend an ear to this encouragement, and were coming a little to themselves, when the same voice broke out again—not this time singing, but in a faint, distant hail, that echoed yet fainter among the clefts of the Spyglass.

'Darby M'Graw,' it wailed—for that is the word that best describes the sound—'Darby M'Graw! Darby M'Graw!' again and again and again; and then rising a little higher, and with an oath that I leave out, 'Fetch aft the rum, Darby!'

The buccaneers remained rooted to the ground, their eyes starting from their heads. Long after the voice had died away they still stared in silence, dreadfully, before them.

'That fixes it!' gasped one. 'Let's go.'

'They was his last words,' moaned Morgan, 'his last words above-board.'

Dick had his Bible out and was praying volubly. He had been well brought up, had Dick, before he came to sea and fell among bad companions.

Still, Silver was unconquered. I could hear his teeth rattle in his head; but he had not yet surrendered.

'Nobody in this here island ever heard of Darby,' he muttered; 'not one but us that's here.' And then, making a great effort, 'Shipmates,' he cried, 'I'm here to get that stuff, and I'll not be beat by man nor devil. I never was feared of Flint in his life and, by the powers, I'll face him dead. There's seven hundred thousand pound not a quarter of a mile from here. When did ever a gentleman o' fortune show his stern to that much dollars, for a boozy old seaman with a blue mug—and him dead, too?'

But there was no sign of reawakening courage in his followers; rather, indeed, of growing terror at the irreverence of his words.

'Belay there, John!' said Merry. 'Don't you cross a sperrit.'

And the rest were all too terrified to reply. They would have run away severally had they dared, but fear kept them together, and kept them close by John, as if his daring helped them. He, on his part, had pretty well fought his weakness down.

'Sperrit! Well, maybe,' he said. 'But there's one thing not clear to

316

me. There was an echo. Now, no man ever seen a sperrit with a shadow; well, then, what's he doing with an echo to him, I should like to know? That ain't in natur', surely?'

This argument seemed weak enough to me. But you can never tell what will affect the superstitious, and, to my wonder, George Merry was greatly relieved.

'Well, that's so,' he said. 'You've a head upon your shoulders, John, and no mistake. 'Bout ship, mates! This here crew is on a wrong tack, I do believe. And come to think on it, it was like Flint's voice, I grant you, but not just so clear-away like it, after all. It was liker somebody else's voice now—it was liker——'

'By the powers, Ben Gunn!' roared Silver.

'Aye, and so it were,' cried Morgan, springing on his knees. 'Ben Gunn it were!'

'It don't make much odds, do it, now?' asked Dick. 'Ben Gunn's not here in the body, any more'n Flint.'

But the older hands greeted this remark with scorn.

'Why, nobody minds Ben Gunn,' cried Merry; 'dead or alive, nobody minds him.'

It was extraordinary how their spirits had returned and how the natural colour had revived in their faces. Soon they were chatting together, with intervals of listening: and not long after, hearing no further sound, they shouldered the tools and set forth again, Merry walking first with Silver's compass to keep them on the right line with Skeleton Island. He had said the truth: dead or alive, nobody minded Ben Gunn.

Dick alone still held his Bible, and looked around him as he went, with fearful glances: but he found no sympathy, and Silver even joked him on his precautions.

'I told you,' said he, 'I told you you had sp'iled your Bible. If it ain't no good to swear by, what do you suppose a sperrit would give for it? Not that!' and he snapped his big fingers, halting a moment on his crutch.

But Dick was not to be comforted; indeed, it was soon plain to me that the lad was falling sick; hastened by heat, exhaustion, and the shock of his alarm, the fever predicted by Dr Livesey was evidently growing swiftly higher.

It was fine open walking here, upon the summit; our way lay a little downhill, for, as I have said, the plateau tilted toward the west. The pines, great and small, grew wide apart; and even between the clumps of nutmeg and azalea wide-open spaces baked in the hot sunshine. Striking, as we did, pretty near north-west across the island, we drew, on the one hand, ever nearer under the shoulders of the Spyglass and, on the other, looked ever wider over that western bay where I had once tossed and trembled in the coracle.

The first of the tall trees was reached, and by the bearing proved the wrong one. So with the second. The third rose nearly two hundred feet into the air above a clump of underwood; a giant of a vegetable, with a red column as big as a cottage, and a wide shadow around in which a company could have manoeuvred. It was conspicuous far to sea on both the east and west, and might have been entered as a sailing mark upon the chart.

But it was not its size that now impressed my companions; it was the knowledge that seven hundred thousand pounds in gold lay somewhere buried below its spreading shadow. The thought of the money, as they drew nearer, swallowed up their previous terrors. Their eyes burned in their heads; their feet grew speedier and lighter; their whole soul was bound up in that fortune, that whole lifetime of extravagance and pleasure, that lay waiting for each of them.

Silver hobbled, grunting, on his crutch; his nostrils stood out and quivered; he cursed like a madman when the flies settled on his hot and shiny countenance; he plucked furiously at the line that held me to him and, from time to time, turned his eyes upon me with a deadly look. Certainly he took no pains to hide his thoughts; and certainly I read them like print. In the immediate nearness of the gold, all else had been forgotten; his promise and the doctor's warning were both things of the past; and I could not doubt that he hoped to seize upon the treasure, find and board the *Hispaniola* under cover of night, cut every honest throat about that island, and sail away as he had at first intended, laden with crimes and riches.

Shaken as I was with these alarms, it was hard for me to keep up with the rapid pace of the treasure hunters. Now and again I stumbled, and it was then that Silver plucked so roughly at the rope and launched at me his murderous glances. Dick, who had dropped behind us and now brought up the rear, was babbling to himself both prayers and curses, as his fever kept rising. This also added to my wretchedness, and, to crown all, I was haunted by the thought of the tragedy that had once been acted on that plateau, when that ungodly buccaneer with the blue face—he who died at Savannah, singing and shouting for drink—had there, with his own hand, cut down his six accomplices. This grove, that was now so peaceful, must then have rung with cries, I thought; and even with the thought I could believe I heard it ringing still.

We were now at the margin of the thicket and more light shone through the trees.

'Huzza, mates, all together!' shouted Merry, and the foremost broke into a run.

And suddenly, not ten yards farther, we beheld them stop. A low cry arose. Silver doubled his pace, digging away with the foot of his crutch like one possessed; and next moment he and I came to a dead halt.

Before us was a great excavation, not very recent, for the sides had fallen in and grass had sprouted on the bottom. In this were the shaft of a pick broken in two and the boards of several packing cases strewn around. On one of these boards I saw, branded with a hot iron, the name *Walrus*—the name of Flint's ship.

All was clear to probation. The cache had been found and rifled: the seven hundred thousand pounds were gone!

There never was such an overturn in this world. Each of these six men was as though he had been struck. But with Silver the blow passed almost instantly. Every thought of his soul had been set full-stretch, like a racer, on that money. Well, he was brought up in a single second, dead; and he kept his head, found his temper, and changed his plan before the others had had time to realize the disappointment.

'Jim', he whispered, 'take that, and stand by for trouble.'

And he passed me a double-barrelled pistol.

At the same time he began quietly moving northward, and in a few steps had put the hollow between us two and the other five. Then he looked at me and nodded, as much as to say, 'Here is a narrow corner,' as, indeed, I thought it was. His looks were now quite friendly; and I was so revolted at these constant changes that I could not forbear whispering, 'So you've changed sides again.'

There was no time left for him to answer in. The buccaneers, with oaths and cries, began to leap, one after another, into the pit, and to dig

319

Silver doubled his pace, digging away with his crutch like one possessed.

320

with their fingers, throwing the boards aside as they did so. Morgan found a piece of gold. He held it up with a spout of oaths. It was a two-guinea piece, and it went from hand to hand among them for a quarter of a minute.

'Two guineas!' roared Merry, shaking it at Silver. 'That's your seven hundred thousand pounds, is it? You're the man for bargains, ain't you? You're him that never bungled nothing, you wooden-headed lubber!'

'Dig away, boys,' said Silver, with the coolest insolence, 'you'll find some pignuts and I shouldn't wonder.'

'Pignuts!' repeated Merry in a scream. 'Mates, do you hear that? I tell you, now, that man there knew it all along. Look in the face of him, and you'll see it wrote there.'

'Ah, Merry,' remarked Silver, 'standing for cap'n again? You're a pushing lad, to be sure.'

But this time everyone was entirely in Merry's favour. They began to scramble out of the excavation, darting furious glances behind them. One thing I observed, which looked well for us: they all got out upon the opposite side from Silver.

Well, there we stood, two on one side, five on the other, the pit between us, and nobody screwed up high enough to offer the first blow. Silver never moved; he watched them, very upright on his crutch, and looked as cool as ever I saw him. He was brave, and no mistake.

At last Merry seemed to think a speech might help matters.

'Mates', says he, 'there's two of them alone there: one's the old cripple that brought us all here and blundered us down to this; the other's that cub that I mean to have the heart of. Now, mates——'

He was raising his arm and his voice, and plainly meant to lead a charge. But jest then—*crack! crack! crack!*—three muskets shots flashed out of the thicket. Merry tumbled head foremost into the excavation; the man with the bandage spun round like a teetotum and fell all his length upon his side, where he lay dead, but still twitching; and the other three turned and ran for it with all their might.

Before you could wink, Long John had fired two barrels of a pistol into the struggling Merry; and as the man rolled up his eyes at him in the last agony, 'George,' said he, 'I reckon I settled you.'

At the same moment, the doctor, Gray and Ben Gunn joined us, with smoking muskets, from among the nutmeg trees.

'Forward!' cried the doctor. 'Double quick, my lads. We must head 'em off the boats.'

And we set off at a great pace, sometimes plunging through the bushes to the chest.

I tell you, but Silver was anxious to keep up with us. The work that man went through, leaping on his crutch till the muscles of his chest were fit to burst, was work no sound man ever equalled; and so thinks the doctor. As it was, he was already thirty yards behind us, and on the verge of strangling, when we reached the brow of the slope.

'Doctor,' he hailed, 'see there! No hurry!'

Sure enough there was no hurry. In a more open part of the plateau we could see the three survivors still running in the same direction as they had started, right for Mizzenmast Hill. We were already between them and the boats, and so we four sat down to breathe, while Long John, mopping his face, came slowly up with us.

'Thank ye kindly, doctor,' says he. 'You came in in about the nick, I guess, for me and Hawkins. And so it's you, Ben Gunn!' he added. 'Well, you're a nice one, to be sure.'

'I'm Ben Gunn, I am,' replied the maroon, wriggling like an eel in his embarrassment. 'And,' he added, after a long pause, 'how do, Mr Silver? Pretty well, I thank ye, says you.'

'Ben, Ben,' murmured Silver, 'to think as you've done me!'

The doctor sent back Gray for one of the pickaxes, deserted, in their flight, by the mutineers; and then as we proceeded leisurely downhill to where the boats were lying, related, in a few words, what had taken place. It was a story that interested Silver; and Ben Gunn, the half-idiot maroon, was the hero from beginning to end.

Ben, in his long, lonely wanderings about the island, had found the skeleton—it was he that had rifled it; he had found the treasure; he had dug it up (it was the haft of his pickaxe that lay broken in the excavation); he had carried it on his back, in many weary journeys, from the foot of the tall pine to a cave he had on the two-pointed hill at the northeast angle of the island, and there it had lain stored in safety since two months before the arrival of the *Hispaniola*.

When the doctor had wormed this secret from him, on the afternoon of the attack, and when next morning he saw the anchorage deserted, he had gone to Silver, given him the chart, which was now useless—

given him the stores, for Ben Gunn's cave was well supplied with goats' meat salted by himself—given anything and everything to get a chance of moving in safety from the stockade to the two-pointed hill, there to be clear of malaria and keep a guard on the money.

'As for you, Jim,' he said, 'it went against my heart, but I did what I thought best for those who had stood by their duty. And if you were not one of these, whose fault was it?'

That morning, finding that I was to be involved in the horrid disappointment he had prepared for the mutineers, he had run all the way to the cave and, leaving the squire to guard the captain, had taken Gray and the maroon, and started, making the diagonal across the island, to be at hand beside the pine. Soon, however, he saw that our party had the start of him; and Ben Gunn, being fleet of foot, had been dispatched in front to do his best alone. Then it had occurred to him to work upon the superstitions of his former shipmates; and he was so far successful that Gray and the doctor had come up and were already ambushed before the arrival of the treasure hunters.

'Ah,' said Silver, 'it were fortunate for me that I had Hawkins here. You would have let old John be cut to bits, and never given it a thought, doctor.'

'Not a thought,' replied Dr Livesey cheerily.

And by this time we had reached the gigs. The doctor, with the pickaxe, demolished one of them, and then we all got aboard the other, and set out to go round by sea for North Inlet.

This was a run of eight or nine miles. Silver, though he was almost killed already with fatigue, was set to an oar, like the rest of us, and we were soon skimming swiftly over a smooth sea. Soon we passed out of the straits and doubled the south-east corner of the island, round which, four days ago, we had towed the *Hispaniola*.

As we passed the two-pointed hill we could see the black mouth of Ben Gunn's cave, and a figure standing by it, leaning on a musket. It was the squire, and we waved a handkerchief and gave him three cheers, in which the voice of Silver joined as heartily as any.

Three miles farther, just inside the mouth of North Inlet, what should we meet but the *Hispaniola*, cruising by herself. The last flood had lifted her, and had there been much wind, or a strong tide current, as in the southern anchorage, we should never have found her more, or found her stranded beyond help. As it was, there was little amiss beyond the wreck of the mainsail. Another anchor was got ready, and dropped in a fathom and a half of water. We all pulled round again to Rum Cove, the nearest point for Ben Gunn's treasure house; and then Gray, single-handed, returned with the gig to the *Hispaniola*, where he was to pass the night on guard.

A gentle slope ran up from the beach to the entrance of the cave. At the top the squire met us. To me he was cordial and kind, saying nothing of my escapade, either in the way of blame or praise. At Silver's polite salute he somewhat flushed.

'John Silver,' he said, 'you're a prodigious villain and impostor—a monstrous impostor, sir. I am told I am not to prosecute you. Well, then, I will not. But the dead men, sir, hang about your neck like mill-stones.'

'Thank you kindly, sir,' replied Long John, again saluting.

'I dare you to thank me!' cried the squire. 'It is a gross dereliction of my duty. Stand back.'

And thereupon we all entered the cave. It was a large, airy place, with a little spring and a pool of clear water, overhung with ferns. The floor was sand. Before a big fire lay Captain Smollett, and in a far corner, only duskily flickered over by the blaze, I beheld great heaps of coin and quadrilaterals built of bars of gold. That was Flint's treasure that we had come so far to seek, and that had cost already the lives of seventeen men from the *Hispaniola*. How many it had cost in the amassing, what blood and sorrow, what good ships scuttled on the deep, what brave men walking the plank blindfold, what shot of cannon, what shame and lies and cruelty, perhaps no man alive could tell. Yet there were still three upon that island—Silver, and old Morgan, and Ben Gunn—who had each taken his share in these crimes, as each had hoped in vain to share in the reward.

'Come in, Jim,' said the captain. 'You're a good boy in your line, Jim, but I don't think you and me'll go to sea again. You're too much of the born favourite for me. Is that you, John Silver? What brings you here, man?'

'Come back to my dooty, sir,' returned Silver.

'Ah!' said the captain; and that was all he said.

What a supper I had of it that night, with all my friends around me;

and what a meal it was, with Ben Gunn's salted goat, and some delicacies and a bottle of old wine from the *Hispaniola*. Never, I am sure, were people gayer or happier. And there was Silver, sitting back almost out of the firelight, but eating heartily, prompt to spring forward when anything was wanted, even joining quietly in our laughter—the same bland, polite, obsequious seaman of the voyage out.

A NUN'S STORY

Lawrence Wilson

One fascinating thing about human life is the way in which genius crops up in the most unexpected places. It is not confined to the families of the rich or famous. Far from it. Admittedly Sir Winston Churchill was descended from the Dukes of Marlborough and St Francis of Assisi was the son of a wealthy cloth merchant; but the father of the poet John Keats had been a stable-boy, the artist William Turner was the son of a barber, Charles Dickens son of a clerk in the navy pay office, the composer Tchaikovsky son of an inspector of mines—and Mother Teresa of Calcutta was the daughter of an Albanian peasant.

The family, surnamed Bejaxhiu, consisted of one son and two daughters and lived in Skopje, Yugoslavia. Teresa's real name was Agnes, and she was born in 1910. At the age of twelve she became convinced that God was calling her to become a nun and that this vocation would in some way involve serving the poor. To start with, the idea did not appeal to her because her life in the family was so happy, but while at school in the following years she heard a great deal about the work of Christians helping the poor in India and became eager to follow their example. At eighteen she went to Ireland to prepare for her work and joined a religious order there called the Loreto nuns. A few months later she was sent to India.

As a nun, though, she had to do what she was told, and for some years there was no question of her working with the poor. In fact the opposite occurred. She was sent to a beautiful place called Darjeeling in the foothills of the Himalayas to teach geography and mathematics to the children of rich Indian parents. She found she enjoyed teaching very much and so, some years later, was glad to be sent to another convent school at Entally, a suburb of Calcutta. The place was clean, well organized, and set in a beautiful garden. But just beyond the convent wall was one of the worst slums in the city where people were literally dying in the streets of leprosy, malaria, tuberculosis, cholera—and starvation. 'Teresa' saw them and knew at once that here were the poorest of the poor that God had sent her to tend. What she did not know at that time was that in a city of seven million inhabitants (including the suburbs) there were nearly half a million of them.

At one time Calcutta was the capital of British-ruled India, and it is still a busy port and industrial centre. There have always been strong contrasts of wealth and poverty there, rich merchants' houses jostling slums where ragged poverty-striken people live and die in the streets or huddle together in makeshift shelters, their only possessions the odd cup and a few rusty cooking pots to be used when—and if—they have anything to cook. Only half the city has proper sanitation, otherwise sewage runs in open drains beside the streets. In the last four decades the squalor and poverty have been made much worse by an influx of refugees, including Hindus fleeing from the newly created state of Bangladesh (East Pakistan) and the victims of flood and famine in Calcutta's swampy hinterland. Already in 1946, when Teresa looked beyond her convent wall, the situation was bad enough—too bad for international or government aid to make much impression.

Yet here was a small, rather frail cloistered nun deciding that she alone had to do something for those desperate people. Men priding themselves on their sanity might well have called her crazy, and she would have agreed with them had she intended to compete with international airlines flying in sacks of wheat or those organizing large-scale relief. But she wasn't. There was a difference, and in this difference lies the crux of her story.

Right from the start Mother Teresa was determined to give the poor not only material help—food, shelter, clothing, medicines—but also love from person to person, believing that without it they would always feel rejected as outcasts. Let her speak as she did in 1970, after long experience:

'I have come more and more to realize that it is being unwanted that is the worst disease that any human being can ever suffer. Nowadays we have found medicines for leprosy and lepers can be cured. There's medicine for TB and consumptives can be cured. For all kinds of diseases there are medicines and cures. But for being unwanted, except there are willing hands to serve and there's a loving heart to love, I don't think this terrible disease can ever be cured.'

So, back in 1946, after the day's teaching was over, Mother Teresa would slip out into the streets to bring food and her loving concern to the starving people personally. Some weeks passed, and then, on a train journey to Darjeeling, she felt that God was calling her to give up teaching and devote her whole life to the poor. Two years later the Pope gave his blessing on her enterprise and she left the convent for ever. She had exactly five rupees (25p) in her pocket.

First, friends helped to send her to another town where she took a crash course in medical training. Then, back in Calcutta, she was given shelter by another order of nuns, the Little Sisters of the Poor, and started work immediately in the slums. Sister Agnes, now her principal assistant, remembers: 'She didn't know where she was going or what she was going to do in the future. Nothing. But she was not frightened. She knew God was calling her and would lead her where he wanted. She used to go out every day carrying something: a little bread, some medicine, things like that. And she used to walk from slum to slum to slum. Always working. Then always she would go to pray and eat the little food she had left, if any; she probably gave it all away.'

The work was hard and Mother Teresa made it even harder because, as she says, 'to be able to love the poor and to know the poor we must be poor ourselves.' This means that, to this day, she and her helpers exist on the barest necessities of life: the simplest food, hardly any personal possessions, no money of their own and, for clothes, a length of cheap white cotton wrapped round the body, like the sari which Hindu women wear. But in those early years, before her name became known throughout the world, many of her former pupils came to join her, promising to devote their whole lives to her work, some even while still studying for their exams. Surprisingly, a few were high-caste Indian girls who normally would have refused to go anywhere near the 'untouchables', as they were called by the Hindus.

Soon Mother Theresa set up a slum school for young children in an open space among dilapidated huts, teaching them at first only how to keep clean and some signs from the Bengali alphabet. These had to be written in the mud with a stick because there were no blackboards, and there were no chairs or benches either. But on the second day someone donated a table, then a chair, later a cupboard.

From the start she refused to accept payment from anyone, assuming anyone was able to pay, nor would she accept government money. As it was God's work she believed God would provide. and money certainly came, from friends, from people touched by the obvious value of her work, always enough, just enough to help her do what she wanted —and she wanted to do a great deal more. For the growing number of her dedicated helpers, the Missionaries of Charity as they were now called, she needed a place where they could live, a Mother House, and this was provided by a well-wisher at a nominal rent.

Above all, she needed a home for the dying. She knew that from personal experience. Once, when still teaching at Entally, she had picked up a sick woman in the streets, taken her back to the convent and given her her own bed. Then she found another woman with her feet half eaten away by rats and ants. Teresa had somehow got her to hospital and simply refused to leave till the doctors had taken her in. They were not callous or indifferent, but Calcutta's hospitals are always overcrowded, bursting at the seams. There is never room for everyone.

Now Teresa was determined to have a place where at least some of Calcutta's half-million derelicts could die in dignity, tended with loving care. They had to know they were wanted and loved, at least for the few hours left to them in this world. She had no desire to set up a big rescue operation, even if she had had the resources, because she knew that persons would be lost in sheer numbers and become simply mouths to feed. 'I do not agree,' she has said, 'with the big way of doing things. To us what matters is the individual.' And in the individual, however disgusting his or her sores and sickness, however repellent the personality, she sees nothing less than the spirit of Jesus Christ.

In 1952 the city corporation offered her a place for the dying. It had been a rest-house for pilgrims visiting the temple of a Hindu goddess and was at that time a doss-house for thugs, thieves and drug-addicts. They did not like having to move out and they made a lot of trouble, even threatening to kill her. 'All right,' she said, 'then kill me, but let us have an end to this nonsense.' Incredibly then they gave way and the home was set up and called Nirmal Hriday, 'The Place of the Pure Heart'.

When journalists visit the home today they are scared to start with, but after they have seen the long rows of mattresses, on each a dark figure quietly awaiting his time to leave this world, the Sisters flitting to and fro giving a drink here, a word of comfort there, and have felt the atmosphere of love, all agree that in Nirmal Hriday there is an indescribable sense of peace. In nearly twenty years 23,000 people have been taken there from the streets, most of them in the last stages of illness and disease, so that inevitably nearly half have died. But that is what the place is for: to give final comfort to the dying.

But to Mother Teresa this was by no means enough. She had only to go into a Calcutta street or one of the big railway stations to see there were thousands still uncared for. In the main hallways, instead of the bustling passengers seen in London, there were pathetic groups squatting everywhere, whole families living, dying and being born—among them many lepers.

Leprosy is a terrible infectious disease which attacks the central nervous system until bit by bit the whole body becomes involved. Deep ulcers form on the skin, fingers and toes lose their feeling and drop off, even the lungs and vocal cords are affected, so that the sufferer can barely speak. At one time, and still today in many places, when an Indian family saw the tell-tale patch on a member's skin they were so scared of infection that they simply pushed him out to wander the streets or the countryside. Whole colonies of these poor people would then cling together in utter hopelessness because there was nowhere among the fit and active for them to go. So Mother Teresa started to help, first with a humble shed in one of the slums for leper children, then with proper settlements in other areas where the lepers could be treated and given light work. Mobile dispensaries were set up, later still a hospital and rehabilitation centre entirely for lepers.

It would seem horrible as well as dangerous work being with such people, but Teresa's flock of nuns, ever growing in numbers, coming now from all over the world, strictly trained and dedicated, go about it with positive joy. Like her, they say quite simply that Jesus guides them and it is Jesus they serve in the lepers. Even in the most disreputable characters they can see something good. Recently a journalist was shown round a leper settlement. A patient was introduced. 'He's a murderer,' said the Sister cheerily. 'He has been in prison. He's deformed, but he has a heart of gold. Only yesterday he told me, "You Sisters have defeated me. You love even the wicked".'

The poor, the starving, the sick and small children—all come within the net of Mother Teresa's loving concern. She has set up homes for children abandoned in the streets, left with her by their parents, sent from hospitals, even rescued from dustbins. Many of the babies are born prematurely and when brought in are too feeble even to suck, so they have to be fed through the nose or by injection. Though the homes are crowded so far no child has ever been refused.

Slowly the work of the Missionaries of Charity became better known and began to spread throughout India and the rest of the world. Men as well as girls began to volunteer and went through the same strict training, took the same vows of poverty, chastity and obedience, with the same object: to give love and succour to the poor. By 1975 sixty-one centres were operating in India and more in other countries, in the slums of London and Belfast, in the USA, Australia, Italy, Israel, Bangladesh, Jordan, Venezuela, Peru, the Yemen, Mauritius, New Guinea, Tanzania and Ethiopia. Now, too, there are the Co-Workers of Mother Teresa, people everywhere, even in small English villages, who collect clothing, blankets, cigarette coupons, trading stamps and money for the great cause. School-children in England give money to buy bread for the starving; in West Germany they give the equivalent of a glass of milk per day or per week.

Mother Teresa has been nominated for the Nobel Peace Prize. Many other awards have been showered on her. But she shrugs it all off. All this recognition, she says, is not for her but for the poor whom she serves. And here once more we have to recognize the difference between international relief organized impersonally and what she and her helpers are doing throughout the world. They do not try to convert anyone to Christianity, but they themselves are committed Christians, believing that God gives them his own love to pass on to suffering individuals and that beneath their sores and the often hideous diseases the spirit of God is in them too, waiting to be served.

So from the conviction of one twelve-year-old girl, first felt over fifty years ago, that her destiny was to serve the poor, has grown a mighty world-wide band of helpers, joyous and powerful in their faith and self-sacrifice.

DICING WITH DEATH

Rider Haggard

Deep in the rock beneath a gigantic mountain in eastern Africa lay two secret, connecting chambers—the Chamber of the Dead, housing the ancestors of the Kukuana tribe, and the Treasure House of King Solomon, where tons of gold, diamonds and ivory were stored. To this frightening but intriguing place three Britishers had come in search of a lost comrade: Allan Quatermain, the narrator of the following story, Sir Henry Curtis and Captain John Good, of the Royal Navy. Despite warnings from Infadoos, a friendly officer in the Kukuana Army, the three had allowed themselves to be led into the Treasure House by an aged sorceress. Now this treacherous crone had lowered a heavy stone slab, barring the entrance, and they were trapped.

I can give no adequate description of the horrors of the night which followed. Mercifully they were to some extent mitigated by sleep, for even in such a position as ours wearied nature will sometimes assert itself. But I, at any rate, found it impossible to sleep much. Putting aside the terrifying thought of our impending doom—for the bravest man on earth might well quail from such a fate as awaited us, and I never made any pretensions to be brave—the *silence* itself was too great to allow of it.

Reader, you may have lain awake at night and thought the quiet oppressive, but I say with confidence that you can have no idea what a vivid, tangible thing is perfect stillness. On the surface of the earth there is always some sound or motion, and though it may in itself be imperceptible, yet it deadens the sharp edge of absolute silence. But here there was none. We were buried in the bowels of a huge snow-clad peak. Thousands of feet above us the fresh air rushed over the white snow, but no sound of it reached us. We were separated by a long tunnel and five feet of rock even from the awful Chamber of the Dead; and the dead make no noise. The crashing of all the artillery of earth and heaven could not have come to our ears in our living tomb. We were cut off from every echo of the world—we were as men already in the grave.

Then the irony of the situation forced itself upon me. There around us lay treasures enough to pay off a moderate national debt, or to build a fleet of iron-clad ships, and yet we would have bartered them all gladly for the faintest chance of escape. Soon, doubtless, we should be rejoiced to exchange them for a bit of food or a cup of water, and, after that, even for the privilege of a speedy end to our sufferings. Truly wealth, which men spend their lives in acquiring, is a valueless thing at the last.

And so the night wore on.

'Good,' said Sir Henry's voice at last, to the captain, and it sounded awful in the intense stillness, 'how many matches have you in the box?'

'Eight, Curtis.'

'Strike one and let us see the time.'

He did so, and in contrast to the dense darkness the flame nearly blinded us. It was five o'clock by my watch. The beautiful dawn was now blushing on the snow-wreaths far over our heads, and the breeze would be stirring the night mists in the hollows.

'We had better eat something and keep up our strength,' I suggested.

'What is the good of eating?' answered Good; 'the sooner we die and get it over the better.'

'While there is life there is hope,' said Sir Henry.

Accordingly we ate and sipped some water, and another period of time passed. Then Sir Henry suggested that it might be well to get as near the door as possible and yell, on the faint chance of somebody catching a sound outside. Accordingly Good, who, from long practice at sea, has a fine piercing note, groped his way down the passage and set to work. I must say that he made a most diabolical noise. I never heard such yells; but it might have been a mosquito buzzing for all the effect they produced.

After a while he gave it up and came back very thirsty, and had to drink. Then we stopped yelling, as it encroached on the supply of water.

So we sat down once more against the chests of useless diamonds in that dreadful inaction which was one of the hardest circumstances of our fate; and I am bound to say that, for my part, I gave way in despair. Laying my head against Sir Henry's broad shoulder I burst into tears; and I think that I heard Good gulping away on the other side, and swearing hoarsely at himself for doing so.

Ah, how good and brave that great man was! Had we been two frightened children, and he our nurse, he could not have treated us more tenderly. Forgetting his own share of miseries, he did all he could to soothe our broken nerves, telling stories of men who had been in somewhat similar circumstances, and miraculously escaped; and when these failed to cheer us, pointing out how, after all, it was only anticipating an end which must come to us all, that it would soon be over, and that death from exhaustion was a merciful one (which is not true). Then, in a diffident sort of way, as once before I had heard him do, he suggested that we should throw ourselves on the mercy of a higher power, which for my part I did with great vigour.

His is a beautiful character, very quiet, but very strong.

And so somehow the day went as the night had gone, if, indeed, one can use these terms where all was densest night, and when I lit a match to see the time it was seven o'clock.

Once more we ate and drank, and as we did so an idea occurred to me.

'How is it,' said I, 'that the air in this place keeps fresh? It is thick and heavy, but it is perfectly fresh.'

'Great heavens!' said Good, starting up, 'I never thought of that. It can't come through the stone door, for it's air-tight, if ever a door was. It must come from somewhere. If there were no current of air in the place we should have been stifled or poisoned when we first came in. Let us have a look.'

It was wonderful what a change this mere spark of hope wrought in us. In a moment we were all three groping about on our hands and knees, feeling for the slightest indication of a draught.

For an hour or more we went on feeling about, till at last Sir Henry and I gave it up in despair, having been considerably hurt by constantly knocking our heads against tusks, chests, and the sides of the chamber. But Good still persevered, saying, with an approach to cheerfulness, that it was better than doing nothing.

'I say, you fellows,' he said presently, in a constrained sort of voice, 'come here.'

Needless to say we scrambled towards him quickly enough.

'Quatermain, put your hand here where mine is. Now, do you feel anything?'

335

'I *think* I feel air coming up.'

'Now listen.' He rose and stamped upon the place, and a flame of hope shot up in our hearts. *It rang hollow.*

With trembling hands I lit a match. I had only three left, and we saw that we were in the angle of the far corner of the chamber, a fact that accounted for our not having noticed the hollow sound of the place during our former exhaustive examination. As the match burnt we scrutinized the spot. There was a join in the solid rock floor, and, great heavens! There, let in level with the rock, was a stone ring. We said no word, we were too excited, and our hearts beat too wildly with hope to allow us to speak. Good had a knife, at the back of which was one of those hooks that are made to extract stones from horses' hoofs. He opened it, and scratched round the ring with it. Finally he worked it under, and levered away gently for fear of breaking the hook. The ring began to move. Being of stone it had not rusted fast in all the centuries it had lain there, as would have been the case had it been of iron. Presently it was upright. Then he thrust his hands into it and tugged with all his force, but nothing budged.

'Let me try,' I said impatiently, for the situation of the stone, right in the angle of the corner, was such that it was impossible for two to pull at once. I took hold and strained away, but no results.

Then Sir Henry tried and failed.

Taking the hook again, Good scratched all round the crack where we felt the air coming up.

'Now, Curtis,' he said, 'tackle on, and put your back into it; you are as strong as two. Stop,' and he took off a stout black silk handkerchief, which, true to his habits of neatness, he still wore, and ran it through the ring. 'Quatermain, get Curtis round the middle and pull for dear life when I give the word. *Now.*'

Sir Henry put out all his enormous strength, and Good and I did the same, with such power as nature had given us.

'Heave! heave! It's giving,' gasped Sir Henry; and I heard the muscles of his great back cracking. Suddenly there was a grating sound, then a rush of air, and we were all on our backs on the floor with a heavy flagstone upon the top of us. Sir Henry's strength had done it, and never did muscular power stand a man in better stead.

'Light a match, Quatermain,' he said, as soon as we had picked our-

336

I heard the muscles of Sir Henry's great back cracking . . .

selves up and got our breath; 'carefully, now.'

I did so, and there before us, heaven be praised! was the *first step of a stone stair.*

'Now what is to be done?' asked Good.

'Follow the stair, of course, and trust to providence.'

'Stop!' said Sir Henry; 'Quatermain, get the bit of biltong [dried meat] and the water that is left; we may want them.'

I went, creeping back to our place by the chests for that purpose, and as I was coming away an idea struck me. We had not thought much of the diamonds for the last twenty-four hours or so; indeed, the very idea of diamonds was nauseous, seeing what they had entailed upon us; but, reflected I, I may as well pocket some in case we ever should get out of this ghastly hole. So I just put my fist into the first chest and filled all the available pockets of my old shooting-coat and trousers, topping up— this was a happy thought—with a few handful of big ones out of the third chest. Also, by an afterthought, I stuffed a basket, which, except for one water-gourd and a little biltong, was empty now, with great quantities of the stones.

'I say, you fellows,' I sang out, 'won't you take some diamonds with you? I've filled my pockets and the basket.'

'Oh, come on, Quatermain, and hang the diamonds!' said Sir Henry. 'I hope that I may never see another.'

As for Good, he made no answer. And curious as it may seem to you, my reader, sitting at home at ease and reflecting on the vast, indeed the immeasurable, wealth which we were thus abandoning, I can assure you that if you had passed some twenty-eight hours with next to nothing to eat and drink in that place, you would not have cared to cumber yourself with diamonds whilst plunging down into the unknown bowels of the earth, in the wild hope of escape from an agonizing death. If from the habits of a lifetime, it had not become a sort of second nature with me never to leave anything worth having behind if there was the slightest chance of my being able to carry it away, I am sure that I should not have bothered to fill my pockets and that basket.

'Come on, Quatermain,' repeated Sir Henry, who was already standing on the first step of the stone stair. 'Steady, I will go first.'

'Mind where you put your feet, there may be some awful hole underneath,' I answered.

'Much more likely to be another room,' said Sir Henry, while he descended slowly, counting the steps as he went.

When he got to 'fifteen' he stopped. 'Here's the bottom,' he said. 'Thank goodness! I think it's a passage. Follow me down.'

Good went next, and I came last, carrying the basket, and on reaching the bottom lit one of the two remaining matches. By its light we could just see that we were standing in a narrow tunnel, which ran right and left at right angles to the staircase we had descended. Before we could make out any more, the match burnt my fingers and went out. Then arose the delicate question of which way to go. Of course, it was impossible to know what the tunnel was, or where it led to, and yet to turn one way might lead us to safety, and the other to destruction. We were utterly perplexed, till suddenly it struck Good that when I had lit the match the draught of the passage blew the flame to the left.

'Let us go against the draught,' he said; 'air draws inwards, not outwards.'

We took this suggestion, and feeling along the wall with our hands, whilst trying the ground before us at every step, we departed from that accursed treasure chamber on our terrible quest for life. If ever it should be entered again by living man, which I do not think probable, he will find tokens of our visit in the open chests of jewels, the empty lamp, and the white bones of poor Foulata.

When we had groped our way for about a quarter of an hour along the passage, suddenly it took a sharp turn, or else was bisected by another which we followed only in course of time to be led into a third. And so it went on for some hours. We seemed to be in a stone labyrinth which led nowhere. What all these passages are, of course I cannot say, but we thought that they must be the ancient workings of a mine, of which the various shafts and adits travelled hither and thither as the ore led them. This is the only way in which we could account for such a multitude of galleries.

At length we halted, thoroughly worn out with fatigue and with that hope deferred which makes the heart sick, and ate up our poor remaining piece of biltong and drank our last sup of water, for our throats were like lime-kilns. It seemed to us that we had escaped death in the darkness of the treasure chamber only to meet him in the darkness of the tunnels.

As we stood, once more utterly depressed, I thought that I caught a sound, to which I called the attention of the others. It was very faint and very far off, but it *was* a sound, a faint, murmuring sound, for the others heard it too, and no words can describe the blessedness of it after all those house of utter, awful stillness.

'By heaven! It's running water,' said Good. 'Come on.'

Off we started again in the direction from which the faint murmur seemed to come, groping our way as before along the rocky walls. I remember that I laid down the basket full of diamonds, wishing to be rid of its weight, but on second thoughts took it up again. One might as well die rich as poor, I reflected. As we went the sound became more and more audible, till at last it seemed quite loud in the quiet. On, yet on; now we could distinctly make out the unmistakable swirl of rushing water. And yet how could there be running water in the bowels of the earth? Now we were quite near it, and Good, who was leading, swore that he could smell it.

'Go gently, Good,' said Sir Henry, 'we must be close.' *Splash!* and a cry from Good.

He had fallen in.

'Good! Good! Where are you?' we shouted, in terrified distress. To our intense relief an answer came back in a choky voice.

'All right; I've got hold of a rock. Strike a light to show me where you are.'

Hastily I lit the last remaining match. Its faint gleam discovered to us a dark mass of water running at our feet. How wide it was we could not see, but there, some way out, was the dark form of our companion hanging on to a projecting rock.

'Stand clear to catch me,' sung out Good. 'I must swim for it.'

Then we heard a splash, and a great struggle. Another minute and he grabbed at and caught Sir Henry's outstretched hand, and we had pulled him up high and dry into the tunnel.

'My word!' he said, between his gasps, 'that was touch and go. If I hadn't managed to catch that rock, and known how to swim, I should have been done. It runs like a mill-race, and I could feel no bottom.'

We dared not follow the banks of the subterranean river lest we should fall into it again in the darkness. So after Good had rested a while, and we had drunk our fill of the water, which was sweet and fresh, and washed our faces, that needed it sadly, as well as we could, we started from the banks of this African Styx, and began to retrace our steps along the tunnel, Good dripping unpleasantly in front of us. At length we came to another gallery leading to our right.

'We may as well take it,' said Sir Henry wearily; 'all roads are alike here; we can only go on till we drop.'

Slowly, for a long, long while, we stumbled, utterly exhausted, along this new tunnel, Sir Henry now leading the way. Again I thought of abandoning that basket, but did not.

Suddenly he stopped, and we bumped up against him.

'Look!' he whispered, 'is my brain going, or is that light?'

We stared with all our eyes, and there, yes, there, far ahead of us, was a faint, glimmering spot, no larger than a cottage window pane. It was so faint that I doubt if any eyes, except those which, like ours, had for days seen nothing but blackness, could have perceived it at all.

With a gasp of hope we pushed on. In five minutes there was no longer any doubt; it *was* a patch of faint light. A minute more and a breath of real live air was fanning us. On we struggled. All at once the tunnel narrowed, Sir Henry went on his knees. Smaller yet it grew, till it was only the size of a large fox's earth—it was *earth* now, mind you: the rock had ceased.

A squeeze, a struggle, and Sir Henry was out, and so was Good, and so was I, dragging the basket after me; and there above us were the blessed stars, and in our nostrils was the sweet air. Then suddenly something gave, and we were all rolling over and over and over through grass and bushes and soft, wet soil.

The basket caught in something and I stopped. Sitting up I hallooed lustily. An answering shout came from just below, where Sir Henry's wild career had been checked by some level ground. I scrambled to him, and found him unhurt, though breathless. Then we looked for Good. A little way off we discovered him also, jammed in a forked root. He was a good deal knocked about, but soon came to himself.

We sat down together, there on the grass, and the revulsion of feeling was so great that really I think we cried with joy. We had escaped from that awful dungeon, which was so near to becoming our grave. Surely some merciful power guided our footsteps to the jackal hole, for that is what it must have been, at the termination of the tunnel. And see, yonder on the mountains the dawn we had never thought to look upon again was blushing rosy red.

Presently the grey light stole down the slopes, and we saw that we were at the bottom, or rather, nearly at the bottom, of the vast pit in front of the entrance to the cave. Doubtless those awful passages, along which we had wandered the lifelong night, had been originally in some way connected with the great diamond mine. As for the subterranean river in the bowels of the mountain, heaven only knows what it is, or whence it flows, or whither it goes. I, for one, have no anxiety to trace its course.

Lighter it grew, and lighter yet. We would see each other now, and such a spectacle as we presented I have never set eyes on before or since. Gaunt-cheeked, hollow-eyed wretches, smeared all over with dust and mud, bruised, bleeding, the long fear of imminent death yet written on our countenances, we were, indeed, a sight to frighten the daylight. And yet it is a solemn fact that Good's eyeglass was still fixed in Good's eye. I doubt whether he had ever taken it out at all. Neither the darkness, nor the plunge in the subterranean river, nor the roll down the slope, had been able to separate Good and his eyeglass.

Presently we rose, fearing that our limbs would stiffen if we stopped there longer, and commenced with slow and painful steps to struggle up the sloping sides of the great pit. For an hour or more we toiled stead-fastly up the blue clay, dragging ourselves on by the help of the roots and grasses with which it was clothed. But now I had no more thought of leaving the basket; indeed, nothing but death should have parted us.

At last it was done, and we stood by the great road.

At the side of the road, a hundred yards off, a fire was burning in front of some huts, and round the fire were figures. We staggered to-wards them, supporting one another, and halting every few paces. Presently one of the figures rose, saw us and fell on to the ground, crying out for fear.

'Infadoos, Infadoos! It is we, thy friends.'

He rose; he ran to us, staring wildly, and still shaking visibly with fear.

'Oh, my lords, my lords, it is indeed you come back from the dead! Come back from the dead!'

And the old warrior flung himself down before us, and clasping Sir Henry's knees, he wept aloud for joy.

THE STOLEN CUBS

Ronald Voy

Cairncross was up with the lark that morning, and he found the trail of the vixen in the dew. He could see where she had passed through the long grass, the drag of her body clearly marked in a thin dark line leading straight from his homestead after her usual visit to explore the hen-house—the vixen who had already stolen three of his prized Orpingtons, and who, by her stealth and cunning, promised to annihilate the whole roost. He guessed that she would be nursing her cubs not far off, and now was his chance of tracking her to the den. He took his rifle and a couple of traps with him. If he found her at home he would smoke her out, and shoot her; if away, he would set his traps at the den mouth, so that she would encounter one or both of them on her return. Even though she knew traps were there she *would* return to carry her cubs out of the danger zone, so the settler's hopes were high.

The man moved briskly and noiselessly, with the elastic swing of one accustomed to great distances in the stony places. His rifle hung in the crook of his arm, as though it was a part of his person, and only his keen eyes, which scanned every bush and thicket, indicated how alert he was for any moving form. For he knew that as he drew near the den, the vixen might show herself in the hope of diverting his line of travel.

So across the stream, from which he drew his drinking water, through the fragrance of the blueberry patch, and in and out among the jack-pines, then down into Red Valley, where the timber became denser among the boulders. This was a likely spot, and any moment the trail might cease at the den mouth. Silent in his sodden moose-hide moccasins, the man slackened speed and increased his vigilance. Luckily for him, too, for a warning came.

What shape it took he did not know. He heard no sound, saw no movement, but suddenly he stopped dead in his tracks, and the rifle slipped down into the palm of his hand. His gaze became sharply focused on the thicket of a hemlock branch two feet above his head and twelve paces away. But that his woodland instincts were so keenly sharpened he would, a second or two later, have passed immediately under that branch.

At first Cairncross could see nothing, then he discerned a crouching outline—an outline which might, indeed, have passed for a shadow. It was long and low, and at one end of it there was a suggestion of a rounded scalp and of two keen eyes fixed upon him. He could not see the eyes, but he could feel their stare, and instinct told him that the thing had slipped along the branch only a second or two ago, and that it was waiting for him—waiting for him to pass below.

The rifle slipped lower, then slowly, almost perceptibly, it began to rise. Cairncross felt that the crouching shadow in the leaves of the hemlock was tense and quivering, ready to launch itself, and he lost no time. Probably less than five seconds elapsed ere the sharp report smote the morning, yet in the man's movements there was no suggestion of haste, no jerky motion of the kind the Wild Folk see and distrust. The 30–30 spoke, the echoes came and went from slope to butte, and away off into immeasurable space. The branch teetered a little, there was the sound of a body moving swiftly, and the shadow was gone.

Cairncross knew that his shot had told. It was rarely *his* shots did otherwise, and just before he pressed the trigger, the huntsman's knowledge had come to him that his victim was doomed. Truly she had departed ably enough, yet he knew that she would travel less than a hundred yards, and now he heard a sound which left no doubt in his mind. It was just a short, dry cough.

344

'Huh!' muttered Cairncross. 'Old mountain lion, eh, and me thinking it was a fox!'

He swung back a matter of forty paces into the centre of an open patch, no trees near, and sat himself down on an ant-infested log. No sound came to his ears, save the crystal bird sounds of the morning and the gurgle of the stream back across the blueberry clump. Still he did not hurry. He took out his tobacco tin, rubbed up a fill, and proceeded to smoke—and listen. Thirty minutes elapsed ere he rose and went to the place where the mountain lion had crouched. Yes, there was blood—much blood. So much that he considered it safe to follow, but he did so foot by foot rather than yard by yard.

Ten minutes later he stood at the mouth of a hole under a rock. She was in there, he knew, but no sound came from within. It was a dark, natural hole, and he could not see the end of it. He took an electric flashlamp from his pocket, and switching on the light, poked it in, his rifle following the rays, for any ordinary man would have considered this a deadly risk. If she came out, as a wounded cougar might do—well, she would be on top of him ere he could act, but Cairncross was reckless in his familiarity with the Wild Folk, and had so long escaped a mauling that he thought little of risks. Lowering his face into the line of fire, he saw a bundle of fur about ten feet in—her hind quarters evidently, her head away from him. That fact alone indicated that she was dead, for a live cat, any cat, invariably turns its eyes in the direction of danger.

Cairncross rose. The skin at this season would not be worth much, and so long as she was dead that was all he cared. He went back to the point at which he had originally seen her, rubbed up another fill of tobacco, then for a full hour sat absolutely motionless—listening.

At length the sound for which he was waiting came to his ears. It was very small and very thin, and a minute or more elapsed ere he could judge its direction. A plaintive wailing, which rose and fell—clearly the wailing of little things whose stomachs bade them call for their mother.

Cairncross stole in the direction of the sound, readjusted his line, lost the sound, found it again, went back to the starting point, and thus spent another twenty minutes ere he stood at the mouth of a hole under a rock—a very similar hole to the one into which the mother cougar had crawled. Not the same one, of course. It is not the way of wild woodland mothers to betray their children thus.

The man lay flat and thrust his hand into the hole. He judged that the kits were too small to harm him much, and here, at any rate, he was wrong. The nest was within arm's reach, and his naked hand was greeted by a fusilade of vicious blows from claws and fangs, while the wailing turned to explosive hissings and rumblings.

Cairncross cursed, and looked at his fingers. They were dripping blood. The back of his hand was badly lacerated, but by a miracle no arteries were torn. He had been a fool, of course, but he was angry rather than remorseful. He wanted those kits, and he wanted them alive, for healthy cubs would fetch at least twenty dollars apiece.

Anyway, it was not worth while getting mauled, so he tried to stop the bleeding with moss, then he closed the mouth of the hole with stones, and went back for his mitts and the iodine. In the cabin he mopped himself up and bound his injuries, which were even worse than he had thought. It looked as though he were going to have a very sore hand for some days, but he lost no time in returning to the den with his mitts and with a stout bag to carry the kittens home.

When Cairncross got them out, he was surprised at their first savage resistance, for their eyes were only just open—little fluffy, staggering things, which, now dazed by the light, offered no resistance whatever. He dropped them one by one into the bag, three in all, then hurried home as pleased as a schoolboy.

Cairncross kept a cow, so he anticipated no trouble in rearing the youngsters, and, strange to say, having now become accustomed to the man scent, they offered no objection whatever to being handled. He fed them one by one from a teaspoon—a long, sloppy business— and as each cub obtained its fill, it fell asleep between his knees, forth- with to be dropped into the hogshead, lined with an old shirt.

Not a sound came from the tub till milking time, when the cubs struck up an unearthly wailing, which would have carried half a mile. Cairncross left them at it while he brought in the cow, but milking proved rather a protracted business, since his wounded hand was stiff, and his grip sorely taxed. When he had finished, the pain made him feel sick, and he was glad to have the kittens fed and to remove his crude bandages and examine the wounds.

No, they did not look very nice, but another dab or two of iodine and some boracic powder would probably help matters. He went to

He fed there one by one with a teaspoon.

bed with the fading of the light, but not to sleep, for his hand throbbed like a pulsometer, and he began to fear trouble with it. At midnight he got up for a dose of quinine, and scarcely was he settled again when those wretched cubs struck up a fresh chorus to be fed. Cairncross left them at it, hoping they would fall asleep, and so ten minutes passed, when suddenly Cairncross found himself sitting bolt upright.

He could swear he had heard some one 'hallo' down the trail which led to the cabin—someone coming to visit him, no doubt, and calling out for him to show a light. He listened, and again the sound came—a distinct 'hallo', yet so indistinct that he could judge neither its distance nor its direction. It might be a loon, and again—it might not.

Cairncross rose. If anyone were about, he would be glad to see them, for his nearest neighbours were seventeen miles away, and he could do with a helping hand till his wounds improved. He went over to the door, intent on giving an answer. Outside it was brilliant moonlight. The kits were howling louder than ever, and scarcely had Cairncross raised the latch when he received the fright of his life.

The door was half open when something whisked past his face, missing him by the merest fraction of an inch. He felt the wind of it as it smote the door with a force which all but sprung the hinges, and at that same instant Cairncross saw half of a rounded scalp silhouetted against the sky and peering down at him from the roof of the cabin two feet from his face.

With a startled cry he slammed the door to, and began to grope round for his rifle. His head swam, and he felt half drunken. He could not find the rifle, but he found a candle and lit it, then stood listening and pondering. What had happened anyway? If that old cougar had recovered it was a miracle, for he was dead sure that the beast which had struck at his face and hit only the door was a strong and healthy one. The father? Cairncross would have pooh-poohed the idea. With his knowledge of the wild, he set wild fathers at a discount, especially where any of the cat tribe were concerned. He knew of no wild fur-clad father—barring the dog fox—who was worth two cents where the safety of its cubs was concerned. Father be hanged! But—what then?

Still he pondered, and the silence of the night seemed to hiss in his ears. Not a bat squeaked, not an owl disturbed the woodland quietude. If the old cat were still on the roof, which he doubted, she evidently had not stirred since she struck at him. She was still waiting, but—he guessed that she had dropped to ground and made off, scared at her own boldness. If she had crossed the roof, he would certainly have heard the timbers creaking.

Anyway, there was nothing more to be done, so Cairncross went to his bunk, leaving the candle burning, and in spite of everything, including the cubs' spasmodic caterwauling, he fell into a profound sleep.

When he awoke the sun was streaming in at the window, and the candle had spread its last liquid remains over the bench. He knew from the sun's position that it was towards midday, and the three cubs were at it harder than ever. The biggest of them, a plump male cub, had contrived to scramble out of the tub, and sat squashed up on one corner among a bundle of rusty traps.

As Cairncross sat up his head throbbed most abominably and the blood seemed to gush into his legs. He looked down at his feet. They were red and swollen. His injured hand felt oddly numb and cold, and recalling what had happened, he looked at it and started in horror. From the elbow down, the limb was tremendously swollen, and the knowledge came to Cairncross that he was a very sick man, and likely to be a good deal sicker before he was through with it.

Bad luck this! Outside the old cow was lowing and rubbing her nose against the latch, waiting to be milked. He had made a mess of things and no mistake, for he felt in no fit shape for travelling to solicit the help of his neighbours, and the next problem was how to carry on. He must milk the cow at all events, so he staggered out.

Here another unpleasant surprise awaited him, for the old cow also was sick. She was shaking like a jelly, and across her right flank from the shoulder blade down, extended four deep, lurid scratches, obviously where the great cat had viciously dabbed at her.

Cairncross never knew how he got through his milking that morning, nor how he finally dragged himself back to the cabin. He found himself propped up against the bunk, the door wide open, while the wretched cubs were still holding forth good and strong.

With an effort he managed to clear his mind. That he could not feed them was certain, and he did not want the poor little varmints to starve to death. He had no love for mountain lions, yet he had stolen them from their mother, if such it was, and it was up to him to play the game.

It would take him all his time to feed himself, and moreover, so long as those kits kept on calling, there was a danger of the old cat coming back. That she would come back so long as she heard them—that, indeed, she was circling within earshot even now—he was quite sure, and on the whole it seemed that his best plan was to abandon his idea of selling the captives for what they would fetch. Why not give them back to the old cat, who evidently wanted them?

With an effort Cairncross rose, and, as he did so, again that long, hollow 'hallo' smote his ears from the distance. It seemed to come from the timber edge not far from the cabin, and he knew now that it was the answering call of the parent cougar to the whimperings of the cubs. He took up one cub which had escaped, and dropped it back in the tub; then tilting the tub on edge, he rolled it across the verandah and emptied its sprawling contents over the step and into the sunshine. If she wanted the cubs—well, they were there. He and his cow and the survivors of the hen roost would be glad to be quit of them and her. They were heartily sick of mountain lions. So Cairncross went back to the cabin, and three minutes later the wailing of the cubs ceased and he heard a soft, deep rumbling, such as a mother mountain lion makes.

There was a strange sequel to this. Two or three days later, Cairncross, down and out with blood poisoning, awoke at midnight to the knowledge that he was dying of thirst. He had finished the jar of milk he had placed within reach at the last milking, and how long ago that was he did not know. It seemed to him that since then he had made several circuits of the earth, and had explored the dim and twilight regions which are beyond the earth's boundaries.

Now he wanted only one thing—water. He must have water. Every tissue of his warped and suffering body cried out for it. His tongue burnt, his throat was on fire. He dragged himself up, intent on creeping to the creek, but he knew that it would be his last journey. Water, my God! Water! He pictured himself lying at the sandy margin, drinking, drinking, quenching that internal fire which consumed his throat, plunging his burning hands and his swollen, throbbing face into it. He would never be able to creep back, of course, but he would not want to creep back. All that remained of him was that anguished, throbbing resolution to creep there and lie there with the sounds of the water in his ears.

But now, even as he strove to rise, the sound of water came to his ears—a steady lap-lap-lap, dabble-dabble-dabble. The sound was within the very cabin, and as his gaze probed the darkness he saw a dim outline in the light which came through the open door—the outline of something drinking from his water-bucket. His water-bucket, of course! Thank heaven!—he had forgotten its very existence!

Cairncross dropped from his bunk with a strangled cry, and as he did so two green points of light flashed in his direction. He was struggling on all fours towards the drinking bucket, and as he struggled, the thing which was drinking there bounded lightly over him, clearing him by a foot or more, tapped the centre of the verandah, and was gone—the old mountain lion, the cougar!

His neighbours found him lying across the floor beside the half-empty bucket, and when later he told them that the old cougar had saved his life by reminding him that the bucket was there, they simply smiled. Of course they did not believe that there had been any cougar, and one of them as good as said so.

'If you shot her,' he said, 'how could she come back?'

'I did shoot her,' replied Cairncross. 'You'll find her under the rock.'

Again they smiled. 'Then supposing she came to life,' they went on. 'Why should she come back when you had returned the cubs? Surely she would make clean away, having got them safely, glad to be quit of the place? She would not come back just to look at you and to take a drink from your bucket when there was a creek forty yards away?'

'Unless it was the father,' put in the first disbeliever. 'He might come back for a drink. No telling!'

But Cairncross gravely shook his head. 'Cougars is queer things,' he stated. 'There's no telling what they'll do. Anyway, you can take it from me there was two of them—father and mother. The one I shot must, I reckon, have been the father, and it was the mother who came back to the cabin when she heard the cubs call.'

So, for the sake of interest, the men went to the rock and recovered the body of the dead cougar. They found it to be the mother, so Cairncross was wrong. For it was the father who had braved all and come back to the cabin in search of the stolen cubs. So much for wild fathers!

351

Acknowledgements

The editor and publishers express their acknowledgements to agents, publishers and literary trustees in permitting the use of the following stories and extracts:

THE ESCAPE OF KING CHARLES AFTER WORCESTER and THE ESCAPE OF PRINCESS CLEMENTINA from *A Book of Escapes and Hurried Journeys* by John Buchan, Thomas Nelson & Sons Limited.

RIKKI-TIKKI-TAVI from *The Jungle Book* by Rudyard Kipling, The National Trust and the Macmillan Company of London and Basingstoke.

MIRACLE NEEDED from *The Hundred and One Dalmatians* by Dodie Smith, William Heinemann Limited. US edition © 1956 by Dodie Smith, reprinted by permission of the Viking Press.

HIS FIRST FLIGHT from *The Short Stories of Liam O'Flaherty*, Jonathan Cape Limited, and from *Spring Sowing* by Liam O'Flaherty, reprinted by permission of Harcourt Brace Jovanovich, Inc.

THE WHITE-RUFFED VIXEN by H. Mortimer Batten from *Every Girl's Story Book*, William Collins Sons & Company Limited.

MY SHIP IS SO SMALL from *My Ship Is So Small* by Ann Davison, Peter Davies.

THE MAN WHO COULD WORK MIRACLES from *The Short Stories of H. G. Wells*, The Estate of the Late H. G. Wells.

MY FIRST FLIGHT IN A STORM CLOUD from *The Sky My Kingdom* by Hanna Reitsch, The Bodley Head, and *Flying is My Life* by Hanna Reitsch, © 1954 by Hanna Reitsch, reprinted by permission of G. P. Putnam's Sons.

THE TAMING OF PERCY from *Three Singles to Adventure* by Gerald Durrell, Hart-Davis MacGibbon/Granada Publishing Limited, published in the USA as *Three Tickets to Adventure*, © 1954 by Gerald Durrell and reprinted by permission of The Viking Press.

RESCUE OPERATION from *Gara-Yaka* by Desmond Varaday, E. P. Dutton and Co. Inc.

THE FIRST LADY OF FLYING from *Air Adventures* by Graeme Cook, Macdonald and Jane's Publishers Limited.

THE STOLEN CUBS by Ronald Voy from *Every Girl's Story Book*, William Collins Sons and Co. Limited.

Every effort has been made to clear all copyrights and the publishers trust their apologies will be accepted for any errors or omissions.

The editor and publishers acknowledge the contributions of the following artists:

David Godfrey 17, 106, 175, 205, 244, 293, 337
Bob Harvey 190, 260
Sandy Nightingale 52, 147, 224, 347
Lee Noel 29, 120, 237
Mike Woodhatch 73
(*all the above represented by David Lewis*)

Kevin W. Maddison 36, 78, 83, 140, 264, 320
José María Miralles 129, 303
Phil Stevenson 68, 162, 216, 278, 309